Jayne Lisbeth was born in New York City in 1949. From there, life took her to New Jersey, Vermont, Massachusetts, California and finally Tampa, Florida where she resides with her artist husband. Ms. Lisbeth is an avid grave-stone rubber who has pursued her craft in cemeteries from New England and the Southeast US to the West Coast of California and Oregon. Ms. Lisbeth has been published in the *Pomfret, Vermont News, Sacramento Magazine, Monterey News, Monterey Peninsula Magazine, Phoenix Anthology,* and *Pages of My Life Anthologies.* She has received awards at the local level for her short stories and poetry. Her first book, *Writing in Wet Cement,* has been well received as a 'deeply personal memoir', revealing the depths of pain and elevation of joy by sharing her most intimate life experiences through sensually evocative words and painterly writing which resonates with all readers. Her blog, 'Food for Thought' explores women's roles in sensitive, provocative portrayals of the difficulties and joys women experience through all stages of their lives. 'Food for Thought' appears on Ms. Lisbeth's website, jaynelisbeth.com, as well as on her Austin Macauley website, jayne lisbeth.ampbk.com.

Raising the Dead is dedicated to my dear friend, Fran, who believed in my writing long before I did. Fran left this world too early but lives in my heart forever.

Jayne Lisbeth

RAISING THE DEAD

Illustrated by Tim Gibbons

AUSTIN MACAULEY PUBLISHERS™

LONDON ∗ CAMBRIDGE ∗ NEW YORK ∗ SHARJAH

A CIP catalog record for this title is available from the British Library.

ISBN 9781035830978 (Paperback)
ISBN 9781786291066 (ePub e-book)

www.austinmacauley.com

First Published 2023
Austin Macauley Publishers Ltd®
1 Canada Square
Canary Wharf
London
E14 5AA

To Tim, my partner in life and love, who patiently encouraged me throughout the writing and editing of *Raising the Dead*. Tim improved *Raising the Dead* enormously through his astute insights, suggestions and constant loving support.

To my amazing editor, hand-holder, shoulder to lean on and dear friend, Paula Stahel of Breath and Shadows Productions. To all my first readers, who gallantly undertook the massive task of reading my original manuscript and provided valuable and vital editing.

Prologue

The home and surrounding plantation, *Hill Haven*, was the brainchild of Mildred Hanson, widow of Hans Hanson. Hans, a wealthy London shipping magnate,had made his fortune off the backs of sailors. He imported tea, spices and silks from all over the world to his vast warehouses in London. His untimely death in 1827 at the age of 43 came at the height of his career. His demise was the result of his failure to pay his crew their wages on a return from an especially disastrous voyage. High seas, wind and towering waves had battled his largest ship, the *Hail Mary*. Losing all of its precious cargo and a few members of its crew, the *Hail Mary* limped back to London.

Hans made the fatal mistake of visiting his favorite pub, The Fox and Dove. There, he addressed his crew's complaints of non-payment of wages, 'should be happy to have returned with yer lives stead of grousing about lost wages'. A brawl erupted when his crew cornered him. His reasoning that his crew would not be paid due to the loss of the shipment infuriated the sailors. In their cups, they muttered angrily. Hans insisted he had no money to spare. Londoners and sailors knew he was flush from past shipping endeavors. The debate was abandoned when fists, wooden bar stools and finally a broken bottle embedded in Hans' cranium ended the altercation and Hans' life.

At thirty-five, Mildred was not a grieving widow. She had once been called a *bonny lass.* The years with Hans had stolen the joy from her eyes and the smile from her lips. Too many discoveries of his dalliances with servants and harbor wenches had changed her. Now she was *handsome,* no longer a *bonny lass.* Once, her raven hair, marine blue eyes and ivory complexion complimented by full red lips were striking. Now, her stern, angry countenance added premature lines to her face illustrating the eviction of joy from her life. She remained a well-recognized figure on the London docks, statuesque with her commanding height and posture. She was known to be fair in business, stern when necessary, and genuinely kind to those in need. Her kindness was not wasted on Hans.

After the births of their three children, Mildred had had enough. She kept her distance from her husband, not sharing his bed nor his life. She continued to manage their import business and knew Hans' finances to the last farthing. She also knew Hans to be a cheat, liar and philanderer. Mildred lost no tears or words at Hans' grave. She had nothing kind to say, so said nothing at all.

Unlike Hans and most of London society, she supported the downtrodden and strove to be altruistic. Her Quaker upbringing, morals and ethics gave her tolerance and open-mindedness. Kept hidden from most was her belief in the abolition of slavery, which others called that *unfortunate custom*. While others ignored the injustice of slavery, Mildred seethed within. *How was it possible for one human being to own another? To beat them and work them to death with no wages?* She kept her heretic thoughts to herself.

With Hans settled in his grave, Mildred was free. She was an independent, intelligent woman with three children. She was also enormously wealthy, due to the Hanson Shipping Enterprise she had managed for fifteen years. Mildred had always been the force behind the ships and the men who worked them. In return for handling all financial matters, she had insisted on being made full partner of Hanson Shipping Enterprises, with fifty-one percent ownership as an added safety guard. With Hans' death, the business was hers. Mildred immediately took control of her late husband's fortune. She paid the angry crew and within months set sail to begin a fresh enterprise. She was done with London.

Boston had piqued her interest. In 1828, she landed in the thriving Boston Harbor with her three children Chastity, twelve, Ezra, ten, and Jacob, eight. Mildred soon made the acquaintance of William Sawyer, a well-known and respected gentleman of trade with vast knowledge of shipping lanes and oceans. He became a ready and helpful friend, providing Mildred with his experience and assistance as she further developed her *Hanson's Shipping and Imports* enterprise. With William Sawyer's tutelage and guidance, she began shipping tea, spices, silks and luxuries from Havana, South America, Europe and the West Indies to her new warehouses in Boston. *Hanson's Shipping and Imports* was soon becoming known in her newly adopted country.

In the wild Boston Harbor, Mildred worked alongside her men in her warehouse office. The Harbor was fraught with thieves and charmers. Mildred was a trim schooner in the company of blustery ships and roiling waves. She sailed through the most difficult and stormy situations, earning respect from wizened captains and ship owners. Known for her reputation for fairness, pecuniary dedication and financial wisdom, she was said to be 'one tough broad'. Mildred cherished her new moniker. She had survived London and Hans. She could certainly survive her new Boston home.

The glow of Boston eventually dimmed much like the wavering glow of sputtering tallow. By 1835, Mildred was no longer enamored of the Boston docks and the shipping industry. In true Quaker fashion, she didn't desire more money. She craved greater peace. Her daughter, Chastity, was learning to be anything but chaste from lessons taught by handsome young men working in the Boston docks. Ezra was following in his sister's errant tracks, roaming the streets, breaking precious glass windows and consorting with street urchins and women of low repute. He had no interest in Boston gentry and was far happier with the underpinnings of low society. Jacob, her youngest, spent most days curled up in the window seat of Mildred's warehouse office, reading books as though he were starving for bread. He was Mildred's last hope. It was time for her to take stock of her life and family.

As the sun traversed the sky through dusty warehouse windows, Mildred watched Jacob. The whispery threads of light gilded his curls as he bent over his reading. His latest book, *Diary of a Madman*, troubled Mildred. *Oliver Twist*, reminiscent of their London life, was another of Jacob's favorites not shared by Mildred. She longed to spend her time educating Jacob in the finer arts of languages and romances far from the realities of the Boston Harbor. She strove to fill his mind and their bookshelves with the elevated aspects of life. Jacob became Mildred's goal, her greatest enterprise, and her impetus. Her burning mission was to prepare her children's future. This could not happen in Boston. She was determined to find a less raucous and inhospitable, unhealthy environment for them.

In the past, Mildred had traveled from Hampton to Scotland. She knew the world and its most horrific and utopian environs. She searched the world around her, leaving her children in the care of their old nanny, much to her children's dismay.

Mildred sailed up and down the Eastern seaboard, searching for the best climate in temperature and temperance for her family. She spent a fortnight in Philadelphia, drawn there by its strong Quaker community, progressive ideas and excellent care of the poor by Quaker physician, Dr. Joseph Parrish. Dr. Parrish was called a 'saint' in Philadelphia for his work with the impoverished in helping to end the 1805 yellow fever and 1832 cholera epidemics. The Pennsylvania

Society for Promoting the Abolition of Slavery had been established by the Quakers of the city, further enticing Mildred. The Quaker community was strong but when Mildred visited the Arch Street Free Quaker Meetinghouse she was surprised by their avoidance of the topic of slavery and its abolition. The minister who sat on the facing bench seemed to ignore the topic rather than promote it. Even by Quaker standards, this reticence to speak of Mildred's most important goals was disturbing. She ventured into the streets and marketplaces of the great city, walking over the cobblestoned and dirt avenues until her feet complained and forced her to return to her lodgings.

Mildred quickly learned there was an undercurrent against abolitionists in the city. Even in this northern city, there were those who believed in the *peculiar* institution of slavery. An increasing number of landowners and merchants did not want to see the practice abolished. In the marketplace, Mildred quickly learned of the dangers to Quaker women. Their plain brown and gray dresses and unadorned bonnets proclaimed their beliefs as they shopped. Mildred witnessed Quaker women being shoved, their baskets laden with market goods overturned, their feet spat upon. Watching one woman lose her balance and crash onto the filthy Philadelphia streets finally convinced Mildred; Philadelphia was not to become her new family home. The streets were 'repugnant and not fit for her children'.

She traveled further south to the Virginia Coast, 'moved by my inner compass'. It was in Virginia where she discovered her earthly heaven in Charles Town, Virginia, named after George Washington's brother, Charles. The village was close to the James River and was graced with fertile land. Charles Town became the needle on her compass. With easy access to the Atlantic via the James River, if necessary, Mildred could make the occasional trip north to Boston. The peace of the valley and the richness of the soil convinced Mildred that she had found her family's new home and life. She hired her most trusted ship's captain as overseer of all shipping affairs, keeping her main operation at the Boston Harbor. William Sawyer gave his word that he would keep an eye on her enterprise.

In late May, 1836, Mildred and her family moved to the rolling deep green hills whiskered by forests of pine, oak, aspen, maple, cypress and willow. Her new world was filled with grassy green expanses and golden sunlight, the violet of twilight and the ruby hues of dawn. This world appealed to her far more than the incessant blues and grays of ocean waves, surrounded by nothingness.

The fertile acres above nascent Charles Town were the perfect home for the rest of Mildred's years. To build her empire she bought slaves from outlying plantations throughout Virginia, West Virginia, Tennessee and Alabama. She then promptly set them free, enraging Charles Town citizens. Freed slaves built her first dwelling on her 400-acre plot of rich soil atop a high plateau.

This first domicile was a large log cabin, roomy enough for her family. Mildred installed unheard of luxuries in her cabin: glass windows, fireplaces, a large kitchen and pantry, a wood stove and a library. It held bedrooms for Mildred, Chastity and Jacob. The completed cabin was built with a parlor and library, embellished with a window seat for Jacob to while away the hours. In his library nook, he devoured books and pursued the education his mother oversaw. Her eldest son, Ezra, remained in Boston to assist in the oversight of Hanson's Imports and Shipping Enterprises. For the time being, it was all Mildred, Chastity and Jacob needed. Ezra preferred the charms of Boston cosmopolitan life to living in a log cabin on a farm. He remained in Boston throughout the rest of his life.

The second building Mildred constructed was a Quaker Meeting House which would also serve as a schoolhouse. Education was a passion for Mildred she was determined to share with all who lived under her employ and roofs.

The inhabitants of Charles Town and Vienna seethed under Mildred's queendom. They were enraged when overseers were removed from Mildred's employ for 'beating, obfuscating or fornicating' with her 'staff'. In addition, her employees only worked ten hours a day, and had Sundays off. Mildred was untouched by the enmity directed toward her in waves from Charles Town and nearby Vienna. She happily settled into her peaceful existence with Chastity and Chastity's husband, her grandchildren and Jacob.

Mildred's neighbors continued to rant. She paid her 'nigras' a fair wage for building her homes and outbuildings, clearing her lands, planting and harvesting her crops. The worst insult was Mildred's rewarding her employees by providing each family with the means to build their own cabins. They were permitted to harvest lumber from Mildred's dense forests. She encouraged her employees to build their cabins on the remainder of Mildred's acreage in the valley below her woods and fields. Her only requirement was that each cabin was to be built to her exact specifications and blueprints, overseen by a master carpenter, hired from nearby Charles Town.

The cabins were unheard of luxuries for her overseers and farm workers. Mildred's goal was 'to encourage freedom, friendship, family, faith and education'. Along with their cabin, each employee was given a deed to their property with ownership rights in perpetuity as long as at least one descendant of the original family owned or lived in their cabin. Each cabin built to Mildred's plans was spacious yet cozy. A small porch led to the kitchen. The kitchen included a fireplace, hearth and settle constructed for large families. Over years, wood stoves would be added for ease in cooking and heating. Each home embraced a parlor for entertaining, and for weddings and funerals. There were two rooms for sleeping on either end of a central hallway. A ladder to the sleeping loft under the roof was spacious enough for the children's sleeping quarters, no matter how many family members there were.

Mildred's proudest addition to each cabin, inspired by her bibliophile son Jacob, was a library. This largest room at the back of the cabin boasted much to make the room inviting. At the rear of the room, a wide door allowed breezes to circulate from the front kitchen door to the back library door on even the hottest of Virginia days. A fireplace was installed to warm the room during the cold Virginia nights. The logs of the room were interspersed with real glass windows. A window seat in an inglenook nestled beneath the largest of the windows, was surrounded by floor-to-ceiling bookcases. "But missis, we cain't read…what we be needing bookshelves for?" her employees complained.

"You will learn to read and write. My son, Jacob, and I will instruct every man, woman and child of our community."

Mildred helped to fill their bookshelves and their minds. Much to the disgust of the villagers and the delight of her staff and their children, every person in Mildred's community was educated to her and Jacob's standards. Mildred's spirit was instilled in each of the cabins she so lovingly created from her Utopian dreams. The essence of her independence, her savoir faire attitude, her fierce Quaker dedication to education, women's and underlings' freedoms and rights were infused into each family and cabin. Every log, each carefully laid stone, each glass window, each window seat and each bookcase were a testament to Mildred's spirit.

The townspeople continued their grumbling. The plantation above their homes became forever known as 'Mildred's Folly' and the cabin development 'Heretics Holler', which Mildred promptly named 'Heavenly Hollow'. Her beans, corn, peaches, grasses, lavender, cows and poultry thrived with her sharp wits and constant oversight. Mildred's employees flourished in their cabins and within Mildred's protective embrace. Above her acres and cabins with her magnificent views of the surrounding land Mildred paid little attention to the villagers below.

By 1840, with the coming of more grandchildren and the installation of Chastity's 'ne'er-do-well husband' her family had outgrown their log cabin. Mildred built her dream home on the highest peak overlooking the valley and Charles Town. She happily settled into her peaceful existence with Chastity, her grandchildren and Jacob. At forty-eight years of age, Mildred was ready to relax. Even the Lord rested on the Sabbath. It was time for Mildred to follow suit.

She had accomplished much. Her mansion, Hill Haven, was cradled in the hills with a lofty view of Heavenly Hollow below. She anticipated more grandchildren and a restful retirement. Her idyllic vista of the valley below with its meandering streams, cabins, woodlands, natural pastures and farmland quieted her heart and soul. She removed herself from the shipping industry, tide charts, storms and the price of salt. She trusted her son, Ezra, her ship's captains and overseers to run the business well, which they did, as long as they received part of the profits.

Mildred continued to enjoy her life and that of her family until her death at the age of 79, with Jacob at her side. After her death, Heavenly Hollow residents swore Mildred still rustled through the rooms of the old cabins, checking on the inhabitants, gliding silently through their homes, tending to the ghostly upkeep of her dreams.

* * *

Chapter 1

One hundred and fifty-five years after Mildred Hanson's death, Randy Upswatch carried his bride, Emeline Jannison Upswatch, across the threshold of Cabin #25. Randy gently set Emeline down on the heart pine kitchen floor. The windows let in bright splashes of the morning light through the wavy old glass. An antique black wood stove squatted in a corner, next to a small fireplace with an open hearth. The original porcelain sink had been retained but over the years the plumbing had been modernized. Across the room, an old gas stove nestled adjacent to a vintage Frigidaire. A scarred wood plank shelf was built into the wall between the stove and refrigerator, with drawers installed beneath. Knotty pine cabinets and shelves provided plenty of room for Em's collection of antique bowls and pitchers. Next to the fireplace, a pantry with floor to ceiling shelves completed the kitchen, empty storage begging to be filled.

Emeline's heart lifted, then sank, when she remembered the days she and her mama, Cleo, had filled their own pantry shelves. Mother and daughter would process their Sacramento Delta crops into jeweled jars of vegetables, relishes, jams, pickles and chutneys. Her eyes teared up, which she quickly hid from Randy. She scolded herself. *Damn, girl, it's been two years since Mama's passing – isn't it time for you to move on?* She thought to herself.

"Sure, wish I'd paid more attention to Mama's cooking," she said aloud.

"What?" Randy asked.

"Oh! I didn't realize I said that out loud. Just thinking that Mama always needed my help with jamming and canning, but never taught me to cook. She really wanted her kitchen all to herself."

But Randy didn't hear this response as he was busily exploring the rest of the cabin. "Holy Shit, Em, lookit this!" he exclaimed. Emeline followed Randy down a central hallway leading to other rooms. At one end of the central hall was a large bedroom. Windows sparkled as lacy light fell through the trees surrounding the cabin. A smaller bedroom at the opposite end of the hallway seemed forlorn. A large tree shadowed the room, darkening the interior. In the center of the hallway and next to the kitchen was a small bathroom boasting an enormous clawfoot tub. *A window over the tub with a deep sill would be perfect for African Violets and geraniums*, Em thought.

Off the center of the long hallway was the living room. It was just big enough to hold their old couch, her mama's ancient Lincoln rocker, and two end tables. An old black stove, sitting on a raised platform of bricks was nestled in a corner of the room. At the far end of the room were glass French doors, obviously an addition to the original structure of the cabin. Throughout the cabin, light scattered through many antique windows. Emeline pushed Randy aside and walked through the French doors. "Randy, it's the best part of the cabin!"

Through the doorway, she had spied bookshelves. Views of the surrounding pastures were idyllic portraits framed in the old windows. Directly in the center of the room was another door to a back garden. It would be perfect for cross ventilation when both the kitchen and library doors were opened. Wildflowers of all colors were woven into the bucolic pasture in the distance. The flowers gently danced in the spring breezes from the surrounding hill, transporting the outside world into this inner sanctum. Shadows from a large willow tree quivered as the tree shook its slender green leaves on delicate branches, nearly touching the ground. Em was reminded of children around a maypole, all wearing long green dresses. "Oh, Randy, there's a window seat!"

The inviting seat under the large window was laced between the bookshelves. A stone fireplace beckoned in the corner. Em lifted the lid of the window seat and a smoky scent of old fires wafted up to her. It was the most peaceful room in the cabin, exuding warmth and history. Em imagined the hours other occupants had sat on this window seat, immersed in a book. She walked to the door. "Randy! It's a Dutch door!"

"A what?"

"A Dutch door, see, the top and bottom open separately. We can just open the top and get the breezes and leave the bottom latched. Oh, I've always wanted a Dutch door!"

Em turned to Randy and enveloped him in her arms. "It's a perfect home for us. It's beautiful. This room is where I bet I'll be spending my time. It's the jewel of the cabin. What a special place. It's a library, Randy."

"Oh, yeah. My mom told me the lady who built all these cabins insisted her people led educated lives. She had a little school where she taught the kids how to read. Imagine that, teaching slaves to read, even giving them places like this to live. Mom said everybody in the town thought the old lady was nuts. They couldn't stand the way she treated her slaves. She didn't even call them slaves! She actually paid them, as her 'employees'.

"That was 200 years ago. Things have certainly changed since then," Em said thoughtfully. Emeline felt as though she were in the middle of a pumpkin with the cabin's knotty pine walls, the colors of burnt sienna and sunsets. She felt the rooms had been warmed by years of sunlight, woodsmoke and the fingertips of many inhabitants, completing the warm embrace of each room.

Emeline caressed the beautiful wood paneling as she returned to the living room where Randy stood next to the small Franklin stove. "I had no idea these cabins were so lovely. Mom just said they were old. She didn't tell me anything about what great shape they're in." The glow on his face helped to light up the room.

"We should set up our bed and try it out in our new home, don't you think?" Randy said with a bright smile.

Em's mind was elsewhere, busy with all she would do to make their new home a nest she could feather with her dreams.

They returned to a slower examination of all the rooms. The antique pine floors creaked beneath their feet. In her mind's eye, Em began placing their furniture in each room.

She lingered in the smaller of the two bedrooms as Randy left to retrieve boxes from their U-Haul. The entire cabin was infused with rainbows of light except for this small room at the end of the hallway. This room was darker, more somber. An enormous tree towered above this end of the cabin, blocking out the sunlight. The room seemed more silent than the others, with their creaking floors and squeaks. This room had a sad, lonely, uninhabited feel to it.

Randy returned to the kitchen depositing the first box marked 'kitchen, fragile' onto the wide wood counter. Their cats, Scarlett and Rhett, wandered into the kitchen after bursting from the cab of the U-Haul. Their feline family consisted of two calico cats, Rhett and Scarlet, sisters from the same litter. The two had been patient throughout the trip. Now they were anxious to be released after ten days of travel and being locked up in hotel rooms and the cab of the U-Haul. Cautiously, they examined and sniffed the corners of every room.

"Em? Em?" No reply greeted Randy. He found her in the small bedroom, rapt in thought. She wore that haunted look of sorrow he knew all too well. A flame of anger and resentment flared in Randy's mind which he quickly extinguished. He wrapped Emeline in an enormous hug, rocking her in his arms. She rested her head on his shoulder.

"Come on, Sweetheart. You're dead tired. Why don't I find your box of lady things and draw you a nice bubble bath in that big clawfoot tub?"

Em laughed. "You mean that tub that takes up half of our tiny bathroom? I love the old bricks under the tub and the little window over it. And the toilet! I haven't seen a pull chain toilet like that one since the Ryde Hotel."

Randy laughed. "Well, who cares if the bathroom is small, at least it's inside! It was probably part of the pantry off the kitchen before they had indoor plumbing."

Em wobbled in Randy's arms. "I am tired. Over 2800 miles from Little Holland City to Charles Town was a long trek."

"Yeah, but it was fun, too, wasn't it? Traveling from California to Virginia, seeing the country. How many people do you know who have done that?" Emeline saw the hope in Randy's eyes and crushed her rising fear and homesick sorrow.

"You're right, sweetheart. It was a good trip. The last part though, driving up this rutted washboard road nearly jolted the teeth out of my head!"

Em tried to smile with reassurance she did not feel. Every part of the Sacramento-San Joaquin Delta, where she had grown up, was gone; except for her memories. She felt as though she had died and been buried along with her mama and papa in the *Sailor's Last Delight* graveyard. She hoped the geraniums she had planted on Mama and Papa's graves would survive. It was well over two weeks since she had planted them. She felt dead, unknown, a stranger to all but Randy. An orphan, a motherless, fatherless child with no identity. It was a feeling she had been unable to escape since her mama's death, two years after Papa's. Her two brothers, David and Alexander, many years older than Em, seemed part of another family. She rarely saw them. They were busy with their separate lives and families in San Francisco and San Jose. She had no one. Only Randy.

Why had Emeline not argued more forcefully to remain in California? Why had she turned her back so completely on their delta home and everything she knew? She had loved growing up there, with all the vicissitudes, contentment, flooding and hazards to crops. Even the worst days held a beauty she missed. It had been the only home she had ever known. She had obediently agreed to all of Randy's and his mother's plans. She was nothing more than flotsam, floating along on the river of their lives and expectations. She drifted along, with no interest, purpose or meaning. She thought leaving the delta would also leave her grief behind. She had wanted a happy, fresh new life but had brought all her old sorrows with her. She shook the depressing thoughts out of her head. *This is a new beginning* she admonished herself.

"Hey, tell you what," said Randy. "Just help me with the bed and mattress and I'll set it up in our bedroom. Then you get in the tub and we'll take a nap after you soak a bit."

"Oh, yes. Mama and Papa's bed will fit perfectly in our new bedroom. We can put it against the wall across from those big windows."

An hour later, chin deep in bubbles, Em examined their new life. Tonight, she would meet Randy's mother, Margret for the first time. Randy was her only child, and she doted on him. Margret's loneliness and her aging had been the impetus for their move to this little community outside of Charles Town. That, and Randy's inability to make a decent living selling cars in the large and competitive California markets. His attitude toward authority and his arrogance toward customers had been his downfall, yet again.

Em scanned the little bathroom as the lavender scented water rose around her in waves each time she moved. She listened to Randy's grunts and exasperated curses as he continued to unload the truck. She hoped he wouldn't break any of her irreplaceable heirlooms or antique dishes.

The cabin was immaculate. Every necessity had been overseen by Margret prior to their arrival. The electricity, phone and water had all been turned on. All appliances had been checked for flaws and were found to be in good shape, despite their age. Margret had even stocked the old Frigidaire with milk, butter and eggs. A loaf of local bread sat on the kitchen counter along with a basket of fruit. Margret had even put a few cans of soup in the kitchen cupboard. She had thought of everything. Em would let her know how grateful she was when they had dinner with her mother-in-law this evening. As though her thoughts had been transported to Margret the phone rang shrilly in the kitchen.

"Yeah, Mom." Em heard Randy say, "Everything is great. We can't thank you enough." A pause, then his voice, slightly irritated.

"Yes, Mother. We'll see you around five. I'm just setting up our bed now."

Another pause. "No, Mother. Emeline's in the tub right now. You'll see her tonight. There's no need for you to come by now."

Another pause, then a grunt. "She's tired, Mom. It's been a long trip and her first time anywhere but the delta. I made her relax in a hot bubble bath. There's not that much to unload, after all. We don't have a whole lot of furniture."

Em could imagine the other side of the conversation before she heard Randy's reply. "No, honestly, we have all we need. The tiger oak kitchen table, kitchen chairs, our bed, a couple of dressers, the old couch and rocker. We don't need anything else. We only brought what Emeline couldn't bear to leave behind. No, please, don't send your gardener over to help unload. You've done so much already. You've been so thoughtful, taking care of all the necessities."

Another pause from Randy. "I'm fine. Nothing to worry about. Yeah, see you around five."

Just then Rhett and Scarlett entered the bathroom cautiously, tails uplifted, paws tentatively touching the old floorboards. "Well, hey, you two, what do you think of our new home?" Em said. Scarlett mewed sweetly as Rhett flopped down in a puddle of light and began to carefully clean each delicate paw.

"Hey, outta my way you two idiots," said Randy, bringing in a large box of towels along with more of Em's 'lady things'. "I put your suitcase in the bedroom," he said as he sat on the edge of the tub, swishing his fingers in the water, then rubbing his hands over Em's generous breasts.

"Hey, cut it out. We've got work to do," Em said, with laughter in her voice. He continued to dally with Em, breathing in the scent of lavender and that other special Emeline scent. Her damp blond hair settled in curls around her heart shaped face, her long hair off her neck and pinned to the top of her head.

Em smiled provocatively at Randy. "This is heavenly. This tub is big enough for the two of us, you know."

Randy reminded Em of her own admonishment. "You're the one who said we had so much to do. Besides, you know I don't like to sit in a tub. First thing I want to do is rig up a shower. Shouldn't be too hard."

Em bit her lip, then sank beneath the bubbles, only her blonde curls showing above the scented water. She was aware of Randy's lack of plumbing expertise. They didn't have the money to hire a real plumber to fix whatever her husband might break. Randy stood up and stretched, then put a big fluffy towel on the sink next to the tub. Em would have to allay his plumbing plans by insisting they share a candle-lit bath together. She smiled at her planned seduction, anticipating his learning the finer art of bathing.

Em breathed in the scent of fresh towels. "Smells like the delta, doesn't it? Remember how pretty our farm was?" The look that Randy dreaded returned to her eyes.

"It's going to be alright, Em. I promise. This is a new life for us. This was a good move. We'll be happy here, you'll see." He stepped over the cats and left the little bathroom to retrieve more boxes from the truck.

At the moment, the large obstacle in his mind was not just Em's continuing sorrow and lack of enthusiasm, but her meeting with Margret. He knew his mother could be difficult and her overwhelming love of Randy could be territorial. Randy hoped his mom would see past Em's timidity which could make her seem standoffish and cold. He hoped his mom wouldn't take Em's timidity the wrong way. On the other hand, he hoped Em wouldn't blow up over some off-hand innocent remark his mom might make. He had a vague feeling of unease, knowing the two most important women in his life could change in a heartbeat from sweet to sour. He wanted everyone to see Em the way he did: his pretty little bride of two years, with blond curls, violet eyes, curvy body and sweet demeanor. He wished Em could see the good in herself, the essence of who she was, rather than the ignorant delta girl she believed herself to be.

This is a good move, definitely, he reminded himself with each box he unloaded. What could go wrong? They had everything they needed. They had each other. The future looked as bright as any dream he had hoped for in his life with Emeline.

Chapter 2

Em lingered in the delightful steamy escape in their new bathroom, listening to Randy struggle in and out of the cabin. The hot bathwater soothed her complaining muscles. Helping Randy to drag their heavy antique bed, box spring and mattress up the front porch steps and into their bedroom had taken its toll.

Emeline was small but wiry. All those childhood forays running through the tall delta grasses, lying on her stomach watching the activities of fish, turtles and birds had hardened her. Her favorite childhood activity—climbing trees and digging for worms for her papa's fishing trips—had paid off over the years. Combined with the work of helping to care for their small vegetable plot, fruit trees, chickens and pigs had all built her muscles. All those Sacramento delta adventures, even the constant fear of flooding and subsequent muddy fields, filled Em's mind with nostalgia and homesickness.

Em conjured up images of meeting Randy's mom, Margret. She hoped all would go well yet she couldn't quell her apprehension. How would Em feel if she were the mother-in-law, meeting her new daughter-in-law for the first time? She stared out the window over the tub, her eyes capturing clouds racing across the darkening sky. She knew Randy and his mother were very close. His mother depended on Randy for emotional support. Why else would he insist they move almost 3000 miles away from her beloved California home to Virginia where Margret had settled after her divorce from Randy's father?

"If it were me," she told herself, "I'd be so excited to see my son for the first time in two years. I'd probably be cautious about meeting a daughter in-law. I bet I'd welcome her with open arms, though. What mother wouldn't love having a daughter in the family, with only one child, a son?" Em reasoned to herself. She hoped her imagination would match reality. The blanket of scented bubbles relaxed her and eased her nervousness. Yet her fears didn't evaporate along with the diminishing bubbles.

Randy entered the bathroom. "Did you call me? I thought I heard you."

"No, sweetie. Just talking to myself. Do you think your mom will like me?"

"Of course, she will, why wouldn't she? She'll see you the way I do. You're the sweetest little lady in the universe." Em laughed. "Maybe in *your* universe, but not your mom's!"

"Well. I'll admit it. I've told you my mom can be a little touchy, even a bit territorial. She's lived alone for years and isn't used to being around other women. She stays pretty much to herself. Just give her time to get to know you."

Em chewed her lip in thought. Randy urged, "Come on, sweetie, better get a move on. I promised her we'd be at her house by five and it's almost four." Randy picked up a large, white fluffy towel from the sink and held it up for Em as she rose, pink and steamy, from the tub.

Em persisted. "Randy, what if she doesn't like me?" He laughed as he wrapped his wife snugly in the towel, kissing her damp hair. "Don't be ridiculous. She'll love you. Now I've got to find the box with the bedding so we can come home and just crash." *Home,* Em thought. What a nice word. I hope I can make it true. Randy returned to his rummaging through boxes, grunting and muttering.

Wrapped only in a towel Em wandered through their new home, learning its light. She felt the worn wooden floors under her bare feet and wondered how many years of footsteps had preceded her own. The chill of the March temperatures rose goosebumps on her skin. She listened to Randy's muttered swearing as he set up their bed frame. The willow trees waved to Em through the old windows as she moved into the next room, the library. She longed for their first fire to be lit in the old stone fireplace. Tentatively she sat on the window seat and admired its creaking under her bottom. She pulled her knees to her chest and imagined the room filled with a comfortable armchair, her mama's old Lincoln rocker, and Em's collection of handmade rugs. Filling the bookshelves would take more time. Already the room was taking shape, coming alive in her dreamy view.

Reluctantly she rose from her seat and wandered into the vacant living room, touching the old Franklin stove in passing. The kitchen beckoned through the living room threshold. She stood in the center of the light-spattered room. Her eyes became more critical. The old black stove squatted in the corner, immoveable. It challenged her decorator's vision. The large fireplace was the centerpiece of the room. She gently touched the stones and sat tentatively on the flat stone hearth, shivering from the coldness beneath her.

"Em? Em? Where are you?"

"In the kitchen." She smiled to herself, thinking not *the* kitchen, *my* kitchen. She already was beginning to feel at home. Randy stood in the doorway, looking rumpled. He scowled at her towel-clad self sitting on the stone settle.

"Hey babe, what are you doing in here just wearing a towel? I brought your suitcase in. Get on your robe and help me move the box spring and mattress onto the bed. I found the box with the bedding."

Em wove her way between the piled boxes lining the hallway and the bedroom. She smiled at Randy. "*Our* bedroom, honey. I'll make it so pretty. That's the perfect spot for our bed. We can see out the windows and watch the moon and stars. The sun will wake us up each morning."

"Yeah, right. Now help me out." Randy pulled Em's white robe from her suitcase and unwrapped her from the fluffy towel and into her thick chenille robe. Gently he tied the sash around her waist. She lifted her face to accept his kiss as he enveloped her in a hug.

"We're home, Em," he whispered in her ear, her damp curls tickling his nose.

"Yes, our first real home." The vision of her parents' old home in Little Holland suddenly loomed large in her memory. Quickly, she banished the view. "Isn't it exciting? We'll make this little cabin special. It will be a home, not just a place to live. Won't it?"

"Of course, how could it be otherwise? Now let's get this bed made and get yourself dressed. Mom's champing at the bit to see us, you know."

As Randy dragged the big box of bedding into the room Em looked down the long hallway past the bathroom and kitchen to the smaller bedroom looming at the end of the hall. Something about that room bothered Em. She felt a chill that had nothing to do with the cool temperatures of the old cabin. The small room made Em feel apprehensive, queasy. She put her thoughts away, telling herself she was just being silly. It was just a room waiting to be decorated, like all the others, she told herself. Randy's loud voice pierced the moment. "Hey, Em, come help me make up the bed."

Making their bed made Em feel as though they had arrived. The old quilt immediately lit up the room with color and warmth. How many years ago had her grandmother pieced this quilt? Em smiled at the memory of herself as a small child, bringing a spool of thread to her grandmother. She loved to watch her grandmother make tiny stitches, joining the squares of fabric into a beautiful tapestry of color and light. Her grandmother had told her stories as she stitched, pointing out each calico, polka-dotted, floral, striped and solid piece to Em.

"This piece came from a dress your mama loved and wore to death," she had said. "That one is from one of my aprons. This one is from your great-grandfather's own quilt." Em remembered her grandmother's words, "Someday, dear child, you'll be making quilts for your own family." That day never came. Her grandmother had died before Em had a chance to learn how to even thread a needle.

Randy hurried her along. "Em, come on, find something to wear. I don't want to be late." Nagging doubts continued as she dug through her suitcase searching for a mother-in-law-type outfit. *Why was she so nervous about meeting Randy's mom?* She finally settled on a dress she knew Randy loved. *If she looked her best for Randy, surely his mother would approve of her*, she reassured herself.

"Randy, do I look okay?"

"You're beautiful."

"Be serious. I really want to look nice for your mom."

Randy's heart melted to see Em making such an effort to impress his mother. He smiled gently. Em's nervousness was endearing. Meeting his mother for the first time was a challenge, of that he was certain. He hoped his mom would try as hard as Em to forge a mother-daughter relationship.

"I am serious, love. You look beautiful. I always loved that little dress. It shows off your legs." Randy slipped a hand up Emeline's dress reaching for her panties. She deftly pushed her husband away. "Not now. You're the one who said we needed to get on the road. Besides, I want to look nice, not like some slut who just crawled out of bed."

"But I love it when you look that way." Randy laughed and nuzzled Em's neck. Playfully she punched his shoulder. "Enough, Romeo."

By the time they shut their kitchen door, twilight was tiptoeing into the valley. On a whim, Em ran to the field across from their cabin. *Now what?* Randy thought in exasperation. "Just a minute," she called. Quickly she gathered a bouquet of wildflowers.

"Em, what the hell are you doing?" She returned to their old Rambler he had just unhooked from the U-Haul and breathlessly replied, "Getting some flowers for your mom." Randy was again encouraged to see Em paving the way for their visit. "I realized I should have brought your mother a little something. The flowers looked so pretty I couldn't resist." She held a clump of tiny lilies, ferns and delicate blue star-shaped blossoms in her hands.

"She'll love them sweetheart."

"I hope so." Her hopes turned to fear once again. The closer they got to Margret's house the more apprehensive Em became. The half hour drive down their dirt road, through Charles Town and to her mother-in-law's front door ended too quickly. Randy crunched to a halt on the gravel driveway. Em stared out the car window at the imposing two-story white-washed brick house. It was a beautiful old colonial. Black shutters graced the many-paned windows. A plaque over the red front door with its lion's head knocker announced the home's 1869 vintage. Em noticed the ornate flower beds, full of the colors of spring. Azaleas, tulips and crocus embraced the old brick walls at the edge of the garden. Em looked dejectedly at the now-wilting wildflowers in her hands. I'm an idiot, she muttered to herself as Randy gave the lion's head knocker a good thump.

Margret, busy in her pretty kitchen, heard the greeting echoing off the walls and reverberating throughout the house. She quickly washed her hands, checked her image in the oven's glass door, and happily ran to greet them.

As they waited for Margret Em noticed the fanlight over the front door which sparkled in the sunset. Randy waved to his mother as he saw her approach through the leaded glass panel beside the door. Margret threw open the door, clearly thrilled to see Randy, immediately enveloping her son in a warm embrace.

"Oh, my dear son, it's so good to see you, after all this time."

"Good to see you, too, Mom. And here's my Emeline. She's been dying to meet you." Emeline blushed at her husband's fabrication. She resisted the urge to roll her eyes at Randy.

"Mother, dear, remember your etiquette. I've never been a 'Mom'," Margret said as she turned to Emeline, inspecting her from head to toe before pecking her on the cheek. She replied to her son, "Yes, your dear Emeline who I've heard so much about." She smiled at Em, yet her eyes did not smile along with her lips.

"Margret, I brought you some flowers. Wildflowers. They're growing right in the field across from our cabin," Em said, holding out the wilted bouquet.

Margret's mouth opened in a little *O* of surprise. "Why Emeline. I never expected a thing from you. Let me find a suitable vase and I'll put them in water. They look as though they need revival. Thank you." Margret placed her hand briefly on Em's shoulder. "Welcome. Please, come in, come in."

Randy looked around the familiar surroundings. He had helped his mother move in years before. He shuttled Em from the front hallway into a room directly to the left. "Let me show you around the house," he said as he led his wife into the parlor. A large piano dominated the room. On the back of the piano were an assortment of photos of Randy as a baby.

"Oh, look how cute you were, honey." Em remarked, kissing Randy on the nose. She stared at the photos intently, picking up each one. Then, she turned and slowly inspected the room. There were two wing chairs on either side of the piano. On the wall under a row of windows was a thickly cushioned sofa. In another corner was a game table, with a checkers board stenciled on its surface. Randy followed Em around the room, his own memories evoked. He touched the checkerboard's table gently. Then, he opened the little drawer to show Em the worn checkers and chess pieces stored there.

"Mom and I played checkers when I was little. I'm surprised she brought that table with her when she moved. She left behind just about everything else but her clothing, dishes, silver and her favorite pots and pans. That and all these photos."

"Really? Why was that?" Immediately, the antennas of Em's curiosity waved about, like a butterfly pursuing nectar.

"This was Mom's Aunt Clarissa's house," Randy replied, "and it was fully furnished. Clarissa would never give up her antiques and her history. Besides, Mom just wanted to start her life over again. She didn't want to be reminded of her life in California. She sold most of her belongings there."

Margret interrupted their conversation as she entered the room. "I put the flowers on the dining room table, Emeline. They brighten up the room. Can I get both of you a glass of sherry, or wine?" Em's gaze traveled to the room across the hallway, which looked far more inviting than the room they were in.

"Got any beer, Mom?"

Margret gave Randy a withering look. "Mother, Randolph. And yes, I bought beer. It's in the refrigerator."

"Great. I'll get one for both of us," he called to Em as he left the room. Em wandered into the enticing room across the hall. Margret followed her daughter-in-law, studying her from behind.

"You've discovered my favorite room in the house, Emeline," Margret said. "My sun porch. The view out the long bank of windows never fails to lift and brighten my spirits."

It was a lovely and welcoming room. The setting sun lit up the room through the long row of windows. Ornaments glittered on the shelves, seashells on the wide window frames, porcelain scattered here and there on side tables and more shelves over the doorway. Even the polished floors glowed in the light. A white wicker lounge chair sat in the center of the windows, accompanied by two comfy armchairs. The bright splashes of color from floral-printed chintz cushions brought the outside garden into the room. A long glass-topped wicker table dominated the far end of the room. Under its glass an embroidered tablecloth had been placed. Two more windows provided light over the table, decorated with glass paperweights, filled with their own miniature flower arrangements. A desk blotter, an antique pitcher filled with pens and pencils, a brass tray filled with papers and envelopes identified this as Margret's desk. An antique swiveling desk chair sat behind the table.

More shelves were filled with small leather bound books, porcelain, photographs, antique mugs, and a collection of beautifully painted ceramic pitchers. The room erupted with colors, polished by light and age. Em wondered how Margret kept everything dusted.

"I see you've found my little office," Margret said. "This is where I pay my bills, plan my days and contemplate the world outside those windows."

Em picked up one of the photos from the collection of silver framed-portraits on the back of the desk. The photos were in chronological order, and all of Randy. They ranged from his age as an infant to about seventeen. Em studied each one carefully. "Why aren't you in any of the photos, Margret?"

"Well, someone had to take them, Emeline."

"What about Randy's dad, your husband? What was his name, Ernest?"

Just then Randy arrived bearing bottles of Heineken. "Oh, Son. Please. Let me get the Fostoria flutes. You are not drinking beer out of a bottle in my home." Margret left the room. Em's question, hanging unanswered, heightened her interest.

"This is such a pretty room, Randy. Give me a tour of the rest of the house?" *Surely there had to be more photos*, Em thought, putting on her best Nancy Drew detective guise.

Margret returned with the foaming glasses of beer. "Hey, Mom, Mother. Em would love a tour of the house. How about you take her around?"

"Of course," said Margret. "I'd be happy to. Randy, make yourself at home." Margret's voice floated down the central hallway, as she began the tour of her home. "Here's the formal dining room, but I never eat here. Always in the kitchen. I don't need much room. Don't cook for myself as much as I used to. Then there's my bedroom, and the upstairs, of course. Did you know the upstairs has two bedrooms and a nursery, as well as a large bathroom?"

"No. I didn't know that. I'd love to see your bedroom, though."

Margret led the way to her closed bedroom door as Em glanced in passing at the dining room. The table was elegantly set with crystal wine glasses and goblets, fine china and linen napkins encircled by carved wooden napkin rings next to carefully placed silverware. Gold candles waited to be lit in their silver candlesticks.

Margret's bedroom door opened into a spacious room, bright from the many windows lining one wall, much like the sunroom. Thick carpeting graced the wood planked floor. A beautiful antique oak bed, a tall dresser, end tables and another chaise lounge filled up most of the room. In the far corner was a small vanity table with many drawers and a mirror above, which bounced colors and light throughout the room. Ornate crystal and silver filigree perfume bottles decorated the top of the vanity. Margret watched Em as she wandered through the room, noticing the many small treasures which Margret obviously cherished. "Oh, Margret, what a bright and peaceful room. You must sleep like the dead here."

"Well. I wouldn't exactly say that. This was the room my dear Aunt Clarissa died in."

"Oh, I am so sorry. I had no idea."

"No. Of course you didn't, how could you have?" Margret replied softly.

"Randy has never shared his family history. I've always been curious." Em had hoped her remark would open a door into a conversation about Randy's life. Margret ignored her.

Em entered a large bathroom off the bedroom and took refuge there, her face flaming with her remark. When would she ever learn to think before she spoke? It was obvious that neither Randy nor his mother had any desire to share family stories.

A large antique tub resided under a stained glass window. White tile floors and walls sparkled with rainbows erupting through the glass. The sink was antique, with porcelain spigots marked in ornate letters, 'H' and 'C'. A glass cabinet held fluffy flowered towels on its lower shelves with china figurines decorating the top shelf. Expensive boxes of soaps in all sizes and advertising many scents graced the middle shelf. Em felt as though she were in a very fine hotel.

"This is one of the most beautiful homes I've ever visited, Margret," said Em.

"Thank you. I do love it. I kept all of Clarissa's antiques. She was quite the collector. I renovated all the ancient plumbing except the vintage tub and pedestal sink. In the kitchen, I kept the butcher's block counter and shelves and upgraded all the appliances. Then I had the house painted inside and out. The upstairs I left pretty much as it was. Clarissa never spent time there. She couldn't climb the stairs. You're welcome to wander while I get dinner on. You'll see how roomy the upstairs is. It's a complete private apartment, just waiting for new occupants, should you ever grow tired of your little place." Margret smiled encouragingly. Em ignored her not-so-subtle invitation.

Em tried her Nancy Drew approach again. "Randy said Clarissa was your aunt. He never talks about his family, so I don't know much about his history. He's never even told me anything about his dad."

Margret's face immediately turned stormy. "We don't discuss Randy's father. He's out of our lives and we keep it that way. End of story." Em was surprised by Margret's abrupt response. This was obviously another closed door Em hoped to eventually pry open.

"As for Clarissa, she was my mother's younger sister and my last remaining relative in Charles Town. My mother and father were long gone by the time I moved here to help Clarissa. Ten years difference between her and my mother, Prudence. My parents and I visited occasionally. It was a long trip, even on a plane, from California to Virginia. That was in the fifties and sixties. We'd stay for a month in the summer. I loved playing in the old nursery. There's even an attic I used to explore. There were no neighbors or other kids to play with but I didn't care."

Margret stopped abruptly, as though she had said more than she had intended. "Anyway, there's not much more to tell. My parents died in their '80s. Clarissa never married or had children. She had heart problems, degenerative heart disease. When she became too ill to live alone, she refused to follow her doctor's orders to move into a nursing home. That's when she asked me to move in with her. It was perfect timing. I was ready to leave Sherman Island. What do they call it when you feel like you can't get off the island? Island bound? All those smells, the mud, the snakes," Margret said, with a frown of distaste. "I took care of Clarissa until the day she died. She left me the house and all she owned in her will."

Em didn't want to leave the breadcrumb trail of Margret's memories. She tried another tactic. "Who are all these people in the paintings? They look like important people, all dressed up in old-timey clothes. Are they relatives?"

Margret chuckled as she studied the portraits along with Emeline. The images were of stern bewhiskered men in long coats and tight pants, women in ornate floor length satin formal dresses, a child in the center of a herd of sheep and one portrait of two bulldogs. No one was smiling in any of the portraits, least of all the mean-looking bulldogs.

"I have no idea. I suspect Aunt Clarissa just collected antique portraits the way she collected everything else." Margret waved her arms encompassing the room and house. "That woman did put on airs. The portraits make me feel at home, as though they're familiar old friends. They've been here for as long as I can remember. They're not family. At least, I don't believe they are."

"They all look pretty unhappy," Em mused.

"People didn't show their emotions then, in the 1700s and 1800s. They felt feelings should be kept hidden. Letting anyone know what you felt or thought was considered a sign of weakness. And in children, expressing any emotions was downright rude. I can't help but think the early settlers had the right idea about keeping their thoughts and secrets to themselves." Em wondered if Margret's words could be construed as an admonishment, a confession or a warning.

"Enough of this. I'll get dinner on. Please pick up your glass of beer from my vanity. I'd hate for you to knock it over and stain the wood or my carpet." Margret quickly turned and left the bedroom, her heels clicking sharply in a staccato beat on the polished oak floors.

Em followed her mother-in-law. She entered the dining room and noticed that Margret had placed Em's flowers in a large crystal vase that dwarfed her bouquet. The beauty of the vase outshone the flowers. Em felt a stab of embarrassment. She should have known Margret's home would be grand. They could have stopped in town to buy a real bouquet, maybe roses. But who could afford roses? Em picked up one of the dishes from the table and turned it over to read the maker's mark. 'Wedgewood, Autumn Leaves', it read. Randy came up behind Em, placing his arms around her waist. "Having fun?"

"Well, yes, your mother's home is very interesting. So much stuff. But no personal history. She said everything was her Aunt Clarissa's. I couldn't have left my mother and father's special things behind." She laughed. "That, for the memories, and also because we don't own much of anything ourselves."

"Well, Mom did keep all the photographs, of course." He kissed Em. "I'll go help her in the kitchen. You relax."

"Mother, dear, never Mom, remember?" Em chuckled.

"Emeline. Behave, okay?" Randy said, knowing his wife's propensity for inappropriate remarks and flare ups of anger.

"Of course," Em replied with a mischievous grin.

She sat in one of the dining room chairs and examined the heavy silver. It was ornately engraved with the initials MJU, interwoven in a flower pattern. She wondered what Margret's middle name was, assuming the initials were hers of Margret Upswatch. Occasionally, Em heard Randy and his mother laugh companionably, accompanying the musical clatter of dishes and the oven door opening and closing. Em rose and examined the room more closely. It was a beautiful room, as were all the rooms in the house. The dining room table could have seated twelve, many more than the three settings prepared on its polished surface. The walls of the room were rose colored, with pale green chair rails and a wide-carved molding along the top of the walls, adjoining a cream-colored ceiling. A thick Oriental rug lay under the table, bright in shades of reds, violets, greens and golds. Em stealthily removed one of her sandals and rubbed her toes in the thick embrace of the carpet. The house was gracefully elegant. Yet, even with two fireplaces on the first floor, one tiled fireplace in the parlor and a brick one in the kitchen—the house felt cold. Em was reminded of a museum. Margret's home did not feel warm and inviting the way Em would make their little cabin. With all Margret and Clarissa's lovely furnishings, the collections of glass, porcelain, pewter plates, thick rugs and comfortable chairs and loveseats, the house did not feel inviting. It felt unlived in and without personality, except for all those photographs.

Em joined Margret and Randy in the kitchen. "Just in time, Emeline. Randy, fill the water goblets and open the wine. Emeline, why don't you bring the side dishes? I made Randy's favorites, Roast Loin of Pork, Fondant Potatoes, asparagus with hollandaise sauce, and baked applesauce."

"Oh, my mother used to make Hollandaise sauce. Only my dad called it Hollander's Ass Sauce." Em giggled.

"Hmmpf. Yes. I'm sure he did." Suddenly, the kitchen felt like an industrial room, despite the open back door welcoming lilac-perfumed breezes from the yard. Even with the hanging copper and polished pots and pans, the glass cabinets with many sets of dishes, the round table in the center of the room and the old scarred butcher block, the room felt lonely. Yet, Em imagined it was the most used room in the house. She remembered Margret's words that she no longer cooked very much. She sighed as she remembered her mama's delta kitchen, usually messy but filled with garage sale finds as well as her mama's treasured Quimper Ware and Stangl dish collection. Sadness returned to her as she remembered the huge-black enameled canner and the shelves of home canned jars filled with tomatoes, pickles, green beans, beets and jams jockeying for space on her mama's wide wooden shelves.

Em followed Margret into the dining room where Randy had already lit the candles and had settled himself at the head of the table, looking authoritative. Em smirked at his stern countenance. "What?" he asked her.

"Oh, you," Em said. "You look like one of those portraits in the bedroom."

"Just because Randolph looks like a gentleman is no reason to mock him, Emeline."

The rebuke did not sit well with Em. As she opened her mouth with a rejoinder Randy quickly interrupted her reply, "Jeeze, Mother, this looks and smells divine. Can't wait to dig in."

"I was not mocking my husband, Margret," Em said, peevishly. Randy flinched.

"I'm so happy to hear that, Emeline. Randolph deserves only the most loving, supportive, and respectful treatment from his wife."

Randy stepped in to smooth the troubled waters. "Em treats me better than you can imagine, Mom. She's the best wife any man could hope for." Em blasted Randy with one of her enormous dimpled smiles.

"Well, time will tell," Margret said.

Randy deftly tiptoed through the battlefield, anticipating every step. Emeline's face had reddened dangerously. She refused to hold her tongue and waded into what felt like alligator-infested waters.

"Margret, I would never hold Randy in any disrespect, now or in the future. Would you do so to your own husband? By the way, exactly what was Randy's father like? He never talks about him at all. It's as though he doesn't exist. Isn't he remarried and still living somewhere in California?" *Tit for tat, score one for me*, Em thought.

Margret's eyes drilled into Em. "I told you. He's long gone. We don't discuss Randolph's father. He's not worth the breath to do so."

Randy came to his mother's rescue from further discussion. "Emeline, we just don't like to talk about the man. He's been gone for years. We don't know where he is."

Em was surprised by the stern warning in Randy's voice. She realized too late she had gone too far, treading into deep and treacherous waters. *What the hell was this all about?* she wondered, vowing she'd investigate and excavate this skeleton from the family closet.

No other problems arose until the Chocolate Mousse was served. Em's eyes lit up. "I do so love chocolate pudding." Margret gave Em a withering look. "Chocolate Mousse, Emeline. Not pudding." She then began another foray into battle. "You know, Randolph, Emeline would learn so much from me if you lived under my roof, instead of that…shack."

The challenge had been thrown. Em immediately picked up the proffered bait. *Shack?* The word screamed in her mind. As new as it was to her, she already adored their cabin.

"You're the one who found us that 'shack', Margret," Em retorted. "It's a beautiful little cabin. I'm going to make it cozy and a perfect home, I promise you. Randy told me you said the cabins in Heavenly Holler were prized homes, built by the original owner of the land. Valuable historical cabins, is what he called them."

Randy sensed that his mother's goodwill, and certainly Em's, was coming to an end. His mother did not like being lectured to by her daughter-in-law. Of that, he was certain. He got up from the table and started clearing the table.

"I'll get started with the dishes, Mother."

"Shouldn't Emeline help, dear, so you can rest?"

"Hey, speaking of rest, you're right. We'll have to leave soon. We're both dead tired." Margret piled up the rest of the dishes. Randy followed his mother into the kitchen. He hurriedly kissed his mother goodbye. Em realized she had overstepped the bounds of good behavior and goodwill. Contritely, she approached Margret.

"Thank you so much, Margret," Em said. "Honestly, I can't remember a more delicious meal. And thank you for sharing your home with me. Most of all, thank you for all the special touches and all the help you gave us to make the move in so easy. Even fresh bread, groceries and fruit. That was so very thoughtful of you, not to mention turning on the electricity and even the phone. Next time I'd love a tour upstairs, okay? And as soon as we're settled in, I'll cook dinner for you." As she gently kissed Margret on the cheek, she admonished herself for offering to cook. She hadn't yet learned to do much more than make mac and cheese and grilled cheese sandwiches.

Randy distractedly ran his hands through his Brylcreemed locks, following Em out the door. "Bye, Mother. Absolutely, next time Em will make dinner for you at our house."

Margret waved from the front door as she watched them depart. Randy and Em walked down the driveway, arms around one another's waists, heads touching, engrossed in talk. Randy laughed over something Em had said. He turned and kissed her before they both settled in their old Rambler.

Turning from the door Margret caught the image of herself in the mirror next to the front door. I used to be that young, that beautiful and that much in love, she said to herself, suddenly enveloped in sorrow. Her reflection in the antique mirror over the petticoat table was so different now. When she was Emeline's age, her hair had been raven black. It fell to her shoulders in soft waves. Now, her eyes which were once deep green seemed to have faded into the wrinkles surrounding them. Her lips were set grimly, unused to smiling as they had once been. She slapped at the jowls around her chin, as flabby as her cheeks had become.

Suddenly a childhood memory floated up to her from her past. The remembrance brought a burst of joy to her tired countenance. She had been playing her favorite game, hiding under the petticoat table making faces at her reflection in the mirror below the table. Suddenly Aunt Clarissa appeared behind her.

"What on earth are you doing under my petticoat table, child?"

"Nothing," Margret, then called Maggie, had replied. Guilt graced her child's features.

The look on her face brought Clarissa to laughter which Maggie shared in a wide grin.

"Auntie, why do you call this a petticoat table? And why is there a mirror under it?"

"My dear, it was the last thing any lady of refinement would check before walking out the door. Her petticoat in that mirror could not show beneath her skirt. Her mother would check, as no lady would allow even the tiniest bit of lace to show beneath her dress. It was considered shameful if any undergarment, even a trace of lace, appeared. No young lady would be allowed to leave the house showing lace, as her behavior would be considered scandalous, indecent and flirtatious. Many a girl would try to slip out of the house without her mother stopping to check her appearance in the mirror over the table and the petticoat mirror beneath it."

Margret continued to smile over the memory. She had always loved her Aunt Clarissa's stories. She shook the memory from her mind, recalling that she was now about the same age as her Aunt Clarissa had been when she had offered her niece this life's lesson.

"You're just an old, foolish, lonely woman rattling around in this big empty house," she told her reflection.

She turned from the mirror and returned to the dishes, busying herself with the washing up. As she straightened up the dining room, she noticed the flowers Em had brought. The small colorful bouquet gave her unexpected pleasure. I'm sure she's a sweet child. And Randy certainly adores her. I'll have to do my best to be in her good graces. "She is your son's wife, never forget that," she said out loud to her silent musing.

Unexpectedly exhausted, Margret left the room. She retrieved a book from her bedroom and settled onto the chaise lounge on the now darkened sunporch. Sitting with the book unopened on her lap her eyes studied the photographs lining the shelves in her most treasured room. Her voice was the only sound in the silent room.

"History. All just history, not worth sharing. I've got all I need with my son. I'll get to know his wife and we'll be one big happy family." She advised the photographs staring back at her. She hoped her prediction would come true.

* * *

That first night Em awakened and was completely disoriented. Where was she? Then she remembered. She and Randy were in their new home. Images of Randy's mother fluttered to the surface of her mind. She hoped they would become friends.

She had to find the bathroom, but the world was black. Randy snored gently as Em crept from beneath her grandmother's old quilt. Feeling around the boxes and the unfamiliar walls she made her way to the antique pull-chain toilet. As she re-entered the hall, dim light drew her into the kitchen. The window above the kitchen sink glowed and sparkled. Em leaned forward, her nose nearly touching the glass to see what lit up the field across the street. The glow was beyond the road Em and Randy had so recently traveled. She noticed the waving grasses and the deep shadow of a large tree. The distance was black and unknown, menacing and unfamiliar. Suddenly, there were lights. One. Two. Three. Six. Ten. Flicking on and off. Tiny lights mysteriously chasing away the darkness. Fireflies. They were fireflies. Em rejoiced in this vision she had never seen. She was truly home, welcomed by glowing lights in the darkness of the future. For better or worse, she was home.

Chapter 3

Night after night, Em returned in her dreams to her beloved Sacramento delta home. Once again, she had dreamt of her mama, who had been standing over Em, shaking a finger at her. Mama had clearly been angry. "Don't you sass me, gal. You're not too big for my wooden spoon." Above all, Em feared her mama's punishment of a smart smack on her bottom with her mama's favorite kitchen utensil.

When was that day? As she struggled into the new day suddenly that long-ago morning returned to her. It had been one of life's lessons taught to her when she was barely old enough to know what sass meant. The day had begun happily enough, then quickly had turned to near disaster.

"You have to be really smart to be stupid," Cleo had said. The words returned to Emeline, rattling her. She sat up, embracing the morning sunlight as she brushed her tangled curls from her eyes. Randy's side of the bed was empty. She smelled coffee brewing. Snippets of that day reappeared as though she were watching an old home movie.

She tried to recall what her mama had meant. Something about Em's pet mouse, Giant. Em did her best to recall every moment of that day and the compilation of other days the dream had evoked. It had been a beautiful summer morning at their home in Little Holland City, on Sherman Island, deep in the heart of the Sacramento-San Joaquin Delta. Remembering the day, Em could almost smell the rich soil of their farm and hear the chickens clucking and scratching in the dirt.

Cleo had studied her daughter as they sat companionably together on their verandah. Her expression was one of love and tenderness. Emeline was a miniature of Cleo. She had her mother's eyes but not their deeper violet shade. Em's eyes were a clear blue, aquamarine, the color of still water lit by the sun in river shallows. Her eyelashes were blond and almost invisible. Her heart-shaped face was surrounded by unruly blond curls. Her mouth was wide with full lips, decorated by dimples. At five, Em still had her baby fat with a rounded tummy, dimpled knees, and chubby fingers, which were usually unwashed. Even for such a young child her beauty was frequently remarked upon and had been from the time she was born. Emeline shirked from any comments on her appearance. It didn't matter to her what she looked like.

Cleo, at 49, was aging gracefully. A tracery of lines had grown around her eyes and mouth, roadmaps of joys and sorrows. She was a strong woman, used to hard work on their farm. She was plump in a sensual way emphasizing her love of good food and happy times. She was an attractive woman who still turned heads. She noticed her daughter's unruly head of curls.

"Time I took a comb to that mass of hair, girl."

"No. Can't make me." Em had surprised herself with her rebelliousness. In a flash, Cleo was up and standing over Em, "Don't you dare sass me, girl. I'll get my wooden spoon, then you'll be sorry."

"Sorry, Mama," Em had sheepishly replied as her mama settled back into her rocking chair. Contritely, she amended her earlier rebelliousness, or sassiness, as her mama called it.

"Not now, please? I'm busy."

Cleo sighed as she watched her daughter play with her pet mouse, Giant. "Before the day's end, I *will* comb and brush your hair, missy."

"Yes, ma'am." They both knew that the threat of hair combing was unlikely to be meted out. Em would hide in one of her secret spots. She would do anything to avoid the painful, scalp-scorching, hair pulling which was the screaming result of her mother's efforts at taming Em's hair. For her part, Cleo never pushed for this interaction. It was understood between Mother and Daughter that they would avoid the hair-raising event until it could no longer be ignored.

On that long-ago morning, Em sang softly as she played with Giant. '*To market to market to buy a fat slug. Home again home again Jiggidy Jig*'.

"It should be a fat pig, sweetie, to rhyme with Jiggidy Jig. Or jiggidy jug, to rhyme with slug. But it is a lovely song and I know Giant must enjoy it. Why don't you change 'jig' to 'jug' to rhyme with slug?"

"Okay. Maybe. I like slugs better. You know, like those big banana slugs in the garden?"

"They're disgusting."

"Besides, Giant loves the way I sing my marketing song so I shouldn't change it." Clearly, Giant did not love the song, nor the jig Em subjected him to as she sang, holding him by his tiny arms as he performed on her knee. It was better than Em's other favorite activity which the poor mouse squirmed to avoid, that of Em dressing him in the tiny outfits she cut from her grandmother's old quilt scraps.

Arnold, Em's father, wandered onto the porch, scratching, stretching and yawning.

"You're up early," Cleo said, as he leaned down and gave his wife an affectionate kiss.

"How are my two favorite girls?"

"Papa. You always say that. We're your only two girls so we have to be your favorites."

"That's so. But even if I had a houseful of girls, I'd feel the same way."

He noticed the growing pile of peeled potatoes in the colander on Cleo's lap. "Fried chicken and potato salad for dinner? Better than that French shit with some Hollander's ass sauce."

"Hollandaise Sauce, dear. And that was on the asparagus, anyway. And I do not cook shit."

Em giggled and whispered to Giant. "Papa said shit again, and so did Mama." Her pet mouse did not reply, instead escaping up Em's overalls to deter his mistress from another harrowing dance or costume fitting.

"Thinking of going fishing tomorrow on the Suisun Bay."

"Oh, Papa, can I go? I'll be so good you won't even know I'm there."

Arnold looked at his daughter, his greatest pride and joy. Their beautiful daughter had been a surprise to them both, announcing her presence to Cleo when they were both in their mid-forties. At her age, Cleo thought it was menopause, not pregnancy.

Arnold never imagined he could be the father of such a beautiful child, who looked nothing like her two much-older brothers, Alex and David. They were both tall with long limbs and tended to be stout, inheriting their father's rounded pot belly. When annoyed with her sons, Cleo called them, fat louts'. Arnold always chuckled at the nickname which fit their lumbering gait perfectly.

Emeline was a small replica of Cleo, resembling a porcelain doll. The only thing she had inherited from her papa was his pudginess. Thoughtfully, her papa rubbed his tummy which stretched out his worn tee shirt. As always, his right hand was hidden in his jean's pocket.

"Not this time, lovie. I'm going with Stan and we'll be gone overnight," he said.

Cleo threw the last of the potato peels to the chickens pecking in the dirt, who fought over the prize. She gave her husband the raised-eyebrows look of admonishment he knew so well.

"Arnie. Go easy on the beer if you're staying on that flimsy wreck of a boat overnight," she said. "You know how unpredictable our delta waters are, flooding in an instant. I don't care what Stan says, with all his blowhard crap about—'I know this whole web of waterways like the back of my hand, from the north delta of Sacramento to the east delta in Stockton to the west delta in Benicia and the south delta in Tracy and I've fished every mile of the Suisun Bay'."

Her papa attempted to deflect Cleo's concerns. "Yeah, of course, I'll only drink one beer," her beloved husband said as he gave his wife a bright smile. "But Stan does know a helluva lot about fishing the Sansun Bay, and he's traveled every mile of the Delta."

She looked up at him directly, drilling her eyes into his. "I almost believe that, on all counts." Cleo tried to appear stern, but she and her husband laughed together. "You know me too damn well, woman."

"Next time, Papa?"

"Yeah, sure. When I go to the Sacramento River. We'll fish from shore."

"When?"

"When I say so. In the meantime, why don't you do some worm pickin' for me?" He dismissed his daughter and turned his attention to his wife. "Coffee left?"

"Some. Should still be hot." He gave her another kiss and ruffled both his girls' curls. As he returned to the kitchen, he treated them to a loud fart.

"Papa!" Em called after him as the screen door slammed on his departure. What neither Emeline nor Cleo noticed was the younger cat, Tristan, escaping through the screen door as Papa entered the kitchen. Tristan was confined inside the house whenever Giant was on the verandah with Em. Being the younger of the two cats and Isolde's daughter, she was the more dangerous and aggressive hunter. Although Tristan did not yet have Isolde's skillful patience, she was quick and brutal. Even though both cats were female, in her contrary way, Cleo insisted on naming them after a tragic romance she had read. "Should have named her Diana," her mama had often said, for queen of the hunt.

Cleo shook her head over her husband's flatulence, then advised Emeline. "Men. If you learn nothing else about them, remember the longer you know them the more uncouth they become."

Em, smiling at the memory, pulled the quilt up to her chin. She had learned from her experience with Randy that her mother's words were exactly true. She recalled other words of her mama's wisdom, "Never underestimate the power of words said in anger. They could be more true than an apology said later." Another of Em's favorites was, "Make that face again and it might just stick to your face forever." Em loved to make faces behind her mama's back when she thought her mama wasn't looking. Now, in her warm bed, Em giggled at the memory of so many years before.

She surveyed their new bedroom, lit with sunbeams dancing around the room. She really should get out of bed. She sat up and looked out their bedroom window. The willow tree branches were performing their ballet in the early morning breezes.

Em snuggled back under the quilts and remembered how on that long ago day disaster had struck suddenly. Em had been sitting against the porch pillar in a warm puddle of morning light. The wrap-around veranda, with its seafoam green-painted ceiling, to 'cool the masses' as her grandma had said, threw the light around the veranda in glimmers of grace. The perfume of the delta drifted to the porch, scenting the early morning coolness.

Giant ran up and down inside Em's worn overalls, eliciting wild giggles from her as her tiny pet tickled her ankles and thighs. Giant's home was a cotton-batting-filled Sacramento Italian peeled tomato can. He slept in Em's bedroom at night. Em always brought the can-nest onto the porch for Giant's playtime and naps.

Giant leaped from Em's overalls, raced into the can, rustled through the cotton batting, and then leaped out and perched on her knee. They would play their game until one of them wore out or Emeline left for adventures elsewhere, depositing Giant in his nest in her bedroom.

Mother cat Isolde slept on the windowsill of the veranda, wrapped in the sun's morning sauna, her tabby coat gleaming in the light. Her chin was tucked onto her front paws, her tail snugly wrapped around herself. She was as happy as any cat had a right to be. Mama cat was unaware of the danger unfolding as her feline daughter hid behind Cleo's rocker. None of the porch inhabitants realized Tristan had escaped. She slithered from behind the rocker, hunting, hiding in the verandah shadows. Every fiber of her body bristled, lusting for Giant. She hungrily watched the mouse cavort directly in front of the happily dozing Isolde. Tristan steeled herself in anticipation. Em finally realized the danger when she heard Tristan's growl as Giant carefully washed his paws and whiskers on her knee.

It had all happened so quickly. Giant had overestimated his protection. Tristan struck Giant from Emeline's knee, plucked him from the floor and popped the tiny mouse into her captive mouth. Emeline's beloved pet managed to escape from Tristan's grip when Emeline screamed and grabbed the cat. Giant's escape was fruitless. His tiny, limp body rolled under the porch swing.

Her little friend was dead. "Mama!" Emeline screamed, as she ran and picked up Giant. Unmoving, but seemingly whole, Giant was slimy with Tristan's saliva. Emeline had interrupted Tristan's plan of playing with and snacking on her trophy catch. The hunter slunk off and hid in safety under the porch steps. It wasn't as much fun to play with a dead mouse as a live one, especially with Emeline sobbing hysterically while holding Giant's body.

Mama had watched quietly, a half peeled potato in one hand, peeler in the other, a lazy smile on her face. "Wait, just wait," she had said softly, in answer to Em's screams and sobs. "Just wait."

Miraculously, Giant moved. Cautiously and slowly, he picked up his little head and looked around. "You're alive!" Em screamed.

"Gotta be really smart to be stupid, Emmy. Tristan just wants to play with any live thing before she kills it. Your little friend seemed dumb to get caught. When caught, he was smart enough to play dead for his protection. Just as in our lives, never overestimate your safety over your enemies."

Mama had put down her potato peeler. She grabbed Tristan from under the steps and threw the criminal into the house slamming the door behind her. Tristan landed with a loud thump and an angry 'YOWL!' on the kitchen floor.

"What the---?" Em heard her papa mutter from the kitchen.

Cleo had picked up her potatoes, colander and peeler. She watched her daughter where she sat cuddling her wet but otherwise unscathed pet mouse. Cleo, glazed in love for Emeline, her final hope for the family said:

"Never forget that, my love. You've got to be really smart in life. If you have to fool others by acting stupid, that's okay. As long as you know who you are, what you are and what you can become. Know who your friends are, and even more importantly, who your enemies are. Learn who will teach you lessons and others who will try to hurt you. Outsmart them any way you can. Acting stupid will cause others to underestimate your power. If ever you're in trouble, or feel threatened, just wait, wait, wait to discover how to outwit any who might seek to harm you."

"But, Mama, who on earth would ever want to harm me?"

Mama just shook her head. "Oh, you'll see. It's inevitable, love, no matter how good a person you are. Jealousy will be one motivation. Even worse, those you love may disappoint you and leave you without you knowing why. Don't be fooled. True love, real family and friends, will always stay by your side. They *want* you to succeed in life. A disappointment is only a passing moment. There's always another day to learn from your mistakes and seek forgiveness for any errors in judgment."

Her mama had always been Emeline's best friend. She trusted every word her mother said as though they came directly from the mouth of God, or the angels. "I'll remember, Mama."

Cleo had chuckled. "Emeline, also remember, never underestimate our animal friends. You'll learn a lot by watching everything they do."

Over the years of Em's education this proved to be true. She had always preferred animals to humans for company. She had been a shy child who preferred solitude to playmates. She loved nothing more than to play quietly by herself. From almost the moment she was born, she had been timid and fearful of people, but not the animal world. When she could barely toddle, she had chased a butterfly, watched it crash onto her outstretched hands, its wings torn. Her mama could not assuage Em's grief as the Monarch stopped fluttering and died. Since then she had been drawn to injured or broken things—be it crockery, a butterfly, or a baby possum.

"Why did the flutterbye stop flying, Mama? Why did the pitcher break? Can't we put them back together again?" Cleo never had an acceptable answer.

The older she became the more Em preferred insects, birds and pets to humans. Neither of Cleo's sons had been so sensitive, so tender, so fearful. Em loved her imaginary friends as well as their real barnyard animals. When neighbors stopped by, she would inevitably retreat to a hiding place in the barn or in her room, settling in with her stuffed animals until everyone departed.

Muriel, Em's grandmother, was the only visitor to their home other than neighbors. Em adored her grandmother. She would climb onto her ample lap, inhaling her lovely Lilies of the Valley scent. Grandma Muriel always brought

45

her quilting and would give Emeline scraps of material. "Someday I'll teach you how to make a quilt, little Emeline," she would say.

"Oh, yes, please, Grandma. I want to make a story quilt with all the animals I've met. Can you teach me that? How old do I have to be?"

"When you're old enough to thread and hold a needle steady and cut material with precision. We'll practice soon, I promise." But she hadn't been able to keep that promise, dying suddenly of a stroke when her granddaughter was only six. Em never became dexterous or patient enough to sew quilts. Her mama kept all her grandmother's quilts and scraps, unable to part with the fabric of Muriel's life. She also promised Emeline, "Someday I'll teach you how to quilt, sweetheart, just like your grandmama taught me." Yet Cleo had her doubts. She didn't think her daughter would ever have the patience to become a quilter. Em loved the mystery of how the pieces fit together but could never master the patient art of tiny stitches needed to craft it all together into a quilt. Cleo would find discarded pieces of material with haphazard stitching where Em had thrown them in a pique of anger. Instead of teaching Em to quilt, Cleo had promised to someday teach her how to embroider and use their old Singer sewing machine for larger sewing projects.

Em's grandfather, Henry, had died before she was a year old. She had no recollection of him. She built her knowledge of her grandfather around the photographs in her mama's albums and the quiet reminiscing chats of her mama and grandmother that always began with, 'Remember the time when Henry…'

Em had always felt as though she was an only child, although she wasn't. Her brothers had left home long before Em was born. Mama affectionately called Emeline's two older brothers, David and Alexander, the 'louts', nicknamed for their lumbering gait and their slow, yet thoughtful, speech. David, the eldest, was the result of her mama and papa's early passion. Cleo had been sixteen, Arnold nineteen when they married, pregnancy being their incentive. The impending birth of David simply brought her parents' wedding date sooner than planned. Cleo would have married Arnold eventually, just not at sixteen.

Her brothers were so far apart in age from Em that she had never really known them. On those rare occasions when she thought of them, Em had been fascinated by her mama and papa's laughter-filled stories of them. David and Alexander now lived close to one another in San Jose and San Francisco. "Too far for visits to the delta," they said, knowing it wasn't true.

Em's brothers were a mystery to her. At her mama's funeral, David and Alexander's three children seemed as fascinated by Em as she had been by her brothers. At the time, Em was too overcome with grief to do more than watch her 'other family' from a distance. If they had lived closer to the delta perhaps, she could have been her nieces and nephew's doting auntie instead of an absent and unknown relative.

David, her elder brother, had become a successful IBM sales executive. He lived in a gated San Jose community with his wife, Anne Marie, and their two daughters, Chloe and Christine. Her closest brother to her in age, Alexander, lived in San Francisco with his wife, Heidi and their son, Sidney. Alexander was in real estate. Heidi had confided to Em at the funeral that his real estate position made them either fabulously wealthy or devastatingly poor, depending on sales. Their son, Sidney, was a genius, Alexander had boasted to Em. He had skipped two grades and was due to graduate high school at sixteen.

Who was this family she had never known? Clearly, they were not louts. They were close to one another and visited each other often. Em noticed that Heidi was as likely to retie a ribbon in her niece Chloe's hair as she was to straighten her own son, Sidney's tie. They were a unit, these distant family members. Em knew them only through funerals and Mama's Christmas cards enclosed with the annual family photos. They were part of her, yet they were not.

Cleo did not want Em to follow in her footsteps. As their daughter entered her teens both parents watched Em's developing curvaceous body anxiously. She was becoming a voluptuous and beautiful young woman. By the time Emeline was fifteen, her mother frequently reminded Em of the necessity of preparing in life and not making the same mistakes she had made. She instructed Em that it was she, Cleopatra, who had been her own mother's greatest hope. Cleo had crushed her mother, Muriel's dreams with her pregnancy and early marriage. Muriel finally had accepted Arnold with open arms when she realized how happy her daughter was.

Cleo hoped for a brighter future for Em, college, adventure, travel, maybe becoming a veterinarian, with her love of animals. Anything but early marriage. The torch had been passed. Emeline, Cleo's dear bright and beautiful daughter had become her hope for a stellar future. There were so many lessons to teach Emmy. A lifetime of talks and confidences were her mother's tools for shaping her daughter's education.

Em's dreams dispersed, the smell of coffee tempting her from under the quilts. Randy was up and about, getting ready for his job at Bert's Best Buddies Pre-Owned Vehicles.

She shuffled to the kitchen and poured a thin stream of brew into her heavy white mug. Lacing her coffee with a curl of cream she watched as it blended into the brew. She loved that moment when the cream created a Rorschach pattern in her coffee. The fat globules caught the light, exploding into a rainbow as she stirred.

Randy watched from the doorway, noticing the way the light made his wife's curls form a halo surrounding her heart shaped face. How did he get so lucky?

"I just know it, Em. I can feel it. First day on the floor actually selling, not just watching the other guys. I'll sell more cars than anybody. After just hanging around for three weeks walking through the lot, today I'm finally going to be on the sales floor. I'm sick of just watching the other guys trying to sell cars."

Emeline smiled with a brightness she did not feel. Randy, freshly shaved and dressed, sat down across from Em at their scarred antique table. She studied her husband. She still thought he was the most handsome man she had ever met. At 6', he towered over Em. She loved to bury her face in his chest inhaling his warm scent. His dark curly hair was always a mess unless he greased it into place with Brylcreem. His chocolate brown eyes, laced with gold, his aristocratic nose and wide lips could melt her heart. She ignored his ears which were prominent, and had prompted many teasing insults as he was growing up. She hoped his prediction of success on the sales floor would come true.

Em was worried, though, aware of Randy's past employment history. She hoped this time he would succeed. He had blown all his previous positions with his arrogance and failure to listen to the advice of older, more experienced car salesmen and co-workers. She sighed and buried her concerns.

Randy nattered on and on. Em sipped her coffee. Her husband's words were the background music she could easily filter from her mind as her imagination led her elsewhere, everywhere. Her thoughts were on her mother today— indeed—she seemed stuck in memories of her childhood. She picked up the box of Wheaties and poured some into a bowl. She planned her day around the sound of Randy's voice, pushing memories from her mind. *What should I make for dinner? Guess I'll do laundry. Maybe iron.* Em traced the stripes in the old tiger oak table as Randy slurped up his bowl of Wheaties, Breakfast of Champions.

"God, I love you. You're so gorgeous, even this early in the morning," Randy said.

"Thank you, honey. But I think love corrupted your vision in high school when we first met." Randy reached out and wound one of her recalcitrant curls around his finger.

"What are you going to do today?" he asked, seeming to read her mind.

"I don't know. Maybe after I do housework, I'll take a walk through the neighborhood. Meet our neighbors." Maybe she'd even climb up the hill to explore the rich old plantation house Margret had said was up there, overlooking their valley.

Randy grunted, "Sounds great." He looked at his faux Rolex watch, jumped up and put on his tweed sports jacket. He straightened the collar of his freshly starched and ironed blue Oxford shirt and turned toward the door.

"Gotta flash." He picked up his briefcase which only held a battered, but current 1979 Blue Book, two pens, a pencil, and a pristine legal pad which had never known the imprint of words. He had brought all his car sales information in the same briefcase from his last job in Antioch. At least, now he didn't have to take a bridge to get to work, as he had done to get from his home in Sherman Island on the delta to the car lot on the mainland.

"Wish me luck, sweetheart." He kissed her goodbye.

"Break a leg, sweetie. Or better yet, sell a car," she said, watching him jauntily walk to their reconditioned Rambler. Dust filled the yard as he sped down their dirt road.

Randy would never admit it to Em, but he was nervous about his first day on the sales floor at Bert's. He knew he had exaggerated his talent at selling cars during his interview with the manager. Now he'd have to prove himself. He noticed his worried expression in the rear-view mirror and began to whistle, bolstering his confidence. He gave himself a pep talk. "Come on Randy, you're a big shot, you got this," he told his image. Momentarily, he believed it himself. "King Randy the Dandy, right?" *If only he could believe his own words*, he thought.

Em was also worried. Randy was reluctant to talk about his new job. It's probably just because the job is so new, he's got nothing to say, Em reasoned. She knew how Randy liked to brag about non-existent accomplishments. When Em pestered Randy with questions, all he would ever say was, "You know, I'm still feeling my way around, getting to know the guys and the ins and outs of the job. They know I'm great at selling cars, that's all that matters." *That, and actually selling cars*, Em thought. She chewed her lip and put her worries aside, knowing eventually he would tell her more. She just had to be patient. He *had* to be successful this time. Their livelihood and happiness depended on it.

Rising from the kitchen table she critically assessed their home. Em had worked tirelessly since the day Randy had carried her over the threshold a month before. Since moving in, she had cleaned each nook and cranny, moved furniture around, decorated and had made curtains from her mama's antique dish towels. She was happy she had brought the old pedal Singer sewing machine from California, despite Randy's complaints about 'that old thing'.

"Yes," she had replied. "We're bringing this old thing. It still works and I'm not much for hand sewing."

"So glad I didn't get rid of anything of Mama's," Em told her cats, as they wound around her ankles. She opened the kitchen door to let them out and looked across the road and into the field and woods beyond. She sighed deeply and hoped for the best for their little home and new life.

* * *

Em and Randy had settled into a daily routine. While Randy was at work, Em did the housework, cleaning their little home until every surface shone. In the evenings, she and Randy ate dinner, then watched TV. While watching TV, Em braided rugs from the old wool scraps she had thrown into a box at the last minute of their move. She also planned to begin a new embroidery project.

Em had made their home pretty and comforting with whatever little she and Randy had brought from Little Holland City. When they had moved, Em hadn't been able to part with the treasured antiques, the old battered couch, and her mama's dishes. They had taken everything they could fit in the UHAUL. Now that she was finished moving into and decorating their home, there was nothing on the horizon to spark her interest.

Randy had brought home dinners from KFC or Burger King for the first week until Em started cooking scrambled eggs or Mac and Cheese for dinner. Em was proud of their home, but not her lack of skill in the kitchen.

The sun blasted through the little curtains which gaily framed the old wavy glass kitchen windows. The wood-planked floors were polished. The living room with its used TV set and side tables were dusted. Em had carefully covered the stains on the sofa arms with antique doilies, giving the room a warm and inviting look. Her favorite room was the library with its built-in bookcases, window seat, fireplace, Dutch door, and many windows. The room was her remaining challenge. The bookcases were empty. The only furnishing in the room was the latest braided rug she had woven from cast-off wool scraps. She hoped the library would become her oasis of peace, her sanctuary, her refuge. The room's bookless shelves and waiting window seat beckoned her. She nibbled her lip imagining what the room could become. She had never bought books, a luxury she couldn't afford with Randy's meager salary. She had already read the three books she had borrowed from the library on Monday and it was only Thursday morning. The Charles Town Library was Em's favorite escape, although she hadn't explored the little town much further. Days after their arrival in Heavenly Hollow they took time out from unpacking and cleaning. Randy had been sweet to take her into town, showing her around. He shared all the places he had visited with his mom when he had helped move her into Charles Town. As yet, Em had not explored by herself.

This day, Em was left alone with nothing to do. Their little cabin felt like a vacuum in the backwoods of Virginia. Their home was close to Charles Town, the James River, Jamestown, Spring Grove and Cabin Point. Further north was Vienna. Randy said they could even take a ferry to Scotland. She had laughed at his words. "Really? I had no idea we were that close to Europe! Scotland *and* Vienna?"

Em longed to visit the surrounding towns but with only one car it was difficult. To do so she'd have to get up early and drop Randy off at work. She was determined to venture further from Heavenly Hollow and explore Charles Town. She wanted days to herself, savoring whatever private adventures she might discover.

She was bored and didn't feel like beginning her morning chores, instead she moved onto the front porch. She sat comfortably in the Appalachian rocker Randy had discovered in a refuse pile in Charles Town. The field across the street from their cabin beckoned her with its wildflowers and blooming trees. Em wondered what they were, Apple Orchards? They looked much like their old orchard in California. Em found peace on the porch. As she rocked, she was once again overcome with memories. She couldn't seem to escape from her past on this bright spring morning. Her mama wouldn't leave her mind just as she would never leave her heart. She had died in late 1977 and Emeline still missed her as much as on the awful day she had watched her mama slip away from her. Thinking of her departed parents brought Em's sorrow back. Days like this her grief made her feel like a small child, the wounded prey of catastrophe. Whenever possible, she pushed her memories and grief aside. Not today.

Her papa had left this earth two years before mama. After his death, Mama had lost her spark. Her departed parents haunted Em. Lessons in life she had not understood at the age of five, or six, or sixteen, became realized in her world of today. "Better to be subtle than audacious. Gets folks' attention when they have to listen closely to your words," advised her mama on more than one occasion. Mama had been correct in all of her teachings. Except grief. Em didn't have lessons for coping with her broken heart. She sorely missed her family home. Randy tried his best to lift her from her dark moods—he was excited with their new life and home. But to Em, Virginia was still terribly unfamiliar. She constantly compared their two worlds in her mind's eye, the California delta and Virginia. She still had one foot and at least half her heart on Sherman Island. She knew every part of that island and of the San Joaquin and Sacramento Rivers. She missed every inch of their family home in Little Holland. She couldn't jump enthusiastically into their new life in Virginia as Randy had.

On the delta, she knew the seasons by what was planted, grown and harvested. There was always something to do, either in the garden or tending their chickens and pigs. The emerald fields of rice, corn, soy beans, Bok choy and lettuce had been Emeline's playground. She had loved running through the rows of tasseled corn, escaping from the world, hiding in the scent of growing vegetables and rich earth. Even the snakes making their watery trails in the blue and green river waters was a beautiful sight. She missed everything about the home where she had grown into her twenty-year old-self. The river smells, that wet, yeasty, earthy fragrance, was a longed-for perfume. Em yearned for the local farms, the fresh produce by the side of the road, the bunches of flowers she would pick for her mama. She even missed her farm chores. Now, her household chores were completed in less than an hour. She had no visiting neighbors to interrupt her time alone.

She wished she were a Sandhill Crane, making its annual migration returning to family nesting grounds on the Suisun Marsh and the Sherman and delta islands and waterways. She imagined she was flying west, across the country, back to California. The images floated into her consciousness. She remembered the jungle-like foliage surrounding their home on Sherman Island and the way the green shadows wavered in the mist and rain. The fear of flooding was always present on Sherman Island but never worried Em. To her, it meant easier 'worm pickin', as her papa called it, when he asked her to gather bait for his fishing trips. After yet another torrential storm flooded their farmland, Em recognized the fear on her parent's faces. They knew the danger of muddy water rushing onto their land and ripening fields and into their home. It was a ghost gnawing at the back of her parents' minds. How would they ever have been able to leave their home in the event of a major flood, cut off from neighbors, and the world, from roads and the bridge to safer ground in Antioch on the mainland?

Em rose from her rocker and planned the rest of her day. Maybe I'll paint my toenails? Red or pink? Maybe I should get pregnant. She giggled to herself. Maybe not. Randy's departure settled over her like a cloak of loneliness. She loved Randy with all her heart but wondered why she thought of him negatively at times. Her worries over his new job returned to Em. "He'll do just fine, stop worrying. No one knows about his other jobs in California. This is a new start," she admonished herself.

It was also time to put her memories and sorrow aside. "That was then. This is now. Focus on today!" She lined up several shades of nail polish, like small soldiers on the table next to her chair. *Red or pink polish?* she wondered. The day stretched before her like one endless mass of acres to be ploughed through on their delta farm. She had nothing to do but decide on the color of nail polish and eat peanuts. She was already halfway through the bag Randy had brought home from the greengrocers yesterday. *Wonder how fattening peanuts are?* she mused.

Suddenly, Em was disturbed from her caloric musing to see a thin, tall woman appearing from around the bend in their road. The woman was in no hurry. A fat orange cat followed her. In her arms, she carried a large wicker basket.

"What on earth?" Emeline muttered to herself. "Where did she come from?" Em rose and brushed the peanut shells from her shorts.

"Lo, darlin'," said the stranger upon arriving. *Don't darlin' me*, Emeline thought suspiciously. Her concerns were quickly replaced by curiosity and vanity. Maybe she was a friendly neighbor, come to welcome her to Heavenly Hollow? Wonder if I have peanuts stuck in my teeth?

"Just stopped by to pick your magnolias, darlin'. With your permission, of course. Been doing this for more years than you've lived." The tall woman looked at Emeline admiringly. "Lots and lots more years, in fact, I'd say."

"What magnolias?" Em asked.

The tall, gray-haired, thin-lipped, granite-eyed woman stopped dead in her tracks. "The *magnolias,* deah. Don't you ever look up? Can't you smell that magnificent scent? *Those* magnolias," the woman said, as she pointed a long, bony finger upward.

Emeline looked up at the towering magnolia tree, which had only been, up to this moment, a tree shading the front porch and darkening the small bedroom in their cabin. "Oh, yeah. That tree. Never noticed the flowers before."

"Oh, my," the stranger replied.

Emeline's two calico cats, Scarlett and her sister Rhett, objected to the big orange intruder. Hissing and growling, noses down, haunches up, fur rising and tails coiling under their behinds, they backed up. Usually kind to visitors, or at least curious, they turned and raced under the porch. *Now what the hell's gotten into them?* Em thought, as she examined the woman more closely.

"So unusual to have not one, but two, calico cats, my deah," the elderly woman said, noting the noses of the two cats poking out from under the porch.

"I know," replied Em. "They're both females. Male calicoes are pretty much non-existent. Mama and I found them hiding in a woodpile next to our house on the delta. They were wet and scraggly, and looked as though they hadn't eaten in days. We figured they were related to my mama's calico cats, Tristan and Isolde, with maybe a black or orange male thrown into the mix. Mama adored Tristan and Isolde. They lived to be twenty-one and died a day apart. Mama said they couldn't live without one another." Em grew silent, thinking of her mama and papa, who couldn't live without one another, either. She returned to the present.

"I named my calicoes Rhett and Scarlet. I was reading *Gone with The Wind* in high school. They got along with other cats just fine, unlike the real Scarlet and Rhett." Em giggled. "Well, anyway, none of our neighborhood cats fought or loved the way Scarlet and Rhett did in that book."

A question furrowed the older woman's forehead. "Goodness. You're very new to our little holler then. What delta? I only know of the Mississippi and Louisiana Deltas. Where did you grow up, deah?" the stranger said, then walked over to where the cats were hiding causing them to scurry more deeply into the dark recesses under the porch, giving Em time to think over her answer.

Bending over, the older woman addressed Em's two cats, "Oh, well. Perhaps someday we'll all become friends." She waved her fingers under the porch, tempting the cats but they would not be seduced so easily. The large orange cat stretched and yawned completely unimpressed with Scarlet and Rhett, or their history.

The older woman looked questionably at Emeline, awaiting her answer. "Oh, yeah. I grew up in a tiny town, Little Holland City, on Sherman Island, in the middle of the Sacramento-San Joaquin delta," Em said, pride coloring her voice. "We had a farm, not a big one, but big enough to always have fresh veggies and fruit and even share with a few neighbors. Sometimes Mama brought tomatoes and corn to the local farm stands and markets in Antioch and Locke. She canned the rest. It was a perfect, wild place to grow up. My papa taught me to row a boat on the waterways almost before I could walk. I loved every inch of that delta." Em stopped her conversation abruptly, then brushed the tears from her eyes. "Well, that was then, this is now," Em said, dismissing her memories, yet again.

The tall, thin woman looked at Em closely and decided it was best to drop the subject, for now anyway. Silence grew between the two women as they examined one another. Emeline noticed the woman was as old as her attire. She wore faded-blue wrinkled pants with a worn blue and white striped blouse and stained, beat-up Keds. She held tightly to her woven basket. She appeared as ancient as the surrounding hills. "Wow. You're really old." The words escaped from Em's lips. She was immediately embarrassed by her audacity and bit her lip but didn't apologize, hoping her remark would not be noticed.

The older woman took no offense, and even seemed proud of her age. "Yes, deah, that I am. Older than you can imagine. I've earned all these wrinkles, old baggy eyes and droopy jowls life has given me. Not to mention this old body. I'm Felicity, deah. Who are you?"

"Emeline. My mother named me after a song she loved when she was growin' up. But then she found out the name in the song wasn't Emeline. It was Irene. I think." Now why had she told a complete stranger so much about her history? She'd never told that story to anyone before. Not even Randy.

"Irene, yes, a lovely old song. *Goodnight, Irene, goodnight, Irene, I'll see you in my dreams*," the tall woman sang in a high, quavering voice, then smiled, obviously proud of herself.

"Well, darlin', Irene or Emeline, you're a beautiful sight for these old, tired eyes."

Em's manners returned to her. "I'm sorry I called you old. That was rude. Randy always says there's no space between my brain and my mouth. I have a tendency to talk without thinking."

Felicity smiled as she replied, "What does it matter, Emeline, if what you say is true? I *am* old. I respect honesty. Who's Randy?"

"Oh. Randy's my husband. He's at work right now at the Auto Emporium of Pre-Owned Vehicles. It's out on the Meridian Road."

"That used auto place? I thought that it was called Bert's Best Buddies Used Car Lot. Have they changed the name?"

"No, the name's the same. Only Randy calls it the Auto Emporium of Pre-Owned Vehicles. He says that's what he's going to call it when he buys the place. But I don't know how that's going to happen. Today's his first day on the sales floor. He's gonna have to sell a hell of a lot of cars to buy the place." Em could feel the scowl on her face which she hoped the older woman didn't notice.

"It's wonderful to have ambitions," said Felicity as she began deftly plucking magnolias from the lowest hanging branches of the tree, filling her basket with their enormous, waxy white, voluptuous blossoms. Em marveled that she had never noticed the enormous flowers before. But then, she hadn't ventured outside much until Randy brought home the old rocker she was sitting in. This old lady, this Felicity, was right. The magnolia flowers did smell heavenly.

"Did you ever wonder why Georgia O'Keefe never painted magnolias, deah?" asked Felicity. "They're so worthy, so sensual and elegant. However, they don't grow in the desert. That must be the reason." She continued to pluck the blossoms from the ancient tree's lower branches laden and heavy with their beautiful bouquets.

"Who?" asked Em.

Felicity stopped her plucking to gaze warmly at Em. "Georgia O'Keeffe. Have you never heard of her? She's an astounding and very famous artist who lives in the desert and paints the beauty of the floral world in quite, um, an unusual and graphic, sensual manner."

"No. Never heard of her. I don't know much about artists. Or much of anything, I guess."

"Oh, my," the elderly woman said again. "I'm sure that's not quite true. But I will say you have a lot to learn and I have a lot to teach."

"That's what my mama always said." Felicity looked over her shoulder from her task of collecting magnolia blossoms. She smiled at Emeline. "Never too late to learn, darlin'." Her basket filled, she placed it on the ground and sat companionably in front of Emeline on the porch step. Emeline lazily stroked Felicity's orange cat, whose name she learned was Zuma. Scarlett and Rhett watched cautiously from under the porch.

"You're awfully young to be married, aren't you? Why, you can't be more than twenty."

Em didn't reply immediately, thinking over her decision to marry Randy. It had seemed like the best idea after she was left alone after the deaths of both her mama and papa. But Em hadn't counted on Randy moving them across the country to 'take care of Mother' in Charles Town, Virginia. The closest waterways to them were the James and the Chikahominy, miles away. The biggest nearby cities were Ruthville and Vienna. Emeline felt marooned, so far from her beloved California Delta, with not a hint of the perfume of the sea to revive her. Maybe the move was all a mistake. Here she was, living 3000 miles from her childhood home and all that was familiar. She was stuck in this backwoods village with no future she could discern. *No, it was not a mistake,* she thought, her loyalty to and love of Randy overwhelming her. She smiled as she returned to the conversation.

"Turned twenty on my last birthday, March 15. The Ides of March, Mama always said. Mama hoped I wouldn't marry young, like she did. I was eighteen. But Mama had passed, and I was all alone. Papa had died two years before Mama. I was never much for having girlfriends. Mama had always been my best friend. Didn't trust girlfriends or girly things much. I was always a tomboy. After Mama died, I was so lonely. Randy and I had been together since I was fifteen. So, I figured, oh, what the hell. Why not get married. What else do I have to do?"

The true story behind Em's blithe remarks went much deeper than her words. Em found herself drifting back into her memories. One bright day everything seemed perfectly normal. Within a moment, everything changed forever. Her papa had crashed to the bedroom floor with a heart attack. The doctor said he was 'probably dead before he hit the floor'. It was the worst tragedy, so unexpected and horrific, that Em or her mother had ever suffered through. No one had even known that Arnold had a heart condition. Their grief was so excruciating that neither she nor her mama could discuss that life-changing day. They avoided all talk of her papa which only made Em grieve more deeply. She accepted her mama's silence knowing she was too crushed to admit the depth of the agonizing sea change in their lives. It was as though both Em and her mama had died along with her papa of broken hearts. His death had been Em's first experience with grief, pain and sorrow, multiplied by her mama's devastation. Mama had changed overnight. The light, the spark, had been extinguished from her eyes. Only Em could bring joy back into those beautiful violet orbs. Despite her attempts to help her mother, sorrow would not leave her haunted eyes, no matter what Em tried. Cleo just didn't seem to care about anything—eventually, not even Em.

Then her mama began showing signs of exhaustion where she had been energetic and lively previously. Her face had turned gray and her hair limp. Even her eyes seemed to lose their color. Emeline had imagined her mama was just lonely and still deeply grieving for her beloved Arnie. No wonder she had let herself go.

Cleo's constant cough had worried Em. She had reassured herself that Mama had always coughed. Her habit of smoking a pack a day of unfiltered Lucky Strikes would certainly cause that raspy cough. Finally, Emeline decided to broach the subject.

"Mama, you don't look well, like your usual self," she said one day. "Are you okay? Maybe you should see our doctor?"

"I'm healthy as a horse," her mama had replied— "just can't get rid of this chest cold. You've always been a worrywart."

Em remembered how she had continued to nag her mother to take better care of herself. She admonished her mama for not getting enough rest, saying that she needed to rest to get over her chest cold. Eventually Cleo told Em the truth. She had been to their family physician, Dr. Waggoner. Cleo trusted Dr. Waggoner who had known her for most of her life.

"Emmy, I think I felt worse for Dr. Waggoner than I did for myself. His worried face and tearful eyes told me the truth before he said a word. 'Cancer is what I think, Cleo, after seeing the x-rays. But I can't be sure. You need to get another opinion from an oncologist. They'll run more tests'."

Her mother had chuckled then, which began another bout of coughing. Finally, she continued. "I told him I don't need another doctor to tell me what we both know."

It was too late for Mama to do anything but die. It was as though Cleo just didn't want to fight the disease. She was worn out by grief. She didn't seem to care about anything. She didn't have the strength, or desire, to live.

Em refused to acknowledge the possibility of her mother's death. An admission of such enormous loss and loneliness made one vulnerable, open to catastrophe, like falling off a cliff. Cancer made the decision for Mama as to whether she wanted to continue living without her beloved Arnie. She didn't. Opting for radiation was out of the question for Cleo. The disease took her mama away without her mother even seeming to care that she was leaving.

Days before her death, in the pure white sterile hospital bed, Cleo had rasped her hopes to her beloved daughter. "I've taught you all I know, my love. Time for you to spread your wings and find out what life is about. I'll always be looking out for you. Just look for me in your heart. I'll be there." Soon after that, her mama slipped into a coma and was gone. At seventeen, Em had become an orphan. She had been devastated, crushed, blackened to ash by her mama's death, just two years after Papa died. Randy became her rock. He adored her and listened to her. Still did.

"Emeline? Where did you go?" Em realized she had gone off into the past again, disappearing into her thoughts right in front of Felicity. Belatedly, she remembered her manners.

"Oh, I'm sorry. Just thinking about the past. I've been doing too much of that lately."

"It's always important to remember our roots, child."

Em ignored Felicity's remark and returned to the present. "Anyway, Randy couldn't make a good living where we came from, selling cars in Antioch, the next biggest city over the bridge from Little Holland. Mostly people bought tractors and trucks. He started out by going to Technical School for auto mechanics. He didn't want to go to any community college and the closest one was in Sacramento, anyway. I know it was because he didn't want to leave me. He did learn a good trade though, fixing cars, and he was great at it." Em smiled at the memory of him with his head under the hood of an old truck. "He said, 'I don't like getting my hands dirty like some dumb old mechanic. I want bigger things'. So, he started selling cars. He was always a better mechanic than a salesman. When he got fired from the used car lot in Antioch, we figured maybe it was time for a change. We came here about a month ago. Figured it was a better place to make a living, and Charles Town seemed like a good choice.

Besides, Randy's mom missed him. She found this place for us. We moved clear across the country to be closer to his mama after I'd lost mine. I'd never even met Randy's mother."

"Hmmm. The first time meeting a family member is always fraught with nervousness. Have you met her yet? And, if so, how did the visit go?"

"We went over for dinner the day we moved in. She did everything to help us get settled in. Her name's Margret, and of course she adores Randy. She's a little uppity. One of the things she said over dinner was, 'Have I told you that I'm related to George Washington's brother, Charles, who Charles Town is named after?'" Em scoffed at the memory, then continued. "That was the only family information Margret has shared with me. I don't even know if that's true. She wouldn't tell me anything about Randy's childhood or his father. I really don't know much about Randy's family. He never talks about them, either."

Em chewed her lip, remembering their visit with Randy's mom. She asked Felicity, "Do you know if that's true? Is Charles Town named after George Washington's brother? Do you think there are relatives of the Washingtons living here?"

Felicity chuckled. "Well, I don't know about that. But certainly, George Washington and Thomas Jefferson, along with other early settlers and diplomats lived all over these hills. But back to you. That's quite a story about your family. And look at you, barely twenty, married and living in one of my favorite cabins, #25. You lost your mama but gained a mother-in-law. I'm sure she'll warm up after she gets to know you better."

Emeline snorted, remembering her first encounter with Margret. Em had been her usual timid self and was a bit fearful of Margret. She had wanted to make the best impression and wondered if she had succeeded. She shouldn't have become angry with some of Margret's remarks and hoped her mother-in-law hadn't noticed. Em felt the jury was out on Margret and vice versa. She resented Margret yet was grateful to her for all she had done for her and Randy. It was an odd mix of emotions which Em didn't bother to untangle. She was glad of the miles between their cabin and Margret's big house. She worried that Randy's mom would never approve of her. She wasn't nearly as elegant as her mother-in-law. And Margret was a great cook, Randy always said so. Em could barely boil water for the macaroni and cheese she relied on for their dinners. Maybe her mother-in-law looked down her nose at Em because she couldn't cook. *She could certainly open cans as handily as the next girl*, Emeline thought. I guess I really should learn to cook, Em mused.

Felicity looked puzzled as she again broke into Em's meandering thoughts. "Emeline? You look like you're a world away. Would you like a few magnolias from my basket?"

"Oh, thank you. Yes, I would," said Em. "I wish they'd been in bloom when we visited Randy's mom for the first time. They would have been a better bouquet of flowers than the little wildflower bunch I brought over." Em studied her visitor as she took the proffered magnolias from her. "Where do you live? It must be close by since you walked here, and you know our cabin."

"Oh, yes. I've lived in these hills forever." Em longed to prod the woman into revealing more, but for once, she held her tongue. If Felicity wanted to tell Em more about herself, she would have.

Felicity returned from the magnolia tree to again sit comfortably on the porch steps, silently studying Emeline. She seemed in no hurry to depart, and Em was happy for the company and conversation. Rare for Em, she suddenly couldn't stop talking to this old lady.

"Now, sometimes I wonder," she said. "Maybe I did get married too young." *There I go again*, thought Emeline. *Why am I telling this old coot, this stranger, my life story?*

"Yes, indeed you should. Wonder, that is. About life and marriage. Oh, all sorts of things," said Felicity. For a moment longer, she examined Emeline, so young, fresh, Pollyanna pretty and naive. For several moments, the two sat in silence. Emeline picked up the bottles of nail polish. She examined the colors carefully.

Felicity said, "Go with the red, darlin'. It suits you and is far more elegant than pink. Pink is a child's color. You need the shade of a woman on you."

"Elegant." Emeline snorted. "That's a good one. Do I look elegant? In my worn-out shorts and scrappy tee shirt covered in peanut shells and cat fur? There's no one worth seeing out here anyway to admire my nail polish."

"Don't I count? And what about your Randy, doesn't he count?" Felicity said with a warm smile. To Em's surprise, Felicity reached out and touched Em's warm hand with her cold and wrinkled fingers.

Felicity's words struck a chord in Em. The older woman seemed to be reading Em's mind, just as Randy had earlier in the morning. Was she so transparent? She continued to study Felicity. She was old enough to be her grandmother, yet she seemed ageless. Em couldn't guess at the number of years she'd lived. She didn't want to repeat her thoughtlessness by asking Felicity's age. The older woman's face was lined, her skin papery thin and pale. Yet she appeared filled with light generated by those steel-gray eyes. Her nose was long, providing a stately Roman profile. Even her lips were thin and pale. Her face was haloed by her recalcitrant mass of short gray curls. Em guessed she must be 5'8", at least six inches taller than petite Emeline. Her body was long, thin and almost manly. *She looked as though she worked outdoors a great deal and she probably walked wherever she wanted to go,* Em thought. It appeared as though she'd been dropped into Emeline's yard from another era. Em tried to pluck from her memory where she'd seen such an outfit before. Slaves picking cotton? A laundry lady? Who knows. Em shelved the thought away for further examination later.

"Well, darlin, I better get these lovely blossoms in water," said Felicity. "My thanks for letting me pick my bouquet. Come on now, Zuma, let's get on home so Emeline's cats can come out from under the porch." The big orange cat gave one last look at Scarlett and Rhett. In disdain or farewell, she flicked her tail and sauntered after Felicity's departing figure.

"Bye, now," Felicity called over her shoulder, lifting her hand, like a flag, behind her. She quickly disappeared down the dusty lane. As Em watched her depart, her new friend seemed to evaporate in the bright glare of morning sunlight. The meeting had been so unexpected and left Emeline feeling lonelier than ever.

"Wonder where she lives?" Em asked Rhett and Scarlett, who had crept cautiously from beneath the porch. They didn't reply other than to stare angrily down the road after the orange interloper.

Returning to the kitchen, Em retrieved one of her mother's antique Stangl pitchers from a shelf and filled it with water for the magnolias. They *were* beautiful. Why hadn't Em noticed them before, right over her head? Randy would be pleased to see her bouquet tonight. Their scent immediately filled the kitchen.

Em sat at her grandmama's old kitchen table, picked up the red nail polish and began to paint her fingernails and toes. *Hmmm,* she thought. Red, elegant. You know, I think she's right about that. After her polish dried, she busied herself putting her little house in order. She made their bed, swept the worn wood floors, washed and put away the breakfast dishes and opened all the windows.

As Em completed her housework Felicity kept returning to her mind. She wondered again where the old woman lived. She hoped she would return to visit again. Emeline was unfamiliar with friendships with women and perplexed by her feelings for Felicity. Would friendship come creeping into her life, opening doors she had always preferred to remain closed? Em didn't like missing people. Friends had no place in her life. Her mama had always been her only true friend, her confidant.

A stray breeze ruffled the dish towel curtains Em was so proud of. She caught a whiff of the magnolias through the open kitchen windows, the scent mingling with the magnolias on her table, inundating the kitchen with their strong, sweet scent. *Now why didn't I notice that magnolia tree, right here in the yard?* she wondered. She couldn't get Felicity out of her mind. Her words kept coming back to Em. "You have a lot to learn and I have a lot to teach," the older woman had said, somehow lifting Emeline's spirits. The thought that Felicity might return excited her, like a new adventure.

After she finished ironing Randy's work shirts, she retreated to her favorite room, the library and settled in the window seat. "Bet I'm going to like that old lady," she said aloud to Rhett and Scarlet, splashed in sunlight as they lay entwined together on the braided rug. "Hope she comes back." Both cats perked up their ears and looked at her. Did Em imagine it, or did she notice fear? Of Felicity's orange cat, Zuma? Or was it disgust on her cat's faces? Stop being stupid! She told herself. Cats just eat and sleep. They don't understand a word I'm saying. And they sure don't care. "You two are just like Randy," Em said, insultingly. "But just like him, I love you, too."

Em found herself wondering what the future would bring, years down the road. Nothing important was on the horizon; that was certain. Ambition in her life was simple and small, but meaningful. Eventually, she would start filling up those beautiful empty bookshelves. She would sit in her mama's beat up old rocker as she read, mended socks or embroidered pretty peasant blouses for herself. She'd fill up the pantry shelves with canned vegetables and jams. For now, she'd just sit in the rocker and look out the windows to the meadows beyond the wavy glass.

Eventually, Em returned to the kitchen and wondered again what she should make for dinner. In a desultory fashion, she peered into the contents of the refrigerator. Only eggs, cheese, bread and wilted lettuce greeted her. She should throw the lettuce out. She hated making salads and was surprised Randy had brought some Romaine home from the green grocer.

Guess it'll be grilled cheese sandwiches again. Wish I had some tomatoes. Should she call Randy at work and ask him to bring some home? No. Why bother?

It would be a long, lonely, uneventful afternoon. Again.

Chapter 4

Just by the look of Randy's hair Emeline knew it had been a bad day. Running his hands through his Brylcreemed brown mass too many times made him look like a disgruntled porcupine. He slumped dejectedly on the front seat of their faithful old Rambler. He needed a minute to collect his thoughts before facing Em. It had been another day without selling a car. The other guys on the lot seemed as though they didn't like him. He had tried his best to let them know he was a man to be reckoned with, a guy with a great history selling cars in Antioch. But Antioch was nothing like Charles Town. Instead of farmers looking for a new tractor, these were wealthier men wandering the car lot, looking for deals on convertibles and luxury vehicles. "I'll show them." Randy told himself. "Just wait and see. I'll outsell them all."

In a huff, he got out and slammed the door making the old Rambler shudder. Em knew he hadn't sold a single car, again. Not the red Impala. Not the blue Nova. In the last week, other sales reps had sold. Not Randy. He was a buffoon. She felt her anger rise over her husband's real, or imagined shortcomings. "I better not have to get a job myself," she angrily muttered.

That cruel word, buffoon, reminded Em of her mama's name for her papa, which she said under her breath only when she was very angry. Mama would never hurt Papa with unkind words or insults. Well, almost never. OMG. She suddenly wondered, have I married my father? She pushed the thought from her mind. No. They were nothing alike. Papa was accomplished, smart in his way. Nothing like her Randy, who was tender and sweet, and who needed her. He just wasn't the best salesman.

She quickly retreated from the kitchen before Randy stomped up the porch steps. Em busied herself in their small living room rearranging the afghan and doilies covering up the holes and stains on the threadbare sofa. The longer she stayed out of Randy's way the more time he would have to invent a fairy tale describing the events of his day.

Em's heart strings were strung tight. As though it were yesterday she suddenly remembered the first day they had met in high school. She never would have imagined that she would someday end up in Virginia with the same boy who had walked into Mr. Wisegar's General Science classroom in her freshman year of high school.

As usual, Emeline had been paying little attention in class. Instead, she was engrossed in watching a pair of robins building a nest outside the classroom window. This lesson was much more interesting than electrons and neutrons. And birdwatching was certainly part of science, Em reasoned.

A timid knock on the classroom door interrupted the science lesson. Em dragged her eyes to the open door. The vice principal entered the room followed by a tall, lanky, freckled, dark-haired boy about Em's age of fourteen. He reminded Em of an Ibis as he awkwardly shifted from one foot to the other. His unruly dark hair stood in a ruffled mass above a high forehead. His eyes were golden brown, the color of a Carolina wren's plumage. His expression was stern with tight lips, clenched jaw and distrustful eyes. He didn't smile as he looked around anxiously. Clearly, this boy didn't want to be in the classroom any more than Em did.

"Mr. Wisegar, this is your new student, Randy Upswatch. I'm sure your class will provide him with River Bottom High School's special welcome." The vice principal looked at Mr. Wisegar hopefully.

"Yes, indeed. Class?"

In dull monotones and with some high-pitched teasing voices, the students shouted in unison:

"Welcome to the friendliest school in the Delta, Randy Upswatch." Some boys mispronounced his name to Randy Upshitz. A fierce warning glare from Mr. Wisegar ended that mispronunciation, for the moment. The poor guy couldn't have looked more miserable as he retreated to an empty desk Mr. Wisegar directed him to in front of Em. She surreptitiously examined the new kid as he made his way down the aisle to his seat. Cute freckles, slim, nice eyes. She wondered what he would look like if he smiled.

Em usually behaved in her designated back-of-the-room seat, fearful of any inattention discovered by Mr. Wisegar. The punishment of being moved to the front of the room directly under Mr. Wisegar's desk was more than she could bear. She knew her teacher's hawk-like eyes would end her daydreaming and inattention. Em had never tried to be friendly to the students around her. She listened to and enjoyed the camaraderie of the boys and other girls, but never joined them. Until that particular day.

The undertow of the boys' insults aimed at Randy continued. "Hey, Upshitz, where'd you get that shirt and jeans? Goodwill?"

"Probably the dumpster." This drew a few chuckles from Em's fellow students.

"Hey is that shit spatter on your face? Where didja come from, the Halfway House?"

"Quite the little piss-ant, ain't ya?"

That final insult brought Randy to full-throttle rage, which he tried desperately to control. 'Piss-ant'. His father's favorite name for Randy for as long as he could remember, beginning the night when he was only four and had been awakened by a loud argument in his parents' room.

It was the first time he suspected his father didn't love him the way his mother did. His mother had always said his father just had trouble showing affection. That night Randy learned there was much more to his mom's excuses for his father's coldness toward him.

Randy had been awakened from a dream by the shouts coming from behind his parent's bedroom door. He crawled out of bed and walked toward the loud yelling, carrying his teddy in his arms. He heard his mother crying. He couldn't hear her words but he recognized the pleading in her voice. It was the same voice Randy used when begging for another cookie. The words his father shouted stunned him.

"You fat pig. You're nothing but a ruined fat hog. And to think I once thought you were beautiful. Stupid me. I thought you were a catch. Ha, what a joke."

Randy moved closer to the door to hear his mother's voice. "Please, darling, please. Don't leave me again. Stay with me. I'll lose the weight, I promise."

"Oh, right. I've heard that for over four years. You'll always be nothing but a fat, disgusting pig."

Randy sucked his thumb, felt the clot of sorrow in his throat as he tried not to cry. He knew his father hated to see him cry. It always made his daddy angry. Randy knew exactly what a 'fat pig' was. His mommy had taught him animal sounds from his picture book. 'Moo' says the cow, 'cluck, cluck' says the chicken, 'oink, oink' says the pig. His mama wasn't a pig. Why did his daddy say that? She was his beautiful mommy who smelled like flowers when she held him close in her arms.

Randy jumped back when the bedroom door flew open, the light from the room lit up like a spotlight shining on his small, cowering body. He held his teddy closer. Through the open bedroom door he saw his mother doubled over on the bed, sobbing. His father glared at him, his face dark with rage.

"You stupid worthless little piss-ant. I wish you'd never been born. You ruined everything." His father pulled teddy from Randy's arms and threw his cherished stuffed animal on the floor. "What a baby you are. You're too big for stupid teddy bears." Randy erupted in screams and tears. His mother had raced from the room, scooped Randy into her arms and held him in her warm, soft, pillowy breasts. "It's okay, baby. Daddy's just angry because he has to leave. He'll be back tomorrow. He didn't mean anything."

As his father walked to the front door, he spat words over his shoulder. "That's right, piggy, take that worthless piss-ant to bed with you. Better him than me." Randy watched tears streaming down his mother's face as his father hurried out the door, slamming it behind him.

"What's a piss-ant, Mommy?" Randy could barely get the words out of his mouth. He knew whatever his daddy had called him wasn't good, but he had no idea what it meant. Was his mommy a pig and he was an ant? His mother's soothing voice calmed him. "It's nothing, sweetheart. Pay no attention. Come on now, back to bed. There's lots more hours of sleep to catch before morning."

Over the years, watching the battles between his parents, listening to his father jeer at him, "Hey, piss-ant, you're a real buffoon, you know that?" Randy finally realized those insults defined all he would ever be to his father. His mother always said 'piss-ant' was an affectionate term for a little boy. Randy knew better by the tone of his father's voice. When he finally read the definition in the dictionary in third grade, he understood the full extent of his father's disgust toward him.

'Piss-ant: vulgar slang for an insignificant or contemptible person or thing'. Randy looked up every unfamiliar word in Webster's definition. That's all he was, 'insignificant and contemptible'. At that moment, Randy made a vow. "I'll show him. I'll show them all. I'll just make sure everyone knows I'm no piss-ant. I'll be the biggest, baddest, smartest kid in my whole class. They'll see who I really am, a king, not a piss-ant. From now on, I'll be 'King Randy the Dandy'. And from that day forward that was who Randy pretended to be, a big kid who could do anything. Even though his grades or his size didn't prove it, his wild stories would show the world he was a force to be reckoned with, King Randy the Dandy."

Randy's thoughts returned to Mr. Wisegar's classroom. The students around him came into sharp focus as they stared at him. Randy clenched his teeth, tried his best to control his anger. He'd show them.

The laughter of one boy pushed him further to the boiling point. "Got kicked out of Washington, huh, Upshitz?"

"I've lived here all my life, assholes. Just changing schools is all."

Em could stand it no longer. Here was a wounded bird being pecked by malicious crows. She knew what it was like to be ridiculed. She had learned long ago to ignore the nastiness of her classmates. She recognized that Randy was fragile, a soft-shelled crab in the midst of molting and moving into a new home. Em understood. It had taken her years of hardening her own shell to become who she was today.

Her intervention was swift and startling, even to herself. "Why don't you all just shut the fuck up and leave him alone?"

"Ooooooh, she speaks! Didn't know you had a voice, Curly Cutie. And she swears!"

Em threw her General Science workbook at the largest member of the mob.

"You bitch, that hurt," he said, rubbing his head.

At that moment, Randy fell instantly and permanently in love as he watched Emeline being sent to the Principal's office.

Mr. Wisegar's shocked countenance hurt Em more than the eviction from his class. His stern voice would not leave her ears. "Emeline. I never would have imagined such behavior coming from you. I am very disappointed. Book throwing *and* swearing? You've always been such a quiet, refined young lady. I think a discussion in the principal's office is what you need right now."

"That idiot deserved a book in his face and more," she said under her breath. Em turned at the door and gave Randy a long look before departing. Her clear aquamarine-blue eyes, insouciant smile and rebellious posture gave Randy courage. New school or old, he'd found a friend. His heart flipped over. He knew he'd love this cheeky girl forever, no matter what the future held. As for Em, she had someone to protect and watch over.

Since her earliest school days, Em's education had been sketchy and varied. She had been moved to several different schools by her mama whenever Cleo felt Em was threatened. The earliest move resulted from the first time Em, in fourth grade, had been marched to the principal's office at Lincoln Elementary.

She had been standing in a circle on the playground with classmates Priscilla, Mary and Heather. The wind ruffled the leaves of the Plum trees at the edge of the asphalt where the woods closed in around the playground. The shadows of the trees sheltered and shaded the swings, bleachers and baseball field from the heat of the sun. Emeline's favorite place was at the edge of the woods, protected, unseen by playground monitors. She held court there with her three friends sharing opinions and knowledge her mama had provided to her, as well as her own observations.

"We don't have to worry about the playground monitors," said Emeline. "This is their recess, too. They don't care what we do, as long as they can smoke. We're just girls. The only thing they have to watch out for is boys fighting." She was solemn in her wisdom.

"I don't like it when they fight," Priscilla said anxiously, pushing her glasses further up on her nose. "It makes my tummy ache."

"You're just a sissy." Mary interjected. "I like it when they fight. It's fun to see who wins."

"I like it better when they get sent to the principal's office," Heather said, giggling, through a chocolate smeared grin.

"Why don't you ever share your chocolate candy bars, Heather? We always share with you," Emeline scolded.

"Mama says I can't."

"Bullshit."

The utterance of the forbidden word caused all three of Emeline's friends to gasp.

"Emeline! I'm gonna tell. You can't say those words," Priscilla screeched.

"She can say whatever she wants, Prissy," said Mary. "Bullshit. Bullshit. Bullshit. So there." Mary stuck out her chest in pride at her own swearing. Priscilla wasn't listening. She was watching two dogs at the edge of the field.

"Look at those dogs! They're fighting! We should help them!" All eyes turned toward the spectacle of the dogs.

"No, they're not fighting. They're loving, they're mating, making puppies. My mama told me all about it." Emeline recited her facts with authority. The three girls looked at her in horror.

"What? What are you talking about?" Heather asked with aroused curiosity. Encouraged, Emeline explained the facts of life to her audience of three. "My mama told me everything about where babies come from. We have lots of animals on our farm, you know. I've seen animals loving all the time." Emeline expounded, not with complete honesty.

"Wow. My mama doesn't tell me stuff like that," Heather said, awestruck.

Priscilla threw up on Emeline's new sneakers and then ran off crying and screaming to the recess monitor.

"Yuck," said Emeline, looking at her sneakers as she wiped them on the grass. She ignored Prissy as she ran off. Em returned to the subject. "Well, where do you think you came from? Where do you think all babies come from?" Emeline sneered.

"Storks," Heather said importantly.

"Now you're in trouble," Mary predicted, watching Priscilla cry and scream to the recess monitor, pointing her finger accusingly at Emeline. Still fascinated, Mary returned her attention to Em. "Is that really true?"

"That's gross," Heather said. "I'm going to ask my mom. I think you're making this whole thing up. My mother and father would never do such things. No clothes on and all that in and out stuff? Gross."

By now, the dogs had separated and the male was lovingly licking the smaller female. They touched noses and ran off deeper into the woods. An infuriated recess monitor, who was also the girl's fourth grade teacher, marched toward them.

"Uh oh. Told you. Now you're in big-time trouble," said Heather, slouching off toward the playground as their teacher clasped sobbing Priscilla's hand and advanced toward Emeline. Mary stayed put to watch the action as Emeline was dragged off. There was no mistaking the fury in Miss Persnik's red face as she yanked Emeline's arm.

"Told ya," Heather said when Mary joined her friend after Emeline's departure. Heather was proud of her knowledge of school rules and enjoyed reiterating her wisdom whenever possible. She and Mary ran toward the cafeteria door just as the recess bell rang.

Emeline sat silently in the Principal's office waiting for her mama to come pick her up. When she arrived, she told Emeline to wait outside the office while she 'discussed this matter' with the principal. Although Em was sitting outside the glass enclosure of the office, she could clearly hear arguing, then shouting, behind the principal's office enclosure window.

"Provincial ignoramuses. Stupid morons." She heard her mother shout.

"Tender young minds…" the Principal retorted.

'Free speech, education, open minds, life' were some of the words Em caught from Cleo, in furious exploding tones. Emeline couldn't hear everything but she got the gist of her mama's rage. She dared to inch closer to the glass window and watched her mama leaning over Mr. Ignoble. The principal had stretched back and away from Cleo. He seemed to shrink in the swiveling chair behind his desk. Mama's thrusting finger barely missed hitting him in the face. She stormed out of the office, grabbed Emeline and screamed, as she retreated, "Provincial cretins! All children should be educated! Education is being honest, not pussyfooting around facts. Storks! Fools! Idiots! My obligation is to be truthful with my child unlike you Victorian vaporous vipers! Ever heard of freedom of speech?"

Mama is so poetic, Em thought proudly as she and her mother raced down the long hallway and out the school door. It wasn't often Emeline had seen Mama so furious. She was usually quite calm.

"Mama, am I in trouble?" she asked tentatively.

"No, sweetheart. Your friends and the school just don't believe in sex education at such a tender age." She snorted. "Come on, let's get ice cream cones. You're not going back into that classroom or school. I'm moving you to the advanced fourth grade at Montessori. The kids are smarter, more open, and allowed to learn through experience and artistic endeavors. Just the way you need to grow up."

That was the end of Emeline's friendship with Mary, Heather and Priscilla. Sometimes their paths crossed. She and Heather would wave to one another, nothing more. Em occasionally saw Priscilla or Mary from a distance. The last place Em had ever thought she'd encounter Priscilla was outside the Locke movie theatre one afternoon a year later. Her mama didn't notice as she was arguing with the ticket attendant over the price of a child's movie ticket.

Priscilla spat at Emeline. "No one likes you. My mother said you're trash, nasty. No one's allowed to play with you anymore."

"I don't care, anyway," Em told Priscilla. And much to her surprise, Em found she didn't. She had learned friends weren't to be trusted or depended on. Anyway, there was too much life to explore around their farm, on the island and on trips to the mainland with her mama. Mama and Papa were always there for her. Who needed friends?

By the time Em entered River Bottoms High, she had learned to remain aloof from other girls and their attempts at friendship. She confided in no one except her mama. As she grew from a child into a naive young woman, she kept to herself. She was largely uneducated by the State of California's public school system. She had become oblivious to the efforts of her teachers and did whatever she needed to get by. What captivated and instructed Emeline was the delta. The farms and waters of the South Fork of the Mokelumne, the Joaquin and Sacramento Rivers kept everyone apart on Sherman Island and the delta, which was just fine with Em's family. They enjoyed the occasional visits of neighbors, but did not encourage their friendship.

In the months following Randy's entrance into her freshman class at River Bottoms High, the taunts and ridicule continued. He adopted his secret 'King Randy the Dandy' persona. His pretentiousness and pompousness was his defense against their insults. His boasting made Em wince. He became more and more outrageous and ridiculous.

Her classmates relished telling her 'Randy' stories, knowing Emeline's protection of him. On the bus rides home, she'd be forced to listen to the insulting voices of the girls around her.

"You'll never believe what that idiot Randy…said, or did, on any day." Em would listen to them absentmindedly as she watched the Sacramento River sparkle in the late afternoon sunlight along the Slough road. Willow trees lining the river dipped their branches alluringly into the fast flowing water, reminding Em of fairy tales. The willow branches looked to Em like sprites bending over and dropping their long tresses into the flow of the river. Occasionally she would laugh along with her bus-mates but stopped when guilt overcame her. She knew Randy had a crush on her. Instead of the stories of Randy's foolish escapades hardening Em toward him, they had softened her heart. She felt tenderness, protectiveness and concern for him.

After they began dating, Emeline had convinced herself those feelings of tenderness were love. Her emotions and needs changed slowly as she began to trust Randy more and more. Tentatively, she confided in him, usually after he sensed her sorrow or anger. He gently coaxed any suspected problem from her, helping her to sort out her feelings. She had never trusted anyone except her mama, and the only secrets Em kept from her were problems at school. Em was too old to have her mother marching down the corridors berating teachers and the principal.

Randy's tales of bloated accomplishments and bravado were charming, sweet and pitiful. Defending Randy was what her mother called, 'your mama cat fierceness'. It was true. Em would go to considerable lengths to defend Randy from himself and the laughter of others. As time progressed her acceptance of his fabricated tales embarrassed her. His escapades had become less humorous and more pathetic. Em had no idea that the shadow of Randy's father was always above him, mocking him. It was rumored that Randy's dad was a big-shot in Sacramento, a lawyer working on the Governor's staff. Em didn't know if that was true and Randy never talked about his father. He would clam up the minute Em brought him, or his mother up. "I don't like talking about my family, Em. That's all there is to it."

Em didn't push Randy to confide in her. *He would when he was ready*, she thought. But her motherly feelings prevailed. His behavior tugged at her emotions. He was like a baby bird fluttering its wings for food and attention. His sweetness towards her, his obvious love-sickness had won her over. When they became 'steadies', Em continued her oversight of Randy. She had endured more than one battle over his continued taunting by their classmates. When one kid or another pantomimed Randy as he attempted to pull off a cosmopolitan air, she became infuriated but kept her anger well hidden. To show anger or attention would show she cared. Instead, she remained aloof from all those classmates, as though they didn't exist.

There were times when she winced over his antics. On one occasion, Randy had leaned so far back in his chair that he fell onto the floor. Sprawled on the floor, eyes on the ceiling, desk on his chest. He could not have appeared more ridiculous. Randy's telling of the tale was far different from the reality she had already heard described. She felt overwhelming sorrow as she listened to his version of the event.

"You should have seen me in World History class today, Em. I cracked everybody up! Pretended I was so bored that I fell asleep. I started snoring and then pretended to fall off my desk. I was a riot! Everyone hollered and laughed. Pissed off that nasty old Mrs. Ruday, which made everyone laugh even more." Em bit her lip, then plowed forward, accepting his fairy tale as she wove one of her own.

"You have such an amazing sense of humor, honey. You're a comedian. You should move from the Delta to Hollywood."

"Yeah. I'm pretty good, huh? Bet I could do a show like that Laugh-In guy…Rowan Andy Martin?"

"Dan Rowan and Dick Martin," Em corrected.

"Yeah. That's him," Randy replied, ignoring Em's comment.

When a rebel thought would creep into Emeline's consciousness, "What if everyone's right and he really is nothing but a fool?" She would force the idea out of her mind, recalling their last encounter. The sweetness of his overwhelming love, his concern and kindness were more important than ridicule. She was often in a muddle of emotions over her boyfriend. Anger, sorrow, laughter, humiliation and tenderness overtook any concerns over their deepening relationship. Eventually, she became consumed by the heat of their high school romance. She was in love. Nothing else mattered.

Now here she was, married to her high school sweetheart, living in Heavenly Hollow instead of the delta. Em shook the past from her mind as she tidied up the living room.

Randy's voice floated to Em from the kitchen, announcing his calmer demeanor. "Em? Emeline? Where are you, sugar? Your man's home!" By his voice Em knew he had come up with the day's fiction. She entered the kitchen just as he was reaching into the fridge for a Pabst Blue Ribbon beer.

"Get one for me, too, sweetie."

"What's for dinner? I could eat a horse, or a cow, better tasting!" He chortled at his joke, which Em had heard at least a thousand times.

"Mac and Cheese."

"Again?" Randy complained.

Emeline felt herself flush. They'd only had mac and cheese once in the past week. "It's special this time. I added peas and little pieces of ham."

"Oh, sounds great," he replied unconvincingly.

"Hey, I got a great idea. Let's go to Mom's this weekend. Just relax, lay back, and let her cook for us. You know how she loves to spoil us." *Spoil you, more like it*, Em thought sarcastically.

She saw right through his ruse. He missed his mother's cooking. Em took the proffered invitation as an insult. "I could cook every bit as good as your mother. I just don't want to. Don't have the time."

"Time? But what do you do all day?"

"*Do*? What do I *do* all day? Lots of things! Cleaning the house, doing laundry, ironing *your* shirts, sewing curtains, lots of stuff." Em realized she should change her repertoire of household responsibilities as she hadn't sewn anything in weeks.

"And I take care of Scarlett and Rhett. These cats pester me all day long. They leave piles of cat hair all over the house. I'm constantly cleaning up after them. Not to mention the hairballs they throw up."

"I could eliminate that cat problem in a minute," Randy said, as he gestured with an imaginary rifle. "Pow, Pow."

Em grimaced, knowing Randy's dislike of the attention she bestowed on her beloved furry children. *Just like Papa and his hatred of Mama's cats,* she thought.

As she was growing up Tristan and Isolde had added to Em's animal husbandry education. Mama's allegiance to their cats was a long-running feud between her parents. When Tristan or Isolde would return from their night-long hunts, they would proudly deposit their 'contributions' as Mama called the variety of mangled rodents and snakes they victoriously brought home. Sometimes just a mouse or a rat, or just the head of either would be gifted to the family. Occasionally they'd proudly display a snake, the worse for wear.

"Kitties like to play with snakes, dear," her mother had instructed Emeline. "It's more fun for them, but it takes teamwork to catch a snake. That's why they arrive so torn up." The worst times were when one or the other cat brought home part of a baby bird. Emeline always wondered how the mama bird felt, watching her baby being torn apart by their beloved cats.

Her father's fury had been particularly fierce one August morning. His face was red and blotchy, as he screamed at Mama. "You're disgusting. You jeopardize the health of this family by your revolting 'praise' of those two damn cats when they bring home dead rodents."

Her mama had fluffed up, like a cold chicken, trying to find warmth in its feathers. "They deserve to be acknowledged and rewarded for their contribution to this family," mama had scolded.

Em remembered the incident clearly, her Mama's words ringing in her memory. "Tristan! Isolde! Wonderful! Astounding! How long did it take you to catch that rat?" Mama clapped her hands as the cats swirled lovingly around her ankles. "Which one of you fabulous hunters brought us this delectable meal?"

"As if we'd actually eat this?" Papa had yelled, pointing to the decapitated body of a small rat her mother had just plucked from the welcome mat at their porch door. She placed the decapitated rat on one of the family's best 'Rambling Rose' dinner plates.

"There, There," Mama had said, as she kneeled down to pick up and cuddle Tristan, the superior hunter of the two. "I'm so proud of you for catching us breakfast. And what a nice fat rat it is, too, sweetheart. Where's its head, love?"

Emeline had watched in fascination as the fresh carcass bled onto the rose pattern on the antique plate. The entrails, thin, worm-like bright red stripes, decorated the delicate china. Papa jumped angrily from his chair. "God fucking dammit! That's it!" Papa had shouted, after stepping on the rat's head, hidden under the kitchen table. The head had been generously placed there by Isolde for a late morning snack.

"Oh, wonderful! You found the head! What a delightful treat! Arnie, thank Isolde."

"I will do no such fucking thing!" Mama's 'thanking of the kitties' ritual was what most infuriated Papa in their otherwise peaceful existence. Mama watched calmly as Papa ran down the porch steps, muttering about getting breakfast in town. She refused to change her ways to please him. With shoulders hunched, he jumped into their old beat up Ford truck and sped away.

Mama caressed both cats, happily nestled in her arms. Tiny flecks of blood decorated Tristan's chin which the cat was contentedly washing from his whiskers. Mama watched her husband depart. She sighed and muttered to herself, "He'll never respect the true nature of animals." Em heard her remark and filed it away, promising herself that she would always listen to her mother's lessons and respect for the animal world.

"Never forget the downtrodden, Em, be they animal or humankind," said her mama. "Praise those who least expect it for their everyday deeds."

It was true that mama always bestowed more praise on the cats, the struggling person at their back door asking for a handout, or imparting advice and hope to the woman selling herself on the dark side of the delta. Mama rarely praised Papa or Emeline for any of their accomplishments. That was fine with Emeline. She liked to stay out of the limelight, knowing that praise of any sort turned on the bright lights. Emeline would rather stay hidden in the dark, just as she was now, hiding on the sofa awaiting Randy telling her of his latest escapade.

"EM! Perk up! Your ever lovin' honey is home!" Her husband stood in the living room doorway, holding out a bottle of PBR, which Em happily accepted. He ran his hands through his hair again. Em knew from experience his agitation prefaced the fiction he was about to deliver.

"How was your day, honey?" Em sweetly asked, enveloping him in a hug.

"Great! Great! Was THAT close to selling that '75 Lincoln. Guy took my card, said he'd be back. Had to talk it over with his wife. But that damn Stan didn't want to go for the deal I cut with the guy. A great deal, too. How am I supposed to sell anything with no bargaining power, I asked that dope of a manager. He ruins every sale of mine. I think he's just jealous of me. Afraid I'll show him up with my superior sales expertise. Maybe I should check out some other dealerships."

Em's heart lurched as she set the table. If he quit, or was fired, we'd be hogs on ice, thrashing about. We'd have nothing. Margret would work on Randy to move him and Em in with her. She'd use that old sob story: "Ever since your father and I divorced and Aunt Clara died, I've needed you more. I don't have any friends here, and everyone is too backward. My family is all dead. You're the last family to me, Randy. I need you. You're my only child."

Charm was always Em's best defense which she worked like a spell on her husband. "Now, sweetheart. Don't be rash. You're probably right. Stan is just jealous of you. Where's the harm in that? Isn't jealousy the greatest form of respect?"

"Yeah. I guess so." Randy muttered into his Mac and Cheese. "Another PBR, sweetie?"

She plunked the bottle in front of him, opened it with a sharp crack from their vintage iron rooster bottle opener. Something about the old rooster bottle opener reminded Em of Felicity. She was surprised at how often she had hoped to see the older woman walking up their lane again. She wondered where she lived. Felicity, with her old fashioned cotton pants and shirt, and her Southern plantation lady-of-the-manor drawl made her seem like a mirage from a distant era. Was she real? Had Emeline imagined the whole meeting? Then she remembered Zuma, Felicity's large, unfriendly and arrogant cat who Scarlet and Rhett detested on sight. *I did put on red nail polish like she said*, Em thought, examining her now chipped polish. Nope. She's real. Just some crazy old lady from down the lane who has no friends. Like me. Em reminded herself. Why on earth am I missing an old lady I've only met once?

"Em? Any dessert?"

Boredom plagued her. She had to get out of the house. She planned her escape.

"Hey, sweetie," she said to Randy. "What if I take you to work tomorrow so I can have the car? I'll go to the grocery store, the library and run some errands. Okay?"

"Yeah, sure." Randy replied. Em cleared the table and noticed the peas from his mac and cheese hidden under Randy's plate. She said nothing, just gave him a rueful smile as she placed a bowl of chocolate-chip-mint ice cream before him.

"How about I call mom and see if she's free on Saturday? Or Sunday. She'd love us to visit. You know how lonely she is." Em recognized Randy's proffered bargaining chip. He continued to plead his case. "Em, my mom only has us. After my father left, too, you know." Randy said quietly, under his breath, "You have no idea of what my father was like or what he was capable of. Glad the bastard left."

Em remembered the local gossip before Randy's father departed. Ernest, Margret's husband and Randy's father had done everything he could to get rid of Margret, even moving to Sacramento. The open affair with his buxom secretary had finally sealed the deal.

"Mom really cares about you, like you're her own daughter, Em. She had a hard life with my dad."

"Well, maybe I'd know more about your dad and would be more sympathetic if you and your mom shared your history! Why are you both so secretive?"

"It's not secretive. I just can't stand him. He was such a shit to mom and never cared for me, not ever. Big man around town, all right. The only time he ever acknowledged our existence was at some special event he was hosting."

"That can't be true. No father dislikes their own child, especially an only son to carry on the family name."

"Em. Enough. I'm not discussing this now."

"But…"

"Enough. Just leave me alone about it. When I'm ready, I'll tell you exactly what he was like. Not now. I've had a rough day. All I want is to watch TV and eat ice cream."

Em knew she couldn't press the matter further but the conversation left her angry. She hid her feelings.

"Okay. Fine. We'll see her this weekend. We owe her dinner. Maybe next time we can invite her here?"

"Yeah. Sure. I'll pick up some KFC." Randy turned to the living room. Em chewed her lip. She really did want to invite Margret for dinner, but Randy was right. If she wasn't able to impress her mother-in-law with a home-cooked meal, they could call the invitation a 'picnic'. They'd have Kentucky Fried Chicken with all the fixins on the porch. That would make it seem like a fun event, not an avoidance of Em's non-existent culinary skills.

"I'll pick up a recipe book at the library. The next time your mom visits, I'll cook her a real meal, something gourmet. I promise. Maybe we won't have to get KFC."

Randy shuffled off to the TV in the living room, smacking her bottom on the way out of the kitchen. "Yeah, right." Randy patted the couch cushion next to him. "Come on, sweetheart. Sit with me. Stop worrying. Everything's fine."

"No, let me do the dishes first." Even the blare of the sports channel couldn't obliterate Em's thoughts as she let her hands rest in the warm soapy water. She had always loved washing dishes, especially with her mama. The act of washing, rinsing, drying and stacking was a well performed dance, leaving her mind free to wander.

It was through their many dishwashing talks that Em had learned of her parent's courtship, subsequent pregnancy, birth of the Elder Lout, as Mama liked to call her brother David, and so much more. For most of Em's childhood, her mama had been a housewife and stay-at-home mother thanks to her papa's generous monthly disability and workers' comp checks. Her father's injury was one of Em's favorite stories.

"Tell me again, Mama, about the time Papa smashed his hand in the sausage maker."

Her mother's laugh would always precede the eventual retelling of the tale. "Haven't you heard that enough?" she would say, passing a dish to Em to dry. But she always wistfully retold the story.

"Well, your papa had been working at the sausage factory from his junior year of high school until after graduation. It paid real well, being the only meat packing plant in the delta. But you know your dad, always fooling around. He worked on the line with Merika Poplovitch. She was Polish, you know. Later changed her name to Mary Ann after she married that old cranky Dutch guy, Harvey."

"Mama, the smashed hand story?"

"Right. Anyway, Merika wasn't much to look at, kind of a flat face, wide mouth, ears that stuck out. But did she ever have big boobs! They always jiggled yet stood up at attention. Never did figure out what size bra she wore. Thirty-eight? Maybe even forty? For sure she was a D cup."

"Mama…"

"Okay. So your dad, like all the other guys, just couldn't get enough of Merika's boobs. Let me tell you, she was popular with the boys. We all knew why. She put out. But I knew your papa's heart belonged to me. We had been dating for months." Her mother giggled. "In all honesty, I guess Merika wasn't the only one putting out."

Em glared at her mother and slammed a dish into the drying rack.

"Alright already! So, one day on the line, as usual, your dad was paying more attention to Merika's boobs than the sausage casing he was supposed to be feeding into the machine. Somehow his hand went into the press along with the sausage meat. It would have been solely his fault, had there been a working 'off' switch on the machine. But there wasn't. Your poor papa's right hand was smashed flat like a pancake by the time they turned the main power off. Sultry Delta Sausages owners were afraid your papa's parents would sue. You remember Grandma Mary and Grandpa Jake? They didn't have much in the brains department. They just yelled and screamed at Arnold for losing his job, forcing *them* to lose *his* income. When Arnie and his mom returned from the hospital, Jake even slapped your papa upside the head, as I recall. Now, Jake didn't run on nine volts but he knew he had a diamond in the rough. He swore he *would* sue Sultry Delta Sausages if they didn't compensate his talented son. 'Coulda pitched for the Angels but for his ruined right hand', Jake had insisted. Sultry Delta Sausages paid Arnie $100,000 if he wouldn't file a workers' comp claim and blow the whistle on the little sausage empire. Arnold and his parents took that money, put it in the bank and promptly filed a workers' comp claim. Your papa won, got a monthly check for life for the injury and then filed for disability. You know, your papa, my Arnold, he's real smart. He got a good lawyer out of Sacramento and got a 60% disability judgment for life with future prospects of more as he aged."

Em sighed with contentment. She loved that story of how Papa had supported their family. Through his own ingenuity he had provided them with money from the $100,000 he invested in annuities for retirement. His disability checks and workers comp checks took care of all their expenses. And that was *before* he and Mama started collecting Social Security.

"Wow. You were lucky, Mama."

Her mother continued. "Course, soon after Papa's accident I found out I was pregnant with the Elder Lout. Merika or any of the other girls chasing after your papa's money never had a chance. And we've been happily married ever since. HA!" Mama erupted with a screeching laugh.

"I heard that, you bitch." Papa had yelled from the living room. Mama just smiled affectionately at his pretend insult. Em's parents teased and baited one another constantly, which seemed to have been a big plus in their marriage.

"After he got his money, your papa never had to work. He learned to do all the important stuff with his left hand. Only thing he couldn't do anymore was shoot pool. Just couldn't master it with his left hand. He always missed that."

"I still don't understand why you kept working at the Ryde Hotel. You didn't have to work."

"Well, I started in high school before we were married, and Papa had his accident. And I liked the job. Lucy was always so entertaining. So, on and off I worked part-time when the Ryde needed extra help."

Mama insisted that Lucy, the resident ghost, was a personal friend. She claimed that Lucy had taught her how to dress by describing what the 'red light' ladies wore while waiting for clients in the enormous candle-lit ballroom.

"I always did love vintage clothing. Maybe I shoulda opened a shop? As for my working at the Ryde, your papa was always good at watching over you, so I just kept on working part-time."

As much as her parents bickered, Emeline knew they had a happy, loving marriage. Pestering and picking on each other, constantly questioning one another in their perennial battles of one-upmanship had never fooled Em as to the status of their marital bliss. She knew their forays were just their form of entertainment. Em had come home from school earlier than expected on more than one occasion to hear them cavorting in bed. Em would walk back out the door, loudly slam it, and call out, "I'm home." Silence would immediately replace the bedroom jousting and her Mama's giggles. Em would wait until the inevitable whispers would subside.

"Just spring cleaning the bedroom, dear. Your papa's helping me move the furniture to mop the floors," her mother would call out.

"Yeah, right." Em would mutter to herself. Living with as many animals around as they did Emeline was aware of sex for as long as she could remember. The sows especially instructed her. The dumb fat pigs wouldn't even bother to move from the feed trough when the large boar would grunt and mount the female for a few quick seconds of rapture. Mama was always happy to tell Emeline the physiological and sexual facts of life.

When she and Randy finally consummated their eighteen-month relationship, Em remembered the sow at the feed trough. After barely two minutes, Randy had rolled off her, saying, "Oh, that was fantastic, wasn't it Em? I love you so much. Now we're truly married in our hearts." Within seconds, he was snoring as Em asked herself, "That was it? Where's the rapture? The flights of ecstasy? The quivering of her heart and nether regions?"

Em realized her mistake immediately. Better to have put up with Randy's constant complaints of 'blue balls'.

"You can die from sexual repression, babe, did you know that?" was his favorite line. She had provided hand jobs and the occasional blow jobs and that should have been enough. Much better than an imagined life-long commitment through sex.

Within a month, her mama had sized things up. One evening after an especially long, provocative phone call with Randy, Mama had knocked loudly on her bedroom door. Without waiting for a response, she barged into Em's room, sat down on her bed and handed her a little round disc with tiny yellow pills.

"I don't care what you're doing as long as you're protected and don't get pregnant at sixteen like I did."

"Thanks, Mama," Em had said sheepishly as she accepted the round disc of birth control pills. She looked at her mama closely. Should Em feel guilty? Embarrassed? She realized she didn't feel either. She was sorry she hadn't confided in her mama, which had probably hurt Cleo's feelings. Em's face flushed and tears came to her eyes.

"Sweetheart. It's okay. I just don't want you to make the same mistakes I made. Remember, I was young once, too." Tenderly Mama had brushed the curls from Em's forehead and wiped the tears from her cheeks.

"Now you're all grown up, a full-fledged woman. That doesn't mean you have to marry the first boy you're serious about, though, my little changeling."

Em knew she was referring to Randy. Mama had always thought she could do better, although she didn't come right out and say so.

That was the end of Em's and Mama's fears about Em becoming pregnant at sixteen.

"You're my hope, my last, my changeling baby." Cleo had said as she kissed the top of Em's head and left the room.

Em loved it that her mama called her 'changeling baby'. Her mama had told her that her pregnancy with Em at forty-three was completely unexpected. Cleo just thought she was going through 'the change'. Her own mama, Muriel, had been forty-two when she went through menopause. When Cleo started putting on weight and unexpectedly felt the familiar flutter, she knew. She was not going through any change except pregnancy. Emeline, a surprise to her mama and papa, was swimming contentedly in her mama's womb. Five months later she was born, making her papa 'the proudest papa in the Universe'.

After her mama died, Em looked at marriage differently. By then, she and Randy had been having sex for over a year. What was the difference between being married in our hearts to being married on paper? Because of her own pain, grief and loneliness, Em couldn't bear to be by herself. Randy, for all his foolish ways, strutting and bravado, was the person she had chosen to spend her life with. He understood, deep in his heart, Emeline's pain. He knew who she was, through and through, and accepted every part of her. He would do everything he could to wipe any sorrow or disappointment from her eyes. A year later they were married.

"EM! Emeline! What the hell are you staring at? Haven't you heard me calling you?" yelled Randy, his voice puncturing her memories. "Get out of the kitchen and come watch the tube with me."

Randy was right. She had to get herself out of the past and pay more attention to her husband and the present. She hung up the dish towel and dragged her eyes away from the beauty of the magnolia tree outside her kitchen window. The tree glowed in the moonlight, mesmerizing her. She turned to see Randy staring at her from the kitchen doorway, a worried expression on his face.

"Take the car tomorrow and get some more books at the library, like you said. Go shopping, get yourself something pretty. Get outta the house. That'll cheer you up." He kissed her forehead, put his arm around her and led her out of the kitchen. "Come on, love. Let me give you a nice foot rub. Come sit on the couch with me." She looked into his dear, sweet face. She should be as good to him as he was to her. After all, she had no one else in her life. Besides, he was the dearest, kindest man she had ever known.

As she walked with Randy into the living room, she felt the excitement of a Charles Town adventure. "Oh, sweetie, I can't wait. I'll even go to the grocery store and see if I can pick up something different for dinner."

Randy kissed her. "If you want to, that would be great." They settled in to watch their favorite show, *All in the Family.* Life was good.

Chapter 5

The next morning Em arrived, breathless with anticipation, at the library door. It had been too many days since she had visited her favorite haunt. She entered the sanctity of the old rooms, dust motes falling through sunlight from the stacks and stacks of welcoming books, every one of them a waiting gift to open and treasure.

Em made her way to the romance section and then, on a whim, entered the sale room first just inside the double library doors. An image of her empty book shelves floated into her mind. She had promised herself she would pick up a cookbook and began rummaging through the cookbook section in the small 'Library Sales' room. Books were placed haphazardly on the shelves. Suddenly a fat book fell at her feet, barely missing her vermillion-coated toenails.

Jeeze! She exclaimed to herself. That could've landed on my foot, ruining my fresh polish! Damn librarians can't put books on the shelves properly. Wait till I fill my own library, she proudly reassured herself.

She picked up the book at her feet. *Cooking for the Soul: Recipes for the Down-At-Heart*. The title intrigued her.

Gingerly, as though the book of old recipes could magically scorch her fingertips, she thumbed through the worn, stained pages: Sweet Candied Yams, Sunny Day Morning Biscuits, Home-On-The-Farm Fried Chicken, Grandma's Secret Ingredients Fried Okra. Emeline now sped through the pages, finding familiar recipes. *My mama used to cook like this*, she thought excitedly. Southern Tennessee Pecan Pie, Company Coconut Cake, Lemon Bars Fit for Royalty. Emeline marched to the library desk with her stack of books to check out and pay the $1 purchase price.

"Oh, that's a great recipe book," said the librarian warmly. "You can really learn to cook with her recipes. They're easy to follow." The librarian was auburn-haired, tastefully made up, and wore a casual pants suit.

"Yes, well. I need to learn to do something worthwhile, you know?" said Em. "And eating is something we all need to do right, so…I figured…"

The librarian, whose name tag announced her as Ms. Ogelthorpe, looked at Em hesitantly as she checked out her books and collected her $1 placing the bill carefully into an old tin deed box.

"Well, you got a real bargain here. She's a local author, Miss Magnolia. We're very proud to have her in our little community. But you know, sad to say it, she's out of print."

"Out of Print?"

"That's correct. Almost impossible to find this cookbook anymore." The head librarian noticed the way Emeline was chewing her lip with worry.

"Anything wrong dear? Do you not want to purchase Miss Magnolia's book?"

"Oh, no, I mean yes, I do. I just wonder if the recipes will be too hard for me to follow. I've never really learned to cook. My mother only taught me to can vegetables and make jam."

"Well, my dear. Then you're certainly not a novice chef. I'm sure you'll have no trouble becoming an expert, just like all the other young ladies who have perused these pages."

Em brightened. "You think so?"

"Of course. You'll learn these recipes in no time at all." Charged with confidence, Em vowed to begin her new culinary education the following day.

The next morning Em's confidence did not match her efforts to follow what she felt was the simplest of recipes: Biscuits. By her second failed biscuit attempt, all confidence had fled, leaving her close to tears with a sinkful of blackened, burned biscuits.

She had just dumped the coal lumps of biscuits into the porcelain sink. *Now she'd have to scour the sink too*, she thought dejectedly. She licked her burned fingertips, the result of rushing to remove the cause of the smoke-filled kitchen from the oven. *Why* could she not learn to make biscuits?

With the inferno of ruined biscuits tucked safely under running water, Em took a moment to rest her eyes on the view outside her kitchen window. And there she was, appearing out of nowhere. Felicity was walking up the drive followed by her big orange cat. What was her cat's name? Zuma?

Felicity's musical voice announced her arrival. "Yoo Hoo, Darlin'. Smells like somebody's been baking. Or perhaps baking overlong?"

For a moment, Em was so happy to see her new friend she forgot about her burned fingers and buried her biscuit disappointment. She ran to the kitchen door and shouted into the yard, "Burned. Not baked. Blackened. The biscuits I tried to make Randy for breakfast. Again. From that stupid cookbook. What a disaster."

Felicity gave a deep, throaty chortle. Em thought the sound resonated from somewhere long buried within the depths of her being. Her voice sounded earthy and other-worldly, as though Felicity had traveled generations, not steps, to her door. Em wondered how often Felicity laughed. Maybe her laughter was rusty from not being used? What a silly thought, she admonished herself. Her mama had always said Em heard things others never did due to her high level of auditory perception. "You can tell a hawk from a blue jay or an osprey from fifty feet," she would tell Em. Em had scoffed at her mother's remarks, yet was proud of her talent for identifying birds. Maybe Em did have good hearing but she sure couldn't figure out Felicity. She smiled as her friend approached. *Definitely*, she thought. Felicity enjoys life and laughter.

"Now, Darlin'. Learning to cook takes time as with any important venture in life."

"I'm useless."

"That's not so, deah. Every life has meaning and purpose. You just have to find out what yours is."

Em thought over Felicity's words for a long moment, gnawing on her lip, reminding herself of a cow chewing its cud. Finally she retrieved her manners.

"Would you like to come in for a cup of coffee? Or tea? I think I might have some of that, somewhere…"

"Well, since you've invited me into your home, I'd be honored to set with you awhile. No coffee or tea for me, darlin', though I thank you for your hospitality. Zuma, you stay on the porch. Emeline's feline friends don't appear to relish your company."

She's right about that, Em thought, as she watched Scarlett and Rhett high tailing it, literally, into the living room. She saw them disappear under the couch.

Felicity settled in one of the worn ladderback chairs at Em's antique kitchen table. She was as proud of this table as her mama and Grandmother Muriel had been. How many words had been shared, shouted and loved across this old table?

"What cookbook are you using in your epicurean quest for knowledge?" Felicity finished her words with an almost indiscernible giggle.

Em read the title, "It's Miss Magnolia's recipes. *Cooking for the Soul: Recipes for the Down at Heart*. Supposedly a local author and a great chef."

"Oh, yes. I know her recipes well. Many in our community have learned to become culinary experts through her cookbook. Quite a number of dinner parties in these parts over the years owed their success to Miss Magnolia. As for the biscuits, what kind of shortening did you use? Lard or Crisco? Did you use milk or buttermilk? And has your oven been properly calibrated?"

Em quickly scanned the flour splattered Sunny Morning Biscuit recipe from her cookbook. "What? Well, the recipe called for lard, whatever that is. I didn't have any. I used margarine. I did pick up Crisco for making pies, like Mama always used. And I don't have any oven calibration. Mama never did teach me to cook. We only canned and jammed together."

"Now, why is that? It sounds as though your mama certainly knew her way around the kitchen."

"Oh, she was a tyrant in *her* kitchen. It was completely her territory. She guarded everything as though she were a queen. Well, I guess she was." Em chuckled to herself, memories overcoming her once again, this time happy ones.

"Mama insisted on making dinner for Papa and me every night. Once a week she'd make a special meal, which she called, 'chef's choice'. Papa usually grumbled over Chef's Choice night. 'Why can't we just have chicken fried steak or meatloaf?' he'd say. Mama hated his complaining and would wince, as if his words actually caused her pain. 'Because we're not entirely provincials, love'. Then she would whip up something with some sauce slathered all over it. It was always delicious, just like her meatloaf and chicken fried steak. Mama could cook anything. But she didn't want to share her recipes, her kitchen or cooking with me, except during the canning season. That's when she really needed my help. Whenever I complained that she should teach me all her favorite recipes she'd say, 'You're made for the finer things in life, sweetness'. I never did figure out what those finer things were. Anyway, we had fun canning and making jam together."

Felicity smiled encouragingly. "Well, back to following recipes. Using margarine instead of lard or Crisco, dear, there's your problem, or a few of them. You must use exactly the ingredients and amounts called for in each recipe. When you become more skilled, you can experiment to a greater degree. That's what all great cooks do. But for the time being, perhaps you should learn the basics. Calibration is how hot your oven is. True to its degrees, as they say. You know that old adage, never cry over spilt milk, or burned biscuits, for that matter.

After all, it's the thought that counts. I'm sure your husband, Randy, is that his name? I'm sure he was pleased with your culinary efforts."

"Yeah, I guess. He felt as bad as I did. For me, not for the burned biscuits." Em remembered how sweet Randy had been over her most recent failure, kissing her tenderly as he left for work. "I'm not hungry anyway," he lied to spare her feelings.

Felicity interrupted her thoughts. "Now, dear, until you are a highly skilled chef, I would suggest you don't attempt to use the wood stove."

"The what?"

"The wood stove. Your Down Home Stove, one of the finest wood stoves ever created. Any Down Home stove is a valuable antique. Yours, with its beautiful nickel plating, water reservoir and griddle is the centerpiece of your lovely kitchen. Set against that brick wall it commands attention. And the fireplace hearth, beautiful. All old craftsman's work, you know."

"Oh, you mean that black thing? Randy said it was a Franklin Stove, but I wondered. For now, I just put all the houseplants on it. Collects the sun."

"Perfect utilization of an old friend. I've known these cabins for years and years. Most aren't as well kept as yours. Good thing you also have a modern stove."

Silence enveloped the kitchen as Felicity studied the surroundings carefully. She noticed each homespun touch Emeline had added to the room. Em followed Felicity's granite-gray eyes as they traveled. Felicity's gaze lingered over her mother Cleo's collection of Stangl pitchers, hand painted Quimper ware and Delft blue and white figurines. Her eyes moved to the curtains decorating the old windows made from antique embroidered dish towels. Em watched her examination of every detail she had added to her kitchen. She was proud of her curtains and loved the way the morning sun glowed through the tapestry of colors. Next, Felicity bent over and examined the braided rug under the kitchen table, tenderly touching its sewn braids.

"You certainly have a talent for the homey, dear. This rug is beautifully woven. I can't identify the fabric."

"Homely? I'm homely?" Em's face flushed realizing how horrible she must appear. Hair a mess, unwashed face, burned fingers and old jean shorts.

"Homey, darlin'. Not homely. Your home is welcoming, warm, full of character and personal touches. You make guests feel at home. That's homey. You, my sweet child, are anything but homely."

Em tried to take in the surroundings with a newcomer's eyes. It was a pretty room. It held all her improvements and the best of the old life she had brought with her from the delta.

"I guess I do have a knack. Got that from Mama. Along with a lot of her crockery and furniture. But I made the braided rug and curtains. I even sold my braided rugs back on the delta. I made them out of old wool factory scraps. I used to get those scraps by the barrel, braid them into long braids. Then, I'd sew the braids together to fit the size of the rug the person wanted. I'd even do special colors for people if they asked. That was more costly. It took a lot of searching and sorting, matching of colors. It was a Girl Scout project and I guess I just kept doing it."

Silence filled the room again, accompanied only by the refrigerator's humming song. Both women thought over their words. Memories were evoked. The silence was broken when Felicity cleared her throat, as though preparing for a speech.

"You miss your mama deeply, don't you, you poor motherless child."

Em was startled out of her reverie. "What? How do you know that?"

"You told me. Your mama died after your papa and then you married Randy. Moved here, from the California delta, Sherman Island, was it? Here, you know no one. Excepting myself, of course, and Randy's mother. I can see your past in your eyes. There's a grieving aura around you. I hope I'm not being intrusive or impertinent?" Felicity studied Em to gauge her reaction.

Em's emotions overcame her. She felt sorrow and relief, all at once. She chose relief that this strange woman could read her thoughts. She *was* still grieving. Could it be that she had found someone she could trust with her friendship? A woman who recognized who Em was on the inside? A true female friend to talk to and confide in and learn life's lessons from?

The ghost of a thought reminded Em that she had never wanted friends. She never trusted other girls or women. Jealousy often betrayed friendship which turned to cruelty. Now, it was Em's turn to study her new friend. She examined Felicity's open face closely. No, this woman would never betray her. She didn't appear to have a jealous or mean bone in her body. Em was certain. She was nothing but motherly toward Em, someone she could welcome into her life.

"You remembered. Yes. I do miss my mama. And the delta. I should have insisted that Mama taught me to cook. Then I wouldn't have to be trying to learn without any help." Em was surprised to feel her eyes fill with tears. "I should have asked her so many more questions. I could have learned so much from her, like how to make Grandma's biscuits. Mama said Grandma made the best biscuits every morning for breakfast."

Felicity looked at Em tenderly. "I always felt that I was an orphan, too, darlin'. We have that in common. As for learning, I'll teach you whatever you want to know. Including cooking."

Em's interest was awakened. She wondered how Felicity had become an orphan. Immediately, she realized that of course she was an orphan. Felicity was ancient. Em thought another long moment before she finally replied. "I hope you will. Teach me things, I mean. If you don't mind."

"Of course not. It would be my honor and pleasure to be your mentor." Those were the first embers of the growing blaze of their friendship. Em threw caution to the winds. She needed a woman friend in this out-of-the-way backwoods of Heavenly Hollow. The older woman's kindness had already drilled a little wormhole into her heart, like an auger snail hiding in the delta mud.

"Well darlin', let's begin. Where's that old cookbook all of our country gals learned to use to maneuver their way around the kitchen?" After a thoughtful moment, Felicity continued, as though reading Em's thoughts once again. "My deah, true friendships always begin with the sharing of recipes. Let's get started." She patted Em's warm hand with her cold, thin fingers, then took command of the kitchen.

That morning Em learned what a 'calibrated' oven was. She discovered the necessity of following the biscuit recipe, or any recipe, exactly.

"Sift your flour and dry ingredients, salt and baking powder together."

"Damn. I don't have a sifter."

"If you make jam, you must have a strainer. We can use that."

Em retrieved a strainer and handed it to Felicity. She watched as Felicity sifted the flour, salt and baking powder into a bowl. "Now, my dear, preheat the oven to 450 and place the dry ingredients in a large bowl." Felicity scanned Em's collection of bowls and selected one, a blue-striped heavy, well-used antique bowl. "There, this will do nicely. Then mix the Crisco into the flour with a pastry cutter. Do you have one, deah?"

"I have no idea what a pastry cutter even is," Em replied. Felicity chuckled. "Your honesty is refreshing, love. That's not a problem. Always remember that everyday household utensils can double for the real thing. We'll just use two knives to cut the Crisco into the dry ingredients. Until you have a rolling pin, pastry and cookie cutters, a glass, and forks and knives can replace many utensils."

Felicity continued with her instructions. "The lard and flour should become a cornmeal consistency. Then slowly stir the wet ingredients—your buttermilk, milk or plain yogurt—into the dry. Everything must be added in the precise order the recipe calls for. Carefully work the dough with your hands into a nice satiny ball. Your dough should never be too sticky or too dry," she instructed.

Em watched intently as Felicity worked the ingredients into dough. "How on earth will I know that the dough is right? You make it look so easy."

"Practice by touch, my deah, and experience. I have no doubt you'll learn." Felicity handed the ball of dough to Em for her to feel.

Next, Em learned not to overmix the dough and how to roll it out on a floured board using a large unbreakable chrome glass as she had no rolling pin. Felicity taught her young student how to cut the rolled, virgin dough into circles using the top of a glass. "Or, deah, you can form the dough into little balls and flatten them slightly. For today, we'll roll out the dough. Drop biscuits are the easiest, but today I'd like you to learn the feel of the dough as you roll it out."

Felicity showed her how far apart to place the biscuit dough on a baking sheet and when to know when the biscuits were ready. She even calibrated the stove just by reaching her fingers into the preheated four-hundred-fifty degree oven. The heat crawled up her knuckles before she slammed the oven door shut. Em noticed how Felicity clenched her mouth after she slammed the oven door. She turned to Em, a disgusted look on her face. Emeline cringed.

"That darlin' is a poor oven, off fifty degrees at least! Four-hundred-fifty degrees is actually five-hundred degrees! No wonder your biscuits were burning. It's not your fault. It is the fault of this so-called 'modern' oven."

"But, Felicity, the dial said four-hundred-fifty. I turned it to four-hundred-fifty to preheat, just like the recipe said."

"My thermometer says five-hundred, or even higher. I'm never wrong when it comes to oven temperatures. We'll just have to adjust baking temperatures for any recipe down fifty degrees. So, a recipe for four-hundred-fifty degrees should be set at four-hundred. That should work." Felicity knew it all.

After the batch of biscuits went into the oven, "always on the center rack," Felice instructed further. Em set the timer for ten minutes and soon the heavenly scent of baking biscuits filled the kitchen.

"This time you'll make the recipe on your own. I'll just oversee your work and correct you when necessary," the older woman said. With Felicity's assistance, Emeline made the biscuit recipe again. Carefully, she added each ingredient as instructed. "Feel the dough with your fingertips and mind," Felicity said as she scrutinized her junior chef intently. Em was not intimidated. She felt thrilled with Felicity's tutelage. Someone, a woman, was paying attention to her, helping her. She felt the elasticity of the dough. The texture under her fingers was so different from Em's earlier sticky messes. She intuitively understood not just the *word* satin, but the *feel* of satin.

Felicity congratulated her. "You have created a perfect ball of biscuit dough, Emeline. The first of many, I'll wager." Em was nearly bursting with joy and pride.

Companionably the two women cut the second batch of dough into circles after Em had rolled it out with her tall chrome glass. Felicity shook her floury hands over the sink, turned and laughed at Em. "Go look in the mirror, darlin'. You have the look of a true pastry chef about you."

Em did as she was told and laughed at her flour decorated face and hair, dimming the shine of her curls. She returned to the kitchen with a washed face just as Felicity was removing the first batch of biscuits from the oven. They were beautiful golden globes. Their scent wafted throughout the kitchen.

"Go ahead, love. Now, place *your* very first batch of biscuits into the oven while I put these fresh ones up."

Felicity glared at the misbehaving oven one last time as Em carefully placed the cookie sheet on the center rack of her oven. Felicity then turned to the yard. Zuma rested, queenly, in a patch of shadow-speckled sunlight.

Felicity smiled happily at Em. She was sparked with pride as she witnessed the bloom of joy replacing the earlier doubt in her ingenue chef's face. "Now you're getting it, darlin," she said happily. "That's the secret to good biscuits. The dough has to be just right. Never overwork it. Can't get the oven too hot, now, and that's why yours burned. If the temperature is too high, they'll burn on the bottom and the top and the dough will remain raw in the middle. Watch carefully until your biscuits are golden brown on top and soft to the touch. You'll know they're done when their heavenly aroma makes your mouth water. Now, let's keep these warm by placing them in a tea towel in a warmed ceramic bowl. Where are your tea towels, darlin?"

"Tea Towels?"

"Yes. Tea towels. The same kind of towels you used to make your pretty kitchen curtains."

"Oh, those, right here, in this drawer. We always just called them kitchen towels." Felicity selected an old blue and white checked towel, placed it in a ceramic bowl, and carefully nestled the biscuits inside the bowl. Em's first culinary success story, *her* biscuits, were gently placed in the nest with the first batch the two had made together.

"There. Isn't that a beautiful sight? Remember, love, the eyes always eat first. Your biscuits are perfect, tempting and beautiful. They'll keep for dinner."

Em followed Felicity's eyes as they wandered out the kitchen window. Em, too, admired the view outside her kitchen window as well as the view inside her kitchen. Felicity appeared as though she were in an old Vermeer painting Em had once seen in one of her papa's *National Geographic* magazines. He had always subscribed to *National Geographic, Life,* the *Saturday Evening Post* and *Scientific American.* Em remembered the wait around the mailbox when the *National Geographic's* brown paper wrapped magazines were due to arrive. She had been fascinated and astounded by the magazine's explicit photographs, art and scientific articles.

Em returned to the present. "But Felice…can I call you that?" Felicity's smile gave her permission for the shortened and less formal use of her name. "What on earth am I going to do with twenty-four biscuits? Why don't you take some home?—better yet, let's eat some now."

"Oh, I couldn't love. This is your success story and I'm not overly hungry. Besides, I imagine you and Randy will finish them all tonight." She rewarded Em with another one of her deep earthy chuckles.

Emeline was stunned by the success of the biscuits. It was so easy. She could do this.

Perfect biscuits, she, Emeline, had created. A miracle! "Thank you so much. Would you like to see the rest of the cabin?"

"Love to, darlin'. I'm always interested in the special touches each homemaker adds to their abode." For the next hour, Emeline happily showed off each room of the cabin.

"What a lovely old Spool Bed and where did you ever find that antique quilt?" Felicity asked as they viewed the bedroom.

"The bed was Mama and Papa's. Too small for a queen size mattress like Randy wanted. He hoped to buy one of those big beds with shelves and drawers underneath but I wanted none-a-that. I'm attached to the bed where I know Mama and Papa made me."

"And well you should be. One must always hold onto and respect one's past," Felice advised sagely.

"As for the quilt, my grandma made quilts. I've got a bunch," Em said.

"Beautiful. And the Clam Broth glass lamp next to the bed, a true and rare antique." Felicity gently reached out and touched the white glass shade.

"Doesn't give off much light but I sorta like the white glow, like moonlight, you know?"

A long pause ensued as Felicity studied Em closely. The spell finally ended when Felicity gently touched Em's face, tucking a stray strand of curls behind her ear. Em noticed how gentle and delicate Felicity's touch was, like a butterfly's wings.

Felicity murmured, as though speaking to herself. "Yes, exactly, like moonlight, a perfect description. You have an artistic eye and a poetic voice."

In each room, Felicity found fresh treasures, rediscovered by Emeline through Felicity's eyes. "That's End-of-the-Day glass, my deah," noted Felicity as she picked up the little sculpted glass bowl swirling with all the colors of the rainbow. "It's very rare. End-of-the-Day glass is what glassmakers pour, using all the glass refuse at the end of the day, creating that lovely little sculpted vessel." Em watched in amazement as Felicity moved from room to room. How did Felicity know so much and Em so little?

"That is a Lincoln rocker, from the late 1800s, I'd reckon," Felicity said, spying the old rocker.

"That old thing? It's trash Randy always says. He keeps telling me to throw it out. But something makes me hang on to it, even though it's all busted. I can't sit in it without a bunch of pillows to cover up the ruined seat. I guess memories are all that hold it together. Mama used to rock in it, all those nights she couldn't sleep in their bed after Papa died. Then when she got so sick and hurt so bad, she couldn't sleep ever."

Em thought for a minute and wondered how much to confide in her new friend, then continued. "You know, after Papa died, Mama was broken-hearted. The only thing that could lighten her mood was the hope of seeing Papa again. She thought their strong bond of love would last after death. My mother, Cleo, believed in ghosts and used to say she'd communicated with them at the old Ryde Hotel in the delta. Everyone said it was haunted. I'll never forget Mama saying,

'I know he'll come back to me. We'll talk and laugh like we always did. Death won't end us'."

"But Mama never saw Papa again, and I think that's what finally killed her. She just didn't care anymore about anything."

Felicity's eyes warmed Em's heart, as though she could look right into her soul. "My deah. When the dead are ready to go, they depart. If they have unfinished business, or something that compels them, they hang around. Apparently, your papa was ready to go. He had no unfinished business. He knew how much your mama loved him. He didn't need to come back to tell her that."

"I guess you're right. Mama's never come back to me, either. I know she was ready to go. Still, it made me angry that she didn't try harder to live. Then I was just sad, all the time."

"I well understand your grief. Letting go of a loved one is the hardest thing a person can ever do in life and in death. But we never really let go, do we? Look at all your beautiful treasures from your parents' and grandparents' homes. Each one has a story and a memory attached to it which will live forever through you."

"Huh. I've never looked at it that way." Em's eyes drifted off into her memories of watching her grandma make quilts, including the one on her mama and papa's old bed.

Felicity's tone changed abruptly into a business-like voice. "As for that Lincoln Rocker, you're right to hang onto it. That can never be replaced, they're not made anymore. However, little Emeline, with a lot of cane and a bunch of wooden pegs, we'll fix it up good as new. I'll teach you how. You can braid, embroider, and sew. No reason why you can't add caning to your list of accomplishments."

Em marveled at Felicity's words and loving warmth. It was like they had known one another for years, for all of Em's life. It was as though Felicity had been waiting in the shadows of Em's existence.

"You can teach me how to cane? I thought only blind people could do that."

"No one is truly blind, deah, anyone can master any craft. You see not only with your eyes, but with your heart, your memories, and your fingertips, along with your strength, hopes, and dreams. We'll make a master homemaker out of you yet. You'll be the envy of all of the neighborhood, of old Mildred's valley, here in our little Cabin Village. Or the Flats, as those in Charles Town prefer to call our neighborhood."

"Heavenly Hollow is what my mother-in-law calls our cabins."

"Yes, I know our little village by that name, also. Much more appropriate than the Flats." Em smiled with her whole being. "I'll look forward to whatever you can teach me. I promise I'll do my best to be a good student."

"Yes, I'm certain you will be. You have a will to learn and see where others might not. Now, time for me to depart before that beloved of yours returns, Randy."

"Oh, Randy." Em giggled. "I forgot all about him. I was having so much fun."

Felicity glanced worriedly at Emeline. "You've only been married for two years, Emeline. Surely, you're still happy?"

"I guess. At times, he can be so annoying and such an idiot. Sometimes I even wonder if I did the right thing in marrying him so young." Felicity's look deepened, creating furrows in her forehead and darkening her eyes. "Well, that's a conversation for another day," she said.

With that, Felicity returned to the kitchen, walked out through the screen door, flashed Emeline a brilliant smile and departed into the lowering sun. The magnolia tree was the backdrop of her retreating figure. Felicity became silvered by the sunny universe surrounding her. Her loose blouse caught the light. The breeze billowed shades of greens, blues and pinks on Felice's blouse painted by the colors of the surrounding sky and foliage. Her old blue cotton pants turned white, her hair turned into a silver halo. She looked like a design in an old silver nitrate photo or daguerreotype, maybe a chrome hood ornament on an old Bentley. Her strength was in her long stride as she walked down the road with confidence. Zuma ended the spell, bits of her bright orange fur merging into Felicity's wake, floating on the late afternoon breezes. Em admired the vision in light and nature, color and friendship. The scene ended abruptly. Felicity turned and was Felicity again, not a hood ornament or a silver sculpture or an old portrait.

"Well, darlin', ta-ta till next time," she called over her shoulder.

And with that farewell she and Zuma disappeared around the bend in the road, evaporating into another world Em felt she had only briefly glimpsed. Even after her departure Emeline continued to feel Felice's presence. Her new friend had left Em's home but had embedded herself more deeply into Emeline's life. An hour later Randy skidded into the driveway to find Emeline still rocking on the front porch, uncharacteristically immersed in thought.

"Hey, Sweet Pea, whatcha doin?"

"Nothin. Just setting, rocking and thinking."

"Thinking about what?" Randy said as he retrieved his briefcase from the front seat of the Rambler.

"Not much. Randy, have you ever noticed the way the colors of the day change with the light, at different hours? And how each change brings different sounds, vibrations, and breezes? Even different birds show up at special times. Like they have appointments." Em chuckled at her words. Birds with appointments? She remembered Felicity telling her she had a *poetic voice.*

"No, I don't. Sounds pretty foolish," he said crossly. He was hungry and tired and didn't want to talk about poetry or birds with appointments.

Instead, he asked, "What's for dinner?"

Em continued to rock gently. Her cats napped nearby, their tails avoiding the rails of the Appalachian rocker.

"Biscuits."

"Biscuits? I thought you burned them all this morning. Now we have to have them for dinner? You tell me you've been home all day while your man's been out working and sweating and all he comes home to is burned biscuits?" Em threw him a venomous look and said, "That's so, is it? What have you been sweating over all day?"

Em then rose to her full five-foot-two height. She stood defiantly in front of Randy, poking him in the chest as she emphasized each word.

"I've been (poke) calibrating the oven. I've been (poke) cleaning up burned biscuits. I've been learning…things. My new friend, Felicity, came by. She's going to teach me how to cook. So there. I made you *fresh* biscuits. For dinner, along with leftover mac and cheese." She poked Randy painfully once more, ending their conversation.

Randy's concerns grew. Why was she making friends with some flighty old lady from the neighborhood? She probably had dementia and wandered around looking for naive girls to talk to and impress with her crazy ideas.

"Oh, what do you care, as long as you get fed?" Em's anger rose to match Randy's frustration. "And stop treating me like I'm a two-year-old!" she continued angrily.

"Now sweetheart, I didn't mean nothing…" Randy stammered.

Her response was a slammed screen door, sending her feline friends to hide beneath the porch yet again.

Randy shook his head, ruffled his hair and muttered to himself, "Damn women. Who can understand them?"

"Now, sweetheart," he tried again, as he raced into the kitchen, "That's all fine. I do so love biscuits and your mac and cheese."

Em slammed plates on the table. "Felicity says I have talent in homespun arts. She's going to keep teaching me all it takes to become a true master homemaker."

"Felicity, huh? That old lady who's been stoppin' by? That old biddy you keep harpin' about?"

"YES! That old lady who thinks I'm worth teaching things to, like cooking, and calibrating."

"Now, lovie, you know I think you're worth your weight in gold," Randy said hopefully.

Em continued to crash around the kitchen, finally removing the ceramic bowl from the oven and placing the still-warm biscuits, nested in their tea towel, on the table. Randy unwrapped the bowl and the aroma of biscuits filled the room. The vapors infused the kitchen, circulated by the *tick-tick* melody of the old ceiling fan above. The twilight breezes lifted the biscuit perfume further throughout the cabin. Randy imagined he was standing in front of a bakery in some ancient, out-of-the-way market.

"There. See if this meets with your approval while I heat up the mac and cheese," Em said. Inside the bowl Randy discovered a most wondrous sight—big, fluffy, golden globes of beauty. Em heated the leftovers as Randy ate one, then two more biscuits with butter, than a fourth with butter and jam. His taste buds exploded in ecstasy.

"My dearest," he said, with a face full of crumbs leaking onto his rumpled, once crisply ironed shirt, "I've never loved you more." And with that, he welcomed Felicity into their lives and kitchen, whenever she chose to visit. "Whatever Felicity wants to teach you, whenever she wants to visit, I welcome her to our home."

Em turned from the stove and gifted Randy with one of her luminous smiles. She realized that was the true beginning of her friendship with Felicity, cemented by Randy's approval. *As if I need his approval*, she thought, as she dug into the warm nest of biscuits herself.

"Who needs mac and cheese when we've got biscuits, right?" Randy happily chortled as he dug into the bottom of the bowl. "You know what they say, sweetheart, the way to a man's heart is through his stomach. You've won my heart in every way possible."

Sometimes her husband did say the sweetest things. She reached across their old table and held his hand. His smile convinced her she really had made the right decision in marrying him. She wanted this moment, this mood and love to last forever. With all her heart, she hoped it would.

Randy noticed the sweet look of contentment on Em's face. *Maybe she's finally getting over her sorrows*, he thought hopefully. Perhaps against his better judgment, he forged ahead with what was on his mind.

"Sweetheart, you know this weekend we're going to my mom's. She was really unhappy we didn't make it last weekend and she's already planning dinner."

Em thought over Randy's words. She should be kinder to Margret. After all, she had done so much for them. It wasn't really her fault that they had moved from Em's beloved delta to Virginia. Guilt, along with a little cream, flavored her enjoyment of her after dinner cup of coffee.

"More coffee, honey?" Em purred. She leaned over Randy and enfolded him in a hug, leaning her head on his shoulder. "I'm sorry, sweetheart. I don't think your mom and I hit it off that well on our first visit. It's my fault. I felt as though she was looking down at me."

"It's not that, honey. She's just not used to being around younger women. She's not very sociable. Never had many women friends. I guess that makes her seem uppity."

Just like me, Em thought. "I'll try harder with your mom, I promise. We'll invite her here for dinner soon? I can show her my new culinary skills, as Felicity calls cooking."

"Oh, Em, that would be great. She'd really love that."

Em chewed her lip, realizing once again she was out of library books and needed groceries. It had been almost two weeks since her last visit to town.

"Let me have the car tomorrow and I'll drop you off and run some errands. You know, go to the library, get groceries for dinner. How about I pick up some hamburger meat and make your favorite casserole tomorrow?"

"Dogfood?" Randy said hopefully. Em slapped him playfully. "Not dog food, you idiot. Hamburger Helper."

Randy warmed at the thought as he rose and kissed Em. "Sure, that would be great. I don't have to go to work until later, anyway."

"Oh, why is that?" Em said without allowing her anxiety to enter her voice. Surely Randy wasn't doing so poorly that they were thinking of firing him, or cutting back his hours?

"Nothing special. There's a baby shower for one of the office girls and they're having a big to-do. Stan had said he'd hang out and take care of business while the girls decorated for the party. He told the rest of us that we could come in at one."

"Perfect. We can have leftover biscuits for breakfast." Em said happily. "I think there's about six left."

"Ouch. Did I really eat that much?"

"We both did, sweetie," Em said as she patted her rounded tummy. "Sign of a good chef, right?"

"I couldn't agree more," Randy said. Em smiled over her newfound domesticity. It had been a perfect day.

Chapter 6

Em could have recognized every twist and turn of the drive from their cabin to Charles Town even if she had been blindfolded by the way their little Rambler navigated the rutted road. Their cabin #25 was set back from the road, with a long dirt driveway leading to the dusty, washboarded Heavenly Hollow Lane. In the evenings, Em loved to watch the distant cabin lights flickering like fireflies through the darkness. During daylight hours, she noticed every turn in the road on their trips into town, noting the fields across the road, filled with wildflowers. Some fields held growing vegetables, tidy rows of corn, lettuce and tomatoes or fields of hay. Some cabins embraced the road with barely enough room to park a vehicle. Eventually, the cabins disappeared and more trees appeared: elm, shimmering Aspen, stately Oak, delicate Willow and ancient Maples lined the road at various points.

The skittering of the Rambler at the bottom of the long Heavenly Hollow Lane after the worst of the washboard ruts announced their arrival to civilization at the intersection of Heavenly Hollow Lane and Charles Town Road. The smooth asphalt welcomed the Rambler's worn shocks and put an end to the teeth chattering drive.

Like spokes on a wheel, roads led off the main Charles Town Road in all directions. They first passed Little Lake Road. In the distance, Em could spy the small lake, its mirror-like surface reflecting the sun and clouds, with a few cozy cottages nestled at the far end. Walkways led from the cottages to weathered docks, with moored boats bobbing in the water. Next were fish shacks and cabins, listing into one another with repairs in makeshift patterns of wood and tar paper, while others had fallen into their stone foundations. The views changed from cabins to farm houses, picturesque in fields of growing vegetables. The largest lots were scattered with tractors and old rusting farm equipment, a tribute to long histories of farming. The backdrop in distant pastures were cows and horses grazing peacefully. The pastoral scene changed as the road progressed, exhibiting larger stone cottages, prettily covered with vines and walkway trellises, covered with blooming roses, bougainvillea of all shades, and purple trumpet flowers. Emerald lawns were trimmed and carefully tended, bordered with more flowerbeds or vegetable patches. Entering the Village Green in the center of Charles Town the largest homes appeared, those of the wealthiest in the community. These homes were much older than the smaller cottages, and had probably been the center of Charles Town when it was originally established. Some were whitewashed brick like Margret's or all shades of red, burnt sienna and umber colored brick. Some houses were two stories tall with pretty wooden gingerbread adorned verandahs and porches decorating lower and upper stories. Many had two, even three stone chimneys climbing majestically up the sides of the largest mansions. Long drives were gated, discouraging the curious and intruders.

As they entered Charles Town Em's favorite place, the library, sat directly across from the center of the village green. The stately courthouse, two imposing stories high, rose next to the library. Two field stone churches, one at each end of the Green, invited Lutherans and Catholics to Sunday services and Wednesday Bible studies. Beyond the Green small shops lined the two main streets of town: Elm and Maple. The shops crowded together in brick, wood frame and stone, leaning against one another like old friends, bulwarked by their history, bracing for whatever the future held. Ornate and hand-carved and painted signs announced their wares: Sew What? Going Places: Fine Leather and Luggage Specialists, Book Nook, Flaky Foreigners Bakeshop, Thrifty Threads, Prim and Proper Women's Apparel and Antique Lives. The Inn and Out Diner was at the far end of Elm Street, housed in its small wooden building, beckoning visitors with quaint red and white gingham curtains. Em peered into the diner which held few customers. She hadn't explored all of the stores yet, but looked forward to doing so.

On their way out of town toward Meridian Road and Bert's Best Buddies Pre-owned Vehicles was the Piggly Wiggly, the large modern supermarket where Em shopped. The Charles Town High School, 'Home of The Panthers' resided on one side of the supermarket. A mile further Washington Elementary School appeared. Its large billboard announced, 'PTA Spaghetti Dinner! First Wednesday of Every Month!' The rest of the drive to Bert's was uneventful and unattractive, filled with car lots, manufacturing plants, lumber and farm stores. When they finally arrived at Bert's, Em had grown anxious to get on with her day. She hadn't planned on visiting but Randy insisted she say hello to his boss, Stan. She had only been inside the building once before and knew the interior was a painful attempt at imitating a major car sales enterprise. There were balloons, half deflated, hanging from the ceiling. Hand-made signs announced 'HOT DEALS' and 'NO CREDIT NO WORRIES! YOU GET IT ALL AT BERT'S!'

On this day, there was a gaggle of women at a round blue and pink beribboned table in the center of the break room. The remains of a large cake announced the end of festivities. The recipient of the baby shower was waddling around the cake splattered table placing her baby gifts in a plastic bathtub.

Randy grabbed Em's hand and dragged her off to greet Stan, his manager. Surreptitiously, she studied the other salesmen. She wondered if things had improved between Randy and his co-workers in the ensuing weeks since her first visit.

Stan's office was in a glass walled cubical with a large desk littered with papers, fast food containers and 'In' and 'Out' boxes. He grunted a hello to Randy and treated Em to a warm smile.

"Hey, little lady, nice to see you again. How are things out in the sticks?" Em had no time to respond as Monica, Stan's secretary, entered the small room. She fluttered around her boss, handing him a sheaf of papers to sign. Monica wore dresses so tight Em wondered how she could sit down. But she had to admit Monica certainly had the body to fill out those dresses. The young secretary could usually be found flirting with customers in a seductive, gum snapping way, her tongue advertising her talents. Randy and Em returned to the show room.

Em noticed that Randy's co-workers appeared to have arrived at work before 1p.m. The four men were sitting at their desks, residue of frosting smeared paper plates and discarded forks decorating each desktop. Her stomach gave a lurch as she wondered if they had been invited to the baby shower leaving Randy out of the festivities. "Hey, Randy, grab yourself some cake while there's some left." Em recognized Jason, who had befriended Randy, taking him under his wing. "Yeah, thanks, I think I will," responded Randy, straightening his tie as he approached the table, walking with a slight swagger.

"Everyone's met my beautiful wife, Emeline, right?" Emeline wanted to shrink inside her skin, but she said, "Oh, Randy, I have to run, I've got so many errands." She noticed the gaze of one of the men, who was imagining her naked, Em guessed, by his leer.

"Yup, Randy, you're one lucky guy all right. Hey, sugar, have some cake with us."

"No, I really have to run. But thanks." Em kissed Randy perfunctorily on his cheek and turned to leave. "Now, honey, I bet you can do better than that for a kiss. Want me to show you how it's done?" said the leering guy whose name Em learned was Ray. Monica poked her head from Stan's office, gave her gum a loud snap, stuck her tongue out at the salacious salesman and returned to the office.

Em felt that she couldn't get out of the place fast enough. As she departed she heard Randy's voice as he launched into one of his grandiose speeches. *Oh, please*, Em thought. Please don't make a fool of yourself acting like someone you're not. As she walked toward their Rambler, the unwelcome thought floated into Em's mind: why had Randy been told to arrive at work at 1pm when the party had begun earlier? She shuddered at the thought that he could be so disliked by everyone but Jason. Why, oh why, did he have to put on such ridiculous airs? Just like high school, she reminded herself. He can't help himself.

As she drove Em's thoughts turned to her mother-in-law. Perhaps when they visited Margret on Sunday she could pursue facts of Randy's past life from Margret. She shook her head. No. Margret was as reticent and secretive of their history as Randy. Em now knew that her mother-in-law was the last person Em would beg for confidences or family history. She'd just have to discover things on her own.

By the time Em arrived at the Village Green, she felt an enormous sense of adventure and freedom. It had been too many days since she had last wandered between the tall stacks of books at the Charles Town Public Library. She entered the quiet sanctity of the cavernous room. Windows high above illuminated the old stacks of unread stories. She breathed in the wonderful scent of old paper. Every book was a potential gift to open for the exploration of new worlds, words, and treasures.

Suddenly, Em was overcome with emotion. She remembered the scent of their attic where she would hide as a child. As if it were yesterday, she saw her mama sitting in their old rocking chair on the porch, going through her weekly stack of library books. Close by, her papa would be immersed in one of his Science magazines, or snoring loudly, head thrown back, mouth wide open. *Why does missing Mama and Papa never end?* she wondered. The answer came to her: It was because she had no guide, no hand on the rudder of her life. Em hadn't asked her mama enough questions and now it was too late for answers to the thoughts that assailed her.

How did Mama feel when she first found out she was pregnant at sixteen? Elated or fearful? What did Em's grandparents say? Were they angry with her out-of-wedlock news? What were her grandparents like? What was their history? Did her grandmother Muriel teach her mama to cook? What was her mama's favorite meal when she was growing up? What about her great-grandparents, who she had never met? What was it like for them to have lived in Brooklyn, New York, and then to have picked up and moved to California during the Gold Rush years? Did they ever find gold? There were no answers, only more questions.

She put her memories aside and dove into the *Romance* section. She discovered two 'bodice rippers' as her papa had called her mama's favorite choice of fiction. He had teased Cleo whenever she brought home a new stack of her bawdy books. Her papa preferred his magazines to books for reading pleasure. He scolded Cleo for her lack of interest in other forms of fiction or nonfiction. She would reply, "You know perfectly well how much I learn from my so-called 'bodice rippers'. Listen to this, quivering thighs, arching back, she dove into her passion as her lover…"

"Okay! Enough!" her papa would shout, covering his ears. Em giggled at the memory of her parent's sparring, which raised the eyebrows of the head librarian, Ms. Ogelthorpe. I bet she's never had quivering thighs, Emeline muttered under her breath. She then laughed outwardly which brought the second librarian, Adrian, from behind one of the stacks which he had been pretending to dust. He grinned and shook his finger at her in mock chastisement. Em appreciated his tall and handsome presence. During her first and subsequent visits to the library they had begun to tease one another. Their friendship continued to develop.

Adrian retreated behind the stacks as he danced a little jig, using his duster as a baton, waving it over his head. Em chuckled at his outlandish behavior. Yes, definitely. She'd have to get to know him better.

She settled on two bodice rippers: *Down Under Love: Australian Secrets* and *Passion Unfettered*. To Em, they were not just tawdry books, they were an education gleaned from provocative passages. Such books had enormously improved her and Randy's love life. She chuckled over their most recent delightful and fulfilling romp. That encounter could easily have been included in the repertoire of the books she now held in her hands. Her third choice was made on impulse, a children's book whose title intrigued her, *Best Friends*. The beautiful illustrations on the cover and inside the book enticed her. Making her way to the checkout desk she felt foolish clutching her choices of a children's book along with two provocatively titled and illustrated covers.

Adrian checked her out. She teased him for his flamboyant choice of outfit. "What on earth are you wearing? I just love that print. It would make great curtains."

"How right you are complimenting my ensemble," he replied with a smirk. "This lovely Hawaiian shirt was inspired by the island of the same name. Its magenta, turquoise and lime green are perfect contrasts of color, wouldn't you agree?"

Em snorted. "Yeah, I guess. Those colors would look better on a window than me, though. I could never imagine wearing anything that wild."

"Hmm. You're correct. You don't have the *chutzpah* to wear such an outfit. Besides, your blond locks would clash with these hues. As for me, with my darkly tanned complexion, lime, turquoise and magenta bring out the best of my handsomeness and green eyes, don't you concur?"

Em rolled her eyes. "Sure, if you say so. I must admit, you look a bit Rhett Butler-ish today."

"My, my. M'lady's been reading *Gone with the Wind*." He smiled at Em proudly, as though she were his child and protege. Adrian had recognized the early bibliophile in Emeline as he had spied her wandering the stacks. He saved treasures for her, books meant for sale or the dust bin, stealthily adding his finds to Em's weekly check-outs. He was the co-conspirator to her edification. Em always knew he had a treat for her when he began looking around furtively for Ms. Ogelthorpe. Satisfied they were not being watched, he would sneak a book or two into her pile.

"You'll love this one, sweetie. The back cover is only half there but I have a feeling *Rebecca* will resonate with you."

"Adrian, won't you get in trouble if that old hag finds out you've been giving me all these books?"

"Frankly, my dear, I don't give a damn." They both erupted in giggles as Em gathered up her treasure trove. "Oh, and by the way, Sir Adrian. I read *Gone with the Wind* in high school. I'm not entirely uneducated, you know. I even named my cats after Scarlet and Rhett even though they're both females."

She struck a pose imitating Ms. Ogelthorpe on rounds, nose in air, slapping recalcitrant books back into their rightful places. "Emeline. Stop it this instant," he whispered, looking to see if Ms. Ogelthorpe had witnessed her mimicry. "You want to get me in trouble?" Em smirked as she replied, "oh, poor frightened Adrian." He slapped her wrist for good measure. "Watch out or I'll stop saving you books, you little vixen."

As she exited the library, Em decided to check out the Inn and Out Diner: 'Service in a minute or linger longer'. She could at least afford a cup of coffee. The gingham curtains on the windows were irresistibly welcoming. As she opened the door the musical notes of a jingling bell announced her presence. Inside, there were only two tables filled. A plump waitress was bustling about between the diners and the kitchen. Em settled in a small table for two at a front window. "Be with you in a minute, honey," the waitress said as she handed Em a menu.

It was closer to five minutes, not one, before the waitress approached Em again.

"Sorry for the wait, honey. Damn cook drank too much again last night and didn't show up, so I'm working the kitchen and the tables." She wiped at the perspiration on her brow and shoved a loose strand of hair from her ponytail off her face. "Lunch was a mess, but since we're near closing at three, I can slow down some."

Em studied the woman more closely. She was round figured and not much taller than Em. She certainly did look frazzled. Her brown hair was unkempt and falling out of its ponytail. She had a wide face and wasn't very attractive. *Mousey*, Em thought. Her white apron was spattered with stains which coincided with items on the menu: burgers and fries, meat loaf, grilled cheese sandwiches, chef's salad, hot turkey sandwiches and homemade pies. Em brought herself to attention as she noticed the waitress was also studying her.

"Oh, I'll just have a cup of coffee."

"You're new to Charles Town, aren't you, honey? I haven't seen you here before. My name's Sadie. Pleased to make your acquaintance." Sadie held out her hand, then abruptly withdrew it to wipe on her apron. "Sorry. I'm a mess. Glad we're closing soon."

"Oh, if it's too late I'll come back another time," Em said.

"Oh, no, of course not. We always have coffee. And I've always got time." Sadie laughed at her response. She waved goodbye to the last of the customers as they left, the bell on the door releasing Sadie from any hesitation in chatting. She quickly ran to the door and turned the OPEN sign to CLOSED and then returned to Em's table.

"Glad that's over. Tell you what. I'll join you. No one comes in this late anyway. Since I'm the boss today, I can close when I want." She giggled mischievously. "Been dying to sit down and have a cup of coffee myself." Em was surprised at Sadie's forthright manner but hastened to hide her surprise when Sadie pulled out the chair across from Em and sat down.

"You don't mind, do you, honey? I just gotta rest my piggies a sec."

"Of course not. You're right. I've never been here before and I'm happy to meet you, Sadie."

Sadie gifted Em with a warm, dimpled smile. Her whole being was immediately transformed. Her brown eyes sparkled and her face lit up, changing her appearance from mousey to cute. Somehow, her plumpness fit her.

"Oh, my manners," Sadie said. She rose and bustled back to the kitchen. Moments later she reappeared with two steaming mugs of coffee and two large slices of Blueberry Pie.

"It's on me, dearie. After all, I made the coffee, the pie, and everything else today. I oughta be allowed to share the goods." A trilling high, musical laugh erupted from Sadie as she set everything on the table. "What's your name, honey?" Sadie asked, as she plopped herself tiredly into the chair across from Em.

"Emeline. My husband, Randy and me, live out in Heavenly Hollow. I don't get into town much. Only about once a week. Randy usually takes the car to work at Bert's Best Buddies Used Car Lot."

"Well, Emeline. Hope you'll visit whenever you get into town. I can always use a new girlfriend. You must get pretty lonely out in the Flats. Not too many neighbors around you, I bet." Sadie took a generous bite of her blueberry pie, which soon also decorated her apron. "Damn. I always wear whatever I'm serving or eatin'. 'You wear your food well', my ex always says." She sighed as she plucked the blueberry filling from her apron. "Oh well. Bleach wipes out every sin and mistake, right?" Sadie laughed her high trilled laugh again, pleased with her unabashed observation of herself.

"We call it Heavenly Hollow, although I have heard people in town call it the Flats, or worse, Hillbilly Holler. We live in cabin #25. I've only met one neighbor and she's pretty old." Em stopped herself from saying more about

Felicity, who she considered a friend, not just a neighbor. For some reason, she wanted to keep Felicity all to herself. Then, unable to resist any longer, Em dug into her pie. "Oh, Sadie, this is really delicious. Tastes like my mother's pies. She always used to say, 'It's not just what's under the crust, it's the crust that makes the best pies'."

"You're right about that, sugar. I do make the best pies. And everything else in here when that damn cook sleeps his drunk off. But I don't mind. Keeps me busy and out of the house until the kids get home from school. They're Alison, ten and Mary Anne who's eight. Alison's turning into a real hellion, just like her dad, Ralph, my ex. He's a good guy, helps me around the house and stuff. Gives me money for the girls, thank the Lord. We had what you'd call an *amicable* divorce, mostly because he was a lot more *amicable* with half the girls in Charlie's Town than with me. Mary Anne's a sweetheart, got a real good disposition. Nothing fazes her, just like me, everyone always says. Does great in school. *Not* like me. Which I guess is why I'm working here, making hardly any money." In between sentences, Sadie gobbled another bite of pie and gulped her coffee. Em found herself liking Sadie more with each bite she witnessed, each remark spoken. She'd definitely put Sadie and the Inn and Out on her list of things to enjoy in Charles Town.

Sadie gathered up their dishes and headed for the kitchen. On her way, she turned and gave Em another warm smile.

"Hey, I'll tell you what. If you always come in this time, around 2:30, I'll close up and have a cup of coffee and pie with you. I don't have many girlfriends since Ralph pretty much went through all of 'em. Whattya say?"

Em laughed. She couldn't ever remember meeting a woman who was as spontaneous as Sadie. She noticed Sadie was older than she, maybe in her forties. She'd be a great woman to get to know better. "I'd love that."

"Great! Then I'll see you next time." Sadie made her way to the kitchen. As Em left, she heard her singing in a sweet, high voice, "*She'll be coming round the mountain when she comes, when she comes...*" Em smiled and waved goodbye to Sadie through the little window to the kitchen. Sadie lifted a soapy hand from the dishwater and promptly dropped a wet dish onto the floor, which shattered. "Oh fuck, not another one!" Em heard Sadie scold herself as she left the little diner, the bell jingling her departure.

Several days later Emeline's most recent bodice ripper lay at her feet. She sat in her window seat, watching the progress of the sun through her library windows. She was lonely when Randy was at work. The only company she had were her books and cats, until Felice made another appearance. Em lazily picked up *Rebecca,* thinking she'd start that next. What had Adrian said? He thought the book would *resonate* with her? She'd have to read it to find out what he meant. There was so much she didn't know.

Troubling questions had begun to surface from her usually placid mind. Why am I here? What is my value? Who am I, after all? Felicity had told her everyone had a purpose in life. Em hadn't found hers yet. She doubted she ever would. She felt adrift. Tired of keeping house, of cleaning, of tending to her husband and cats, and living her isolated life. She had settled into an existence of anonymity, knowing only Felicity, who she barely knew and rarely saw. She couldn't yet count Margret as a friend, although their last Sunday dinner had gone well. Margret seemed to be making more of an effort with Em. She was warmer toward her, not so superior and stand-offish. Maybe Sadie could become a friend? She vowed that she would have a late visit to the In and Out the next time she went into Charles Town. Her mind wandered back to Felicity's last visit.

She had admired Em's braided rug, her tea towel curtains, her mama's doilies and her embroidery work. Felicity's favorite piece, 'Home Is Where the Heart Is' embroidery, had taken Em months to complete. It was too precious to place on the wall and resided safely in her grandmother's cedar hope chest at the foot of their old Spool bed. Felicity had been excited with the burned wood letters engraved into the chest, 'In This the Art of Living Lies, To Want No More Than May Suffice'. Felicity had remarked on the words and vines, leaves and flowers entwined around the verse, "True craftsmanship, my deah, a very special old piece." The words on the old wooden chest were true. Em and Randy certainly didn't have more than would suffice. They were always low on funds. Em hated when Randy had to ask Margret for a 'loan' of rent money.

Her mind wandered back to their visit the previous Sunday. Margaret had seemed happy to see Em, and had enveloped her in a warm hug, which surprised her. Momentarily, she had nestled in Margret's arms. Her hug felt so warm and loving, a womanly touch Em missed. She spied Randy's proud look over Margret's shoulder and wondered if he'd had a word with his mother about acting more like a mother and less like a mother-in-law.

Margret had then held Em at arm's length and smiled with her whole being. "It's been too long since your last visit. Don't you dare keep my son from me,

Emeline!" Momentarily, Em felt deflated. Had this been Margret's reason for her warmth? To scold her and keep her in her place?

"Oh, Ma, you know Em wouldn't do that. In fact, we want to invite you for dinner next time. Em's been learning to cook. She makes me biscuits most every morning and they're great."

For once, Margret was side-tracked from correcting Randy's use of his moniker for her. She examined Em anew. "My dear, is that why you've plumped up a bit? Or am I to become a grandmother?"

Randy saw the flush on Em's face and knew his mother was on dangerous ground. He stepped in to disarm the minefield. "Em's always been curvy, Mom. That's one reason I love her so."

"Mother, dear, not Mom," Margret said, returning to her usual admonishment.

Em was about to give up on Margret when her attitude changed again. "Well, my dear, why don't you come help me in the kitchen. I've already set the table there, less formal than the dining room and so much easier to clean up."

Em followed Margret down the hall and turned to inspect Randy. *He must be up to something*, she thought. His demeanor was completely innocent as he smiled and followed Em down the hallway into the kitchen. "Mind if I get us beers, Mother? I'll sit on the sun porch while you two ladies slave over your favorite man's dinner."

At that, both Em and Margret laughed. Margret chuckled to Em. "Quite the man of the manor, right? Or so *he* thinks. Just like his father, which is one reason why he's no longer in *my* life." Em was thrilled with this crumb of history thrown so nonchalantly her way after Margret's earlier secrecy about her marriage. Em decided to put off any investigation into Randy's past. With any luck, Margret would reveal more as they grew closer. Em had to admit she hoped their relationship would expand.

Together they worked over dinner. Margret explained to her how easy it was to roast a chicken as she was preparing their meal. "Really, Emeline. It's the easiest and best thing in the world to cook. You just wash it, throw in the stuffing and roast it in a 350 oven for about two hours for a four-pound bird. Oh, and baste it every twenty minutes for the first hour. Makes a nice brown, juicy chicken." Margaret bustled around the kitchen retrieving spices from her spice rack, an orange and milk from the fridge along with butter from the counter. She returned to share her recipe with Em.

"The stuffing is easy. Just use cubed day-old bread, throw in lots of parsley, sauteed celery, mushrooms and onions, maybe a fresh sprig of rosemary if you have any. I use chicken broth, with a little bit of milk at the end. The milk makes the stuffing creamier, but you don't want to overdo it." She handed Em a spoonful of the stuffing.

"Oh, how delicious!" Em exclaimed, licking her lips.

"Yes, I do make fine stuffing and roast chicken. But as you can see, it's not a difficult recipe, just an old proven one. In fact, I first found this recipe in the Michie Tavern Cookbook. You know, that was where Thomas Jefferson, George and Charles Washington and all their political colleagues used to dine. The Tavern is still there today." Em savored that little tidbit of colonial history. She'd have to tell Randy. Maybe they could go there sometime. If not to eat, just to look around.

Em watched carefully as Margret cut the orange in half and rubbed it inside the bird. She then added the stuffing. Before putting it on a rack in the roasting pan, she spread butter all over the chicken. Finally, she generously sprinkled seasoned salt, pepper, ground oregano, paprika, thyme and poultry seasoning over the bird.

"Only baste for the first hour, dear. Then when your chicken is nice and brown, cover it with tin foil. You'll know your bird's done when the legs pull apart from the body easily. Voila! That's it! Roast chicken, one of Randy's favorites. Isn't that easy?"

Em wasn't so sure. Her mama had only made stuffing for Thanksgiving. She never stuffed their chickens. Margret caught her look of trepidation. "You'll get the hang of it in no time. If you can make biscuits, you can make anything. I never was much of a baker, myself." Em was encouraged by Margret's continued confiding. "Can I write down your recipe? I'll never remember all this." Margaret smiled happily in reply.

"I'd be happy to share any recipes you'd like. I'll loan you two of my favorite cookbooks. You can start looking through them while we're waiting for the chicken to roast."

Margret reached to a shelf bearing many recipe books and pulled out a homespun red with white floral decorated book, *Betty Crocker's Recipes for Women*. She muttered to herself, looking through her chef's library. "Oh, there it is." She retrieved a battered cookbook, *A Taste of the 18th Century: Michie Tavern, 1784 Charlottesville, Virginia*. "Of course, this is a remake of the original Michie Tavern Cookbook. I doubt that any first editions exist anywhere. Now run along and keep Randy company while I get the potatoes and vegetables ready."

As Em left the kitchen with the two cookbooks, she heard Margret humming a jaunty little tune as she opened the oven door and splashed chicken broth over the roasting chicken. Em was reminded of Felicity's words, "My dear, true friendships begin with the sharing of recipes."

"Randy, what on earth has gotten into your mother?" Em said, as she settled on the little couch in the sunroom next to Randy, cookbooks in hand.

"She's really not a harsh woman, Em. She's just been through hard times. When she moved here, it was like a new life, taking care of her aunt. It wasn't easy for her and there was no one else around to help. Mom's not used to being around other women. Never was much for friends. No one ever came over. She has her moods, though. Sometimes she's just plain cranky."

"You'll learn to treat her with care when she's in one of her bitchy moods. Just gotta wait for the sun to shine again." His eyes wandered out the window, lost in thought. Finally, he returned to Em. "I'm getting another beer and checking on Mom. Want one?"

"Yeah, sure."

The next two hours passed happily. Em perused the cookbooks and wrote down recipes which looked interesting and not too difficult. She wandered through the downstairs rooms as the wonderful aroma of roasting chicken wafted throughout the old house. Em felt more comfortable in Margret's home and certainly more welcome. She inspected all the photographs and nick-nacks throughout the rooms again. Hesitantly, she looked up the stairs to the bedrooms above but decided not to venture further. Margret might be encouraged to think that perhaps Em was inspecting the upstairs rooms as possible new quarters for her and Randy.

The dinner was perfect. Randy was the center of attention, his two adoring women hanging onto his every word. He regaled them with stories of Bert's in between bites of the delicious meal. Em knew his tales were funny and quirky ones to hide the fact that he still hadn't sold any cars. At least, this month they didn't have to ask Margret for a loan. *Not yet anyway*, Em thought. They left Margret waving at the front door, the colors of twilight transforming the whitewashed brick into purples and pinks. Randy was unusually quiet on the ride home and Em didn't press him. They were both content in their silence.

Over the following days Em settled back into her life of anonymity. No one knew her in Heavenly Hollow other than Felicity, who she hadn't seen in weeks. Em had new friends discovered in the pages of her books. She dove into *Rebecca* and could not stop reading. She was intrigued by the mystery of a new bride frightened and intimidated by her beautiful home, Manderley. In some ways, the woman in the book reminded Em of herself. Alone, falling crazily in love with Maxim, the handsome ruler of the manor. All the young wife had was Maxim and the ghostly presence of Rebecca in the background. Similarly, all Em had was Randy and the ghosts of her mama and papa in her memory and life. Em could barely get her housework completed each day, so immersed was she in the reading of Daphne Du Maurier's tale. She couldn't wait to tell Adrian how much she loved the book and that it certainly did *resonate* with her.

Emeline began to treasure reading over any household activities. More than once she tripped over twigs or rocks, nose buried in *Rebecca* when she took out the trash. She bumped her knees when crashing over tables or chairs, reading while dusting. When feeding Scarlet and Rhett, she found that their meals would sometimes end up on the floor, not in their personal bowls, much to her cat's disgust. When she would finally put her book down to start dinner, she realized what she'd done and apologized to her feline children. They glared at her as she prepared them a fresh dinner.

The words in books spoke to Em, entered her dreams, brought her to life. She dreamt about the characters in her books, sometimes the voluptuous, sexy women in her bodice rippers, other times the nasty housekeeper in *Rebecca*, Mrs. Danvers. She became aware of and encouraged by stories of other women. They energized her. Everything she read was so much more interesting, beautiful and touching than her own thoughts and world.

Some days, Em examined her life while sitting in the library window seat. She felt she was changing, evolving, like a chrysalis growing into a butterfly. She wondered over her past lack of introspection or thoughtfulness. She had rarely examined her inner self. Why was she doing so now? It wasn't so much that her mind was lazy, but rather a vast unchallenged space. She realized it was her new life, which was forcing her to explore areas she had never tiptoed into in the past, books, her new world and new friends. She had begun to flex this great unused muscle between her ears. To her surprise, she became less bored when alone, less lonely for Randy. She spent long moments gazing out her kitchen window. She watched and hoped for Felicity wandering up her lane, but she also was discovering new perspectives. She was gently placing her footprints into this largely untested, unexplored province of her mind and imagination.

Em was discovering the strange and elusive land of contentment, a geography she had rarely wandered into since her mama's death. In the past, she had missed Randy when he left for work. The days had seemed long, empty and boring. In meeting Felicity, Sadie and Adrian her world had begun to expand. Felicity's friendship especially filled out the edges of her landscape. She began to explore further afield in all ways. From the waxy bronze-shaded fallen magnolia blossoms to the colors of the meadow grasses and flowers, her life was being woven into a new tapestry.

Emeline spent long hours on the porch watching the bird world around her. She had always loved birds, listened to them and worked to identify their varied songs. The birds in Virginia were unlike those on the Delta. She studied their actions, noticing the way they flitted about at different times of the day. She watched the feathered families in their daily routines, their arguments and battles and the ways couples winged together across the horizon, swooping in arcs and painting their feathery images across the sky. She was astounded by the amount of life around her. She decided she would ask Randy to install a birdfeeder, high enough to be unhampered by her hunter cats.

Em took her adventures further afield. She began to wander through the surrounding woods and countryside outside their home. At first stealthily, then with greater courage, she walked through the old lanes. Each discovered cabin was a surprise, a gift to her vision. Some were identical to her own but for features added over the years, a wrap-around porch here, lattice work protecting the underside of a home there. One cabin was painted a crisp white, with carved hearts decorating each green shutter. Who lived there and why hearts? Was it a young couple in love? Some cabins had horseshoes installed over their kitchen doors. Had the horseshoes brought luck? Other cabins were in a state of decline, empty with blackened windows, like soulless eyes turned blankly to the dusty road. What were the lives of the forgotten inhabitants like? Families ruined by financial failure or sorrow? Had they moved away to a better life of greater prosperity or downward into obscurity? Did Felicity live in one of these cabins? Surely if she noticed Em walking down the old lanes she would welcome her into her home. Em shied away from meeting any of the inhabitants she saw, not wanting to appear to be an intruder. If there was a movement in their yards, she scuttled off and hid in safety. She preferred her intimate, personal observations, protecting her own identity.

Em gave the cabins names, mapping out her new world: red-roof cabin, lace curtains behind tree-carved shutters cabin, big-yellow-flowering trees cabin. Sometimes she would sit in a field, watching a cabin and its dwellers to learn their habits. Run-down cabin put their laundry on the line on Mondays. From their laundry line, Em imagined they had two children about four and six. The man of the house was a farm laborer, identified by his overalls. The cows were milked at four at the red roof cabin. Kids at the flower garden cabin weren't in school yet and played on a swing set and in their sandbox most of each day.

Surreptitiously, Em examined the gardens and what was growing, reminding her of her delta farm and home. Lettuce of all colors grew next to tall plants with star shaped flowers and small green tomatoes. Vines climbed up tent-like poles, sprouting bouquets of beans. In other gardens, rows of green spidery webs grew everywhere over the ground and one another. Would they become melons? Squash? Another day she discovered an old apple orchard and was reminded of the wonderful apple pies her mama would make. Em promised herself she would return to pick apples in the fall. She was certain there would be an apple pie recipe in Miss Magnolia's cookbook. How thrilled Randy would be!

Em continued to investigate the wildlife around their home. She spent one afternoon in a field at the edge of a neighbor's property. She made a nest in a shady spot under a grove of trees and followed the busy and elusive lives of the birds. At first, they chattered at her presence. Two woodpeckers were especially ardent in their complaints, chuckling at her until her teasing and mimicking them forced them to flee in disgust. The Carolina wrens hopped about, pecking at bugs. The Blue Jays screamed, darted and dive-bombed her, then finally departed losing interest in her as a menace. A sage Mockingbird looked down on her from his perch. He seemed as mesmerized by Em as she was of him. They said not a word to one another. Eventually satisfied with his assessment of Em he swooped off to the top of a tall tree and provided her with a beautiful concert.

Em traced the light through the trees until the shadows told her it was time to return home. She slowly walked down the old lanes toward her cabin as though in a daze. She felt a shiver of discovery in the world around her and her observations, as though an epiphany had occurred within her. She kicked at a loose stone and chastised herself. "Really, you dummy, birdwatching does not a life make. Home, husband and cooking does." She happily returned home to her little cabin.

Em's bookshelves began to fill with each visit to the library. As though they were the most precious of jewels she collected the battered books purchased at the sale bin and contributed by Adrian. One by one her scarred treasures filled her life and library. The dull colors of the covers had been tinted by age and use, creating artful, abstract portraits on the shelves. These were *her* books, which she had read or was waiting to read. They were becoming old friends and she was extremely proud of these new inhabitants in her life. They meant as much to her as her weekly visits to Sadie and Adrian, but it was Felicity she most longed for. It seemed as though the old woman had become a vision she had imagined. The rarity of Felicity's visits made her presence all the more treasured. Em vowed to appreciate every visit with Felice no matter how infrequently those visits occurred.

Em had so much to tell her. "She'll show up when she's damn good and ready. That will just have to be good enough for me," she lectured herself. Emeline gazed out her library windows in the late afternoon light. It was that pearly time when the day and the evening hadn't yet decided to part ways. Time to make dinner. The only activity Em did not do while reading was cooking. She continued to love the challenge and was slowly making her way through Miss Magnolia's recipes.

Em had planned meatloaf, thinking she could recreate her mother's recipe from memory, along with the guidance of *Miss Magnolia.* She gently placed *Rebecca* on the window seat and rose to start preparing dinner. Miss Magnolia's cookbook was her foundation but she added her mama's special remembered touches; a small can of peeled tomatoes, salt, pepper, garlic powder, parmesan cheese and breadcrumbs to the mix along with stale, cubed white bread. She saved the juice from the canned tomatoes to make gravy, as she had watched her mama do. She covered the meatloaf with Parmesan Cheese and then more tomatoes, patted into the top. The wonderful perfume of the roasting meatloaf greeted Randy as he walked in the door.

"Good, God, Em, what are you making? That smells fantastic."

"Miss Magnolia's and my mom's meatloaf recipe, baked potatoes and canned green beans. And gravy." Em couldn't help but allow her pride to color her words. She nestled into Randy's arms for his warm greeting. Life was wonderful. She was falling in love with her husband all over again.

After her successful meatloaf, Em slowly washed the dishes. When this final task of the day was completed, she took one last look at the magnolia tree outside her kitchen window. She noticed how the moonlight made the leaves gleam.

Randy flicked the channels on their old TV. "Jeopardy is on, hon. Hurry up and get in here." She hung up her dishtowel and joined Randy in their sweet living room. Yes. Life was settling in to be as fulfilling as any of the characters inhabiting her library shelves.

Chapter 7

It was an unexpectedly hot and humid June day. Mama would have said, "The dog days have arrived when Sirius, the Dog Star, caused women to fight with their mates, men to go crazy and dogs to attack one another while cats hid in the shadows." Em felt as limp as the leaves on the trees surrounding their cabin. Even the birds seemed hot, their beaks opening, wings fluttering as they bathed in shallow puddles in their rutted road. Others faught over seeds in the new feeder Randy had installed in the magnolia tree.

Emeline sat in her rocker on the porch watching the birds fly about. As much as she loved birds, Em was starving for human interaction, lives touching lives. And the days seemed endless when she didn't have a fresh supply of books.

Her mind turned to the people in her life. She wondered if she should ask Adrian to have lunch with her on her next visit to the library. Would that be crossing a line? Why would it be, she scolded herself. She only wanted a mind to share, not a body. Still, the thought of enlarging her friendship with Adrian and possibly encroaching on social boundaries made her ponder. What would that look like to the world outside the library? "I'm just being stupid," she remarked to Rhett and Scarlet. "After all, I'm a happily married woman."

The sky was the color of violets. A breeze gave the dead leaves on the porch new life, as they fluttered around Em's feet. She felt the storm long before it arrived, from a sixth sense Em had inherited from her mother. She was becoming more tuned in to atmospheric vibrations. She felt the far-off thunderstorm under her skin. Likewise, Em had become more sensitive to the barometric intensity of storms in her life. Her mind wandered to Randy. Would he ever become successful at Bert's? Scarlet and Rhett slunk about, protective of Em but nervous about the unpredictable weather.

"Oh, all right." Em said to the cats when the first lightning flash slashed the sky. She opened the kitchen door. Gratefully, both cats raced to their refuge under the sofa. The storm captured the cabin in a crashing cadence, a symphony playing its rainy music on the old roof.

Em looked through her kitchen window through the curtain of rain. Certainly, Felicity wouldn't be wandering down their drive today. Em found herself frequently thinking of her elusive friend. Who was she? Where did she come from? What was her history? She was a mystery Em wanted to unravel. She admitted to herself that Felice was her closest friend, even though they had only visited twice. During those visits Em had felt as though she had known Felicity forever and could confide in her freely.

Em took refuge on the window seat in the library enjoying the dark solitude of her favorite room. Slowly, the rain ended its song, its violent drum beat on the roof lessening. Hesitantly, the sun reappeared, turning the world into sparkling diamonds. The soothing sound of raindrop's drip-drip-dripping on the roof became a musical refrain. Scarlet and Rhett crept from their hiding places and joined her in the old library. Scarlet jumped onto Em's lap. She purred her love and promptly fell asleep on the soft, warm pillow of her mistress's tummy.

Em was restless. She gently moved Scarlet aside and rose from the window seat and opened the Dutch door. The after-storm breezes were already drying the world, like laundry on a clothesline. The leaves were shimmering on the trees as the meadow grasses swayed.

Her unrest continued. She felt insignificant, an invisible ghost drifting through life. She had no purpose. She counted her friends on one hand. Felicity, Adrian and Sadie. Margret didn't count in Em's tally of friends. She vowed to bridge that gap, especially as it was so important to Randy.

She remembered the motto of the diner, 'Service in a minute or linger longer'. She looked forward to a visit with Sadie the next time she visited Charles Town. She definitely wanted to linger longer.

Scarlet, interrupted from her nap, stretched and yawned, then pounced on Rhett sleeping on the braided rug. "Silly cats," Em said as she stepped over them to make herself an afternoon cup of coffee. The rain was replaced by a mist rising from the dirt road. Through her kitchen window the sun still shone hesitantly, as the wind played with the wet leaves of the magnolia. Scarlet and Rhett followed Em into the kitchen mewling to be let out for an afternoon romp. "Been cooped up too long. Get out and have an adventure," she admonished her little family as she opened the door.

Suddenly and much to Em's delight, Felicity appeared out of nowhere. Her big orange cat, Zuma, trailed behind her up the muddy road. They materialized from the mist like a dream. Before they appeared round the bend in the road, Scarlett and Rhett had run to their safe spot under the porch. *How on earth did they know Zuma had arrived?* Em wondered.

"Lo, Darlin'. Thought you needed a lift, as do I, during these horrific blazing days. The storm does cool things down magnificently, would you agree?"

Emeline's joy at seeing Felicity overwhelmed her. "Oh, yes, I do need a lift. And yes, I am happy it's a tiny bit cooler. Felice, it's so good to see you." Em ran down the porch steps and grabbed Felicity's thin, bony, cold fingers, leading her up the steps.

"Let's sit on the porch where it's dry. You take the Adirondack and I'll grab one of my kitchen chairs." She ran into the house as Felice settled into the old Adirondack rocker."

"Well, darlin, I'm very pleased to see you, too. I wanted to check in, see how you're doing."

Em thumped her ladder back kitchen chair onto the porch and dropped into it. "I'm doing fine, except for being lonely for company. I've missed you!" Emeline blurted out again, surprising herself.

"Yes, darlin, a friend is a treasure to cherish." Felicity's broad smile lit up her face and Em's heart. "That's so true. I was just thinking the same thing. I never realized how important friends are. And this heat. It makes me feel stupid." Both women watched as Zuma settled herself on a patch of drying grass directly in front of Scarlet and Rhett's hideaway under the porch. Zuma stared intently as Em's feline family uttered low growls to the much larger cat. Scarlet and Rhett did not venture from their safety. Three pairs of feline eyes traded threatening scowls.

Felicity chuckled. "Now, Zuma. Be a good kitty." Zuma swished her tail in reply to her mistress, but did not move from her post. Felicity shook her head, dismissing the threat of Zuma, picking up the thread of conversation. "The heat is powerful but not strong enough to make a woman stupid. The humidity is delightful. Makes one glow. So good for the complexion."

"Well, I don't know about glowing or my complexion," Em replied, wishing she had checked her appearance in the mirror before racing down the porch steps.

Felicity noticed the open book discarded next to Em's Appalachian Rocker. Em immediately colored in embarrassment. It was another bodice ripper. She chewed her lip. Not only had she left the book out, but it was soaked in a puddle left by the storm's lashing. She'd have to somehow dry it out before she returned it to Adrian at the library. Thankfully *Rebecca* was safely ensconced on the window seat in the library.

Felicity picked up the book and shook the spattered raindrops from its cover. "*Passion Conquered?* Well, that certainly sounds, ah, interesting. What is the plot, deah?"

"Oh, the usual, like all romance novels. Guy or girl falls madly into forbidden love. He's married, or engaged, or she is. Or one of them has an incurable disease. Or the disease wasn't a disease after all, maybe just a rash. They end their budding love to save their marriages, or as a penance for the disease suddenly being cured. They run into one another in a lot of weird out-of-the-way places. Every time they meet, they fall more passionately in love, despite vowing to be faithful to their mates. Finally, usually during a wild storm, they tear off one another's clothes and their…Em read the title of the book Felicity was holding. *Their passion is conquered.* End of story."

"Sounds like *Wuthering Heights,* darlin', or *Lady Chatterley's Lover.* Those are the books that have changed many a girl's life."

"Wuthering who?"

"Heights. It's a classic Gothic tale of romance, of which you speak. Also, friendship, which turns to love, to hope, to loss…with a ghost or two thrown into the mix." Felicity laughed her deep throaty laugh Em so loved hearing.

"Is it a horror story, then? With ghosts? Mama swore she had ghostly friends at the old Ryde Hotel in the delta. But I've never seen one."

"Well, darlin, you just have to open your mind to all possibilities in life, death and books. Be aware and look for new experiences, new worlds, new stories. With that in mind, my deah, why don't you fetch a pencil and tablet and I'll give you a reading list for your edification and illumination. I suggest, as you like romance, you should begin with *Lady Chatterley's Lover.*"

"Well, I did read *Gone with the Wind.* We had to, in high school. Studying the Civil War, history and stuff."

"And how did you like it, deah?"

"I loved it. Made me laugh and cry. Scarlet was such a spoiled brat but became such a strong woman. She started out acting like a princess and eventually became a queen. That's why I named my cats Scarlet and Rhett. I knew when Scarlet was a kitten she thought she was a princess. Of course, I spoil them both, so no wonder they think they're royalty."

"Yes. Many true life stories have followed that plot. Your tablet, Em?"

"Tablet? I've got my shopping list..."

"That will do."

For the next half hour, Felicity and Em sat companionably at Em's kitchen table. Felicity dictated books, authors and a short synopsis of each. Emeline tried to keep up.

"Start with *Lady Chatterley's Lover*. Then on to *Little Women*, a much longer book, based on the strength of women and family. Then perhaps *Of Mice and Men*. You'll enjoy the return to your beloved California with Steinbeck's vision. Oh, and of course, *Tom Sawyer* and *Huckleberry Finn*. Mark Twain pinpoints friendship, young love, adventure, racism, slavery and the value of fellow man, no matter their color. Same is true with *To Kill a Mockingbird*."

Emeline looked up from her list, fingers growing tired from racing across the pages. "Why would anyone want to kill a Mockingbird? Mama always said she loved nothing more than to hear a Mockingbird sing."

Felicity studied Em, looking deeply into her eyes. "Did I say something stupid?"

"Oh, no, darlin, quite the contrary. You have a quick, avid mind and have discovered the hidden meaning of that title. Indeed, why would anyone want to kill something of such value, joy and beauty? Do you know that in some states it is against the law to kill a Mockingbird for precisely that reason? Many in life never realize that simplest fact of the title and the messages on its pages." Emeline brightened. She loved the way Felicity credited her with positive aspects and intelligence she never knew existed within herself.

Felicity continued. "There are countless wonderful books and authors. Continue with the classics, Faulkner, Hemingway, Fitzgerald. Oh, if you're looking for a higher level of romance, you'll love *Madame Bovary*, although the heroine and her life story are depressing. Perhaps Erica Jong's *Fear of Flying* would be a good choice after *Lady Chatterley's Lover*. And you should be certain to read anything by Gloria Steinem."

"Sounds like an awful lot of reading."

"Once you get started you won't want to stop. One book I think you would especially enjoy is not a novel. It is a handbook for country living, *Living on the Earth* by Alicia Bay Laurel. You'll need to purchase that one. It's a recipe book for living simply." Em furrowed her brows, chewing on her pencil, feeling deflated.

"That's why I go to the library to borrow books and sometimes buy them from the sale room. I can't afford to buy full priced books." Em did not confide that sometimes Adrian stole books for her. "Randy has begun to sell cars lately, but we still have barely enough to get by. All we can afford is groceries and rent. Sometimes we don't even have that and we have to borrow from Randy's mom."

Felicity thought for a moment. "We'll just have to fix that, now won't we deah? Come with me." The older woman marched with determination, scattering Zuma with her abrupt advance from the porch and across the yard. With strong and resolute strides, she led Em to the shed adjacent to the cabin. "Where are you going? Randy's mom said there's nothing in this old shed but a lot of junk. She checked it out before we moved in."

"One woman's junk is another's treasure. Open the doors, love. They're too recalcitrant for an old lady like me to pry open."

The decrepit doors gave way with Em's yanking. The creaking, complaining ancient metal hinges screeched as the doors swung open. *Light splashed through the doorway for the first time in how long*, Em wondered. The rain had stopped but drops splattered through holes in the roof. Dim sunlight lit up the musty interior. Cracks and holes sent blades of light onto hoops and hoops of something that looked like wire. Wooden boxes were piled high, some with faded stenciling on the side, 'Heavenly Hollow Orchards'. Shovels and picks lined one wall along with other small metal rakes and clippers, all rusted. The old farm implements were hung carefully on their long-ago allotted hooks. There were more piles of boxes at the very back of the shed. Emeline felt as though she had walked into a museum hidden away for decades.

"I feel as though we're the first people to be inside this shed for years," Em said, as a mouse scurried past.

Felicity stood silently in the doorway. She seemed lost in thought. It was as though she had become part of the old building. She was in deep shadow, merging into the dim light of the room. She sighed deeply. "Yes, dear Emeline. I'm certain you're correct. Except for the rodents, no one has been in this shed for many years." Felicity perked up, straightened her back. "As for the rodents, everyone needs a home, isn't that so?" Felicity stood in the decrepit building and appeared to become part of it as though she were enveloped in a faded photograph. Whatever timidity Felicity had felt as she first stood in the doorway quickly dissipated. The older woman strode with determined strides further into the shed. She carefully examined the hoops, which were rolled up and hanging from large pegs on the wall. They were of all shapes and sizes. She muttered as she explored dust and cobweb-covered boxes, looking through those on the floor. "Now where is that…where could those pegs be hiding? They have to be here, I know it."

Suddenly Emeline was struck by the beauty of the room. Everything was placed with such care and precision. At one time, everything in this shed had meant something to someone. Who had it been and where had they gone? Had they departed this world? If so, how long ago?

The light caught the varying shades of ocher and lemony shaded coils, placed on each peg according to size. "Ah! Here we go!" Felicity pulled out a box and instructed Em to carry it outside along with one of the hoops from the wall.

When Em picked up the small wooden box, it rattled, emitting a tinny symphony of pings, metal touching metal, and something else…wood? Felice and Em settled on lawn chairs in the shade under the magnolia tree. Em noticed the years of dust collected on the wooden lid of the ancient box. Cobwebs embroidered the hoop Em had retrieved. "What on earth is all this? And how did you know it was here?"

"Darlin, remember I told you I knew each and every one of these cabins. I had lots of friends in these parts. All gone, now."

"Gone, where?"

"Oh, the residents grew old, love. They're up on the hill resting peacefully under their stones in Heaven's Gate Cemetery." Felicity's eyes quickly grew misty with emotion—sorrow, yes, but something more. Unexpectedly, Em was filled with hope. Felicity seemed to know everything about her cabin, the neighborhood, probably all the neighbors. She certainly could teach Em anything she needed to know about living in the country. The younger woman felt as though any wish she made would come true at that moment. She imagined her new friend could make miracles happen and help erase the sorrow that flitted in and out of Em's heart.

Felicity continued to stare toward the top of the hill where she had indicated the former residents of Cabin #25 were now residing. "You mean there's an old graveyard up there? I never would have guessed," Em said, following Felicity's gaze. The shadow of the hill darkened the cabin and woods. Em always looked forward to this time of day nearing twilight. Both women's eyes remained on the shadowed hill beyond. "Yes, indeed. Many rest there peacefully in their homes under the old trees. Heaven's Gate is difficult to find now and quite a trek. The path and graves are all overgrown. It's still possible to find the trail if you know where to look. The graveyard path was never kept up, due to the nouveau neighbors who've moved into the Hollow over the years. No newcomers seem to care about old things and definitely not old graves."

"How can anyone dislike a grave?"

Felicity smiled at Em. "Slaves, darlin, freed slaves live under those stones now, some early residents and more recent residents of our Hollow. Charles Town never supported Mildred Hanson, the original owner and architect of her beloved Hill Haven, Heavenly Hollow and Heaven's Gate. Mildred's view was that all are created equal. She settled these acres and cabins with that heartfelt belief. She lived her values, much to the dismay of the 1840s settlers of Charles Town. Mildred saw no difference in status because of one's skin color, in life or in death. All colors of humanity are in that graveyard. I imagine they enjoy one another's company still, having conversations, remembering their lives and their histories. I bet there are parties and gatherings up there every night." Em looked at Felicity with some suspicion and fear. Was her only friend completely wacky? Felicity laughed at her look.

"Now, Emeline, I'm not crazy. I've just always had an overactive imagination as Mother used to say. I had to, to keep the demons and loneliness away. You know, we make our own special worlds in our minds. We can go there any time to get away from any discomfort, pain or fear. I learned to do that at a very early age. But enough of that. Stories for another day. Today, you're going to learn the tools of your new trade: caning." Emeline's curiosity was piqued, but she realized intuitively that her friend had shut the door on her past. Felicity returned to the present.

"I remember you telling me about caning. Is it like weaving? There was an old blind lady in the delta who did that. Everyone brought her their chairs, some of them couches, even a wheelchair. I didn't think anyone nowadays caned chairs and stuff."

"Caning is a craft for the sighted as well as the blind. I've heard that caning and wicker repair are very relaxing, although challenging. Wicker repair is more difficult. One has to study each part, each curlicue in the pattern, and then recreate each broken piece. You give new life to something others have discarded. You'll learn all that, in time. For now, we'll start with the tools of your trade."

For the next hour, Felicity pointed out and explained everything they had removed from the shed. The different sizes and types of reed, or 'cane', thin, rounded, flat, thick and narrow.

Some widths were as small as ⅛", others as wide as 2". Tiny wooden pegs, small nails, round and square—some as small as a pin, others no wider than twine—were all examined and explained to Em. Felicity scowled at a round wooden ball discovered at the bottom of the box. "Now how on earth did this old darning ball get in here?" She threw the ball into the yard toward Zuma, who promptly ran after it. Much to Em's surprise, Zuma acted as playful as a kitten. Both women watched as Zuma returned to her perch with the ball in her mouth. She sat in front of Scarlet and Rhett, who remained hidden under the porch. Slowly, with one paw, Zuma pushed the ball toward Em's two cats.

"Still think you're a youngster, don't you, Zuma?" Felicity asked her cat. She then turned to Em. "She's got a lot of good years left in her. Not like her mistress."

All at once Felicity seemed to fade along with the weak sunlight. Twilight was tiptoeing across the meadow toward Em's home. "Oh deah, I'm afraid this old body has overstayed its welcome. I'll start your caning lesson on my next visit. For now, I'll toddle off down the road while you return everything to its proper place in the shed." She called Zuma who reluctantly left her spot. Em was astounded to see the ball returned to Zuma from under the porch, swatted by one of Em's cats still in hiding. "Well, I'll be damned. Did you see that?"

"Cats do love to play, deah. Zuma's always been very smart and loves to tease and be teased, until she's had enough. Why, she actually bit me on my bottom one day when I was sitting on the commode teasing her with my toes. She does lose her temper, just as we all do. Still, I imagine someday our three felines will put away their dislike of one another and become compatriots." Felicity suddenly seemed almost transparently pale in her sudden fatigue. Em worried about her friend. She looked exhausted and as colorless as the fading light. "Do you want me to walk with you? You look awfully tired."

"Oh, no dear. I'm fine, just a bit peaked. It's almost 5:00 anyway, probably time for you to start dinner for your Randy."

Before Em could reply, Felicity was on her way, with a backward wave. Zuma trailed behind her mistress, as always, as though protecting her. "Till next time, darlin'." She called over her shoulder, her quavering voice floating to Em as she watched Felicity's departure.

Em mused over their visit. I shouldn't have worn her out. She's so alive and much younger when we're talking that I forget how old she must be. After returning everything to the shed, Em's thoughts continued to trouble her. "I wonder how old she is, anyway?" She asked Scarlet as she wrapped herself around Em's ankles. "But I guess it would be rude to ask, huh?" No reply came as both cats swarmed Em's ankles, awaiting dinner. Her cats darted in front of her through the kitchen door, where Em felt welcomed by the room's warmth. As always, Em admired the room, with all her special touches. She loved returning to their cabin, as though the walls themselves beckoned and held her.

Em continued her conversation with the cats as she scooped food into their bowls. "I'll ask her age next time Felice visits. She won't think I'm rude. I've said stupid stuff to her before. I won't wear her out so much next time. I want to keep her in my life for a long while."

Suddenly Em's heart lurched. People you love can leave your life in an instant. Her mama barely had time to say goodbye when Em finally realized how sick she was. Then it was too late to prolong her life. Em's eyes filled with tears.

"Can't lose Felice, too, now can I? She's the closest friend I have, besides you two and Randy. And Adrian and Sadie." As Scarlet and Rhett devoured their meal, Em continued her conversation with them. "Do you know you two are named after my favorite characters in *Gone with the Wind?*" Their only replies were snuffled chewing.

Over the next two weeks Em hoped for Felice's return. She worried about her friend and missed her. She wanted to share her thoughts about the library books she was reading, based on Felice's suggestions. There was so much she couldn't talk to Randy about. He just wasn't interested. But then, she wasn't interested in his job or the latest scores of his favorite baseball teams, either. Her life's main interests were trying out new recipes, reading, and investigating their neighborhood. There were times when she felt terribly alone and other times she only wanted to be alone. She vowed to share more with Randy. After all, he was her dearest and oldest friend. Felicity was icing on the cake of her life. Randy was the cake.

Over the next weeks as she read *Lady Chatterley's Lover* Emeline began to appreciate the differences between the overblown, obvious writing of *Passion Conquered* and the more delicate nuances and tenderness of words sculpted, not blasted, onto pages. She was beginning to exercise her brain as well as her imagination. She applied new discoveries in books to her own thoughts and words. She surprised herself when an author's writing began to color and enlarge her own conversations and experiences. She had never been introspective. Now she began to examine her inner self more deeply. As she read she felt as though she had entered a new world. She began to live in books as though the characters were actual people in her life. She wondered what Lady Chatterley would do next. She worried over her developing feelings for the groundskeeper. She feared the inevitable, when Lady Chatterley's trysts would be discovered. What would her husband do? Was she in love with the man she was having an affair with? Or was it just a fling? The words in books spoke to Em, entered her dreams, brought her to life. She became aware and encouraged by the stories of other women. They energized her. Everything she read was so much more interesting, beautiful and touching than her small world.

Randy was at first amused and teasing about the change in his previously quiet and predictable wife. "You're a regular bookworm," he would laughingly say. At times, he felt uneasy, as though a stranger had moved into his home and life. Yet he had to admit to himself that he looked forward to Em's conversations and ruminations when she included him in her thoughts. She became more interesting, more exciting to him. What on earth would his wife come up with next? Yet at times he grew impatient when she rambled on about some character or other in a book she was reading. There was no way to foretell his wife's actions or words, as there once had been. Em was changing before his eyes. He wasn't yet certain that he liked all of his wife's wanderings in her mind or her walks throughout the neighborhood. He noticed his own irascible behavior, along with an uneasiness, an undertow of fear. Were her new worlds discovered in books an unknown and dangerous harbinger to their future? He worked to quash those feelings. He'd known Em since she was fourteen. He knew her better than anyone. She loved him and he loved her. There was nothing to fear. He was surely just being irrational and would work harder to support her latest adventures, even this caning she talked of. Felicity hadn't yet returned to teach this new craft to Em. He half hoped she wouldn't. The elderly woman was creating sea changes in his wife that made him peevish. He preferred a placid lake to an ocean crashing with waves. Yet, he couldn't deny how important this friendship was to Em.

For now, he vowed to go with the flow and enjoy the ride.

One late afternoon Emeline was lovingly perusing the titles on her shelves. She had given Adrian Felice's reading list and he had contributed to her education by giving her old battered books meant for the dumpster or sale racks. *How Green Was My Valley, Death Be Not Proud, Red Badge of Courage, Huckleberry Finn.* They crowded one shelf, then with more additions, moved onto two shelves. Emeline thought of her book collection as old friends, getting to know one another after a long absence, separated on the Charles Town library shelves and the discard bin. She imagined their voices mingling in the stories they told her. Scout, of *To Kill A Mockingbird*, loved Nancy and Beth from *The Secret of the Old Clock.* Rima, of *Green Mansions*, was frightened of Cathy in *Wuthering Heights*, but loved the moors Cathy and Heathcliff ran over as children and later as ghosts. *Rebecca* was reticent in sharing the mysteries of her life and death.

Em began writing in a small notebook creating a dictionary of her newfound words. She carefully listed each word, its meaning, and in which book she had discovered the word. Her bookshelves continued to blossom and flower. There were so many unread books beckoning her. She longed to share her library with Felice but, once again, her friend had made herself scarce.

Em decided to tackle a new task: completely cleaning the old shed. Wouldn't Felice be thrilled to see the dust and cobwebs gone and the floor swept clean of debris? At first the venture into the light scattered recesses of the dark building was overwhelming. There was so much old *stuff.* Scarlet and Rhett were the first entrants into the shed. They gleefully chased the mice, routing and catching them. Em always praised her cats' efforts as her mother had done with her own cats.

The removal of the antique goods became an adventure. She never knew what she'd find next, feeling as though she was on an archeological dig. *She brought old-world items into the light of day for the first time in how many years?* she wondered. She couldn't imagine their origin. On the grass outside the shed, she lined up the old garden tools and rakes and discarded those with tines missing. She took out all the antique shovels, picks and axes and lined them up like a crew awaiting orders. As she cleaned and stacked more personal items began to rise to the surface hidden by years of neglect. Layer by layer Em unearthed history from the organized chaos of tools, apple boxes, hoops of cane, strange coveralls with hoods, perhaps bee smokers? She stood back to admire her work. Even the floor had been discovered, actual wooden planks hidden beneath layers of dirt. It had taken Em a full day to shovel out and then sweep the years of debris from the wood floors and to place the hoops of cane, garden tools and overalls on their designated hooks and pegs. She was proud of her efforts. Everything was in its place. *Tidy is as tidy does,* she thought, remembering her mama's favorite refrain when their house was in perfect order. Em had even discovered one large rectangular window encased with years of grime. Along the sides of the shed were six more windows, three on each wall, equally encased in decades of dirt. She knew cleaning them would be a dauntless task.

Then came the discovery of an old wooden trunk in the back of the room under the long window. A brass hasp on the aged wooden trunk glinted in the dim light. She was too tired to investigate further, and promised herself she'd think about that tomorrow.

She actually did think of the old trunk the following day. Her curiosity had been tickled.

When she opened the creaking shed door the next day, she was thrilled again with her accomplishments. Rhett and Scarlet raced into the room but found no mice. Bored, they left the building and lay in the sun-splashed clearing in front of the old building. The trunk at the back of the room beckoned. It looked out of place, as though it had been hidden like a pretty woman in the back of the room, protected by ancient farm tools and hoops of cane. She was pleased to walk across the floor without raising clouds of dust, dirt, and dodging mouse droppings. Em went straight to the corner where she had first eyed the old chest. Above her, she noticed a dropped ceiling made of lattice over the chest. When she had swept the lattice work installed on the ceiling clean of cobwebs, she wondered why it had been installed there. Remnants of old vines hung from the lattice work. *She'd have to ask Randy to repair the holes in the roof,* she thought, as she pulled away the vines clinging to the ceiling.She returned her attention to the chest which appeared to be made completely of wood, with its domed lid interspersed with strips of ancient, cracked leather. The chest was perhaps as old as the shed itself. Em imagined it to be an old traveling trunk. Its signature beauty was the large brass hasp. A loop through the center of the hasp most likely once contained a padlock. The hasp winked at her, enticing her. She heard mama's voice whispering in her ear, *Open it! Open it!* Em laughed, knowing that's exactly what her mama would have done.

She carefully and gently pulled the old leather handles at the end of the trunk to bring it into the light of the open shed doors. She was surprised at the weight of the chest, but then, it was made completely of heavy wood. Em sat down on the swept floor and carefully lifted the old brass hasp. As she lifted the lid, scents of lavender and mustiness assaulted her. A sudden breeze arose and expelled the musty scent, leaving only the perfume of lavender.

The first thing Em discovered was a removable tray with small compartments held in place by hooks. Inside one cubby was an old blue and white cotton apron, or overdress. Its fragility burned her fingers, as though her touch would cause it to disintegrate. Beneath was a white cotton cap. Em turned it over carefully. Inside the cap several reddish-gold curls were trapped. She replaced the items in the tray and placed the tray on the floor next to her. She then discovered an old woolen blanket and a beautiful ancient quilt. Beneath the quilt she found lace, which still held the beauty of its original craftsmanship. Beneath the layer of old lace Em discovered a pair of heavy white long johns and a long white skirt and a gossamer white blouse with dainty pearl buttons. Wrapped in the skirt was what appeared to be antique boots, ankle high with little buttons. She instantly had an image of a woman from the early 1900s playing tennis in one of the stylish outfits of that era.

Near the bottom of the trunk Em discovered a crocheted blanket, woven together with many squares of vibrant color. At the very bottom of the trunk was a box with the faded name, 'Hearst Clothiers: The Finest Apparel from Head to Toe'. The box was tied securely around all sides and with string. It was obvious this was an item that was meant to be hidden away, secreted forever. Em felt a chill go up her spine. Clearly, she was trespassing onto private territory. Everything she had unearthed belonged to someone else, someone loved. It had been carefully secreted away by a previous tenant of Cabin #25. That person had either left hurriedly, or died unexpectedly. All but the tightly tied *Hearst Clothiers* box were most likely stored, discarded items which could have come from anywhere. After all, the chest had been hidden for who knew how many years, covered as it was in dust and cobwebs. Hastily, Em returned everything to the trunk and pushed it back to its hiding place. She noticed the delicate lace again and decided that was the only item that was no more than a swatch of material, not something sentimental or sacred. Surely, she could use that, paying tribute to whoever had left the trunk in the shed. She removed the lace and then wondered if she should share the secret trunk with Randy. *No.* For the time being, she wanted to keep this buried treasure to herself. All thoughts of cleaning the windows escaped her as she left the shed and closed the old doors, hinges complaining over their unaccustomed use. She hid the lace in her own trunk at the foot of their bed, 'for safekeeping' she told herself a bit guiltily. She vowed never to open the trunk in the shed again.

Safely ensconced in her library, Em returned to her reading of *The Yellow Wallpaper*. She wondered over the woman imprisoned in the room with the yellow wallpaper. Her reading was turning Em into a feminist. She percolated words from the grounds of books. She eavesdropped on conversations in the grocery store, the library and the *Inn and Out Diner*. She was becoming more and more interested in the women around her and wondered what they thought, who they were on the inside.

She did not notice the changes within herself and her newfound curiosity. Randy did. As Em shared her thoughts and new knowledge with her husband, he continued to feel more nervous than interested. Who was his wife becoming?

Em would become itchy with impatience to share her musings, her ideas, her new-found knowledge. Her mind was flooded. She had so much she wanted to confide. She was a dinghy adrift on her newfound sea of knowledge. Often, Em would assault Randy the moment he arrived home from work. In the midst of preparing dinner, spoon or spatula in hand, sometimes dripping with gravy or mashed potatoes or even freshly made jam, she would launch into her latest discoveries. Some nights Randy appreciated her retelling of the stories in her books. Other times he was more wary than appreciative.

As she shared tale after tale with Randy she felt like the heroine in Arabian Nights, a book her mother had read to her as a child. "Did you know that all cultures have their own ideas of creation?" she asked Randy. "They make up their own stories to explain how we got here. Ms. Ogelthorpe showed me *Seven Arrows*. It's all about Native American legends and culture."

"Who? What?"

"It's true, there are all kinds of ideas on creation, from gods living in the center of the earth, to a bald eagle who created the first man. Then he created the first woman made from one of his feathers! And Shamans! Adrian told me Carlos Castaneda wrote about hallucinogens and shamans, who were the spiritual leaders of their tribes. They took drugs and could turn themselves into wolves, birds, anything!"

"Sometimes I think *you're* on drugs, honey."

"No, no! Not drugs, books!"

"Em, that's all great, but I'm starving. Could we talk about this over dinner?"

At such times, Em was also starving, for attention, which saddened her. She hid her disappointment with Randy's inattention. Were she and Randy living on different planets? Didn't he want to share her new knowledge and discoveries? Didn't he care? The feeling that they were growing apart and moving into different directions frightened her. Randy was her life, her world. There had never been anyone else for her. Her complete dependence on him filled her with concern. She realized she knew just about everything about Randy. *But*, she wondered, *did he really know her?* If asked, how would he describe her? Who was she, inside and out, to him? She had no idea.

Did she know him so completely? The last time she had picked Randy up after her Charles Town trip she surreptitiously listened to the other salesmen in the parking lot. They shared simple thoughts of their daily lives, but did not include Randy in the conversation. As they left, one by one, they waved and bounced fists, only waving at Randy half-heartedly. Em wondered if her husband would ever be invited into their closed circuit. She had told him to open up more, to be more humble, but her advice seemed to have fallen on deaf ears. He continued to brag and bluster.

Em winced, remembering another conversation she had overheard when picking Randy up weeks ago. His voice had come to her in a loud burst through the open windows of their Rambler.

"You know you can't go wrong with me, Danny. I'm the best salesman around. Going to open my own lot. I'll get you in on the ground floor. This here Ford is a sweet deal. Can't go wrong with my advice. Yup, I'm the best there is. I can give you the greatest deal of your life."

The customer shook his head and said something about 'the wife'. Em cringed at Randy's reply.

"That's fine, if you can't make a decision on your own. This deal will be gone tomorrow, though." Randy huffed.

"That's life," the prospective customer called out as he left the car lot.

She watched Randy angrily kick the tires on the Ford he had been trying to sell. He ran his hands through his hair. Finally he looked up and saw Em waiting for him.

"Hey, babe." He sauntered to their car. "I'll be out in a flash. Just gotta return the keys."

"Hurry up. I've got ice cream and beer in the cooler."

Em grimaced, remembering the rest of the evening. On the way home, Em's happy day at the library and window shopping became completely deflated as she worried over Randy's job. He just didn't seem to gel. Although he had recently sold a few cars, they still had little money. With his abysmal base salary and few commissions, how were they going to survive? Em didn't like to depend on Margret's 'loans' although she knew how necessary they were. Randy had been his usual blustery self on the way home, never realizing Em had overheard the entire exchange between him and the customer. She sat silently, her thoughts tumbling over one another. She counted his familiar words as though she were keeping score on an abacus. "Best car salesman...opening my own lot...sweetest deal you'll ever get."

Em's silence continued as she put away the groceries and started preparing dinner. Finally, Randy noticed.

"Are you mad at me, sweetheart? Did I do something wrong?"

With Randy's timid question, her protectiveness of him returned. She knew what a caring, loving and sweet man he was. She understood his need to pretend he was something he was not. She gently touched his lips, kissed him lovingly, dispelling her mood. Over dinner they laughed together over Em's description of Adrian's attire and Randy's jokes about other salesmen.

They took their bowls of ice cream with them to bed, the final dessert became their lovemaking. When Randy turned to sleep, Em continued to muse over her life with her husband. She compared her happy day in Charles Town, at the Library, the *Inn and Out* and window shopping with seeing Randy at the car lot. His attitude was so different from Adrian and store keepers and owners wherever she visited. Em's anger unexpectedly rose to the surface. She could no longer ignore her boiling tea kettle of emotions. Just as Randy was drifting off to sleep she approached him with her concerns.

"Randy, can I ask you something?"

"What? I was almost asleep, Em."

"Randy, I didn't mean to eavesdrop but I heard you talking to that customer today. The guy who was looking at the Ford."

"Oh yeah. He's an idiot. Had to ask his wife's permission before he could buy a car, for God's sake."

"Maybe that was just an excuse. Maybe it wasn't the Ford he didn't like, but you, your attitude."

The silence lasted so long Em thought Randy had fallen asleep.

"Randy?"

"That's a really shitty thing to say."

"Sweetheart, Randy, I just meant you don't need to show off and be all loud and obnoxious with customers. I know that's not who you really are. That's just an act from your past life. You're the sweetest, dearest man. You're smarter than you think. Remember how you helped me with my essays in high school when I had to read them aloud in class? You've taught me things over the years I needed to know and would never have learned without you. You understand about my missing mama and papa. You never get angry over my moods. And look where we are, in this wonderful home we have. That's all thanks to you."

"Yeah, with mom's help."

"No, not just that. You keep me happy, no easy task."

Silence ruled the room.

Em tried again. "What I meant was maybe you should show that sweet side of you, instead of, well, challenging customers. That might help you sell more cars. You catch more flies with honey than vinegar, you know."

"I guess." Resentment had colored Randy's words. Em realized she should try a more sympathetic, loving attitude. Randy obviously didn't like her suggestions.

"Sweetheart. You're smart, insightful, and you know a lot more than you let on with anyone but me." Em tried again.

"Hmmpf. Sure. If you think so." Soon Randy's snores had filled the silence of the room.

Em felt as though she was on a fractured ancient bridge over a rushing river. She was stuck in the middle of the bridge and didn't know if she'd gone too far, or if she'd be able to get back safely to the other side. She had more questions than answers about how to help her husband show himself to be the man she knew he was. She wondered what their future would hold. That thought continued to worry her until sleep finally overcame her in a restless mass of dreams and strange images.

Chapter 8

Just as she had at every visit, Felicity unexpectedly arrived one morning before the summer's afternoon showers had a chance to dampen Em's drive and spirits. "Felice! Where on earth have you been! I've missed you!"

"I've missed you, too, sweet Emmy. I've come to begin teaching you your new craft. Caning chairs. Meet me in the shed to learn how to choose your cane for the chair."

Em ran and did as she was told, excited beyond measure. She practically skipped to the shed doors. She laughed at herself. Wait till Felice sees all I've done! Felicity waited outside the old shed doors as Em pulled them open, the dark past colliding with the present. "Voila!" she shouted as she stood aside to let Felice view the room. Everything seemed the same as it had been at her friend's last visit. The coils of cane on the walls, the light and shadows erupting from the tattered roof, the old apple crates and boxes, the tools on their pegs and hooks. But everything was different: sparkling clean with the floors swept, the mice evicted, and light shining through the gleaming windows lining the room.

Felicity stood stock still in the doorway. She was silhouetted in light from the windows. The interior was lit with the shadows of trees swaying in the breezes outside the shed. "Oh!" was all the older woman could say. She stood there for an instant longer, and then turned to Emeline. She seemed at a loss for words. "My dear child, what have you done? It's—" Her eyes filled with tears, shocking her young friend.

"Felice, are you upset? What do you think? I cleaned everything, even the windows, which I didn't even know were there, they were so filthy." Em stood, waiting in anticipation of her friend's response, gnawing her bottom lip nervously.

"I am beyond thrilled. You've returned this old shed to its earlier magnificence. You've worked so hard, which will make my task of teaching you to cane all the easier. You're quite the industrious young woman. Now let's get to work." Felicity's mood changed instantly, shutting the door on further conversation regarding Em's efforts. She sat on the park bench under the magnolia tree where Em had carefully placed it when she had discovered it in the shed. She was proud of her discovery. The bench, even with its missing arm, created an inviting, welcoming spot under the shade of the magnolia tree. Felice looked at Em brightly.

"Now, get a large tub and fill it with water." As Em ran to fulfill Felice's instructions she wondered, what exactly had her friend meant by, "You've returned this old shed to its earlier magnificence?" But Emeline realized from Felicity's business-like abruptness that this was not the time for further questions. She fetched the tub and filled it with water. Then, she watched as Felicity unrolled a strip of the cane and gently placed it into the water.

Felicity continued her instructions: "Bring me that small chair with the broken seat, dear. It's a noble antique, perfect for your first lesson."

Em watched as Felice set the box with wooden pegs next to the chair. Felicity then nodded her head toward the porch, as through sharing a secret. Em followed Felice's nod. Both women noticed Scarlet and Rhett cautiously peeking out from under the porch. Zuma sat directly in front of them, contentedly cleaning herself, pretending to ignore the two felines. *Uh Oh,* Em thought. She hoped fur wouldn't fly between their cats forcing Felicity's departure. Felice placed her finger to her lips, signaling Em to ignore the cats. "They're just staking out their territory prior to testing the waters of friendship," the older woman whispered. Em grinned broadly at her friend. She was exactly right. Cats, and people, don't jump headlong into friendship. They need to set boundaries before they can trust one another.

Felicity patted the bench next to her. "Come sit darlin'. Let's chat a bit while we wait for the cane to cure in the water." Zuma ended her grooming, turned her back on Scarlet and Rhett beneath the porch and curled up beneath Felicity's feet. Zuma obviously wasn't ready to be more friendly. She was letting Em's cats know that, for the time being, they were not worthy of her attention.

"Cure?" asked Em.

"Yes, love. It has to get a bit softer, more pliable and less brittle so we can begin the weaving."

Em looked at Felice with tenderness. "Oh, Felice, I've thought of you frequently. Why don't you come by more often?"

140

"I come when my strength allows, dear. I'm not a spring chicken. I fade in and out. I have to gauge when I'm strong enough to visit." Felicity quickly changed the subject. "How are your culinary skills developing?"

"Oh, great. I try at least two different recipes a week. I really love cooking. It gives me a sense of peace, of accomplishment."

"Yes, I always found that to be true. Nothing feels happier than sharing a meal you've prepared for a loved one. Speaking of loved ones, how is your Randy enjoying your accomplishments?"

"Oh, he's thrilled. He's even put on weight, and doesn't look so scrawny and gawky anymore," Emeline continued happily. "I love Miss Magnolia's cookbook. I've only had one or two failures. I won't be trying chocolate souffle again anytime soon."

Felice laughed her throaty deep chuckle, then continued, "I'd consider Randy's weight gain a wonderful testament to your becoming an accomplished chef."

"I think so. But there's more to life than cooking, right? I have no one to talk to out here. Randy just isn't interested in all I'm discovering in the kitchen, on my walks, or from my reading. Sometimes I feel we're oceans apart. Then, I wonder..." Em trailed off and gazed at their cabin door, hesitant to continue confiding.

"Wonder what, darlin'?"

Emeline wrinkled her nose in distaste. She had never been one to complain and here she was revealing too many of her inner thoughts. But her words were true. Who else did she have to confide in?

"Oh, nothing. I guess I just get homesick for the delta. And Mama. She always listened to me, no matter how silly my thoughts or ideas were. Some days I'm bursting with everything I've read and thought, and there's no one to share it with. Not Randy. He's in his own world. There's just you, Felice. Why don't you come more often?" Em knew her persistence with Felicity was brazen but she didn't care.

"I come when I sense I'm needed and when I have the strength. These old bones tire easily." Felicity dipped her hand into the nest of wet cane and swirled it through the water.

"Almost ready. Just a few more minutes and it will be pliable enough to begin your first lesson. Never leave the cane in water for more than twenty minutes or it will discolor and become too soft to weave properly."

Em watched a dragonfly flit in and out of the shadows thrown by the magnolia tree and the old shed. "I've been walking all over the roads around here. There's so much to see. Cabins, just like ours, but painted in different colors or not painted at all, just old logs. I've noticed lots of gardens. Next spring I'm going to ask Randy to dig a garden plot for me."

"I could certainly help you plot a garden, deah. I always loved gardening. Had a beautiful and bountiful one every year. How I loved to pick fresh vegetables for dinner. Nothing pretties up a table or whets the appetite more."

Em looked at Felice thoughtfully. She knew so little about this woman whom she considered her only true friend at this end of the world in Heavenly Hollow.

"Felice, where do you live? Every cabin I pass, I wonder if it's yours. I never see you except when you visit me. I'd be happy to visit you. I'd love to see your home."

"Oh, my place is nothing special. Just a cabin up over the hill, like all the others. I'm not one for visitors, I must admit. It does my heart good to visit you, gets me out and about. Now, let's get started on this caning." Felicity counted the holes to be certain where to start. "This will be an easy project. Fewer than seventy-two holes, so you won't get worn out or discouraged. Be sure all the holes are cleared of old cane residue. That makes it possible to insert the wooden peg into a nice, clean hole. Start at the center hole and work your way around the chair. Tap each peg very lightly to secure the cane." Em watched in concentration. "It's really simple, once you get the hang of it," Felicity said.

The instructions continued. "To begin the first layer just push a cane strand down the top of the first hole. Then tap the peg to lodge the cane securely in its hole. Always be sure to leave about 2" of cane free at the underside of the chair. That's so you'll have enough cane beneath the chair to tie off your work. That sounds difficult and it is at first. You have to tuck each strand inside the next loop under the chair. I'll teach you that later, how to finish off the weaving by making a binder strand where the seat's edge meets the newly woven section."

Felicity carefully watched Em's progress before she continued. "Okay, my deah, you're doing fine. You're a natural at this, I can see. You've matched up the center holes at the front and back of the chair, securing the other end of the strand. Be sure to pull the strands nice and tight, but don't pull too hard or the strand could break. Just continue until the whole seat bottom is completed, up and down and left and right diagonally. It's a form of weaving, really."

Felicity rummaged around in the little wooden box where all the pegs had been stored and pulled out a pair of needle nosed pliers. "Sometimes it helps to pull the strands through, especially when you need to continue by weaving each new strand up and over your other existing strands. Holes can get a bit crowded, you see." Felicity leaned over and showed how Em could carefully push the strand over another layer and through the hole without it breaking.

For what seemed like minutes but was almost two hours, Felicity tutored Em in the art of caning. She carefully watched Emeline complete the first layer of weaving the cane and securing it with the wooden pegs into each specific hole. Felicity taught her how to leave 'the finishing strand of cane' to be used at the end of each row, for a nice, finished look. "And don't forget to measure your finishing cane first," she added. "It must be at least 6" longer than the entire circumference of your chair, which will become the binding for your chair bottom."

"Jeeze, Felice, do you really think I can do all this and remember each step?"

"Of course you can, darlin'. You're an accomplished embroidery artist, seamstress and homemaker. This will be as easy as making biscuits, which you've certainly mastered!" They laughed together over their shared memory.

Their silence as Em worked felt comfortable, occasionally interrupted by Felice's corrections. Slowly, a pattern took shape in the frame of the old chair. Felicity occasionally gave directions, "Add more cane to your water bucket dear, you're running out. Be careful to plot your next move. If you miss a hole, you'll have to begin all over again. Remember the shiny side of the cane must be looking up at your pretty face, Emmy."

The use of her mama's pet name for her, Emmy, shocked and thrilled Emeline. It was at that moment that she realized what a dear friend Felicity had truly become. 'Emmy'. It was such a simple thing, yet it meant so much to her. No one ever called her by that name. Even Randy used Em, or Sweet Pea, his favorite name for her. "Emmy," uttered by Felicity, had come so naturally, as though she had known Em forever.

"Watch you don't let that cane sit too long. It will make the reed too soft to weave." Em stopped in her soaking of the cane to stare at Felice in a happy daze. "What is it, dear? You look like you've seen a ghost." Felicity giggled over her words.

"Felice, no one has ever called me Emmy except my mama. It was her special name for me."

"Oh, dear. I'm sorry. I hope I haven't trespassed on your mama's territory."

"Oh, no, no, Felice. I love it that you've used her pet name for me. Such a small thing, but no one's ever called me Emmy except her. Please, do call me Emmy. It's as though my mama has returned."

"Dear, sweet child. I am honored that you compare me to your mother. Thank you for allowing me to usurp a very small part of your life with her. Perhaps in a tiny way I'm filling in for that companionship, although I could never presume to replace your mama, of course."

"Sometimes you come close and I'm happy you do." Em reached out and touched Felicity's hand, hers wet with water from the cane bucket, Felice's cold with age. With that touch, fingertip to handhold, their friendship was cemented.

Em was amazed when she had one layer of cane completed. She stood up to admire her work. The first layer of horizontal strips was in place and tightly secured. She turned to Felicity with a joyous expression. She was proud of learning something new that wasn't nearly as hard as she'd expected.

"Goodness! I must be off," said the older woman, "It's getting late. I feel the coolness of the hours. Make sure all your pegs are tight and your cane is taut, darlin'. That makes for a good, strong seat."

"Felice, why don't you stay for dinner? Randy would love to meet you. I've talked about you so often. He's beginning to think you're just a figment of my imagination." Em laughed at her little joke but Felice seemed lost in thought, then stirred herself. "Oh, no, I couldn't. Besides, I've overstayed. I make it a habit to never be out after twilight. My eyes aren't the best on a darkening day."

"But Randy could drive you home."

"No, sweet child. I love to walk. Now I must be off."

With that, Felicity rose, brushed off her old cotton pants and snapped her fingers to Zuma. She turned, gave Em one of her brilliant smiles and began her trek down the dusty road. As always, Felicity waved goodbye over her shoulder as she walked off, trailed by Zuma. Her voice floated to Em, "TaTa, darlin', till next time."

Em suddenly felt bereft and forlorn as she watched her friend's departure. Why wouldn't Felicity confide in her the way Em did with her? Her friend's life was a complete mystery. She longed to know more about this elusive woman. It was clear Felice kept her life and heart hidden, her secrets unexposed. Emeline knew one thing for certain. Felice had become an important friend, lessening the grief Em felt at her mother's absence from her life. Slowly, Felice was filling in that gap.

Randy arrived home a few minutes later. He was in a great mood, anticipating a customer returning the next day to buy a car Randy had shown him. Em was thrilled to see he was so joyous. She met him in the yard to show off her handiwork of the partially caned chair.

"Wow, how did you do that?"

"Felicity was here. Remember, I told you she was going to teach me to cane chairs? She said there's lots of people around here who would love a neighbor who could repair old chairs. Didn't you see her walking down our road on your way home? She left right before you got here. You must have passed her."

"Nope. Didn't see anyone. Maybe she cut through the neighbor's field." He examined the chair closely. "You think this will ever be a chair somebody could actually sit on?" He pressed gently on the completed layer of cane.

"Don't touch it, the cane is still drying. It's nice and tight, but it has to cure so it doesn't become loose in the pegs. I need to cane, or weave, in all different directions. Like a spider's web."

"Well, well, aren't you the expert!" Randy beamed.

"I will be. And I can get paid for caning, fifty cents a hole, that would be thirty-six dollars. I'd make for this chair. And Felicity said that if a chair has more than 72 holes I could charge more, a dollar twenty-five, or even a dollar and forty-cents a hole. Then on top of the caning work the customer pays for the caning supplies. Except for the pegs, of course. I keep them to use on each chair."

"Holy shit, Em! That's fantastic! You'll be making more money than me." He stopped from saying more, but worry was clearly etched across his face. This left Em feeling momentarily guilty. Then she admonished herself. *Why should I feel guilty because he makes so little money?*

"Hey. I'm hungry. When do we eat?"

"Soon. I'll just heat up the leftover stew." She knew a full stomach always chased away her husband's concerns for their future. As she was putting dinner on the table she thought again of Felicity.

"Randy, are you absolutely certain you didn't see an old lady with faded blue pants and a big orange cat walking down the road?"

Randy sat down at the table. He turned and looked at Em closely. "Of course, I'm sure. From what you say she'd be hard to miss. You okay? You look, I don't know, weird." Em pushed her hair from her forehead and tied it off with a rubber band, then placed the heaping plates on the table. "It's just so strange. She left right before you got home. It isn't like she could just disappear."

Randy looked at Em questionably and with some annoyance. "Of course, I'm sure. Are you okay? Maybe you've been working too long on this chair caning thing."

"Don't be ridiculous." It wouldn't be the first time Em said something strange and Randy was certain it wouldn't be the last. *As long as she was happy, he was happy*, he thought, as he dug into his meal. "Oh, baby. You are the best cook." She treated her husband to a sloppy kiss, full of potent possibilities for the rest of the evening.

The following morning, thoughts of Felicity continued to nag at Em. She was deeply troubled that Randy had failed to spy Felicity on their dirt road, moments after her departure from their cabin. Could that mean Felice lived close by? Maybe even a next-door neighbor? "She couldn't just disappear, like Randy said. So where did she go? Why won't she confide in me?" she asked Rhett and Scarlet aloud as she was cleaning up the breakfast dishes.

Rhett eyed her mistress suspiciously. Usually when their 'mother' spoke in this harsh tone no good came of it. "Why is she so secretive? That's just plain mean. She doesn't trust me. That's it. Or does she think I'm too stupid to be trusted with her life's tales, her secrets?"

Scarlet yawned magnificently, showing off her sharp little teeth. "Oh what would you two know, anyway. Now I'm asking cats for advice! Okay, so I'm being the mean one in trying to trespass on her life, which obviously she doesn't want to share, yet. I'll leave her alone until she wants to confide in me. So there."

The cats ran off when Em slammed Miss Magnolia's cookbook down on the oak table. She was looking for a special recipe for her mother-in-law's visit that Sunday. Em recalled their recent conversation regarding her mother-in-law. Randy never reprimanded her unless she had done something outrageous, like the time she set fire to a placemat from overuse of candles. She noticed Randy's assertiveness when discussing anything Margret related.

"I think we should have Mom over at least once a month. She's getting older, and more frail, Em. I want to keep a close eye on her." Em had wholeheartedly agreed but she still dreaded Margret's visit. She wanted everything to be perfect.

Em gazed out her kitchen window at her favorite view. The magnolia tree's leaves were limp with the heat and dust of the July morning.

Em's mind returned to Felicity. "I've willingly told her everything about me and my life. I've spilled my guts to Felice. Yet she never confides in me. I don't even know where she lives," Em said, with a touch of sorrow in her musing. A tiny voice answered from within. *You spilled your guts. That doesn't mean everyone does.* Em tried out one of her new words, "Reticent. That's it. Some people are shy. They're afraid to share their lives. If I'm patient, and give her reason to trust me, I'll bet she'll come around."

Satisfied with her conclusion, Em began her morning chores. With each dish washed, each broom sweep through the cabin, each dusting of shelf and table, Em continued her discussion with herself. Finally, she came to a fresh image of her friend. She was hiding a secret too painful to reveal. Em would have to be patient. After all, Felice was her only close woman friend. She seemed to genuinely care for Em. Felice was sweet and kind, and wanted Em to succeed in life. She had taught her how to cane chairs, an important future source of income, Em hoped.

"I'll be Nancy Drew." She admitted to her bookcase as she admired her growing collection. "I'll pick up on the clues she drops. Maybe I'll follow her home, through the woods. I'll find out where she lives. I'll figure out her life. Felice is too important a friend for me to damage our growing friendship by scaring her off with too many questions."

Em returned to the kitchen to peruse her favorite cookbook. "Pot Roast. That's what I'll make for Margret. Sounds easy and all I'll have to do is cook it for a long time." As she wrote her grocery list, she remembered Randy's words. She would be warmer toward Margret. After all, she was old and no doubt lonely. She vowed to be kinder to her mother-in-law. "You get more bees with honey than vinegar," Em advised Rhett who had returned, in search of a snack, followed by Scarlet.

"I'll be a better person. After all, she is Randy's mom."

Their meows unanswered, her feline family gave up on the hope of snacks. They lay down lazily in a patch of sunlight on the braided rug, their calico coats seeming to melt into one another.

"Wow! Maybe I'm growing up? Finally getting wiser and learning patience?" Her cats refused to answer or be drawn into further conversation. Rhett began lovingly grooming Scarlet, her tiny pink tongue making her sister's fur glisten.

Em admired her kitchen, two happy cats settled in the sun, everything glowing with her efforts and love. She was reminded of her mother in their pretty little home on the delta. Em distinctly heard her mother say, "That's my girl, that's my darling."

She brushed the tears from her eyes when she realized her cheeks were wet. She whispered, "Thanks, Mama."

The following Sunday, Em waited for Randy to arrive with Margret. He felt it was safer for his aging mother and other drivers for her to be off the roads, especially in the evenings. Alone in her pretty kitchen Em critically assessed the room. The windows were sparkling, the curtains freshly laundered and ironed, the plants on the old wood stove watered.

"DAMN you, Scarlet!" Em screamed as the offending cat jumped from behind Em's Boston Fern, which Scarlet had shredded. Em could imagine the fern screaming in pain, with nothing left but mangled stumps where healthy fronds had been. Scarlet loved chewing on the pretty fern much to Em's dismay. Quickly, Em hid the poor damaged plant behind the big Philodendron. "Just wait till I get my hands on you, you rotten fern-chewing cat!" Scarlet was well hidden and not about to come out from the depths under the couch to be scolded.

All else looked perfect. Em had set the table with her favorite cutwork and embroidered placemats and matching napkins which she and her mother had purchased so many years ago in Locke. Mama's favorite dishes, the Country Rose pattern, sat primly on each placemat, adorned by her grandmother Muriel's silver flatware. A bouquet of wildflowers filled her antique Stangl vase decorating the center of the table. The pot roast perfumed the room, bubbling its sweet scent, nestled in her mama's Dutch oven. Carrots, mushrooms and onions were bathed in the juices from the roast. Sadie had suggested adding one undiluted can of cream of mushroom soup, mixed with one packet of Lipton's Beefy Onion Soup Mix and half a cup of beef bouillon. She had splashed red wine vinegar over the top of the browned roast which she remembered her mama doing. For good measure, she poured a little burgundy wine over the roast. She had splurged on the wine to serve with dinner. Grandmama's crystal wine glasses sparkled, waiting to be filled. All that was left to do was steam the fresh peas, another luxury as Em usually purchased canned ones. Em had followed another of Miss Magnolia's suggestions, for 'red cabbage, the perfect accompaniment to an authentic German Pot Roast dinner'. The red cabbage lit up the cut glass bowl into a banquet for the eyes with its deep purple shades. She would sprinkle the wide egg noodles with parsley, butter and fresh ground pepper, creating a portrait in simple ingredients from her kitchen. Felicity's words returned to Em as she appraised her table, "Remember, dear, the eyes always eat first."

Em had gone way over her budget with the burgundy at $3.99 a bottle. It was worth it, plus $2.49 a pound for the bottom round roast. She was pleased with how tantalizing the roast smelled, displacing the worrying extravagance of its cost from her mind.

Randy arrived with Margret in a cloud of dust. He waited for the dust to settle and then helped Margret from the old Rambler. Em had been amused to see Randy washing their tired old car that morning and sweeping out the inside. He even wiped down the seats and removed all the accumulated candy wrappers and clutter from the floorboards. But he was unable to hide the loud *SCREECH* of the passenger door's opening. The sound caused Margret to jump, launching her and Randy into laughter.

Em waited at the top of the porch steps. "Emeline!" Margret greeted her. "What a divine scent is coming from your kitchen." Em glowed as she reached out a hand to help Margret up the porch steps and into their home.

"Welcome, Margret. I'm so happy you're here. Your first visit to our home, now that we're fully moved in. I'm making pot roast from Miss Magnolia's cookbook, along with some of my mama's special touches that I remember. I hope you'll like it."

"Yes, well, I'm happy to have been invited." Margret's warm smile did not betray any sarcasm or contrariness on her part. Over Margret's shoulder, Randy's eyes begged Emeline to not to rise with any combative reply. Em saw his look and remembered her own vow to be kinder to her mother-in-law. "*Remember, you catch more flies with honey than vinegar,*" the voice in her head reminded her. Em's welcoming smile and her hand on Margret's shoulder warmed Randy's heart as he followed his mother into the kitchen. Margret stood completely still as she advanced into the room, inspecting everything. Her hands rose to her chest. "Oh, Emeline, how very lovely you've made this cabin." Em was thrilled that things were going so well. "We have made a lot of changes," she said, her words tinged with pride.

"I can certainly see you have, my dear. I'd hardly know this is the same cabin I discovered. You changed an empty shell into a home."

"Yup." Randy joined the conversation. "Em's a real master of decoration and homebody skills. She made all the curtains, waxed the floors and pine paneling, made the braided rugs, she did it all."

"*Mistress* of decoration, Randolph, not *master*. While Emeline is a masterful decorator, she is the mistress of your delightful little cabin." Em was shocked when Margret enveloped her in a warm hug. She felt as though she had reached a pinnacle of success in her mother-in-law's eyes, something she never could have imagined when she first met the older woman.

Randy smiled broadly at Em, in further congratulations of her successful efforts at making their rustic cabin into a home. "I'll give Mom the tour, Sweet Pea." He took Margret through each room, pointing out every special touch they both had installed.

"Look at the shower I rigged up Mom…Mother."

"You always were so handy at plumbing projects, dear."

Em rolled her eyes, knowing Randy's ineptitude and dangerous repairs of all things related to plumbing or electricity. She had to admit it though, surprisingly the shower *had* been a success. Finally Randy and his mother settled in the library, she with a glass of wine and Randy with a beer. They sat close together on the window seat as Margret admired the view inside and outside the room. Scarlet had come out from under the couch, and she and Rhett inspected Margret's toes. Satisfied, they flopped onto the braided rug and curled into one another, quickly falling asleep.

Em bustled about her kitchen, working on all the final preparations for dinner. When everything was ready and waiting to be served, she walked through the living room toward the library to ask Randy to carve the pot roast. As she approached the library the scene before her eyes stopped her dead in her tracks. Margret's head was gently resting on Randy's shoulder. She appeared to be crying and distressed. Randy's arm nestled her. He held one of her hands in his own.

"Shhh, Mom. It wasn't your fault. He just was who he was. He was never going to change."

"I realized that when that floozie showed up at the house, saying she was pregnant with his child. That's when I finally said, 'that's it. Enough is enough. No more'. All the years of him philandering with other women, ignoring you, speaking or yelling at you only to say how worthless you were, not an '*important man*' like him. I couldn't count the number of times he told you you'd never amount to anything. And look at you now. A beautiful home and a sweet accomplished wife."

"Dad's in the past, Mom. Forget about him."

"I can't forget all the mean things he said over so many years. Telling me I was a liar when I first became pregnant with you. He and I both believed my doctor's diagnosis that I'd never be able to have children. 'narrow hips'? What an idiot that doctor was. But I later learned that was one reason Ernest chose to marry me. That and competing suitors saying, '*You could be a movie star, you're so beautiful*'."

"It wasn't even six months after our marriage that I was thrilled to discover I was pregnant. He was hateful. All his insults that being pregnant ruined my body, that he'd never touch me again. He didn't even drive me to the hospital when I went into labor. I had to get a cab. You know what he did while I was in labor? He bought himself a motorcycle and went on a long drive up the Big Sur Highway to Carmel. A long enough trip to miss your birth, ten hours later. He hated me and you, his own son. His neglect all those years. I should have left him earlier knowing how cruel he was to you. Knowing he would never change."

Through the open French library doors Em listened in astonishment as these secrets were revealed. She silently retreated toward the kitchen, straining her ears to catch the rest of their conversation.

"I put up with all that until that floozie showed up. That was the same day he hit you in the face, hard, his handprint red on your cheek. I'll never forget the way you stood up to him. Only thirteen, but you'd finally had enough, too. I'll always remember the way you screamed at him. 'You fucking bastard. I hate you', you said. It made me realize how much I hated him, too." Margret was unable to stop her words and Em couldn't stop listening.

"Ernest was a snake and I'd known it for years. You gave me the strength, the impetus, to get out. That day decided everything, our future. I finally found the courage to leave. I demanded money from him to support us and I filed for divorce. Smartest thing I ever did. I have to admit, I was so happy when Aunt Clarissa asked me to help her out a year later. You grew up fast, darling. Only fourteen and living on your own. But I had to leave. You understand, don't you, Son?"

"I wasn't living on my own. We had a housekeeper who lived with me, remember?"

"Yes, of course, Hannah. She was a jewel. Did all the cooking and cleaning for a pittance, just because I gave her a place to live after her husband died."

"Mom, I was glad you left. All those years of watching you hope. All those nights I heard you cry yourself to sleep when he was gone. I never blamed you for anything. I was glad that he was out of our lives forever."

Em realized she had trespassed on a very personal and private confession, not meant for her ears. She wondered what to do next. For now, she'd ignore the damaging words she had overheard. If it had been meant for me, Randy would have shared this part of his life, she told herself. Obviously, he wasn't ready to reveal his past, nor was Margret. For now, she'd keep this to herself. She loudly entered the living room and stood at the open French doors, "Dinners ready! I just need you to carve the roast, Randy."

Silence reigned in the library. Margret turned her face to the window and wiped her eyes, which Em pretended not to see. Then her mother-in-law sat up straight, chasing any sadness from the room. "I can't wait, dear. Randy, remember to cut the roast across the grain to assure tenderness."

She smiled warmly at Em as she walked to the kitchen. "I'm so happy to be here, dear Emeline. You've made a beautiful home for my son." Much to Em's astonishment, she placed a gentle kiss on Em's cheek as she made her way to her place at the table. Randy was bursting with joy and pride, any sorrow gone from his eyes. He smacked Em soundly on her bottom as he moved into the kitchen to carve the roast.

The meal was all Emeline had hoped it would be. The conversation was light and joyful, as Margret told tales of her Aunt Clarissa and her idiosyncrasies, her collection of portraits of unknown people, her hysterical fear of spiders, her talking in her sleep. Randy told stories of the people he met at the car lot, mimicking their voices. The conversation was full of laughter, three family members enjoying one another's company. By the time Margret departed, a bit tipsy from the wine, Em knew the evening had been a complete success. Before leaving, Margret enveloped her 'daughter' as she had begun calling her at dinner, in a warm embrace. The evening had been perfect. But the scene Em had witnessed between her mother-in-law and Randy continued to trouble her. She was determined to discover all of his history, carefully. Tiptoeing through the Tulips, as Tiny Tim had once sung so endearingly.

That night as Em tried to drift off to sleep the music of Randy's snores kept her awake. With the secret conversation between Randy and his mother crisp in her mind, she began to examine her relationship with her husband. She loved him and knew he adored her. How would *she* behave if she were married to a mean, philandering bastard? She knew Randy was nothing like what she had heard of his father. Still, small doubts, cracks, began appearing in the mirror of their life. She wondered over their future. Would they always live in this cabin? Would that be such a bad thing? What if Randy met some woman he was attracted to at the car lot? She thrived in her pride of having made such a perfect nest for them. She loved her accomplishments and their home, but was that enough?

Em couldn't turn off her mind. Her thoughts kept her awake. She chided herself over their dependency on Margret for rent money when they were short. She fervently hoped her learning to cane chairs would result in extra income. She could help with their bills, weaning them from Margret's assistance when they were broke. Randy seemed content with their life. Until recently, Em had been also. Now she began to wonder about what lay in the years ahead. Should they start a family? Did she want to trade the independent and happy wanderings and unpredictability of her days for a baby? Was this all there was in life? Em raced from that question and buried it in her 'I'll-think-about-that tomorrow' file. She remembered her mama's advice: 'The future always takes care of itself. Worrying about it won't change a thing'.

Em went over their finances in her mind. She vowed to start a garden in the spring. They'd save money on produce. Randy could dig up the old plot next to their home, which according to the faded seed packets on sticks, had once been productive. Her secret tours of other gardens convinced her that she could certainly grow a garden of her own. Felice had told her she could help to plot her garden. Her mama had taught her how to can vegetables and her jam making had been successful. She certainly had farm knowledge. In the meantime, Em would pick the late wild strawberries she had noticed in the field across the road. They were so tiny and sweet. Each strawberry was a miracle, an explosion of magic to her taste buds. The jam would be delicious. Em drifted off to sleep, the image of strawberries in her mind.

The next morning Em was quieter than usual. She had so much to think about, returning again to the conversation she had overheard between Randy and his mother. Randy noticed. He held Em in his departure hug longer than usual. Then, he held her at arm's length. "Everything okay, sweetie? You're so quiet this morning. Your dinner last night was fantastic. You've really won my mom over. Did you see how she kissed you goodbye? And called you her daughter?"

"Yes, I did. Thanks, love. I *am* proud of myself. Everything went better than I ever could have expected." Em thought a moment longer before broaching the subject foremost in her mind.

"Did you have a good time with your mom? I noticed you two had a long conversation together but I didn't want to interrupt. Is everything okay with her?" Randy immediately changed the tempo of their conversation, from warmth to brusqueness, as though he were shaking raindrops from a wet coat. "Sure, everything's fine. Guess she just wanted a mother-and-son chat. She's okay, nothing to worry about."

"You'd tell me if there was anything to be concerned about, right?"

"Of course. I gotta get to work. Jason told me he'd help me with the latest sales techniques today. Something about customer psychology."

Em was instantly thrilled. Maybe her little talk with Randy a few weeks ago, which had at first angered him, had borne some fruit.

"Oh, sweetie, that's great. I'm so glad he's taken you under his wing."

"Well, I wouldn't go that far. It's not as if I don't know how to sell cars, and I certainly don't need anyone to take me *under their wing*."

Em backtracked. "No, of course not. I didn't mean that." Her words were lost as her husband ran down the steps. So much for Randy becoming more humble and learning from others, Em thought as she watched her husband's departure.

She put her displeasure out of her mind. Just like Mama said. Don't worry about something you can't do anything about. That was certainly true of her husband. She doubted he would ever change. "But I can always hope, right?" she asked Scarlet and Rhett as they raced out the open screen door.

Em laughed at them. "Well, at least you two are always predictable." She turned to her kitchen and her mood immediately brightened. "I'll work on finishing up that chair today."

Again, she clearly heard her mama's words, echoing from years past. *That's my darling, that's my girl.* This time, Em smiled at the memory.

Chapter 9

With a shock, Em realized she was beginning to love her life—her days spent alone while Randy was at work—in ways she had never imagined possible. Some days she felt her life was filled with one success and lesson learned after another. In the past, she had missed Randy when he left for work. The days seemed long and empty. She had been bored. In meeting Felicity, her world had begun to expand. The older woman filled out the edges of her landscape with discoveries of the world without and within. Em began to explore further afield in all ways. From the waxy bronze-colored fallen magnolia blossoms to the colors of cane, her life was being woven into a new tapestry.

Except for Felice, who remained a mystery. Em donned her Nancy Drew persona, determined to discover where Felicity lived. How would she recognize her residence even if she stumbled on it? Em investigated the hills and valleys surrounding their cabin, always on the lookout for signs of Felice or Zuma. She continued to spy on her neighbors while searching for the secret that was Felicity. Occasionally she thought she had caught a glimpse of Zuma through the trees but the sight always disappeared before Em could confirm the big orange cat's roaming grounds.

As she traveled through the neighborhood she realized she was discovering more than neighbor's cabins. She was learning more about herself and the strange elusive land of contentment, a geography she had rarely wandered into since her mama's death. The apple orchard she discovered reminded her of the wonderful apple pies her mama used to make. Em imagined the faded and deteriorating *Heavenly Hollow Orchards* crates in the shed were used for the apples from that orchard. She promised herself she would return to pick apples in the fall. She would make a pie from a recipe in Miss Magnolia's cookbook. How thrilled Randy would be!

The following week she remained close to home. She couldn't wait for Randy to leave the house every morning. By the third day, Randy was becoming suspicious. Why did Em seem to be rushing him out the door? What was she keeping from him? He became more and more nervous. By Friday, he purposely took longer than usual over his coffee and eggs. Em was fidgeting in her impatience, drying dishes already dried and wiping counters already sparkling clean.

Randy was certain. His wife was keeping something from him. Every evening that week his subtle questions had gotten him nowhere.

"What did you do all day?"

"Oh the usual."

"Did you go on one of your walks around the neighborhood?"

"A little."

By the time he left that Friday morning, Randy was convinced Em was hiding something from him. Had she met someone in the neighborhood? The thought made him shiver and tightened up his stomach with alarm. Just being stupid, as usual, he told himself as he drove to work that morning.

Em was indeed keeping something from him, her new enterprise: chair caning. Although Randy had admired her first layer of cane, she wanted to surprise him with the completed chair, which was slowly taking shape. There had been setbacks during the week when she had become so angry she wanted to scream and break the chair into pieces. Twice the cane broke because she hadn't allowed it to soften long enough in her tub of water to become pliable. Once she had placed a strand in the wrong hole and had to tear out all the strands she had woven after that one, then redo them all. Looping the cane from under the chair to the top was her greatest challenge, along with weaving the finishing cane around the edges and under the loops. Yet, she persisted. She wouldn't give up. Her back ached and her fingers were cut. She was proud of every day's accomplishments. She walked slowly around the chair at the end of each day and inspected her work. She hoped Felicity would be as proud of Em as she was of herself. Every day before Randy came home she squirreled the chair away in the shed. By Friday, it was completed. She was thrilled beyond measure. The chair looked perfect. It was beautiful. She had brought the old antique back to life, along with its usefulness and grace. She couldn't wait to surprise Randy with her first success.

When her husband pulled into the drive that evening, Em was aglow with excitement and anticipation, her eyes sparkling with joy. She glowed in her happiness.

Now what, Randy thought. His wife had become entirely unpredictable. Happy as he was, there were times he longed for the old grief-stricken Em who relied on him so completely. Em ran to greet Randy and enveloped him in a warm hug when he got out of their Rambler.

"How was your day? Did you sell anything?"

"Maybe that clunker of a jeep none 'a the other guys would go near. I almost felt guilty for showing it to this young girl, her first car, she said. But in the whole lot the jeep was the only thing she could afford. I'm half tempted to tell her it won't last a year."

Randy eyed Em with suspicion. "What are you so happy about? What have you been up to?"

"Oh, this and that." She led him up the porch steps to where she had draped a tablecloth over the chair. She raced to the chair, unable to contain her excitement a moment longer. She stood in front of her surprise and grinned like a Cheshire cat.

"Crazy place to dry a table cloth, Em," said Randy. "This weekend I'm going to hang a clothesline for you. I promise."

She laughed in his face and pulled the tablecloth from the chair, holding it aloft. She felt like a magician who had just pulled a rabbit out of a hat.

"TaDa!"

"Where the hell did that come from?"

"Me! I did it! Remember, I had started it with Felice. I finished it all by myself. I caned this chair!"

"Holy shit, Em. Really?" Randy walked around the chair as she watched him. He picked the chair up and looked underneath it, noticing her neat handiwork. "You did this? Did Felicity come by to help you?"

"No. She taught me the basics that first day and I wrote down all her instructions. Then I just worked it out on my own." Randy laughed in relief over this innocent secret being revealed and Em's exhilaration in sharing it. He put the chair down and was about to sit on it when Em screamed, "No! Don't sit on it! I don't want to try it out until Felicity comes by to approve my work."

"Oh, okay, sure. It's beautiful, darlin'. It will be a sweet little side chair. We can put it in the living room, next to the couch. So, this is what you've been so mysterious about all week?"

157

She hugged Randy again. "I wanted to surprise you. And I wasn't even sure I could finish it by myself, so I didn't want to say anything. After I finished my chores, I worked on it every day while you were at work. What do you think?"

"I couldn't be more proud of you, sweetheart, honestly. You've done a fantastic job." Em smiled proudly. Those were exactly the words she had hoped to hear.

* * *

Two days later Em was happily sitting across from Adrian at the Inn and Out, where Sadie had just served them lunch. Em reached out and snagged a fry from Adrian's plate.

"You gonna finish those?"

"Well, yeah. I was planning on it. Just because I invited you to lunch doesn't mean you could eat mine, too." He playfully slapped Em's hand as she reached for another fry on his plate.

"Is this why you showed up at the library a half hour before my lunch break?" Em chuckled evilly. "Well, maybe. But honestly, I've missed you and our talks."

"So have I. What have you been up to, buried in that backwater in the hills? What's it called? Hell's Holler?"

"Heavenly Hollow, you imbecile."

"My, how your vocabulary has improved. Which I also wanted to talk to you about. What's with all these women's and feminist books you've been checking out? Gloria Steinem? *Wifey*? Maya Angelou, something about caged birds singing? Are you having problems at home, love?"

Em dropped another of Adrian's fries into the puddle of ketchup on her plate just as Sadie arrived with a coffeepot. Em smiled happily at Sadie as she poured their coffee. Their tired friend sat down with a grunt. "Oh, my aching back."

Em continued the conversation with Adrian. "Well, I don't know if I'm becoming what you might call a feminist. I've just been reading some weird stuff. I read this one really short little book I found in the discard bin, *The Yellow Wallpaper*. Do you know it?"

"I'm not into decorating anything but myself, love."

Sadie snorted. "Ain't that the truth."

Em looked more closely at Adrian and wondered, *what did his apartment look like?*

She brought herself back to the conversation. "No, silly. It's not about decorating. It's about this lady in the 1800s whose husband thinks she's crazy because she wants to write, to work and not have kids. So, he locks her up in this room with barred windows, like a jail cell. It has yellow wallpaper. Then she really goes nuts. She thought there were other women trapped behind the wallpaper. She picked off the wallpaper to discover the people she thought were hidden underneath. She went crazy only because her husband controlled her and wanted her to be part of 'polite society' where ladies didn't act the way his wife was acting."

"Wow. Now I'd call that feminist literature. What saved her? Writing? Did she ever get out?" Adrian leaned toward Em, his chin on his hand. Em saw that he was genuinely interested in what she was saying.

"Not really. She figured out she'd never get out of the prison of her marriage."

Sadie agreed. "I hear ya, honey. Not much of a reader, myself. But I know marriage can be a prison." She sat back, enjoying the company of her two friends.

"Now don't you poison our little Miss Pollyanna with your lurid tales of woe, Sadie."

"Hmmpf. What would you know?" Sadie replied.

Em continued enthusiastically. "I've been reading the autobiography of George Sand. Do you know George Sand's lover was Chopin? Her daughter, Kate Chopin, born out of wedlock, of course, used to sit under his piano as he composed music. When Kate grew up, she also became a writer. Wrote a book called *The Awakening.* I've been reading a lot. I guess one book just leads to another. You know how things happen." Em smiled brightly and took a sip of her coffee. Sadie sat idly by, listening to their exchange.

Adrian studied Emeline closely. Over the past months since their first meeting she had changed dramatically. He wondered what was behind the evolution in her life. Maybe she was having an affair?

Sadie looked around at her other customers. Satisfied that they were all enjoying their meals, she continued to listen in as Em and Adrian chatted.

Em smiled to herself. She was thrilled to see that Adrian was intrigued, he, a librarian, listening to a novice in the world of literature. Encouraged, Em continued. "Did you know George Sand had to use a man's name because she couldn't get published as a woman? She used to dress up in men's clothes, which was pretty outrageous at the time. Women wearing pants, can you imagine?"

"Yes. I can certainly imagine women wearing men's clothes, and vice versa. Oscar Wilde was famous for that. That's one of the reasons I admire him so." Adrian chuckled at Em's puzzled expression as he adjusted his flowered tie. She put a bookmark in that thought and continued.

"I'm learning to cane," Em said, puffing up like a proud Robin with a newly captured worm.

"What? Cane who? Is your hubby being good to you?" Adrian said with a chuckle.

"I'm learning to cane chairs. I love it. You have to think every step of the way from beginning to end. It all gets easier, once you get the hang of it. It's like weaving. Felicity is teaching me."

"Who's Felicity?" Sadie asked.

"Well, she's my new friend, and another reason I wanted to visit with you both. You see everyone who comes into the library and the Inn and Out. I thought you might have seen her at some point."

"The name doesn't ring a bell. Certainly is an old-fashioned name. What does she look like? What does she read? I could ask Genevieve. She knows everyone in town," Adrian said.

"I see everyone around town, and I've never heard of a Felicity," Sadie said, noticing one of her customers waving from across the room. "Oh jeeze," she said, as she rose from their table.

"Who's Genevieve?" Em asked.

Adrian rolled his eyes. "Genevieve, Ms. Ogelthorpe. You've met her. The senior librarian."

"Huh, such an exotic name. French maybe? I never would have guessed her to be a Genevieve."

"Well, she is. You should get to know her better. She can be a real sweetheart to anyone who loves books. She's a great resource."

Emeline reflected. She *should* befriend the elder librarian. After all, what did she have to lose? She might even gain another friend. "I don't know Felicity's last name. She's very well read. She gave me the reading list I gave to you. Just about all the books I've been reading are Felicity's suggestions."

Em thought for a moment, the image of Felice rising, like a cloud, into her mind. She wondered how to describe her. "She's a lot taller than me. Maybe about 5'10". She's old, but I don't know how old. Maybe 70? 75? She's very frail and tires easily. She has short gray curly hair, with white hair, like wings, at her temples. She's kind of bony, so thin, she's almost skeletal. She's pale, but has these amazing eyes. They're dark gray, and they light up with yellow lights sometimes. She's very severe looking until she smiles, and then she's like the sun. She smiles with her whole being. She never wears lipstick. She has a nose like a hawk." Em smiled thinking of her friend. She was surprised by how complete a picture of Felice she drawn from her mind's eye.

"She doesn't sound at all familiar. What does she drive?"

"I've never known her to drive. She walks to our cabin to visit. Her visits are always unexpected. Somehow, she always seems to stop by when I'm really lonely and need a friend."

A note of annoyance tinged Adrian's voice: "Well, you could visit *me* more often. Don't I count as a friend?"

Sadie returned from giving her customers their checks, overhearing the last of the conversation. "Yeah, and what about me? You could visit here more often, you know," Sadie complained. She plopped back into her chair between Adrian and Em.

"Oh, don't get your feathers all ruffled. I can only visit when I get the car away from Randy. But that means I have to get up and out early to take him to work."

"Point well taken. You're forgiven," Sadie joined in. "This lady, Felicity? She does sound interesting. Where does she live? What's her house like? Is she a neighbor?"

"Well, that's the weird thing. I have no idea where she lives. She just appears, walking up the road with this big orange cat of hers, Zuma. She's never invited me to her house. I've been looking all through the neighborhood for any sign of her or her cat. I swear I've walked over every hill and backroad and know just about every place in Heavenly Hollow. I've never seen any sign of her or Zuma."

"Well, I'll certainly keep my eye out for her. But if she doesn't drive the library is too far a walk from Hillbilly Holler."

Em glared at Adrian. "Heavenly Hollow, moron."

"So, what else are my two favorite customers up to lately?" Sadie said. "Besides talking about books and old ladies. Haven't seen you in a couple of weeks, Em. You two are certainly chummy. If I didn't know better…" Sadie chuckled.

Em immediately picked up the innuendo and felt herself blushing. "We're just friends, Sadie."

Sadie laughed loudly, turning customer's heads, whom she should have been serving. Adrian smirked at her.

Sadie took a dirty, damp rag from her apron pocket and began wiping the table. "Well, of course you're just friends. I know that. Addy's not on our team. If he was, I would've jumped his bones long ago."

Adrian posed, fingertip under chin, nose in the air. "I am of the artistic gay bent. Colorful, amusing, bright, poetic…the list goes on and on. And dear Sadie, you're the only woman who could ever tempt me to change teams." He blew a kiss at her and fluttered his eyelashes.

Em's concerns over *crossing the line* by having lunch with Adrian was instantly deflated. *Guess I won't have to worry about imagining romance with him anymore,* she ruefully thought.

"Oh, you're so full of shit, you homo," Sadie said as she smacked Adrian on the arm.

"Why don't you get back to your scullery, you wench. Emeline and I have philosophical things to discuss."

"Yeah, right." Reluctantly, Sadie rose from the table to take care of her customers.

Adrian turned back to Emeline, eyes mischievous, grin wide, noticing the flustered look on her face. He struck another pose, sharing a Mona Lisa smile, his eyes looking dramatic. "What do you think? This is my Oscar Wilde look. Someday I'm going to Paris to see his grave. I've heard the sculpture over his memorial vault is very well-endowed, true to life. He was very handsome. Like *moi.*" Adrian chuckled.

"You're…gay? I've never had a homosexual friend. Of course, I used to see a lot of gay guys in the Castro district of San Francisco. Mama and I shopped there for vintage clothes." Em, no longer flustered, was now curious.

"Well, what did you think? My choice of ensembles was the usual? My dear, of course I'm gay. Did you never suspect the real reason for my going up to Richmond every once in a while? To shop? No! There's no one of my ilk here in little Charles Town. Not to my knowledge, anyway. I just like to mingle with my own kind, search for romance, just like anyone. Like in those bodice rippers you read."

Em felt momentarily disappointed. She had hoped Adrian thought of her as a woman. Now apparently he only thought of her as someone interested in books. She sat up straight in her chair and drilled her eyes into his. In a superior tone, she said, "I know a lot more than you think I do. I no longer read bodice rippers. My literary interests have blossomed, as you well know. After all, you're the one who saves me books from my reading list!"

Sadie came by and settled in again. "Cook's here today, I get to rest a bit between customers." She lifted the last fry from Adrian's plate.

"Hey!" he complained.

"Oh, quit yer bitchin'. You weren't going to finish them anyway. What do you always say? You have to preserve your youthful profile?"

The next half hour the friends chatted happily, with Sadie making forays to and from the kitchen when the cook rang his bell, signifying her order was ready. Finally, Adrian rose to leave. "Genevieve will be all over me if I'm late getting back."

"Genevieve. I don't think I can ever call her anything but Ms. Ogelthorpe. She seems so stern and cranky," said Em.

"Oh, she can be. But she's not all bad, you know. I bet she's got a few secrets of her own hidden away under those pretty blouses she wears. She's got a big, warm heart. You'll see once you get to know her better."

The bell on the Inn and Out jingled merrily as the pair left, Sadie waving and calling to them, "Y'all come back now, ya heah?"

As they walked, Adrian kept up the conversation, intrigued by Em's new enterprise. "Okay. Now tell me more about this chair caning thing. Can you really cane chairs? You know there are a lot of old biddies around here who treasure their antiques. I bet if I put a sign up at the library you'd snag a few customers. What do you charge for a chair?"

"Well. That depends. The asking price is fifty cents a hole."

"Oh, honey," Adrian laughed uproariously. "You better raise your prices. Are you sure you're caning chairs? You sound like an advertisement in the gay district."

"Adrian, I swear. Your mind is always in the gutter. I've been to the Castro district, and I've heard all about the bath-houses there. Back to my chair caning. If you would put a notice on the library board, I'd be grateful. I just finished my first chair. I'm pretty proud of myself. It turned out to be beautiful, nice, tight, even weaving. I've done lots of embroidery, rug braiding and stuff like that, but nothing like chair caning. I'm just waiting for Felice to stop by and let me know if I did a good job."

Adrian smirked, then became more serious. "I have no doubt you'll succeed at anything you attempt, love."

Em rewarded Adrian with a warm smile, then said, "Oh, Addy, *would* you put a notice on the bulletin board? I'd be so happy if I found some customers. It would give us some badly needed extra cash."

"Of course, honey."

On the way back to the library, they stopped in front of the bookstore, The Book Nook, sandwiched between Thrifty Threads Treasures and The Antique Life. They perused the titles of the books in the window: *Sophie's Choice, Birdy, Requiem for a Dream. So many books*, Em thought. She could never read them all.

"Oh, that reminds me," Em said. "Do you know of a book at the library, *Living on The Earth?* It's by Alicia Bay Laurel. Felicity says it's a great book about country living. It's filled with instructions for making your own loom for weaving, recipes, planting gardens, simple clothes making, canning and drying fruit and veggies. Ever heard of it?"

"Yeah. I have. It's kind of like those hippie FoxFire books. We don't carry stuff like that in the library. Maybe you could order it at The Book Nook?"

"Well, no. I can't until I make some money caning chairs. I really can't afford to buy anything but groceries."

Adrian's warm gold-flecked chocolate-colored eyes filled with sympathy. "Oh, honey, been there. Things will look up. How's your Randy doing with the previously owned vehicle sales?"

"Slowly improving. He's not as cheeky as he was when he first started working at Bert's. Dare I say it, I think he's come down a peg or two and maybe learned a bit of humility. He's listening more to his co-workers and bragging less."

Suddenly Adrian's eyes were riveted to the shop across from The Book Nook, called Going Places: Leather and Luggage Specialist. He turned to Em. "Hey, sweetie. Let's take a few more minutes. I want to check out this shop. I've been looking for a leather vest." As they entered the shop Em realized exactly what Addy was really looking for. Arranging a rack of leather pants near the entrance stood the handsomest man Em thought she had ever seen. He was tall and slim, with blond close-cropped curls. It wasn't leather vests that had caught Adrian's eye.

Em smirked at her friend and whispered, "Leather vests, my ass."

"Yes, and isn't it a nice one." Adrian retorted. Em perused a rack of purses while Adrian toured the store, soon catching the shop keeper's attention.

"Is there something I can help you with?" asked the man, turning so that Em was rewarded by more of his movie-star appearance. His brilliant-blue eyes twinkled happily at Adrian. His cupid's bow mouth was curved into a warm smile. His square jaw and high cheekbones made the man look like royalty or a blond Clark Gable.

"Well, yes. I'm looking for a leather vest," said Adrian, as he reached out his hand. "I'm Adrian, by the way, and this is my friend, by the purse rack, Emeline." Em smiled and waved, then turned back to her studious examination of the purses.

The handsome blond took Adrian's hand and shook it warmly. "Pleased to meet you. I'm Nils, Nils Beddekker, owner and lover of all things leather. First time visiting my shop, right?"

"Yes, it is. How intriguing your name is. I don't believe I've ever met a Nils."

"It's Scandinavian, where my family originally comes from. Real Vikings, or so I've been told. But that was generations ago. I've never visited the Scandinavian countries, although it is a dream of mine. Now I'm just a normal little Charles Town business owner who happens to love leather and traveling." He flashed Adrian a brilliant smile which Em was sure made Addy's heart skip a beat. *I bet he's on Adrian's team*, she thought, with a mischievous grin.

Nils and Adrian hit it off instantly, discussing the virtues of Moroccan, Italian, and Western leathers with greater interest than Em thought leather deserved. Maybe, just maybe, Em hoped. It would be nice if Adrian found someone closer to home than Richmond. She chuckled as she listened to their conversation from the far end of the shop. She pretended no interest in anything other than leather as she moved to the belt rack, where she paid rapt attention to each belt and buckle.

"Oh, yes, Italian leather is the softest, in my opinion. You can smell the quality."

Adrian took a deep sniff of the proffered vest. "Oh, my yes. And so delightfully soft."

"But also very strong and supple and noted for its longevity and durability. Italian leather, that is." Nils smiled another brilliant smile, showing bright white even teeth. He pulled out a few more vests for Adrian to inspect.

Adrian's hands fluttered over another proffered vest. "It's important, of course, that I find a vest with just the right fit. Perhaps a little snug, but not too much so. Just enough to show off my physique."

Em snorted, choked on her laughter, and then pretended to be coughing. Adrian shot her a scathing look from across the room. "My dear, are you quite all right? Is the scent of leather offensive to your sinuses? Should you wait outside?"

Em smiled benignly at Adrian. "No. I'll wait for you. You said you had to get back to work soon. I'm sure you won't be long."

Nils ignored Em's remark as he turned to choose a vest from a nearby rack. Adrian nailed Em with a curdling look. She got the message. "Guess you're right, Addy. The leather smell is tickling my senses. I'll wait outside." She winked at her friend and exited the store, watching the action through the window display and listening to their conversation through the screen door.

Nils held a soft buttery-colored vest in front of Adrian. "Well, I think I have just the thing for you, but if you have to get back to work…"

"Yes. Well, Emeline is correct. I work at the library. In charge of stacks, new editions, that sort of thing. I'll come back tomorrow on my lunch break to try on a few. Will that work for you?"

"Oh, of course. I'll look forward to your visit tomorrow. Adrian, right?"

"Yes. Adrian Montagu. My background is French. Pretty close to Scandinavia, right?" Both men laughed, then shook hands again. As Adrian turned to leave, he wiggled his fingers at Nils. "Till tomorrow then."

Em couldn't help but mock Addy. "Till tomorrow then, handsome. You're almost drooling Addy. How can you be so sure he's as interested in you as you are in him?"

"Oh Emeline. You are *such* a naive child. We of the same bent recognize one another immediately. I'm astounded that I've never discovered him before. But then, I rarely go window shopping."

"Well, I guess you can thank me for that, right?"

Adrian put his arm around Em's shoulders and kissed the top of her head. "Yes, my dear, I guess you are good for something, after all. Now. Back to the grind. I'll put your chair-caning business announcement on the board, and we'll see what happens. This could be the start of something big!" He sang in his lovely baritone accompanied by a sweeping waltz around Em.

"You're nuts. Yes. This could be the start of something big. For both of us. Thanks for putting up the announcement." Em quickly wrote her phone number on a slip of paper. "Here, you'll need that for all my future customers. You watch. Soon I'll be caning chairs and making enough money for us to go shopping together for books and clothes. But don't hold your breath."

The two hugged at the library steps. Em headed to the Rambler and then to the grocery store. As she shopped she was overflowing with questions. She felt as though she was an empty vessel that needed filling. There was so much she didn't know. How had she not known Adrian was gay with the clothes he wore and his funny affectations? She knew Adrian liked her, but he had never been flirtatious or the least bit overbearing in a lurid sort of way.

She needed a woman friend to confide in. She wondered if Felice would arrive soon for another visit. She should get Sadie's phone number. Maybe she'd like to chat once in a while, or stop by Heavenly Hollow when she wasn't working.

On the drive home with Randy, Em's mind returned to Adrian. He had become a good friend through the library and books. Em felt as though she could tell him anything. He listened to her and seemed interested in her latest endeavors. Em suddenly realized Adrian was more like another girlfriend than a male friend.

Em turned her eyes to the road when they entered the turnoff for Heavenly Hollow. She stopped chattering to Randy about her visit to town, as her thoughts returned to Felicity. She searched every overgrown avenue for any signs of life or of Felicity walking up the old lanes. She examined every cabin they passed for some hint of Felicity or Zuma's presence. She imagined her friend's delight should Em discover her home and arrive one day with fresh flowers or jam. Em's day dream didn't match the possibility that Felice could just as easily greet her with horror. There was a reason her friend hid herself away, although Em couldn't fathom what it was. Maybe she was ashamed of her home? Prodding Felicity with questions could frighten her elusive friend into further retreat. Felicity could disappear like smoke, never to reappear. She valued their friendship too much to intrude on her privacy. Besides, she had more pressing worries.

Over the weeks concerns over their future had settled over Em like algae on a stagnant bog. Her thoughts nagged her. Randy noticed Em was quieter than usual. He gave her distance and tenderness, certain this mood of hers would pass, as they always did. Best of all, he began paying more attention to her when she started one of her discussions about books. When she told Randy tales of all she had discovered in the neighborhood, he became more interested and began asking questions.

"What cabin was that? Sounds like they have a pretty big garden. Bet they have a lot of kids." He was equally hopeful that her chair caning business would take off. Randy was selling more cars, thanks to Jason's tutelage in what his co-worker called, 'psychological selling techniques'. Randy was slowly learning, becoming more humble and gracious with customers, listening to them with greater attention as to who they were. It was slowly paying off. But Of course, he would welcome any extra income that Em could bring in through her chair-caning.

* * *

Bert's Best Buddies annual employee picnic was scheduled for the first Sunday in September, an event Em had been dreading. Her first meeting with women employees at Bert's hadn't gone well, in her opinion. She remembered Monica's gum-snapping, seductive attitude. Em didn't really want to go to any damn picnic. She wasn't looking forward to hanging out with men like the idiot who had wanted to kiss her and was obviously undressing her with his eyes. On top of that, she had to make a pot-luck offering for the celebration. She decided she'd make Potato Salad. It would be easy and inexpensive to make utilizing her mama's recipe laced with Miss Magnolia's cookbook ingredients. After perusing her meager closet, she decided on a fairly new pair of jean shorts and a blouse she had embroidered with a bright garden of flowers.

The Sunday of the picnic Em was settled on one of her old quilts with the group of company wives. Half-heartedly, she listened to the women's conversation as she watched the men's baseball practice beginning. Randy and the other salesmen had assembled in the vacant car lot next to Bert's Best Buddies. They threw the ball back and forth to each other.

Randy missed catching ball after ball. "I don't have a mitt," he complained. "Now you do," said Jason, throwing Randy a mitt, which he also missed catching. He picked up the mitt and looked at it hesitantly. Then, he tucked his hand into the large leather glove and flexed his fingers. "Fits great," was his reply.

Jason threw the ball to Randy. Randy was embarrassed by not catching it. "Sorry, just rusty." He apologized. He missed the second ball as well, and didn't offer an apology. The men on the team exchanged worried glances. A third ball was thrown to Randy, also not caught.

"Hey, man, didn't your dad ever teach you to play ball?" someone called out. Em clearly heard his response. "No, not really. Not ever." Randy's sardonic laugh broke the silence of the men on the field. "My dad never taught me a thing I couldn't learn myself."

Em realized how telling Randy's comment was. Just as in the conversation overheard with Margret, Em realized Randy really didn't have any relationship with his father. He probably had never played baseball or any other games with him. Her heart went out to her husband. Their childhoods had been so different. Em had received nothing but love from her parents. Randy only had one parent, not two, to love and care for him. She was slowly learning what damage his father had bred into Randy's young life.

The shouts of the men on the field interrupted her thoughts. "Hey, man," Tommy said. "How about this terrific team of ours, Bert's Best Buddies Baseball Team." The men all screamed in laughter. "That's a joke," said Jason. "You think Bert would ever spring for a team? Or anything more than our annual employee picnic? Bert can't even buy food. He always says, Potluck Celebration. What he really means is, Women do all the cooking. That's what they're here for. To cook for us. Don't expect me to pay for anything."

"I got a six pack in the truck and a bottle of whisky," Jason shouted. "Randy, join us? You may not know how to play ball, but I bet you can drink."

"I'll do my best," Randy said happily. Em smiled at his obvious joy at being included in the group. The men wandered off to their cars and trucks in a huddle of voices and shouts. "Hey, Randy, I'll teach you how to hit a mean ball, without breaking any windows!" The men roared as they walked across the field. "Oh yeah, Ralphie. You couldn't hit the side of a barn. You can't teach Randy, or anybody anything, except breaking windows."

Em turned her attention to the gaggle of women around her. One of them laughed and said, "Don't our boys play nicely together? Come on, Emeline, you'll get a numb ass sitting on the ground this long. Join us, now that our 'gentlemen' have brought chairs over."

The women joined in laughter. "Yeah, right, *gentlemen*, what a hoot," Monica said, as she patted the chair next to her. Em joined the group, sipping her

Ripple Wine but not immediately joining in the conversation. For the time being, she was content to just eavesdrop.

"Oh, and the morning sickness," said Tiffany.

"And feeling like a whale," answered Julie.

Marcie, hugely pregnant, said, "I just can't wait till it's all over. I've hated every minute of being pregnant."

"Really? I always loved being pregnant," Joanne remarked.

"Right, Joanne. Is that why you've got five kids? Was it pregnancy or what got you pregnant that you loved so much?" The wives all laughed in gleeful appreciation.

Joanne answered primly, "It's not about sex. Ralph says we have to respect our faith. But then, he changed his tune. 'No more kids cause 'a no mo money'. Praise the Lord for the pill."

The wives laughed uproariously again. "Yeah, thank God for the pill. I hear that!" Joanne said.

As the wives laughed over Joanne's joke, Em was reminded that she needed to refill her birth control prescription. She had no local doctor. Dr. Waggoner was the only doctor and ob/gyn she had ever known. He'd retired right after he gave her a new six-month prescription. She had only one month left and needed to find a doctor soon. She'd have to ask Joanne, who seemed to know something about birth control.

Em felt very much alone, the odd woman out, during this talk of pregnancy and kids. She knew nothing of pregnancy, babies, or how to handle the toddlers crashing about. She didn't know whether she wanted to learn. Her timidity, usually overcome when in the company of women, returned.

Faith, Joanne's oldest daughter, at eight, was being paid to keep herd on the youngest children. She was proving to be unsuccessful, racing after her sisters, Hope and Charity, screaming at them to stay in her sight.

Tiffany noticed Em's silence. "Emeline, where did you find that adorable embroidered blouse?"

Em looked at her peasant blouse and plucked at a loose thread. "This old thing? I found the blouse at a thrift shop and embroidered the bodice myself."

"You embroidered that? It's beautiful. I thought it was some Mexican thing. What thrift store? Thrifty Threads in town?"

"Oh, no. I got this at a thrift store where we used to live, on the California delta."

Tiffany joined in. "Oh, yeah. Jason said you and Randy used to live there. His mother moved here from California, right?"

"Yes. That's why we moved to Heavenly Hollow. To be closer to Randy's mom, after my mama and papa died." Quiet murmurs of solicitude arose from the women. "So sorry...don't know what I'd do..." Tiffany said. Monica commandeered the conversation with her direct, brusque but not unkind questions.

"Is that why you moved here? To get away from that sorrow? I don't know what I'd do if I lost my mom and pops. How long ago was that?" Monica asked.

Em felt herself holding her past close to her heart. She wasn't ready to confide anything more than basic facts to these women she barely knew. "Lost my papa four years ago. Mama almost three. Yes, Randy's mom, Margret, lives here, in Charles Town."

A scream split the air as two toddlers crashed into one another and fell in tears to the ground. Two older boys were on the ground battling in the dirt. Faith ran to her mother.

"That's it. I'm not babysitting anymore. None 'a these kids listen to me. They're all terrible. I'm never having babies. Ever." She ran off toward the back of the field, leaving the adults to handle the melee.

"Damian! I've told you time and again not to bite!" Wanda screamed. Hope and Andrea stood by watching, fascinated with the welt rising on Joseph's arm. Charity wandered off after her sister Faith.

Em couldn't have agreed more with Faith's assessment. *I'm not having kids anytime soon either*, she thought. Just then the battles and tears were silenced by the scream of a Roman candle launched over the parking lot.

"Damn." Arlene exclaimed. "They started the fireworks and booze way too early." The women scattered like hens in a yard racing from the shadow of a hawk. From the distant end of the field, they watched Arlene's advancement toward the men. "That Arlene. She'll take care of them."

Arlene marched to the group of men, who were laughing and slapping one another's shoulders, passing around a bottle of Jack Daniels. Em found herself pleased that Randy was part of the group of men drinking and laughing together. Guiltily, Jason hid the Roman candle he had been about to light. Arlene waved her arms around, ranting.

"Don't you idiots realize there are children here? And pregnant women? What if one of those rockets caught fire?" The men shuffled their feet, looking at the ground guiltily. Finally, Randy surprised Em by speaking up.

"We're sorry, Arlene. You're right. We'll move the fireworks farther across the field. Okay?" Arlene was instantly mollified, her anger dissipating. "Oh, okay, just be careful."

"Yes, Ma'am," Randy replied. Em felt a bolt of pride until she saw the reaction of the men behind Arlene's back. They all made faces and waved their hands at Arlene, as though shooing her from their presence. A couple of the men punched Randy on the arm and Ralph handed him the Jack Daniels.

"That's the way, Randy. Just be polite, sweeten 'em up so they'll shut up."

Shutting up the women? She'd take that up with Randy later. For now, Em wondered if she should be proud of Randy or concerned over the tipping of the Jack Daniel's bottle? Shouts of "That's our man" flavored the moment more than the booze.

Days later Em stood in the yard, once again admiring her first completed caned seat. She patted it gently, afraid to sit in it as Felicity hadn't yet stopped by to approve her work. She pressed harder on the seat and was proud that it held firm, the cane weaving tight, every strand in its place. The finishing strand was evenly secured under the chair bottom, looking exactly as Felice had instructed her. "Your chair must be as neat and tight on the bottom as it is on the top."

Suddenly, Rhett and Scarlet raced under the porch. Em turned to see Felice walking slowly up the lane. Surprisingly, Zuma raced first into the yard, not following her mistress as she usually did. The big orange cat ran to where Em's feline family were ensconced in their favorite hiding place. As the big cat had done at their last visit, Zuma settled herself in front of Rhett and Scarlet and began cleaning her fur.

"Yoo hoo, darlin'. Thought it was about time that I stopped by to see how your new enterprise is coming along."

"Felice, how on earth did you know that's exactly what I was thinking? I didn't want to sit in my chair until I got your seal of approval."

Felicity walked slowly into the yard and Em ran to greet her. She warmly placed her arm around Felice's waist. The older woman briefly stopped her journey into the yard and gently placed her arm around Em's shoulder. "Oh, my deah. What a joy it is to see you, so young and fresh. I'm wilting in this September heat." Felicity seemed extremely tired, worrying Em. She quickly pulled the one-armed park bench closer to her friend, keeping it in the shade of the old magnolia.

"You do look wilted, Felice. Can I get you a nice cold glass of water, or iced tea?"

"Oh, no darlin'. I don't want you to go to any trouble. I'm fine, honestly. Just need to sit in the shade a bit. Usually I'm cold, anyway. The shade will renew me. Now bring over that chair so I can inspect your first caning job." As Em carried the chair to Felice, she felt childlike, awaiting approval. She stood before Felice, chewing her lip, hands clasped behind her back. Felicity pushed on the seat, then turned the chair over.

"Excellent, my deah, you've done a perfect job. The cane is nice and tight, and you've done exactly as I would have hoped, looping the cane tightly underneath and through the top. It has cured beautifully, with a lovely luster."

Felicity looked up at Em, her smile lit her face and warmed Em's heart.

"Oh, I'm so glad. I was worried I might have done something wrong," Em said. The older woman replied, "Dear Emmy, never worry about doing anything wrong. Misdeeds can always be corrected. The same goes for mistakes, in a chair or in life. They can always be fixed with tender care and attention. We must always learn from our mistakes." Much to Em's surprise, Felice touched Em again, this time resting her thin, cold fingertips on Em's cheek.

"Well my deah, this is the moment of truth. Yours must be the first bottom to adorn this newly caned chair as you are the one who has resurrected this relic from the grave and given it new life." She patted the chair seat gently.

Em looked at Felice hesitantly. "Are you sure?"

"Of course, I'm sure. Sit that derriere of yours onto this seat immediately."

Em giggled, then felt pride knowing what a 'derriere' was, having learned the word from her reading. She settled lightly on the seat, then leaned into the back. She picked her feet up and placed her whole weight on the chair. Em laughed, thrilled that the chair had not broken into pieces beneath her.

"Congratulations, my deah. You are officially crowned as an experienced chair caner. Not quite a wicker queen yet, but you're on your way."

"Wicker queen?"

"Oh, that's just an old expression. Ignore my foolishness. Sometimes I forget myself with my aged linguistics."

Em, puzzled, studied Felice intently. Whatever did she mean?

The moment passed and Felice poked Em out of her musing. Felicity nodded her head silently toward the porch. Zuma turned her back on Scarlet and Rhett and curled up under the old park bench at Felicity's feet. Zuma obviously wasn't ready for friendship. Felicity patted the bench next to her. "Come sit with me darlin'. Eventually our feline family will become friends. Friends, just like us. Let's chat a bit." Zuma was letting Scarlet and Rhett know that, for the time being, they were not worthy of her attention. For their part, her cats were slowly creeping out from under the porch, as Em watched in amazement. She then smiled warmly at Felice and reached out and patted her hand again. "Yes, Felice, they'll become friends, just like us."

Em looked lovingly at Felice who returned her look with a tender smile. "These old bones move more slowly but I never stop thinking of another sweet visit with you. As I've told you, I only come when I'm needed. I sensed my dear young friend was feeling the oncoming of fall winds and flying leaves. This time of year always saddens me." Felice had shared a feeling with Em that matched her own. Em always had been filled with sorrow when the delta changed from her summer colors to those of the drab, dark and rainy fall.

Felice had confided in her. Em hoped to open this door to more confidences in the future. She'd retrieve bits and pieces of Felice's life, the same way she was discovering bits and pieces of her neighbors' lives through observation. Em was reminded of the way her grandmother had collected scraps of fabric to create a quilt filled with her stories.

Em then offered a crack through a creaking door to her own past. "It's so different here than on the delta. I'm sure the fall here with the changing autumn colors is beautiful. We never had oaks, aspens or maples, like we have here. We didn't have any real color from leaves changing. All the flowers died along with the ending of the crop season. Mama always said, 'time to put the garden to bed'. Then, everything just got muddy and dark with the fall and winter rainy season." Em chattered away happily, warm in the glow of friendship.

"Adrian said he'd put up a notice on the library bulletin board letting people know I can cane chairs. I told him I'd charge fifty cents a hole, like you said, plus the cost of materials. I hope I get some customers. It would really help our bank account, especially with Christmas just around the corner. I'm so excited. What do you think?"

Felice gave Em the gift of one of her throaty chuckles that seemed to emanate from deep within her body. "Oh, my deah, your enthusiasm brightens my heart. Who is Adrian?"

"He's one of the librarians," said Em. "He's been so good to me. He gives me books that are ready for the sale room. I gave him your list of books and authors. He's become a friend, lots friendlier than Ms. Ogelthorpe. If she found out Adrian is giving me books, he'd be in big trouble with her."

"Goodness, she's still there? She must be ancient. Although as I recall, she began at the library as a stacker when very young."

Em examined her friend more closely. She appeared older, more tired than on previous visits. It was as though Felice was fading right before Em's eyes. She knew Ms. Ogelthorpe. There was a clue worth pursuing. Felice continued the conversation, unusual for her. It was Emeline who usually did all the talking. She was not about to interrupt her friend's musings and continued listening intently.

"I must remark, dear sweet Emmy, how you have changed from our first meeting months ago. You didn't even know what a magnolia tree was and here we sit beneath your magnolia, like old friends. But then, I too have changed."

Em was thoughtful for a moment. "Yes, you have." She decided not to voice her fears of Felice's health and well-being. Her worries might cause Felice to end her confidences. She imagined Felice as a deer, frozen in a glade in the woods, on the verge of bounding off into the deeper forest should any sound frighten it away.

Em continued the conversation. "Funny you should say I've changed. With your help. I think I've grown up in the months since I first met you. I don't know, I'm more content and settled. I do feel like I'm becoming a little wiser. I don't feel so heartbroken over Mama's passing as I did when we first met. I feel as though Mama is always near, even when I'm wandering around our little neighborhood of Heavenly Hollow."

"I've no doubt your mama is always near. Some love can't be deterred by death. Friendship and love remain through time and space. Love defies death and outsmarts the grim reaper."

"Hmmm, I like that thought. I'll have to mention it to Randy. He worries about me missing Mama and Papa. Oh! That reminds me. Margret came to dinner, Randy's mom. It was her first visit since we moved in. I made pot roast from Miss Magnolia's recipe book. It turned out great. We had the best visit ever.

I think Margret is really beginning to think of me as her daughter. She even calls me once in a while just to say hello, to touch base, she says. She tells me how she's feeling, what she's up to. She's making more of an effort to include me in her life. But then again, I guess I'm making more of an effort, too. I was afraid of Margret when I first met her. She seemed so superior and stand-offish. I try to be kinder, to listen and understand her more."

The two friends laughed companionably. "I'm so pleased to hear your visit went well, deah. It takes time to get to know one another, to discover the boundaries between mother and daughter-in-law and to lessen that distance. Which pot roast recipe did you use? The more urbane recipe, or the old timer's version with diced bacon? That's the best one."

"Yes, I did add fried bacon, the old timey recipe. And I added wine. And red wine vinegar over the roast like my mama used to do, to tenderize it. And I added ingredients from Sadie's recipe, using Cream of Mushroom Soup and dried Lipton's onion soup mix."

As she always did, Felice seemed to fade before her eyes. "Well, sweet Emmy, time for me to depart. You have dinner to prepare and I have to toddle along."

Felicity snapped her fingers and Zuma awakened, stretched, and yawned, her pink tongue appearing over her tiny teeth. Felice rubbed her hands over Zuma's fur and the large cat seemed to smile in bliss.

Em examined her friend more closely. She appeared older, more tired than on previous visits. It was as though Felice had begun to fade away right before Em's eyes. Felice's eyes lost their shine and she looked exhausted. She realized once again that she had no idea of Felice's age. In this late afternoon light, it was as though their visit had added years to her life.

Em had the overwhelming desire to hug Felice but worried she would be stepping over the line of her friend's boundaries. Instead, she helped Felice rise from the bench. Much to her surprise, Felice gently touched Em's cheek with her lips, caressing her as tenderly as a summer breeze.

"Until next time, my lovely friend." Em reached out and placed her arm around Felice's thin waist, encouraged by her friend's affection.

"Yes, Felice. Until next time. Your visits are always the best part of my days. Thank you for being my dearest friend."

Felice smiled her radiant smile. Her eyes did not light up as they had in the past but appeared worry-filled. Em knew better than to offer to walk her home.

The older woman turned and made her way down the rutted road. She waved at the turn in the lane with Zuma trailing behind her.

Em picked up her newly caned chair and brought it into the cabin. The vision of Felice's departure remained in her mind long after the older woman had left. I just couldn't bear to lose Felicity. She seems to be getting older and older. If something happened to her... Oh, there I go talking to myself again. Em laughed at herself. Mama? Are you listening like Felice says?

There was no answer. For the moment, Em felt uplifted. She had Felice in her life, along with her mama. Felice had convinced her that her mama would always be there in the shadows of her heart. Em hoped that Felice would always be there for her, also. "No sense thinking about something I can't do anything about. I'll just continue to enjoy every minute I have with Felice." Em told Rhett and Scarlet, who scowled at her, awaiting their dinner.

Another perfect day, Em thought, as she prepared her cat's meals and then hers and Randy's. She began to sing one of her mama's favorite Delta songs:

Way down on the Delta, we're shufflin' and dancin' we're singing and swaying, it's the good ship, Robert E. Lee, that's come to carry the cotton away.

Felice was right: She was certain her mama was listening, and was right there with her, at that moment.

Chapter 10

The phone rang shrilly, interrupting Em and Randy sitting lazily on the couch, a bowl of popcorn between them. The TV was on but Em was paying no attention to *All In The Family*. She was immersed in her book, *Madame Bovary*, about an entirely different kind of family. She ignored the phone which Randy ran to answer.

"Who can that be calling at 8:30? Mom never calls this late." Em could see the worry on his face as Randy raced to answer the phone. She listened with equal concern. Could Margret be sick? Maybe she had fallen? She heard Randy's voice rise when he answered.

"Em? You mean Emeline, my wife? Who is this?"

Em was instantly on her feet, popcorn from her blouse and lap decorating the floor, *Madame Bovary* discarded. She entered the kitchen just as Randy turned to her, a scowl on his face. Clearly, he was not happy.

"It's for you. Some guy named Adrian." Randy handed Em the phone and returned to the living room where he surreptitiously listened to the conversation.

"Hello, Adrian?" Em laughed at his reply, while Randy continued to eavesdrop. "No, of course it's all right. That was just Randy, acting husbandly." Silence, then more laughter from Em.

"Don't be a jerk. You're not on my team, remember?"

More silence, then laughter again as Em stretched the phone cord as far as it could go and sat down at the kitchen table. "Randy is definitely not on your team, either. He's taken, remember? My husband?" She laughed at Adrian's reply. "You're incorrigible. But why on earth are you calling?"

Em's scream filled the kitchen. "You're kidding! Honestly, really? Oh, Adrian, that's fantastic. Wait till I get a piece of paper to write down the number." As Em ran to get her shopping list she spied Randy in the kitchen doorway, looking stormy. She threw him a kiss in passing.

"Okay, I'm ready." She jotted down a message and phone number on her pad. "Oh, Adrian! Great! I owe you a big hug. You're an angel. Okay, yeah, definitely. Lunch then, Wednesday?" Em giggled as she hung up the phone and raced to Randy. "Sweetheart! You won't believe it!"

Randy didn't open his arms to receive Em's proffered hug. "Who the hell was that? Why is some guy calling you at 8:30 at night? And what's this about being on his team? And you giving him a big hug?"

Em sighed deeply. "You're being a moron. That was Adrian. From the library with some great news. Randy, I've told you about him. He's gay, which is what I meant when I said I'm not on his team."

"Oh. Okay. Yeah, I remember," Randy said sheepishly. Em danced around her husband, waving the slip of paper over her head.

"I got a job! I got a job!"

"You've been looking for work? Since when? I thought you were happy staying at home."

Em rolled her eyes at Randy as she walked past him. She retrieved *Madame Bovary* from the floor.

"Randy, don't you ever listen to me or hear anything I'm saying? *Caning*, I got a chair caning job. Some lady has two chairs she wants me to cane."

"Really? Are you sure?" Randy replied, astonishment in his face.

"Well, that's what she told Adrian. She got my name off the library bulletin board. Addy told her I'm excellent at chair weaving, that's what he calls it." Em giggled. "He's such a blowhard. He said I'm highly skilled and do beautiful work." She giggled again and shook her head, her blond curls bobbing around her flushed face.

Em put her hands on her hips. "Randy, the important thing is I have a chair, no, two chairs to cane. I'll call her tomorrow to set up a time to see the chairs and figure out if I can do this." She chewed her lip. "Oh, damn. If only I could get Felice to go with me. But that's impossible."

"I should go with you. I don't like you going to a strange place by yourself."

Em's ire rose. "Oh Randy. For God's sake. This is *my* chair-caning business. Do I hang around Bert's to watch you sell cars?" Em gnawed at her lip again, realizing that's exactly what she had done in the past without Randy's knowledge. Her anger dissipated when she saw the worried expression on her husband's face. "But what if something happens?"

"Like what? She's probably just some old lady with a lot of old stuff. Sweetie, this is just what I've been hoping for. Extra cash, a way to make ends meet." Randy continued to look doubtful, grousing in his uncertainty, "Hmmpf. We'll see."

"I'll call her tomorrow and will let you know how she sounds. Maybe Genevieve knows her. If I'm worried or have any weird feelings, I'll have you go along with me, okay?"

"Okay. Yeah, I guess."

"I'll know a lot more after I talk to her." Em looked at the slip of paper. "Helen Winthrop. Maybe your mom knows her, or her family. I'll call her tomorrow, too."

Em slowly entered the living room. The TV continued to blare with the adventures of *All In The Family.* Archie was yelling at Edith, as usual.

"Honey, please, be happy for me?"

"I am. I will be. You know, I just worry."

"I know, but you shouldn't. I have a good sixth sense for people. Even Felice says so, just like Mama always did. Now, *Madame Bovary* and I are going to take a nice, long bubble bath before bed." Em hummed a Beatles song as she happily left the living room. It wasn't until she was filling the tub and undressing that she realized she had been humming the song "She's Leaving Home, Bye Bye."

But Randy noticed. All these people he didn't know were filling up his wife's life, and her heart? Adrian, Genevieve, Felicity? Was there still room enough in Em's life and heart for him, or was her world becoming too crowded with new people? Was she slowly leaving him behind in the wake of all her new interests? A shroud of sadness fell over him so completely that he felt close to tears. No. He was just being stupid. Still, fear darkened the joy he should have felt for his wife. He walked into the bathroom just as Em was settling under the bubbles, a rolled towel behind her head, book in hand.

"Hey, sweetheart. Is there room enough in that tub for both me and *Madame Bovary*?" Em smiled sweetly and handed Randy the book. "*Madame Bovary* can wait. Get in here, love." By the time they dried one another off from their bubble bath and snuggled under the covers, any fears Randy felt had evaporated. Of course, Em loved him as much as he adored her.

The next morning Em was up bright and early, filling the kitchen with Randy's favorite scents of baking biscuits and coffee. She was still on cloud nine over the possibility of her first chair caning job. "Sweetheart, I was just wondering. If I do start getting some caning jobs, in October, it will be too cold for me to cane outside. How about if we paint the little room, it's so dark in there. Maybe a nice soft yellow? I've got some pretty antique lace I'm dying to turn into curtains. You could just put a dowel up on the windows, and I can thread the lace through that. It would really brighten up the room and would be a great place for me to cane chairs indoors. I can soak the cane in the kitchen sink. What do you think?"

"Randy scratched his head sleepily. Yeah, sure. I guess we can afford a gallon of paint and a dowel after I sold that Impala yesterday." Em's screech of delight was all that Randy had hoped for. "Why didn't you tell me? And here I've been going on and on about me!"

"Well, I wanted to be sure. The guy said he'd come by today to complete the contract after he went to the bank to get a loan. But Stan knows him and said he's good for the money and I shouldn't worry."

"Oh, this is the best day ever! I can't wait to call Helen Winthrop. Do you think I should wait until nine?"

"Yeah, best idea," Randy said, mouth full of biscuits, crumbs decorated his shirt. Em sat across from him and graced her sweet husband with the widest of grins, then worry crossed her face. "Oh, Randy. You believe in me, don't you? You think I can do this?"

"Of course, honey. You did a great job on that first chair. Why wouldn't you be able to do it again? It doesn't seem that hard. Anyway, I'm sure Felicity would help you out if you get stuck." Worry continued to adorn Em's features. "Right, I guess so. Except I never know when she'll turn up and I have no way of contacting her. I don't think she even has a phone."

"It'll be fine. Stop worrying. I gotta get ready. You're taking the car tomorrow, right? To have lunch with Addy?" He smirked at his wife. "That is, if you're sure he's not a guy I need to worry about?" Em slapped Randy playfully as he left the kitchen. It was going to be a super day. She couldn't wait to call this lady and find out where she lived. Then she'd call Margret.

All went according to plan and Em sang her way through her housework. Mrs. Winthrop seemed like a nice woman. She didn't sound old, but certainly gentrified. Em had called Margret who was thrilled to hear from her but didn't know the Winthrop family, but did know the area of town where the Winthrop home was located. "Oh, yes, dear. I know Toby Hill Road. She doesn't live near me, but certainly I know the area. It is an old, well-respected and wealthy part of Charles Town. Do let me know what her home looks like. Of course, they might be newcomers. After all, my family has lived here for generations. We don't know the nouveau people." Em let that slide, knowing Margret had to be boastful, just as Randy did. After hanging up with Margret, she shook her head and said, "After all, the apple doesn't fall far from the tree."

The thought brightened her. "I know what I'll do today." She informed Rhett and Scarlet, who were waiting to be let out. "I'll go back to that old apple orchard. Maybe there'll be some apples ready, and I can make a pie." Her little family ignored her and raced across the porch as soon as she opened the door. They ran into the field where Em could have sworn, she saw Zuma waiting at its edge. "Impossible," she told herself, as she returned to her chores. She pulled out an old warm sweater to wear over her flannel shirt and jeans. It felt wonderful to be wearing fall clothes which she so rarely had an opportunity to do in the delta. She happily set off down their rutted road, the breezes caressing her face as she walked.

Em climbed a low tree to collect apples in her mama's favorite fabric bag. Leaves had begun to change color. The aspens were a glistening bright gold, shimmering in the breezes, painting a stunning backdrop against the scarlet of the maple trees and the azure blue of the sky. The air was crisp and sharp to Em's senses at first, but soon warmed up enough to allow her to discard her sweater onto the leafy ground. When satisfied with her cache of apples Em lay down and looked through the gently swaying branches above her. As always, she admired and chattered back at the birds and squirrels who challenged her presence. The blue of the sky, the white pillowy clouds, the colors and scene above the apple tree gave her a sense of peace. She felt as though she had never been so happy. She was in her own world with a canopy overhead, and anticipating a new life of freedom from financial worry.

Walking home with her bounty of apples the sky overhead suddenly grew dark. She sensed a storm on the horizon. The air felt charged. The light and even the scents were rearranged. The strange weather eclipsed her joy. Suddenly she was overcome with a deep feeling of melancholy. Her life could change as quickly as the weather had, transforming her in an instant. The leaves falling into her path saddened her. She wondered what it would be like in the winter with snow keeping her inside with Randy for long days on end if Randy couldn't drive into work.

Em had rarely experienced snow. Her mama and papa had taken her once to Donner Pass to see the beauty of snow-covered-mountains. At first, it was like a fairy tale. Then everything changed in an instant. The snow grew from fluffy fat flakes to a plummeting, pummeling storm, quickly blanketing the roads and the woods. It was one of the few times Em had seen her father frightened. He drove their car at a crawl down the mountain until they finally reached Stockton where there was little snow. By then, State Troopers had been on the roads advising drivers they could not go up the pass without chains on their tires. It was then Em realized how easily they could have slid off the mountain road into a snowbank. With few people at the top of Donner Pass who knew how they'd get out if that happened? By the time Cabin #25 came into her view Em was thoroughly chilled and saddened. *Were the falling leaves an omen of darker days to come?* she wondered. "You're being ridiculous," she chastised herself as she reached their warm, welcoming little home.

Rhett and Scarlet were not amused with her long-overdue return home. They shivered in a little heap under the Appalachian rocker and raced through the door as soon as Em opened it. Her kitchen cheered her immediately. Its warmth and comfort welcomed her, as did Miss Magnolia's cookbook, open on the kitchen table to an apple pie recipe. Maybe she and Randy could build their first fire this evening? Wouldn't he be thrilled to come home to the scent of an apple pie baking in the oven?

The next day Em followed the instructions Mrs. Winthrop had provided and drove up a long, paved winding road that ended at her home at the top of a hill. It was a house much like Margret's, whitewashed brick, with many windows and beds of late blooming flowers bordering a winding flagstone path. Flaming maple trees topped the hill behind the old house and tall pine trees flanked its sides. Two large pots of bright orange chrysanthemums sat on either side of the brilliant red painted front door. When Em lifted the large dragonfly knocker and let it drop, the sound reverberated behind the door.

Mrs. Winthrop welcomed Em warmly, reaching out to shake her hand. "Please call me Helen, dear." She was not elderly, as Em had supposed she would be. She wore a soft wool plaid skirt and what Em surmised was a cashmere sweater, its pink shade perfectly matching the pink, blue and pale green pastels of her skirt. Em could easily see there was a great deal of wealth in this old house verified by the beautiful antiques and tasteful paintings on the walls. Thick Oriental rugs tastefully decorated the polished wood floors. A delicate orchestra played classical music from a stereo hidden in a tall antique cabinet. Em admired Helen's collection of what she called, 'My dear Tobies'. They were beautiful, yet amusing, with round tummies on the mugs and old-fashioned hats on the heads of the 'Tobies'. Helen expressed no qualms about Em's price of $72 for both chairs, plus the cost of materials. "If you do a good job, my dear, I have many friends with antiques who I am sure would love to have their chairs repaired, also. I'd be happy to recommend you." Em was so thrilled she almost hugged the woman but caught herself. As she walked to the Rambler she restrained her ebullience, adopting a professional demeanor, carefully placing the chairs in the back seat.

That weekend Randy kept his promise and purchased a gallon of pale lemony paint, with the proceeds of his first big sale of the Impala. Together they painted the walls, laughing at all the paint accumulated on their heads and clothes. Randy finally threw Em out of the room. "You're impossible," he laughed. "You've got more paint on yourself than you managed to get on the walls." Evicted from the little room, Em cleaned herself up and settled in the library where she quickly hemmed the old lace she had discovered in the shed. Randy threaded the beautiful lace through a dowel which he hung at the windows. Em was astounded at the change in the room. It was the only room in the house that had actual painted walls rather than pine paneling. A large water stain on one wall announced that there had once been a leak which was probably why the room's appearance had been changed from paneling to plaster. As soon as the paint was dry, Em carried Mrs. Winthrop's two chairs into her 'new' work room. She moved her mama's Lincoln rocker into the room to sit on as she caned.

That evening Em and Randy settled before a fire blazing in the library. They nestled into one another, agreeing that it had been one of the best weekends ever spent in their little cabin. Em hoped this mood, this special time, would last forever. *Why wouldn't it?* she wondered. Yet, that nagging thought reared its ugly head again: nothing, nor anyone lasts forever. This was the most painful fact of life, and that same realization crept into her mind, even in the midst of such joy. Em wanted nothing to end this treasure of a moment. She looked out the window at the falling leaves and shivered. The drifting foliage made her feel uneasy, bringing on a sense of anxiety, or foreboding. Even warming in front of the fire could not dispel this ghost of concern seeping into the edges of her joy or warm the chill in her heart. Her mind suddenly focused on Felice. *How was her friend on this cold evening?* she wondered.

Emeline did not get back to Charles Town for almost two weeks. She had wanted to concentrate on her chair-caning and complete the work as quickly as possible. But after two weeks Felicity had not reappeared and she was lonely for her friends.

Em returned to her favorite haunt, the library, feeling as though she were entering a sacred place. She had followed Adrian's advice on her last visit and sought out Genevieve, who warmly greeted her. Within the library walls, Em felt included in a small and important circle of bibliophiles. She thought of Adrian as her hero of the stacks and Ms. Ogelthorpe as the Wizard of the Library. Em had learned the older woman could find anything on Felicity's book list, no matter how obscure. She had even unearthed an ancient copy of *Green Mansions* by W.H. Hudson. Em cherished the book. Savoring the words Em couldn't bear to read it quickly. Genevieve pointedly ignored the book's overdue status. She listened quietly as Em enthusiastically described the book to Adrian.

"Can you imagine? A little girl grows up in the jungle, alone. She learns to talk to all the creatures, and they protect her. She lives in the treetops, and can jump from tree to tree, like Tarzan!"

"That's crazy." Adrian remarked, shaking his head. Genevieve joined their conversation. "You haven't even gotten to the romantic parts yet, Emeline." Genevieve sighed at the memory. "Such a wonderful story, until the ending."

"Don't tell me!" Em admonished her. Genevieve smiled happily sharing Em's excitement over one of her own favorite books. Reminded of the overdue status of *Green Mansions,* Genevieve admonished herself. Surely a book no one had read in years would not be missed, no matter how long it took Em to read it.

Suddenly, the library exploded in a gaggle of children interrupting the peace of the large rooms. Adrian moved to the front desk, looking impervious to the excited screams and chatter of the children. Genevieve quickly stepped in front of the children and began her tour of the library. Her refined voice drifted over the stacks. "Now children always remember books are arranged alphabetically by the name of the author. If you know the title of a book but not the author, just ask Adrian or me. We'll be happy to show you how to find the author's name in the card catalog."

Em noticed Adrian looked nervous. She sidled up to him conspiratorially. "Can you get away for lunch, Addy? I wanted to tell you about my chair caning."

"Can't go to lunch today, sweetie. You're on your own. I've got desk duty." Adrian added, not without a touch of pride. "Next time?"

"Of course. It will give Sadie more time to gossip with me about you and your love life," said Em with a teasing smile. Then she noticed Adrian's reaction.

"Why Adrian, I do believe you're blushing."

"Oh shut up. Nils and I are just getting to know one another." Em raised her eyebrows. There really *was* someone in his life. "That's the guy you met at the leather shop, right? The reason you keep going back for 'adjustments' to the vest you bought there?"

Adrian immediately brightened. "Well, now that you mention it, we are spending more time together. He loves to cook for me and I love to consume his fabulous meals. And yes, I admit it. He is the sweetest man I have ever met. He's *real*, Em, honest. We spent last weekend together at his tiny apartment. Now that's a true test of any relationship." From Adrian's happy countenance, Em knew Adrian and Nils had easily passed the first test of spending a weekend together. "But for now, we'll just see how things develop. Now, shoo!"

Em became lost in thought over Adrian. She had intuited much. She knew it had been a long lonely time for Adrian before he met Nils just a short month ago. She had noticed the way his eyes lit up and his smile grew when they discussed his new 'friend'. Em made her way to the Rambler where she dropped off her latest load of books. With plenty of time to spare before picking Randy up, she window shopped on Elm Street. She stepped into a shop that had long intrigued her, the Sew What. The windows beckoned Em. Antique woven baskets were filled with beautiful globes of yarn in all types and colors. Knitting needles of many sizes filled a glass vase like a bouquet of flowers. Crochet hooks of varying widths and lengths were artfully arranged on a bolt of cloth. Em entered the shop to see a group of women sitting on a lumpy, well-worn sofa. They were happily knitting items which Em could only assume would someday become sweaters, socks or hats. Their happy conversation and laughter ended abruptly when Em entered the store.

"Welcome to our knitting circle. Did you bring your own yarn and needles or do you need to purchase supplies?" Em was momentarily timid. "Oh, no, knitting is something I haven't learned to do yet. But I can crochet, embroider and braid rugs. And cane chairs."

All eyes turned to Em with interest. The woman who Em surmised was the owner of the shop stood and reached out, grasping Em's hands with both of her own. "Well, knitter or not, I'm pleased to meet you. I'm Mary, owner of the Sew What. This is our weekly knitting circle. If you'd like to learn to knit, you're more than welcome to join us. If you crochet, you can certainly master knitting. You say you cane chairs?"

Em examined the tall woman. She was stunning with raven black hair pulled into a tight bun. Her black eyes were large, and devoid of makeup. Her high cheekbones were naturally bronzed, which complimented her full red lips. Mary looked as though she spent many hours in the sun. The exotic woman wore a long dress of layered pale-blue gauze. A large necklace reached almost to her waist. Em was fascinated by her unusual adornment which jingled musically when she walked. Em looked more closely and saw delicate strands filled with tiny bells, sea shells, ceramic buttons and glass beads. Mary's slim, elegant presence was one of the most exotically beautiful women Em had ever encountered.

One of the women on the couch asked the question all the women wanted answered. "You cane chairs?" Em stood up straight engulfed in her own pride. "Yes, yes I do. And I do all kinds of homespun skills. But not knitting, not yet, anyway."

"I am impressed," Mary began. "One usually doesn't find such a young woman able to cane chairs." The other women on the couch murmured their agreement. One woman, older and somewhat frumpy looking, asked her neighbor, "Maybe I could get that old corner chair finally repaired for Amy."

"Well, ask her. Why ask me?" came the response. All the women giggled.

"Okay, How long would it take?"

Em calculated in her mind. She hadn't yet finished her first two chairs for Mrs. Winthrop and had no idea how long a corner chair would take but she was sure it wouldn't be quick or easy. She hid her discomfort under feigned courage. "Oh, I'd have to see it first. And I am working on two chairs right now. I have to finish those first before I can take on any new jobs."

"Really, whose chairs are you caning, dear? Perhaps we know your customer," Mary asked, her eyebrows raised in curiosity.

"Mrs. Winthrop, over on Toby Hill Road. Helen Winthrop."

"Oh, my," the frumpy woman on the couch said. "Of course, we all know Helen. She's one of Charles Town's matriarchs. I'm sure if Helen is pleased, you'll have more orders than you'll know what to do with." Em blushed, imagining how much money she could make with more orders. "Oh, I do hope so. The chairs are coming along very nicely. But I need to find a supplier of cane. I'm afraid I won't be able to take any more orders until I resupply my materials."

Mary put her hand on Em's arm. "Well, young lady. That's something I can certainly help you with. I'll call some of my suppliers and find out where I can order cane. I'm sure it won't be a problem. I have a lengthy list of contacts for all manner of handwork projects." She graced Em with an enormous smile. "Oh, that would be wonderful, Mary. Thank you so much." She noticed some of the women on the couch had taken up their knitting again and were murmuring among themselves. Em took the hint.

"Well, I'll stop in next week. Helen's chairs should be completed by then. Oh, and here's my number. If you'd like to give me a call to let me know about the cane, I'd be grateful."

"Of course, dear. What did you say your name was?"

Emeline blushed. "Oh, well. I guess I didn't say. It's Emeline. Emeline Upswatch."

Mary's eyebrows raised in surprise as she observed Emeline. "Why, you must be Margret's new daughter-in-law. She doesn't get into town as much as she did when Clarissa was alive, but we all know her. Yes, do give me your number. I'll be happy to call when I find a cane distributor." Em thanked Mary, said goodbye to the women ensconced on the couch and made her way to the Inn and Out floating on a cloud of expectations. *This is the best news ever*, she thought. Not only might I get more caning jobs, but I may even have a place where I can pick up supplies locally.

It was 1:30 when the bells on the door of the Inn and Out cheerily announced Em's arrival. Sadie smiled broadly, spying Emeline as she made her way to a table with a customer's check. Em stood in the doorway, wondering which way to turn. Out the door or bother Sadie when she was in the middle of the lunch rush? She shuffled her feet, listening to the conversation, then moved to a small empty table to eavesdrop on customers. "Great chicken pot pie, as always, Sadie."

"Thanks, Barry. No leftovers for the wife, huh?"

"No way! When you gonna own this place, Sadie? You do all the cooking and work, anyway. Might as well make it official."

"Yeah, right. As soon as Mr. Inverness gives it to me!" They laughed together. "Well, keep your chin up and keep the place running like clockwork. Miracles do happen."

After the bells verified her last customer's departure, Sadie plopped a chef's salad in front of Em. "On the house, honey," she said with a smile, as she settled at the table with a steaming cup of coffee. Em thanked Sadie soundly and then dove into the salad. "You know Sadie, that customer was right. I don't know how you do everything. Getting here at five every morning can't be easy. You're amazing."

"Thankfully, we're only open for breakfast and lunch. It was a lot harder before the kids were in school all day. Now, the bus stops at our door and I'm usually home by 3:30 when the girls are getting home from school. My neighbors all keep their eye on my girls. It works out fine." Em decided to dip her toes a little deeper into Sadie's life.

"Do you ever miss not having a husband?"

Sadie sat for a moment, deep in thought and memories. "Not really. My ex, Ralph, is still around, so he's hard to miss since he's never really gone." Her laughter accompanied her words. "The reality is, I'm better off on my own. I honestly do still love Ralph, sorta like you'd love a distant brother. It's easier to live my life by myself with no one running interference. Ralph was never a big help when we were married. Too busy chasing other women. Although to give him credit, he did try. Or at least he tried after I caught him in yet another 'fling'. Eventually it became clear we weren't in love anymore. We parted by mutual agreement, amicably, as people say. He still comes by when I need a repair or I'm sick or just need a break from the girls. He sees them about once a week, picks them up from school, takes them for ice cream or Burger King in Ruthville. I'm content with my life. If I didn't have this place, I guess I wouldn't be as happy. Here, I have a family other than my kids. All the regulars who come in are more than friends. I've known some of my customers since we were in elementary school together." Em assessed Sadie, looking for any tell-tale signs of fatigue or sorrow and finding none. "You are one of the happiest women I've ever met, Sadie."

"Oh, I have my moods. I just don't show them here." Sadie stirred her coffee thoughtfully. She looked into Emeline's eyes before she continued their conversation toward deeper friendship. Sadie decided she had known Em long enough to feel confident before wading into the waters of intimacy. "What about you? What's your life like? Your caning business is picking up, I hear from Adrian. He said he got you two chairs to cane."

"I might just have another order. I stopped in at the Sew What and met all the ladies of the knitting circle. And I met Mary. She said she'd probably be able to find me a cane supplier. I'm hoping to get more jobs from my notice on the library bulletin board. Mrs. Winthrop's job is two kitchen chairs, just the seats that are small, no arms or back to cane." Em chewed her lip. How could she possibly do a rocker without Felicity's help?

"Mrs. Winthrop, huh? She's a good customer to have. You won't have to worry about getting paid, that's for sure."

"Yes, looked that way from her house." Em continued, opening up a small door into her life as she answered Sadie. "I'm happy, more so than when we first moved here. I've made some friends, you, for one. I loved meeting your girls when they came to pick you up a few weeks ago. How old are they? Eight and ten?"

"Right, exactly. Alison's ten and MaryAnne is eight. They're good girls. But they fight a lot. Drives me nuts." Em ignored the present and tiptoed into the past. "Were you happy when you found out you were pregnant? You and Ralph hadn't been married that long, had you?"

"No, but we both came from big families. Wanted to start our family as soon as we got married. Never regretted my girls for an instant, even though sometimes they make me crazy. And girls are so expensive. They always want a new dress or shoes, you name it." Em and Sadie laughed together in agreement.

Em had encouraged Sadie to step into the forest of Em's life and emotions, without realizing she had done so. "You ever think about having kids?" Sadie asked.

"Well sure, we think about it. Someday, not right now. We don't make that much money. Thank the goddesses for my chair-caning business, if it takes off. Randy's not the greatest car salesman."

"Well, sweetie, he's still pretty new at Bert's. The other guys there have been there forever. They're pretty entrenched in Charles Town and have gone to school with most of their customers. I don't imagine they like sharing sales with your Randy."

"Yeah. I guess." A tiny flame of resentment flared in Em's mind. *Would her husband ever be a success at anything, except the fantasies he wove which had nothing to do with practical matters? He was a legend in his own mind, that was certain.* She squashed her rebellious thoughts. *That simply is not true*, she admonished herself. *Randy was getting much better at sales and was tempering his blustering persona.*

Em changed the subject. "What was it like being pregnant?" The question surprised Sadie. Her eyes grew misty as she thought back through the years. "It was wonderful. I loved every bit of being pregnant once I started showing and got over morning sickness. I wasn't working so that made things easier. Believe it or not, Ralph was a great help through both my pregnancies. I was so tired the first and last couple of months. He'd cook for me, gave me foot and back rubs, even took full control of Alison when I was pregnant with MaryAnne. Ali was only two at the time. Some nights by the time he got home from work, Alison and I would both be in tears, hating one another over some small problem or infraction of rules. Ralph made life so much easier." Sadie smiled, her face brightening and opening up. Her big brown eyes sparkled as she remembered those days.

Em was struck with Sadie's appearance. When she had first met Sadie, Em had thought she was very plain. Her face had a flat look, with a large nose dominated by an incongruously wide mouth. Her eyes were her best feature. She wasn't slim, The Inn and Out's fare, all cooked by Sadie, had softened the edges of her body. But when she smiled, her face changed markedly. She became pretty, like a cherub content with her life. Her happiness was infectious and always lit up anyone in her sights. Em believed Sadie's warmth, maternal attitude and joy were why the diner was so popular and successful.

"Was it the other women that caused your split? Uh, if you don't mind my asking." Sadie was silent for a moment, absently picking up a salt shaker and checking to see if the top was screwed on tightly. "He liked other women more than me, that became obvious. I put up with it for a while since he always said it was a one-time thing, nothing important. Well, those one time 'things of no importance' added up to a lot of lonely, angry nights and days. I don't know. I guess I finally just gave up. As the girls grew older, we drifted apart. It wasn't all his fault. We just never seemed to have anything to talk about. Guess we fell out of love long ago. Then he got a job at the post office and started making good money. When he realized he had enough to get a place of his own and still help support us, it seemed best to part ways. We figured we were young enough to start new lives. Well, Ralph did. Got a new wife and started a second family. I got the same old life here at the Diner. But it suits me. Yes, definitely, I can say I'm happy."

When Sadie put the closed sign on the door after the last customer left, Em helped her friend wipe down the tables, refill the salt, pepper, sugar and ketchup containers before Sadie could admonish her not to. "You know you don't have to help me, but I sure do appreciate your help. Will get me home faster, way before the girls get off the bus."

"It's the least I can do with you always 'forgetting' to charge me for lunch."

"Silly girl. That's nothing. It's like you're in my kitchen, my home, and I've just invited you in for a meal and a chat." Em fought joyful tears as she hugged Sadie goodbye. She had a friend to add to her bookshelf of life. Just as her library was filling up, so was her heart.

By the time Em arrived at Bert's to pick up Randy, it was almost 4:40. Her groceries fit snugly in the cooler in the back of the Rambler. She sat nestled next to her latest pile of library books. She felt content, filled to the brim. A full trunk of groceries, a fresh stack of books, possibilities on the horizon and a happy husband. What more could one ask for in life?

Chapter 11

Her mood changed along with the weather. Em felt saddened for unknown reasons between the seasons. Her melancholy state of mind matched the falling leaves. Finally, Felicity reappeared. The dust in Em's yard made mischief, chasing the older woman's faded, blue cotton pants as she walked up the drive. Added to her ensemble was a large, faded red flannel shirt. Watching her slow advance Emeline came alive. She had a friend *and* a teacher. She had a mentor who would carry her through the swamp of old dreams, lives and thoughts with new endeavors and adventures. Felicity was the only unpredictable anomaly in her life. She never knew when her dearest friend would appear like a dream. She rejoiced in Felice's growing friendship, care and tenderness. Felicity was a treasure, a happy surprise made more precious by the rarity of her visits.

As she ran into the yard to greet the older woman Em noticed the expression on her face. Felice was deep in thought. She carried a walking stick and walked more slowly than Em had noticed in the past. With a start, Em realized how old Felicity must be. Although Felicity had never confided her age, Em imagined her to be at least 75. Em caught Felicity's hands in her own. "Let me help you up the porch steps. Let's rest a bit." Em smiled from her eyes and heart. "I've missed you so, as I always do."

Felice returned her smile tenderly. "Darlin', I've missed you, too. These old bones just move more slowly but I've never stopped thinking of another warm visit with you. And as I've told you, I only come when I'm needed. I sensed my dear young friend was feeling the onset of winter with these cold winds and falling leaves. This time of year always saddens me."

Em shook her head in agreement. Felice spoke after a moment, choosing her words carefully. "This is my time of melancholy, deah. It is the time of departures." Em wondered what the older woman meant, but decided it was best to ignore Felice's comment for the time being. She brightened and switched gears.

"Let me tell you what I've been doing." At that moment, Em clearly heard her mama's voice, teasing her dad. "It's all about me, remember?" The thought did not deter Em from the onrush of words describing her life. Em chuckled, well, right now it is all about me, Mama, she told the voice in her head as she continued to chatter at Felice.

"I got a chair-caning job! From a Mrs. Helen Winthrop, who lives in Charles Town in a beautiful old house on Toby Hill. It's two chairs. Luckily, they're proving to be pretty easy to do."

"Oh, dear Emmy. I'm so happy for you. See, I told you you'd be a success. How much did you charge?"

"Seventy-two dollars, according to the number of holes, plus materials, just like you said." Felice's warm smile as she reached out for Em's hand was all the confidence Em needed, along with Felice's words, "I know you'll be a master chair-caner before you know it, my deah."

"Well, I sure hope you're right. I also went into the *Sew What* and met the lady who owns it, Mary. She said she would be able to order caning supplies for me."

"Well, half the battle's won, then. It's all up to you now," Felice replied warmly.

Em continued excitedly, "I've been learning so much. Not just through reading. I've been exploring all over the neighborhood. You can't imagine all the birds I've discovered. And the wildlife! I saw a red fox one morning when I was sitting under a tree. It was so strange. We just looked at one another, like he was trying to figure out why I was in his fox territory. Then he ran off. And I picked apples and made a pie, the first one all on my own. There are so many gardens in the neighborhood. Randy promised we'll plant a garden in the spring. He still thinks I'm crazy because I talk to myself all the time. I tell him I just like my own company." Em took a breath and smiled, then laughed at herself.

"You are a magpie, my deah. Yet it is so heartening to hear of your full life. You are blossoming. As for talking to yourself, we all do that. Perhaps your mama is listening. Departed souls are never really gone. Still beloved, they linger. They remain with cherished friends, family and places. Their shadows fall on walls, then flee from sight of the living. They appear at unexpected moments. Their souls refuse to depart. They capture joy from memories. They keep an eye on their loved ones. We go about our days, oblivious to their presence."

"Wow, I never thought of that, in just that way. Maybe Mama is listening. You sound just like her." Em grew silent, poring over this new germ of thought.

Felicity turned toward the shed. "You've done so much with little Cabin #25 and that old shed."

"You wouldn't believe how many years' worth of dirt, leaves and mouse droppings I cleaned out. Even a dead bird." Em thought for a moment and then braved her question, despite Felice's intense privacy. "Felicity, have you visited here before?"

"I told you I've known all of these cabins forever. Yes, I did visit here, often. Years ago." She reached out and tenderly touched Em's fingertips. Em noticed how cold Felicity's hand felt. "I remember everything about these parts, these cabins. I'm a good observer. Every person must be an observer of life. Of everything around you. It is only when you observe the outer world closely that you grow in your inner world. That certainly applies to chair caning. If you observe each area carefully before taking your next step, you won't make any mistakes."

"Well, that's certainly true. I've never been known for my patience. Caning is teaching me that." Suddenly Em realized Felicity's faithful companion was missing. "Felice, where's Zuma?"

"Oh, she's tired, just like her mama. She was resting so happily in a patch of sunshine, I let her be." Em wondered if her beloved companion had run off or gotten hurt and Felicity just didn't want to confide in her. She was more emboldened with her next question. "You're always full of secrets, Felice. I wonder if you'll ever invite me to your home."

"Someday, darlin', certainly. That reminds me. I have a favor to ask. Would you mind providing me with a tour of your little home? I'd love to see all you've done with the old place since my first visit." Em was thrilled, not only with the hope of visiting Felicity's home in the future, but of her interest in Em's decorating.

"Well, thank goodness I made the bed and did the breakfast dishes," Em said, laughing as together they walked through the kitchen door. Em stayed beside Felicity as she entered the room, afraid her frail friend would falter, as she had left her walking stick on the porch.

Felicity traveled slowly through each room as Em watched and listed all her accomplishments. "Look at my plants. They love the light on top of that old stove. You were right about putting them there." Her Boston Fern had been rejuvenated, but still was not completely over Scarlet's latest feast on its fronds "Let me show you what we've done with the little room." Em led the way down the hallway but noted that Felice hesitated in following her into the room. She stood on the threshold and seemed uneasy about entering. When she did, she appeared visibly shocked. She stood silent and still in the center of the room, examining every detail. She was drawn to the window, parting the lace curtains and gazing for a long moment through the old wavy glass at the view beyond. She seemed transfixed with the curtains on the windows. Tentatively, she touched the lace. "Oh, my heavens. This beautiful antique lace, Emeline. Where ever did you find it?"

"It was in an old trunk I discovered when I cleaned out the shed. It was there with a lot of other old weird stuff. An old afghan like my mama used to crochet, in squares. An old striped dress, with a matching apron. And a little cap. It still had some reddish curly hair attached to the inside. Very strange. Guess everything's been there forever." Em decided not to confide about all she had found in the trunk, remembering her feeling of trespassing.

As though speaking to herself Felice stood in front of the window, gently caressing the lace with her fingertips. She murmured quietly to herself. "Yes. Of course. You found all that in an old trunk, in the shed."

"What did you say?" Em asked, with some concern. Felice returned to the present and moved from the window. "Oh, nothing darlin'. Just an old lady's musings. What a beautiful window dressing you've created with the old lace. I never would have imagined. You're right to have used lace, which will allow the sunlight to shine through. Light comes brightly through this window every morning from daybreak till noon. It's a great window for African violets. The north windows are better for orchids. How lovely you've made this room. You've painted the walls a moonbeam shade, very soothing. The floor has been waxed—did you use beeswax? It seems to glow. That's what my old friends always used. Now, you need to furnish the room for your guests who I'm sure would love to visit."

Em was puzzled that Felice knew the room and light so well, thinking perhaps Felice's own cabin was nearby, and held the same light each day as Em's did.

She returned to Felice's comment. "I can't imagine who would visit. All my friends live here. We were thinking, well, maybe a baby's room." Felicity

196

brightened, seeming to crackle with electricity. "Oh, my deah, are you expecting?"

"Oh, no, no. Just a thought. We've been talking. We've been married almost three years now. But we've got plenty of time. Although Margret is dying for a grandchild. She always says, "my large hips and breasts mean I have the perfect body for childbearing." Felicity laughed at Em's high-pitched imitation of what she could only assume was Margret's voice. "I don't know. I think I could be a good mom," Em continued. "For now, this will be my workroom for caning chairs in the winter when the weather turns too cold to work outside. That is if my chair caning business is a success."

"Oh, it will be, love. I have no doubt. And one can always cane when pregnant. And embroider. You have many saleable talents."

"For the first time, thanks to you, Felice, I'm beginning to believe that."

Felicity continued, "You are a talented homemaker, Emmy. I believe I told you that the first time I toured your little cabin. I'm always interested to see how each woman pretties up their home. While these cabins are virtually identical, each owner changes the inside to their own tastes in decorating and life. Let's get on with the tour."

Em ran down the hallway, through the living room and into the next room, her favorite, the library. Felice stood for long moments in admiration standing in the open French doors before stepping into the room. She looked through the old wavy glass at the view of the fields beyond full of stirring shadows from the willow trees. Felice seemed lost in thought again, as though she had disappeared into another landscape. Em watched her friend intently. The light from the window haloed her steel-gray curls. She slowly sat down on the soft, pillowed window seat. Em could hold her curiosity in check no longer. "Felicity, you seem to know this cabin so well."

"Oh, my deah, all these old cabins were built exactly alike. But, yes," said Felicity, hesitating as though making a decision, then continuing. "Yes, sweet Emmy. I have been here before. Many years ago, a very dear friend of mine lived here."

"Who?"

"Oh, it was so long ago, and you wouldn't know her name." Felicity rose, clearly changing the subject. She gently touched Em's treasured collection of books. "Goodness gracious! How your library has grown." Em took great pride in her collection. All the authors were arranged alphabetically and she kept the shelves dusted regularly. Felice read the author's names. "Richard Brautigan, Hemingway, Zora Neale Hurston, D.H. Lawrence, Marjorie Kinnan Rawlings, Steinbeck, Steinem. So many books. My deah, you have been busy following up on my literary suggestions. What's this title? *Revelations, Diaries of Women*? I don't think I know that book."

"Oh, I love *Revelations.* It's amazing, about all the wonderful writers who kept diaries and even authored books. Yet they were all so afraid they were worthless, had no talent, nothing of value to say. Every one of them became important authors, yet they doubted their ability to write. Even George Sand."

Felicity looked at Em for a long moment, her gray eyes capturing Em's blue ones. "Darlin', that's you, too. You have no idea of who you've grown into. You've changed from a needy child into a self-confident, assured young woman." Em blushed deeply. "Well, thank you, Felice. You set me on the right path. Books have helped tremendously. I've found new worlds, new words and ideas. You've probably helped me explore more than anyone I've ever known. Except Mama. You've opened new vistas for me. You helped me to rely on myself, to become more independent. Especially by teaching me to cane chairs."

Felicity chuckled, with her deep throaty laugh Em loved so dearly. "Yes, you have certainly learned every lesson well. You don't need the advice of this old lady anymore."

"Oh, Felice, don't say that. I'll always need you and your friendship. Whether you visit me or not." Silence graced the room as the two friends thought over their words. Finally, Em realized it was growing late and she could see Felicity was fading. The older woman roused herself. "Well, let's finish our tour of the kitchen. I long to explore your pantry."

In the kitchen, Felicity carefully examined everything on the shelves, neatly stacked and organized. "Look at all your jam!" The lowering sun lit up the jars on the shelves in colors like jewels—ruby, amethyst and gold.

"Well, jam is so easy to make." Em admitted. "Basically all you do is boil it with sugar. Then I just melt the paraffin to seal the jars."

"Lovely, and delicious, I'm sure. Strawberry, Wild Blackberry, Apple, you *have* been busy." Felicity lingered over each blue glass jar of peas, corn, green beans, next to store-bought cans of veggie mix, potatoes and soups. On the shelf above the jams and canned goods, Em had arranged her spices, also in alphabetical order. "I'd say you've learned your recipes from Miss Magnolia's cookbook very well," Felice remarked.

"Yes. That book is just chock full of so many great recipes and household tips. I swear, it turned me into a regular Miss Magnolia myself!"

"Hmmm, yes, I'd say so…" Felicity replied absent-mindedly as her eyes rose to the highest, empty shelf in the pantry. Her gaze lingered. Finally, she reached up, running her fingers over the vacant shelf.

"I can't reach that shelf so I never use it. Sorry about the dust. I'm not the best housekeeper when it comes to dusting. But you're tall enough to reach up there. I bet you'd have that shelf filled in a heartbeat!"

"Oh, my deah, it's fuller than you can imagine." *Her friend was certainly weird today*, Em thought. She was much more open than in the past which thrilled Em. Perhaps she was finally coming to trust Emeline with her secrets. She wondered if she dared to breach the protected borders of Felice's hidden life. She decided she had nothing to lose.

"Felice, can I ask you something? How long ago was it that you visited here last?" Felice locked Em's eyes with her own, holding her in a hypnotic gaze. She seemed to be making a decision. Em was sure she was trying to decide if she deserved Felicity's confidence. Finally, the older woman replied.

"My deah Emmy, the last time I was here was years ago. I spent countless hours within these walls. This cabin holds my heart. It is my touchstone to the past, the pathway to so many memories. My dearest friend lived here. She's long gone. As I must also be. Zuma will be wanting her supper."

"Can I walk you home? I know you're tired."

"No, darlin'. I prefer my own quiet company and I've kept you too long." Felicity took one last long look at the pantry and the kitchen, murmuring, "How these old walls could talk." She touched Em's cheek tenderly, a smile gently gracing her pale lips. "Darlin', I've so enjoyed our friendship."

Em was startled by the finality Felice's words seemed to convey. "But we'll always be friends. I could visit you. I can see walking is difficult for you. I could even help you out in your home. When will you visit again?"

"Oh, how the chill does get into my old bones. I don't travel much after all the leaves have fallen. You know what they say, 'No birds, no blossoms, no leaves, November!' That saddest of months is only a few weeks away. I'll be staying close to home then, after the end of the month on All Hallows Eve."

"Are you sure I can't help you? Walk you at least part way home?" Em was considerably nervous, almost to the point of fear for her old friend. Felice seemed so fragile, so weak and wavering, more than she had ever been previously. She had never spoken to Em with such finality. Em felt a chill enter her heart, her soul. She simply could not lose Felice. Who took care of her friend during the long winter months? Who brought her groceries and cleaned her home? She had never made any mention of a husband, or children.

"No, sweet Emmy. You have your home and your life and your responsibilities, and I have mine. I've been by myself for many years and have come to enjoy my own company best when no one else is about." She hesitated a moment longer, and much to her surprise, embraced Em in a long hug. Her arms were skeletal and cold. Em lay her head gently on Felicity's shoulder. Felice's chin rested on Em's golden curls. "Sweet Emmy, I'll always be around. I promise you I'll see you in the spring when the weather warms up again. Remember, that's when we first met." She pulled away and looked deeply into Emeline's eyes. "We have been good for one another. You've given me as much as I could ever have given you."

With that, Felicity turned and made her way across the kitchen and out the door. Em followed, picked up Felice's walking stick and helped her down the porch steps. She rested a moment and then walked down the drive. Within moments, she had disappeared, the late afternoon sun following her path, making shadows of her progress. The leaves rose in a cloud, rustling around her, gracing her slow passage down the lane. Em's eyes filled with tears. She found it hard to believe she wouldn't see her closest friend until spring. She knew she'd miss Felice even more, now that her friend had finally opened up to her and shared shreds of her past life. Em remembered her first conversation with Felice when her friend had said, "Oh, my deah, you have a lot to learn and I have a lot to teach." It was still true. Em had learned so much, but she didn't want these life's lessons from Felicity to end. Slowly, she closed the kitchen door against the chill as she wiped her tears away. "Time to start dinner," she said, laughing to herself. "Hope you're listening, Mama, like Felicity says."

Over dinner, Em related the day's events and conversations to Randy. He listened intently. In between bites of Em's Navy-Bean soup and cornbread, he asked questions which Em was happy to answer. "Felice keeps her life very close to her chest. She didn't really tell me much. Only that she had a dear friend who used to live in this cabin."

"How old do you think she is, anyway?"

"I'd say she's at least 75, maybe in her 80s. She's so frail. I worry something will happen. I don't know if anyone looks in on her. She has no family or kids that she's ever talked about. Sounded like she only had one friend who lived here, and who died. She didn't even tell me her friend's name."

After washing up the dishes with Randy, Em brought up the subject of Felicity again. "I swear, she knew every nook and cranny of this cabin. You know what's weird, she seemed so interested in the top shelf of the pantry. There's nothing up there besides dust bunnies. Would you mind dusting that top shelf for me? I was so embarrassed when she ran her hand over the shelf and came back with a handful of crud!"

"Oh, sweetheart, of course, that's easy. You know I can help with the housework. I'd do anything for you, even dust!" Em rewarded Randy with a kiss. She was so happy that they were getting along. Their life had certainly become fuller since he had first carried her over the threshold of Cabin #25. "I'll get the step stool."

Em watched as Randy took a dust rag and dragged it across the shelf and into the furthest recesses in the back. "Hey, there's something here. Way at the back. Feels like a little book. I can just reach it." With a stretch and a grunt, he grabbed the small diary-like book and handed it to Em.

"Oh, what a pretty little book. It's all leather, black with red binding and trim. It looks like a diary." Randy watched intently as Em wiped away the dust and opened the little book.

"Oh, my God," she breathed.

"What's it say? What is it?"

"It says, in the prettiest old-fashioned writing, *The Book of Memories: The Story of a Friendship*."

Randy and Em sat down at their kitchen table and slowly turned the pages in the book, filled with the same neat handwriting. They looked at one another with surprise. Em abruptly closed the book, and then asked Randy, "What do you think, is it okay to read it? Can't imagine how long it's been here. It must have been left by the owner of the cabin. Felicity said she's long gone."

"I don't see the harm in it. Especially if she's no longer alive," offered Randy as he left the room to put the step stool away. "I'm beat, think I'll turn in early." Randy called to Em.

"I'll stay up awhile," she replied to her husband as she heard him rustling around in the bathroom, getting ready for bed.

Em began to read the little book. It was hours later, with Randy long snoring in bed that Em tenderly closed its pages. The diary provided more questions than answers. Em had no idea how she would unravel the tale within.

Chapter 12
The Book of Memories:
The Story of a Friendship

The words on the inside front cover were written in blue ink, perhaps with a fountain pen? Em wondered. The penmanship was old-school, clear and straightforward cursive, not the handwriting world of 1979, that was for sure.

The Book of Memories: A Friendship, Dani and Julia

Immediately Em was captivated. The words flowing across the pages enticed her. She could not put the little book down until she had read the last page.

* * *

"To Dani, from my heart, Julia."

I'll never forget the first time we met. You just 'peared in my yard as I was washing up the breakfast dishes. I spied you from my winder and watched as you walked over to my work shed, as if you owned the place. You opened the door, stepped inside and lookt around for a spell before I caught up with you. Now, I'm just a country gal from West Virginny and don't cotton to nobody, man, woman, dog nor cat, just walkin' inta my yard. Who is this gal and why is she in my shed? I thought to myself. I quickly figgered it out when you started yakking at me.

You stuck your hand out for me to shake in a manly manner. "I'm Danielle. I hate my name so never call me anything but Dani."

I was dumbstruck. The nerve of this lady! Who did she think she was? Your manner was not country-friendly. No 'How Do' or 'Hey Nayber'. What you said next struck me upside the head.

You looked inside the shed again and said, "This will do."

"Do what?" I asked.

I couldn't believe your next words. The gall of you, woman! Why, if I'da had a mind to I coulda' beat you up like a rented mule for trespassin'. But that ain't my way, though you did bristle me with your next words.

"This will serve as my new business of which I will offer you an opportunity. Rent this shed to me, let me do whatever I want with it and I'll pay you $50 a month. Your caning and wicker repair shop will complement my antiques."

I stood like a young'un with my mouth open. You started tapping your foot. Well, I sure din't have any money cept for my savins' from nursing and what little I made with caning and wicker fixin'. Praise the Lord for that! That fifty dollars a month would be a windfall. Then the light came on. *This* lady, if you could call her that, was the one everyone hed gossiped about for years. I'd heard the stories a few times when I shopped in Charles Town. "Crazy," everyone said. But why wouldn't she be, married to that drunk. You *were* famous, in your own way. Here you were in my shed tellin' *me* I was the lucky one to be offered such a great deal, as if I ever asked anyone for a thing. I was happy in the holler and din't need you, or any other body. In a while, I found out you were right. You made me laugh, Dani, then and even now, through my broken heart and swamped with tears.

The next time you walked into my yard, you laid out your plans for your new antique bizness. I had to figger that if our futures were to be commingled we could make a messa money together. My wicker repair and caning business had been goin' slow as molasses. Hell, I thought, what's to lose? And it came to be just as I'd hoped. My caning and wicker bizness grew like a house afire next to your antique business.

Remember that crazy story? You told me you'd bought all that old 'stuff' you din't know what to do with, except fix it all up and sell it. But you din't have a place to sell, that's where I came in. Told some tale of how you'd bought it all from that old lady who lived over that broken-down, rotten place on the outskirts of Charles Town. Somehow, you saw it, the money behind all that old crap. 'Antiques', you called it, 'glass and porcelain, smalls and fancies'. You spent your last $500 on what you called *antiques* but I called 'ready for the dump'. Just looked like a bunch of old dirty broken down stuff. I'll admit the porcelain and glass were perty. "*Fostoria*, Julia, not glass." You corrected me. You always corrected me, taught me the difference between 'West Virginny talk' and 'Virginia *refined* language'. And you were always right. I didn't know Fostoria from milk glass or Anchor canning jars. I never would have dreamed that this joining together of our lives would become such a fruitful venture. But it did. I knew about wicker repair and caning but nothing about the old stuff you sold. You moved in that whole buncha crap quick as a fox. I watched you as you brought everything over. Furniture, boxes and crates of porcelain, china, glass, crystal, *vintage* clothes and jewelry. To me, them clothes just looked like something for the dust bin. And boxes and boxes of books. Who needs so many books? Couldna read 'em all in a lifetime.

Where the hell are you going to put all this stuff? I asked. You had an answer for anything and everything. "Not a problem. Leave it to me. Your supplies don't take up much space and you can always do wicker repairs and cane in the yard or in the house." You looked around *my* shed as though I tweren't even there, telling *me* that *I* could move out. Your smartass ways took my breath away. As usual, you were right. You made my shed into a shop that was the pertiest antiques bizness I'd ever seen. You profited over the years in money made and a life brought back from the dead. You renewed not only your old broken down furniture, Dani, you gave me new life, just like turning old broken down things into pricey antiques.

You could work like a demon, woman, truth be told. I remember how you cleaned out that shed from top to bottom. Put in a new heart pine floor after you'd swiped the wood from somewhere, I was sure, but you wouldn't say. Then you hired those two young'uns, just barely teen boys, to put in the floor on *credit*, no less! And they did it without complaining. After all, they were good ole boys who'd lived in the holler and knew how to build. You had this charm that made people want to do anything for you. We all did, glowing from any praise and love from yourn. You did pay those two kids all the money owed, plus a big tip. But that was months later after we got going with the shed shop, as I called it. Yup. You were ornery, but always fair and honest. I'll give you that.

You hung strips on the ceilin I'd sooner use for a chicken coop. Then you strung little lights and plastic flowers all over the ceilin. She's crazy, I thought, planting a garden in the rafters. But you tweren't crazy. You made that old shed perty as wildflowers in full bloom. Then you painted all the walls hemlock green.

"Sets off the wicker and antiques," you said. By God, it did. Then you tackled the winders. Where you got that old beveled glass door I never knew and thought it best not to ask. Turning that door sideways like a long winder was a stroke of pure smartness. It let so much light into the dark of the shed, a sight for sore eyes. Like magic you turned my old work shed into a shop for selling your antiques and my wicker.

You made up the name, Antique and Wicker Queens. How I laughed over that, which annoyed you. For gawds sake, woman, I told you, 'twas jest a shed shop. I'm no queen and I don't think you are neither. You gave me that queenly look and said, *You can be whatever you make up your mind to be. And we will be the queens of antiques and wicker.* I have to admit it. Once again, you were right.

And glory be, that's how we began. Never dreamed how much more than $50 a month I'd gain through our friendship, which proved to be more love and fun than I ever could have dreamed. Dani, that was the beginning of the deepest, best friendship of my life. It was a way out of the evil kingdom of my loneliness, going over the *what ifs* in my life for so many years. I felt all alone, no one in my neck a' the woods for years to set a spell with. I lived with nothing but my own thoughts. *What if I'd married? Had children? Why did I turn Austin down?* He was a fine man. But then I'd moved here to where the nursin money was better and I just never left. Aunt Tildy leavin me this cabin sealed the deal. Austin never came to Ginia, so here I am, a lonely old maid. *Now what's in this here world for me in the time I got left?* On and on I'd ask myself the same questions which had no answers. But you wiped away every *what-if* and replaced it with what *is.*

And what a grand happy life it became, with the dearest friend who filled me up with smartness, lots mor'n my country learning. Not that I was a dummy, mind you. I had a nursing education and got my certificate to be a full-fledged licensed nurse way back in the 40s. You filled me with wit, laughter, and our loving friendship. Even taught me to talk better and to read books. I tweren't uneducated. I was a nurse, after all. And a good nurse, not just the kind that cleans up bedpans.

Oh, I still groused about the name, the Queens. I thought it was so biggity, but you'd have none a that. You said, "That's what we are, queens of our shop." You did the selling. I did the wicker repairs and all the chair caning just like always. People came to buy antiques and finally my wicker and caning business had plenty of folks likin' what I did. I never could have had so many customers on my own.

Remember the night of our opening party? That was the first time I really learned the queenliness of who you were. You were a sight to see. I just stood back, 'mazed, watched you work your spell on all the uppity folks you invited. None a' them had probably ever been in the holler. They never woulda' ventured here, havin' their big shot lives down in Charles Town.

You told me you knew a lot a folks who loved what a great chef you were. All those years you shared recipes they felt they knew you. Remember? That was another one of your businesses, catering, you called it. I woulda just called it having pie suppers. You gave that up. You said it was too much work trying to please others and you were tired of cooking, anyway. That's when you bought all that old crap, your new business venture, to my shed.

Everyone wanted to see for themselves what the crazy lady was up to now. On our opening night, they swamped us. The lights were all lit up on the ceiling. There were so many candles I worried that you'd burn the place down. My jasmine was blooming, smelled so sweet and strong you could almost taste it. The magnolia was in bloom, too. It was as though the world dressed up and put on fancy French perfume for our opening night.

The wine flowed like a fountain, after you talked the liquor man into giving you a great deal. Tasted like champagne, the way you served it in your Fostoria flutes. It was the first night I seen you glowin' so brightly, like a comet in the sky, with such brightness that I spied the other Dani. Oh, I sniffed around, listened to all the talk 'bout you. Those biggity folk said, "You were elegant, lovely, smart, funny." And you were, talkin in that beautiful old Virginia drawl of yours. Laughter was unending as you made one sly statement after another hilarious with your *double-ontondays* as you called your jokes. Yup. Sly as a fox, circling the chicken coop, which was really what my old shed shop once was. The old biddies pretended to be shocked but their old fart hubbies sure loved your talk and jokin, your great big ole smile, your jesting ways, the way you touched hands and patted shoulders. I remember looking at you 'stounded the way you charmed and laughed your way into the hearts of everyone there, future customers all. To my surprise I figgered out this cranky, demanding Virginia lady was a party girl who sparkled like the champagne she was servin. You floated like a butterfly in that perty spider web dress. You said you'd bought it in the '40s in Paris. I knew it came from a thrift shop. All those party-goers came back to buy antiques, jewelry, vintage dresses and fancies. They'd buy my wicker and then they'd order repairs. You could sell anything. If someone came into the Queens, I knew they'd leave with something. You could sell ice to Eskimos.

I do believe our opening night was the night Frank fell in love with you. He adored you and I know how much you loved him. Like an explosion, a star falling, a bright, brilliant lightning-quick romance. Before I knew it, you and he were bedding down in that old antique bed you'd had delivered to your otherwise empty old broken-down cabin. I was glad Frank had a place in Charles Town you eventually moved into. I was always scared for you in that rickety cabin of yours alone in the holler.

How you and Frank fought! Like cats and dogs! Two strong heads crashing into one another, like rams. Remember that sparkling purple ring he gave you? Amethyst you said it was. A few weeks later you'd had another one of your big rows. One of our best customers came in. She admired that ring. Who wouldn't, it was a beauty. She asked about it and you floored me with your answer. Right then and there you said, "Oh, this? Want it? I'll give you a great price." And you did. Took it right off your finger and sold it. I swear Frank coulda killed you, right then and there when he noticed it tweren't on your finger. You told him, cool as a cucumber, "I sold it." Frank stormed out of your life, I thought for good. But he couldn't live without you. He came back and I tactfully left the shop and went into my cabin. Course, you made up. He was never one to hold a grudge. You were a tough row to hoe, I know that for a fact. Yet the two of you laughed, always, even after that spell about the amethyst ring.

Dani, broke my heart 'bout as much as yours when skin cancer took Frank in less than a year. You kept noticing the big dark patches on his arm. Looked like melanoma to me. Being a nurse, 'a course, I knew how serious it could be. Frank just ignored it for heaven knows how long. Finally, you marched him off to a doctor. By then, it was too late. "Would it have made a difference if we'd come in sooner?" You had asked. "No. Not really," the oncologist said. Six months later he was gone.

You grieved. You were broken, although you'd never admit it. You tried your best not to let me see your hurt. But I knew. You laughed less, talked almost not at all. Your wit, your glow and shine was darkened, covered up in heartbreak. The Antique and Wicker Queens is what kept you going.

You slowly revealed more about your past as we spent those long hours together in the Queens. You told me you certainly didn't grieve when that idiot of a husband finally wandered off drunk in front of a train, passed out on the tracks in the middle of the night. "Didn't cry over him when he cleaned me out and didn't cry over him when he died." I was proud of your strength. All the years you suffered his drunkenness. Everybody in the holler knew of his drinking and messing around. He was famous for all the wrong reasons, like a weasel who moves so sneakily in the night, comes in and ya dint know he was there until mornin you find all your chickens in the coop had their heads bitten off.

I finally figgered out why you had bought all that old furniture. It was because Artie had sold everything you owned for booze. You told me that story without a tear. "Came home one day and my house was empty. He was sitting on a lawn chair in what had been our living room, passed out. All our furniture, even our bed, was gone. I'd be damned if I'd spend another night in that house or put another stick of furniture in there. I slept on an old pile of blankets that night. I wouldn't spend another cent of my life savings for my comfort, or his."

Course, you had nowhere to go. You had to stay in that rickety old empty cabin. You swore you wouldna put anything of value in that house while he was alive. And you dint. I don't know how you survived.

Dear Dani, I was blessed with your strength, like a church meeting with a good preacher. You shared so much with me. Your heartfelt memories and thoughts which you gifted to me, slowly at first, then with more trust. You gave me so much more than I asked for. You had more stories than a book to tell and you told them well. You didn't confide in me like some floozy, spewing her tales. Over long spells spent in the shop together, me working on wicker or caning chairs, you selling, slowly you'd open up. I discovered that your hard exterior was a protective shell. You were hiding the most tender and wounded of hearts. You softened, letting in one tiny shred of a secret, then more and more over the years. Course, first-off you were never one for telling rumors. You have too much integrity for easy, casual secret tellin. Eventually, our friendship deepened with our secret past lives shared. Our lives became completely entwined. Our friendship was like a hedge of wild roses that hid prickly thorns under their colorful beauty and sweet scent. The Antique and Wicker Queens was your shop, completely. You managed it like a general. Anyone who gave you a hard time you controlled with your 'grace and intelligence', you called it. You'd just stand tall and blast them with your brilliant smile. You being taller than most, Dani, if they became 'parsimonious', you'd stare them down and say, 'Do you not recognize the value, the craftsmanship, the loveliness of this piece?' Yet you never talked down to a customer. You always spoke with such grace, kindness and wit that no one ever realized an argument had been fought and won by you, not them.

Our Queens shop, as we started calling it, jokingly, then for real, was more of a success than I ever could have imagined. You were something! From knowing not a thing about antiques when you bought all that old lady's stuff you became the most gifted and well-known antique dealer, first in Virginny, then across the country. You sold the wicker piano stand I repaired to Gloria Vanderbilt! You were written up in books. You told me one time you went into New York to search for bargains and research the big, smarty-ass antique dealers. One antique dealer recognized your name. You said the guy practically fell over himself, acting the fool like a lovesick courtin' kid over you, couldna believe "The Antique Queen" was actually in *his* shop.

It was you who made us so well-off and well-known. Well, I might have been able to repair wicker and cane chairs, but I sure couldn't sell worth a damn. When someone would *overpraise* our little shop or my repairs, you'd brush off the *kudos*. "Just what we learned to do," you'd say. But you had the eye and you always found bargains. With our reputation, you could put a high price on something you paid a pittance for and you'd get your price, after you made that old antique look like new or like it should have been in a museum. Sometimes I'd laugh and tell you, "You entrap people, like a spider with a fly." You took offense to that. You glared at me and said, "They always leave happy, though, don't they?" You chuckled at me then, with that knowing look in your eyes. Guess you entrapped me too.

Me, I admit it, have to say, I was good, even the best at wicker repairs and caning. It was borned of my patience, bred into me by my mama, I guess I'd have to say. I would look at each curlicue of an old piece of wicker. I'd examine it, walk around it, touch it, and finally start working. I learned to take down the right size of coil. I'd work and work until I replaced the exact replica of that curlicue. Then I'd take my tiny hammer and nails and put it back together. No one would ever dream it had been replaced, it was so perfect. And chair caning! Good heavens, I was good at that before I took up wicker. How my fingers flew. Once I caned a Lincoln rocker in two days. Don't know how I did it. But you had told a customer it wouldn't be a problem for your wicker expert to complete. Easy for *you* to say. But the client paid me double, so I couldn't complain.

The only times you would get starched with me was when I'd be studying a piece and figuring out how to fix it. "Oh, for Christ's sake, Julia, just get on with the job, why don't you?"

It was one of the few times you got my back up. "That's exactly what I'm doing," I'd said. "I don't tell you how to sell antiques so don't tell me how to repair wicker and cane chairs." You laughed in my face. I coulda smacked you. "Dear Julia, you're finally showing some fire. You're exactly right. I won't chastise you again."

Over time I realized the secret of your success in selling. You din't just sell antiques and wicker, you also *counseled* people. Women, especially, loved to come in and talk. You listened to them more than probably any other body in their life had. You gave them heart and fixes to their problems, just like you did for your antiques and me.

One day you confided in me after a particularly hard 'session' with one of your crazy lady *clients*. "Julia, you're the only sane friend I have. Everyone who comes in here is cracked. I collect the crazy ones. You know why? Because they're receptive. They listen, like you do, though you're not crazy. But they have their own wisdom." How you made me laugh! One day you told me I was the youngest friend you had, even though I was older than you. *You're the only one who doesn't have dementia or isn't crazy*, you said, with that sly smile you had, your *smirk*, you called it!

Remember the Colonel? That old gentleman who stopped by all the time? I think he thought he was courting you. He always wanted your full, undivided attention. You called him a *misogynist*. Whatever he was, it was clear he was smitten. He'd ooze charm, but he was jealous and prideful, like he owned you. You ignored all that. No doubt he saw himself as a worthy suitor for lucky you. One day he said in a fit of arrogance and anger that you weren't taking him seriously. He got all hot under the collar when you gave all your attention to one of the crazy ladies who had stopped by, instead of to him. After she left, the Colonel acted like the little Napoleon he was. "Why do you always have so many crazy people who stop by here all the time?"

Without missing a beat, you said in that elegant Virginia drawl of yours, staring right into the Colonel's eyes and giving him your sly smile, "Well, my dear. Look around you. You're here, aren't you?" I near 'bout choked trying not to laugh.

Slowly, ever so slowly, you learned to trust me more, tell me more. One day you twere sanding down an old wash stand, getting it ready to stain. I was working on caning that old wheel chair, remember that? The lady said she was going to put a big flower basket in the seat. So why cane it? I asked her. "Because flowers look so pretty up against a woven background." I just thought the lady was nuts to spend that much money on a seat she'd never see. "May as well just leave the seat open and ugly," I said. But, oh, you had your wisdom. Of course, you agreed with the lady and her woven background, Dani. Sure nuff, you sold that caning job, even though I thought it was not worth fixin, being nothin more than a ugly old wheelchair. That was the day you told me about your mother who you took care of. Not the other way around. The mother who couldn't give two hoots about her own daughter.

You said, "Julia, I'll tell you about ugliness. My big old ugly story." And you did. Now there's a story I'll never forget. I listened and you just wove that whole tale. You said all through your childhood your mother was moaning and crying about what a horrible life she had. You never did know your father, he left before you were even born. You were only five years old, and you'd have to be takin' care 'a her. She'd tell you what to cook when you could barely reach the stove. You'd drag wood from the pile, light a fire in the old stove and learnt to make anything in the world with your mother's talkin you through it. Just so *she* dint have to cook, but she still got hungry, dint she? She gave you nothing. All those years of her headaches, her feeling peaked, you helped her without a thought to your own self. All those years of her boyfriends, one after the other. The drunken fights, the ones who tried to take liberties with you, a child.

It was Christmas eve when it all came to a head, well, Christmas mornin, really. You said it was when your life was changed for good and you gave up all hope of your mother ever becoming one who would truly love you as a mother should. All those dreams just blew away like the winter gales. For weeks before Christmas, you had been hoping for the pertiest blue-quilted satin robe with matching slippers and nightgown. You told me you'd wanted that more than you'd ever wanted anything. I think you said you were nine or ten at the time. Every time you went into town from November to Christmas with your mama you'd stand at that Hearst Clothiers store window and stare at that set. Then, a few days before Christmas it was gone. You knew your mama hadn't bought it.

She dint have two cents to her name. You were broken-hearted. But you still dreamed about it. Maybe it would appear on Christmas day like a miracle. And it did. But not quite the way you had wished for.

Your mama had a new boyfriend. They hadn't started into fighting yet so he might end up being a keeper, your mama said. Christmas eve arrived and you were beyond excited. You woke up Christmas morning to a cold house, the stove hadn't been lit all night. You told me you were so frightened, maybe your mother had died during the night, been killed by her latest lover. But it wasn't that at all. There was a note on the kitchen table. You closed your eyes and I knew you were remembering that note exactly. When you opened your eyes, I saw your tears. "Darling Danielle," said the note. "Your gift is here on the kitchen table, just as you had hoped. David and I decided to go away for the holiday. We'll be back the day after Christmas. There's plenty of food in the icebox. You're a big girl and I know you'll be fine. Enjoy your very special gift. Merry Christmas! All my love, your beloved mother."

You said you made a fire to warm up the house and then opened your gift. It was the blue-quilted robe with matching slippers and nightgown. You told me you nearly threw it in the fire but changed your mind. You put it back in the box, slipped it under your bed, and cried the rest of the day. You said you were dead inside. And you never loved your mother again after that day, but you always took good care of her.

"Great goodness. That really *is* one big ugly story. I'm so sorry, Dani. What you must have suffered through."

As always, you brushed it off. "Oh. Just another memory. What doesn't kill you will make you stronger, right? It made me stronger."

And Dani, you are the strongest lady I've ever known. Maybe the craziest, too. You got the idea to stock up your 'book nook' in the shop. You said, "All these old cabins have libraries built in them. Bet you there are first editions out there." I have to admit at the time I dint know or care what a 'first edition' was. But you had to have your way so we visited every cabin in Heavenly Hollow. And you were right. People had stored their old books in attics and trunks, or kept them stuck in their library bookcases and under their beds. You came away with a treasure trove of first editions, from *Uncle Tom's Cabin* to *Jane Eyre* and *Wuthering Heights* to *To Kill A Mockingbird.* You were brilliant. And you made me read them all. "Carefully, Julia, like you would touch a delicate flower. Do not touch the pages roughly. Touch them as you would when weaving a chair."

When I worried that we weren't spending enough time at the shop, you laughed at me. "My dear Julia," you said to me, as though I were a child. "We'll open by appointment only. People will not be disappointed in our hours but thrilled that we allow them into our shop." Once again, you were right. Sometimes our appointments stacked up because your people dint want to leave. Those were the crazies you were *counseling.*

You had always been a strong walker. Six inches taller than me, your strides were longer, faster, like a jack rabbit runnin from a wild hog. Remember? We walked all over these hills and fields, searching not only for books but wild strawberries and mushrooms.

By accident, we found the ancient graveyard on one of those walks. The old wrought iron sign was almost completely hidden by weeds. Heaven's Gate Cemetery it read. How I loved those long walks up the hill to visit those ancient gravestones. Peaceful, it twere. Like a church under the trees.

You said it was us who had to save the cemetery, to honor the dead. "There's no one left but us to remember these old graves. We are the self-appointed caretakers of the long dead."

Heaven's Gate was our weekly date. No matter what, be it jamming or planting or opening the Queens. we made cemetery time. We trekked up the long hill. You always walked it without a problem. Me, I lagged along behind you. We brung our baskets, clippers, cuttings and trowels. My basket was a pretty wicker one, made it myself. We'd shed our baskets and our garden tools and fresh dug out flowering plants from around our cabins. We'd look around the graves before starting to work, seeing who needed what. We'd begin by weeding. Like warriors, we stooped and bent and grabbed those weeds savagely out of their old ruined beds. We planted new clippings and flowers and scrubbed the gravestones till my knuckles hurt. We certainly gave life to those old stones in Heaven's Gate. Once we discovered all the graves we realized how sacred the ground was. We were curious of the names on the stones. The ones that weren't buried under dirt or worn away by time, anyway. It was like a mystery we were trying to solve, thinkin bout those long dead folks under our feet. Who were they? You were stubborn like you are, headstrong, like a dog after a long-buried bone. Once you hit on a plan, Dani, you were never one to give up, like a rat to the cheese. You went to the library and the county courthouse and learnt all 'bout our little holler. Mildred Hanson founded this valley, the living places, Heavenly Hollow, as well as the homes for the dead, Heaven's Gate Cemetery. You discovered this graveyard was the final resting place of slaves, poor whites and the ones with no homes who tramped the countryside until they just lay down and died. All these folks were all mixed up together. "Death knows no boundaries." That's what you said.

It was there you taught me how to lift the names and words from gravestones like magic. Gravestone rubbing, you called it. You taught me how to use Japanese paper, rice paper, taped to a stone. I remember the way the light bounced off the bright white of the paper and lit up your pale face. You showed me how to hold the hard, colored wax in my hand, tracing it slowly, tenderly, carefully across the old stone. It was history, an existence, coming alive under our hands, making a portrait of gravestone words, like a vision. We brought the dead from beneath our knees into sunshine, bringing those long buried back to life. Too bad there were many graves sunken with no headstones we could read, the letters so worn off with age. "We're raisin' the dead," you said, as we stood back to admire the latest rubbing.

"Yes, we are," I agreed.

Sometimes there wasn't even a headstone, just the remains of an old wooden cross. Other times no more than a scattered pile of stones. The saddest stone was the most 'extravagant'. It was a tall, carved obelisk bearing a message from a son to a mother who had died without her beloved son by her side. The stone told of the son's guilt and pain. "I was traveling across the deep blue ocean when my dear mother departed across the River Styx."

Another was the wife of Pastor Goodrich: *A Good Woman,* "She Had Nothing Left To Do But Die." We giggled over that one. Then you said, "And happy I was to go after working myself to death." Oh, if people had heard us screeching with laughter that day they would have thought there were witches and harpies in the graveyard.

Then there was our favorite stone. How we howled over that one: "Damn She Was Good" was all that was written on the face of the stone. We laughed until we cried. Then we began making up stories as we collected the weeds, throwing them into the woods and made the slow trek back down the hill with our baskets.

"Good at what? Cooking? Ironing? Cleaning? Or FUCKING!" I slapped you for saying such a forbidden word. Then we laughed all over again, throwing caution to the winds of what you called, *society-driven euphemisms.* Not making love, but *fucking!* That was another thing our friendship taught me, what you taught me. To throw caution to the wind.

In my mind's eye, that day shines like the sun, the moon and all the stars. It was a moment that took us from that day of pure happiness and overflowing joy to the coming horror. For it was on that long walk down the graveyard hill with the leftovers of begonia cuttings that you first stumbled so badly. I helped you up and clucked over your wounded knees. It happened again and again over the following months as you dragged yourself up the hill. You wouldn't give up. I started bringing bandages and alcohol with me to nurse you when you fell, it happened that much.

"Must be a bad sprain," you said. "You know, how once you hurt yourself it happens over and over again in the same place?" Then your right foot began to trouble you. My worried eyes foretold your future. I was not ready to share my diagnosis with you. After all, I was a nurse, not a doctor, although I did my fair share of doctorin. I remained silent. Was that a good or a bad thing? That is the question that comes to my mind in the darkest hours of the night when sleep is a ghost, haunting me. You made me promise when we first met that I would never lie to you. And I dint, exactly. I just hid my thoughts.

Finally, you could barely walk. Traveling up to Heaven's Gate was impossible. I sorely missed our treks to the old graveyard but you wanted to keep trying. You were always so strong and determined. I don't know if that was good or bad on your part. You refused to give up. You bought that beautiful carved walking stick. Soon, that dint help neither. When your muscles began to waver all up your left leg, we both knew something was terribly wrong. When you got sicker and sicker, we couldn't deny it any longer. I'll never forget your words. "Let's go doctor shopping." So, I dusted off my nursing skills and that's what we did.

Now, that were the perfect chore for me, caring for you, taking you to doctors, with my being a nurse for years and years. Long as I could member back to when I was a kid, I cared for the sick around me at the farm. For my mom and grandma, whenever they felt poorly. Later pa, fore he died. By then, I knew what I was best at in life: taking care of people I loved. Soon as I grajated from high school I went right into the community college nursing program in Raleigh. Worked the whole time at the local hospital. Doctors and nurses all, they liked me. Taught me a lot, they did. From drugs to talking right to patients to helping grief-struck loved ones of those just passed. They knew they could trust me to work as hard as them. Same as at home, I was a hard worker, never shunned anything I was asked to do. As a nurse, I'd do any little or big thing, from dumpin bed pans to watching over patients when the real nurses needed a dinner break. Did my two-year internship, took the nursing boards and finally was a full-fledged nurse. So I ain't no dummy, I did my time, loving every minit of nursin till my back and feet were so bad I had to retire. My great aunt Tildie left me this cabin, me being her only living relative. With my nursin retirement and making what little I could on repairs in the holler I got by. Folks knew I could fix just about anything, from fences to chairs to privvies. Always had as a youngun, my daddy taught me everything he knew, and that was plenty. Livin on a farm with just about no money, you learn to do for yourself. So, twere no one better suited than me to take you to the round of doctors. Put on my nurse's thinkin cap and jumped into whatever had to be done.

I learned mighty quick you were no easy patient. Dani, you were a trial. You fought with every doctor. You challenged em all. When first your left foot, then your right, stopped working. "Must be the rheumatiz," you insisted. I could always tell when you were acting. We both knew there was something more than rheumatiz wrong. I was turrible worried although I dint want to admit that to you. You dint think it was rheumatism any more than I did. One doctor after another insisted it was some sort of neuropathy, nerve damage. My nurse's knowledge kept me on the forefront of all our meetings.

"But there's no pain or numbness, isn't that what neuropathy is?" I asked, knowing the diagnosis of my own poor feet. That darkest thought kept niggling in the back of my mind: *Lou Gehrig's Disease.* The nursing side of me was coming out and taking over, but I was doing my best to shove her back into the closet in my head, not wanting to admit the worst. Until I couldn't hide it any longer, and we both had to face the truth I had long suspected.

We finally found the right specialist, Dr. Baylor. When we left his office that day, we both wished we hadn't learned the truth. Dr. Baylor, a well-respected neurologist, did all sorts of tests, with his little hammer, his electrical wires, holding your feet, flexing your toes, asking you all sorts of personal questions. I laughed when you said you were being electrocuted and tortured, not examined. I felt your pain, in little bits and pieces, far less than what you experienced. Dr. Baylor kept up with his questions which I wrote down, along with the answers.

"How long has this gone on? Do you have stomach problems? Are you constipated?" You answered yes to every question. Then, the most telling one:

"Did you hit your head recently?" We noticed defeat in his voice, like a general knowing a battle was over. He breathed a long sigh when you told him you had fallen off a ladder onto the hard floor of our shop months before.

"How hard did you hit your head? And where?" asked the doctor.

"The back of my head, hard. I had a headache for two weeks, I swear."

"Did you seek medical assistance then?"

"Well, Julia kept nagging me and nagging me until finally after two weeks when the headaches wouldn't stop I went to my doctor. He said I probably had a concussion. He told me I should have come to him much sooner."

And, as usual, you had challenged him, the doctor you had known for years. "What good would that have done? I know there's no cure for a concussion except time." You were right, eventually the headaches did disappear.

That day in Dr. Baylor's office changed everything. After he had asked you all his questions, he closed his little pad, capped his pen, took off his glasses and looked at you. Then, he looked at both of us by turns, holding our eyes tightly with his gaze. Having worked with doctors for years who dint want to provide bad news, I knew he was making a decision. I'll never forget your expression, Dani. You knew something was catastrophically wrong. Maybe you'd known it all along.

For the first time in my recall, you had no words. You sat, holding my hands, and stayed silent. Finally, I said, "What is it, doctor? You can tell me. I was a nurse for years. Started as a Candy Striper when I was only fourteen years old. Honesty is best. Tell us what we're facing here."

"Have you ever heard of Charcot's Disease?" I know my face turned even whiter than yours.

"Yes. Named by Jean-Martin Charcot in 1869? Is that it, Dr. Baylor?"

"I'm so sorry. That's the clearest diagnosis that matches all of Danielle's symptoms."

"Especially the hard blow to her head. Amyotrophic Lateral Sclerosis or ALS. It's also called Lou Gehrig's disease. Have you heard of that? Named after the great baseball player?" I felt as if all the blood had been drained from my body. I could not take my eyes from yours. Your eyes, Dani, your eyes. You dint cry, yet. Those dark orbs were blazing like jewels.

You found your voice, Dani, shaky and choked with emotion. "Yes, of course. Who wouldn't have heard of Lou Gehrig? He was the iron man of baseball when he retired in 1939. He said he was the luckiest man alive for his baseball career. But he had to give up baseball for the good of his team. That's what you're talking about? That's what I have? Lou Gehrig's disease? ALS?" I had never heard a quaver of fear in your voice, until then. My eyes filled with tears.

"I'm afraid it appears that way. However, get second opinions, if you would feel comforted, or if you think I'm mistaken."

You leaned forward in your chair angrily. "We've had second, third and now you're the fourth opinion, Doctor Baylor. Just tell us. What's the treatment and what's the cure? I'll do absolutely everything I can to get better."

The doctor took his time. He cleaned his glasses and put them back on. "I can't begin to tell you how sorry I am. There is no cure. The disease is terminal. How long? It's different with every patient. There have been strides made since the disease was first discovered. The best diet helps, massaging the weakened limbs to keep the blood circulating. It is a debilitating disease. Some individuals stay stronger longer. Others deteriorate more rapidly. It appears the onset of the disease was about six months ago?"

I stuttered. "Y-y-yes."

"And Danielle, you have great difficulty walking? I noticed that when you arrived today."

"Yes."

That's when we both understood, Dani. You leaned forward in your chair and fell into my arms. We both sobbed as though the doctor wasn't even in the room. We dint notice when he left or when he returned and brought his nurse with him. I was so glad you and I were going through this together. No one, not even the strongest woman I had ever known, could have survived this diagnosis by herself.

I wrote down all the information the nurse and doctor gave us. You were numb. Shattered. Dr. Baylor told us what to expect, how long you might have, and what the disease would do. Move from your legs up, then attack in an entirely new place, your back, your neck. Eventually you'd have difficulty breathing when the disease would move to your diaphragm and lungs. Finally, you would no longer be able to swallow, to eat. You wouldn't realize it, but you'd be starving to death. You'd be too weak to notice. You'd just slip off into a coma. At least, that was what we hoped. I felt it in my heart and soul. I knew what his next words would be. He cleared his throat and said those painful words: "May

I ask, do you have someone to care for you, when the time comes, which I think will be very soon, when you can no longer care for yourself?"

I leaned forward and wiped the tears from my eyes. "A course she does. Me. Dani is my dearest friend. I'll be the one to take care of her. And besides being her best friend, I told you, I'm a nurse. Or at least I was."

Your spark returned, if only for an instant, Dani. You shouted at me, "Oh, no you won't. I'm not about to destroy your life just because mine is near over. My future might be disappearing but I won't have your's end, too." I could have slapped you. For once, I stood up to you, stronger than you in my voice and words.

"Don't you dare tell me what to do. You think you're going home alone? Well, you've got another thought coming, Danielle."

When I used your hated name, I knew I had your attention. You came home with me that day. I moved you into my cabin immediately. I made you comfortable, then watched your life being stolen from you. You never went back to your old, broken down old cabin again.

If ever there were conversations we needed to have, but never wanted to have, we had over the next months. We talked about so many things regarding ALS. The end of your life, and how much our friendship meant to each of us. How we would cope, how I would cope, watching my dearest friend waste away before my eyes. When you could still talk, you told me things that were the hardest for you to lose. Being active, loss of movement, walking, balancing, being independent, breathing, eating, sleeping, communicating, digesting, it was all being taken from you, little by little. One horrible step at a time. Except your brain, your mind. You said that was the hardest part. Your entire body was slipping away, but your mind was still just as active, quick and as witty as it had always been. That was the cruelest part of this awful disease. You had to sit by and watch yourself die.

There were days when you were such a spitfire, like a cat in a battle. At first, you hated me for taking care of you, taking control over your life. We both knew you had no choice. You protested, of course. Over and over again. I'll never forget your words in one of your fits of rage.

"I'm walking out that door and going home." You actually tried to rise from your chair and fell straight to the floor. I lifted you and held you while we both cried. "I'm not going anywhere, am I, Julia?"

"No, dear heart. You're exactly where you need to be. I'll keep going by your place and will bring you whatever you want or need. But no, you're not going anywhere. You can see what good care I'm taking of you, right?"

"Yes."

You finally had to accept that the only life you had left was the one I offered you. Then I set down the rules so you'd never be rebellious again. "You will live here. In my cabin, in my life. I promise, I will move you back into your home if a miracle happens and you get well and can walk again." We both knew any thought of your recovery was a liar's game. We had always vowed we would never lie to one another. You knew you would never get well again. There would be no miracle. You would never leave my home. You were always the honest one, Dani. You never learned to lie. If you attempted to, I recognized your dithering. Subterfuge never found a home on your lips.

"I *invited* you into my life because I love you. Your husband died on the railroad tracks, not that he was worth much when he was alive. Good for nothing philandering drunk. How he ever got that last floozie I'll never know. But Dani, even through all this, you got the best, the last laugh. He's dead and you're a queen. Your sales made you wealthy, but he impoverished your soul. We rebuilt both our lives with our little shop. I'll rebuild your soul, if I have to. I'll take care of you until you just drift off. Wouldn't you do that for me, Dani, if the tables were turned?" I asked.

"Of course, I would," you yelled at me in anger. Then, you had to admit I was right. The first thing I did was unearth an old wheelchair hidden back a the shop. I carted you around in it. Just short little walks around the yard, me showing off my flowers, my latest chair caning. Once or twice, we managed to get down my old rutted drive and into the road. We had our little treks until you could no longer travel in the wheelchair safely. Remember how we laughed, we could do nothing more, when you fell out of the wheelchair onto my beautifully waxed kitchen floor? And peed into the bargain all over it? I said, "Well, Dani, I guess it's time I cleaned the floor. Couldn't you just have told me to do so without being so dramatic?" I always made you laugh, at least I tried to. Some days, we laughed until we cried, or just cried. More than once I cradled your head in my lap and just let you sob. Your tears drenched my apron.

Then there was the day I came home from grocery shopping and you had fallen out of the wheelchair again. I found you dragging yourself across the floor. You were trying to pull yourself up into the wheelchair but dint have the strength to do it. For the first time, you looked frightened which scared the bejeezus out of me. You were always the strong one, even with ALS. Then, somehow, you found the courage to say, "I can either lie on this floor after falling again and cry, or I can figure out a way to crawl over to the kitchen drawers and pull myself up on the handles and get back in that wheelchair. I'll go on with life, one way or another."

I said, "That's why I'm here, Dani. To pick you up when you fall." For once, you dint argue with me. You let me pick you up and put you back in that wheelchair. Already, you were so much lighter. You had lost so much weight, nothing but bones you were.

You lived, contentedly I think, until things got so bad. You loved my beautiful little cabin, all vine covered and surrounded by flowers. I loved you being here. I know there were times when I infuriated you, times when you resented me. I was such a mother hen, a true nurse at heart. When you complained that you were taking over my life, my privacy, I scolded you. "Moving you into my home is the greatest gift to me, filling up my life of aloneness. Your presence will never intrude on our friendship Dani. It made me richer. It still does." Until I closed up the shop, I kept our 'appointment' hours and continued to sell your antiques. I gave up my caning and wicker repair, dinnit have time for it anyways. No one ever knew you were here. Course, I'd never been sociable so it was no problem being completely unsociable. I closed up the shop without you knowin and never even left a note on the door. It was as if we had both vanished from the holler. But I knew that was how you woulda wanted it, if I'd asked for your advice. Which I dinnit.

Remember how you loved the light that came through the windows? You'd watch it for hours as I bustled about. Toward the end, you asked me to move your bed into the library. You lay on your cot, right by all my beautiful windows. You could see more there. You watched the sun rise every day and studied the way the shadows in the room told you it had set. You noticed the flowers blooming and then the leaves falling from the trees. You saw the days pass by, the seasons, and your life.

Months after I moved you into the library I sold the good antiques left at your house and left the riff-raff there. I brought your favorite possessions here. I surrounded you with your most beloved objects. We knew it was mostly over. You started calling my library 'your sunny room'. That room gave you so much joy, lighting up what had become your world.

I became your legs and arms. You said no, more than that. "You're my heart and soul, too." That was when you could still talk. I'll never forget all our long conversations. The final secrets of your heart, the reasons why your marriage failed, why Artie became such a drunk. You told me your last, your final confession. Your pregnancy. When you found out you were pregnant, you were beyond thrilled. Yet all through your pregnancy you said something was 'off'. Something didn't feel quite right. But hell, you'd never been pregnant before so what did you know? That was long before we met. If you had come into the hospital to deliver, I probably would have met you then, wouldn't that have been something? I'll never forget your words. "Nine months of hopes and dreams crushed in ten hours of labor." The baby was stillborn. You said it just 'bout killed you. You had all those baby clothes you'd crocheted. I could see the excitement in your eyes when you told me of your hopes, the way you would raise your child, the walks you would take through the holler.

When I clucked over you that day, when the tears came to my eyes, you became angry. "Stop it, Julia. I can't be sad all over again." Then you laughed. "Imagine that. I thought that would be the greatest tragedy of my life." You looked down at your broken body and the tears came in a rush. "Turns out I was wrong. This is."

We talked 'bout the end of your life and how much our friendship meant to each of us. How we would cope, how I would cope, watching my dearest friend waste away. I nursed as best I could, making you feel at home and then watched your life being slowly stolen away from you. You told me your mind gave you hope but your body crushed it. Your brain was fresh as ever, untouched by disease. You were forced to watch yourself die.

Oh, we tried to make it alright for one another, to be sensitive to one another's pain and grief. It was hard to be honest about what was happening, what was to come in the future. We had to face your death, dearest friend. And we did. We talked about how nothing about ALS is right or fair. You said, "This isn't the way I planned on leaving this world, Julia."

Yet you still had your sense of humor. You had always been so full of fun, joy and life. That dry wit of yours made me laugh to the point of tears. You would not allow ALS to take that from you. Even devastatingly sick you always outshone and outsmarted me. When you could still talk you said, "Laughter is the only thing I have left. If I didn't have my sense of humor, I would have nothing. I've reinvented myself so many times I don't think there's anything left to do but die. Just like on that gravestone, but I'm no pastor's wife! I'm not giving up. So while I can still laugh, I will."

You never did lose your sense of humor. There were times we both laughed joyously, uproariously, crazily. Hard to believe now, but we had fun, until you could no longer talk, or laugh or move.

Sometimes your observations startled me. One day you said I was like Irish coffee, laced with whisky. Strong, robust, topped with a dollop of sweetness in whipped cream and a spark of fire from whiskey. "You're like the German word for delicious, *likka*. Just like our friendship. I am so grateful for you, dear Julia." When I reached out my hand to touch yours, you immediately hid behind that shell of yours. You pretended you hadn't said anything so tender. That was you. But we both knew how important those words were.

I had always viewed the world through rose-colored glasses. There were no rose-colored glasses anymore. Then there was the day you asked me to make you oleander tea. That was the only time you came near to showing me you were giving up.

"Oleander Tea? What are you asking me?" I said, my stomach lurching. I felt sickened, knowing what you were asking, any self-respecting nurse would. "Well," you said, "it worked for the Confederate ladies on their plantations when their Yankee captors had destroyed their homes and were about to steal their lives. Those smart ladies served them Oleander Blossom Tea, and that took care of them." You laughed. I dint. "Course," you said, "Hemlock tea would work just as well. Or just make a big fire of Oleander in the fireplace and don't open the damper. Let the smoke fill the house, just be sure you're not here."

I was shocked beyond measure.

My dearest friend was asking me to kill her. I said, "Dani. I love you more than I've loved anyone in my entire life. But I won't murder you. And I wouldn't do well in a jail cell, either, after you're gone."

You dint say a word, but we never talked about oleander or hemlock tea again. I finally realized you just had to try. Maybe you were testing me in the hope that I'd agree. I couldn't. We both knew that we would have to face this together till the end. There was no other way out. Finally, when your speech became slurred and we both knew the end was coming faster than we'd thought possible you told me, "Plant me next to 'Damn She Was Good'. I'll depart in the joy of your love and care-taking. But don't you ever forget me, Julia. I'll come back to haunt you!" As if I could ever forget you. I wish you *would* come back to haunt me.

I admit it: There were many nights I fell exhausted into bed. But the next day you always cheered me. What was I, what did I add to this friendship? Only my love of life, literature, old things. These were all the things you taught me. Dani, you made me so much wiser and more discerning. I learned worlds and words from you. I can never reach the summit of the mountain of your mind and knowledge. You are scorched into my heart and soul. What I loved most about you, dear Dani, was your courage, your sense of adventure, of starting anew with nothing and ending up with a lotta somethin'. Until there was nothing.

Long before you could no longer swallow, you made me promise that I would never force feed you with a tube. You said, "Just let me go." Soon after your speech became too slurred and garbled for me to understand. I gave you a tablet and you wrote down whatever you needed or wanted, even your thoughts. I wiped the drool from your lips, sat by you for hours, reading your words. I recognized the terror in your eyes. One of the last things you wrote was, "Dear Julia, speech is the last to go but I'll always hear your voice. Talk to me until I leave. Read to me until I'm gone."

Another day you wrote, "I love watching your eyes. They're so expressive. I can read you like a book." I laughed at that and said, "Well, I hope it's been a good one." You smiled sadly and wrote, "Yes, dear Julia. The best book I'll ever read." It was the last thing you wrote, and I could barely read your words. What a fast year it was. Finally, your hands grew so weak that you couldn't move your fingers. You could no longer speak or scribble, but you could hear my words. You gave your life to me for safekeeping. No better place for your heart, soul and story than to remain in my little cabin till your last breath.

I decided to write this book for you, Dani. I hid it from you until the very end. When you began having trouble breathing and could no longer swallow, I knew you couldn't last much longer. I wanted the last words you would hear to be the beloved history of our friendship.

You slipped into a coma. I began to read. When I finished reading our *Book of Memories*, I talked and talked. I told you of how much you meant to me, how much I loved you. That last day, you actually opened your eyes. I was astounded. You looked right at me and smiled with your eyes, the only way you could 'talk'. Then slowly, so slowly, two tears escaped from your beautiful eyes, the windows to the soul, people say, and I think it's true. I reached out to wipe your tears away and somehow you lifted your hand and held mine. You gave me one last look with your smiling eyes and then you were gone.

Our friendship began with nothing but a whim and a dream. That's how we met. That's how we ended. With our dreams.

Now I visit you at Heaven's Gate, where we spent so many happy hours. I'll join you there soon, I know. My body is weak and I feel broken. There really was no one I could enjoy life with anymore after you left. I guess I've given up.

We'll have parties in the graveyard at night, just like the stories we made up about all the residents of Heaven's Gate. I'll listen to your wit and humor again and you'll regale all the grave-holders with tales of your life. And we'll all listen raptly. We'll laugh until we cry and the sun comes up to dry our tears.

November 1969. Julia Anne McNamish

Chapter 13

Emeline sat silently, stunned into cold shock as she read the last page of *The Book of Memories*, overcome with sorrow. Her face was wet with tears she hadn't realized she had shed. The house was quiet, interrupted only by Randy's gentle snores. All this had happened in their cabin? Who was Dani? Could Julia still be alive, somewhere in their neighborhood?

Nagging thoughts attacked her. She walked slowly from room to room. Moonlight streamed through the windows lighting her way through her darkened home. She imagined the bedridden dying woman in each of the rooms at each stage of her horrific disease, ALS, the disease that had robbed both women of a future. Em settled in the window seat in the library.

Had Dani died in this room? With Julia her caretaker, her dearest friend? Only Felicity could provide her with answers. She had told Em that a dear friend had lived in this cabin. She had also told Em that she knew every one of the cabins in Heavenly Hollow, having lived here for so long. Felicity, who knew everything about these cabins, might be able to solve this mystery. But Felicity wouldn't arrive again until spring. Em would have to figure out her own answers. Had that been Julia's candy-striper nurse's aide uniform in the old trunk? There were clues, but where were the answers?

Oh my god, Em thought. I used lace from that trunk to make the little bedroom's curtains. She shivered in the darkness. Her next thought was too preposterous. Felicity was her friend, flesh and blood and very vibrant. And her cat, Zuma always arrived with her. Rhett and Scarlet had begun accepting Zuma. No. The theory developing in her mind was too ridiculous. Randy would think she'd finally gone over the edge, or 'round the bend', as Mama used to say. She put her absurd thoughts aside. She would only share what she had read, the only words in the little book that appeared to be true.

"Randy. Wake up," Em said, shaking his shoulder, then crawled into bed with him and tousled his hair.

"Whaa? Baby? It's the middle of the night. Let me sleep. Wait till morning." His snores returned peacefully. Em had no choice but to wait till the sun rose. She retreated from their warm bed and paced the well-worn floors for the rest of the night, into the pale dawn of the day.

When the rosy glow of daybreak finally lit up her kitchen windows, Em had made a decision. She wouldn't share the little book with her husband. Em wasn't ready to confide the secrets it held. She wouldn't voice her thoughts to anyone. Randy wouldn't remember or care about discovering *The Book of Memories*, anyway. For now, this was Em's secret to mull over.

There was no doubt that she had to learn more about Dani and Julia. Em suddenly realized if she could find Heaven's Gate Cemetery, perhaps she could locate Julia's grave next to the 'Damn She Was Good' grave mentioned in the Book of Memories. There was one other person she knew could help her unravel this mystery: Adrian. With his librarian-research skills, he'd know where to look to discover answers. He would know where to find old County records, census, church and graveyard records. At least, she had a date from *The Book of Memories,* November, 1969. That was ten years ago. It was a start. There had to be records of Dani and Julia somewhere, if only in a graveyard. That was the key. She had to find the graveyard. Felicity knew where it was, but had never revealed anything other than, 'up there over the hill'. That was no help. Em was determined to find the graveyard before Felice returned in the spring. Adrian would be her sorcerer's apprentice. He'd find the answers she was seeking. He would help her solve this mystery.

Perhaps Felice was related to a distant cousin or friend of Julia's? Yes. That's it. Everybody in the holler probably knew Julia. Felice would have known the story of her friendship with Dani. Ten years wasn't such a long time ago. I bet she shopped at the Queens, maybe Julia even repaired chairs for her. Randy wandered into the kitchen, having slept late this sunny Saturday morning.

"You talking to yourself again, sweetheart? Coffee on?" She blazed him with one of her radiant smiles. "Yes. Coffees perking. Just thinking out loud. Getting ready to make some biscuits." She handed Randy a steaming mug of coffee as her thoughts tumbled. By the time the biscuits were in the oven, Em had come to a decision. Yes. Adrian. He's the only one who can help me solve this puzzle. "Sweetie, okay if I take you to work on Monday? I need to go to the library."

"Sure. You run outta books already?"

"Yes, and I need to check the bulletin board to see if I have any more requests for chair caning." She took the hot biscuits from the oven, placed them in her basket with the heart-shaped heating stone Randy had found for her at Gillinghams. The scent of the fresh biscuits perfumed the kitchen. Looking out the window, Em noticed how beautifully the light was filtering through her curtains. It was going to be a glorious day. Then she thought of the lace curtains in the little room and how she admired the way the light made patterns on the floor through the fabric. Enveloped in the biscuit-scented glory of her kitchen, Em was reminded of all Felicity had taught her: using what one had at hand, from baking biscuits to coils of cane, to making curtains from castoff fabric.

The jangling of the phone thrust Em from her reverie. She answered and was happy to hear Margret's voice. "Good morning, dear. I hope I didn't call too early?" Em laughed in reply. "Of course not. I've been up for hours." That was certainly true, she admitted to herself.

"Here's our favorite man, Margret. Hope to see you soon."

"That's what I'm calling about, dear." Em heard Margret say as she passed the phone to Randy. "Oh, yes, Mother. That does sound wonderful. Yeah. Uh-huh. Well, how about two? Yes, the weather is perfect. We should see some color along the river, being mid-October. Okay, see you then."

Randy hung up the phone and turned to Em. "I have to say, Mom seems a lot happier these days. I bet it has something to do with her getting to know her new daughter better, as she says."

Em chuckled in reply. She certainly wouldn't dispute that observation. "Are you going someplace?"

"Yup, we all are. Mom had a great idea. She's going to take us out to dinner at the Woodbine Cottage on the James River. It's right near the old James River Plantation. They have beautiful gardens there and we should see the maples turning color when we tour the plantation. Mom used to go to the Woodbine Cottage with her Aunt Clarissa. It will be nice for her to travel that route again and have dinner at one of her favorite old inns."

"Jeeze, Randy. What will I wear?" Randy laughed at her. "You'll figure something out." Promptly at two Randy and Em picked up Margret. She was aflutter with excitement and was waiting at the front door for them. "Oh, Emeline, what a lovely dress. Burgundy is the perfect color for you. Wherever did you get it?"

Em wasn't about to tell Margret it was the dress she had worn to her father's funeral, six years earlier. She was surprised it still fit, although a big snug across her breasts and tummy, which Randy loved.

The drive to the James River Plantation along the James River was all they could have hoped for. The colors of the bright red and orange maples lit the road with their fall beauty. Aspens shivered in their gold glistening attire. The flower beds at the James River Plantation were magnificent with the mums in bloom and the falling leaves decorating and mingling with the landscape. Wisteria, scattering delicate purple blossoms on the lawns, painted the day with more vibrant color. The multi-hued landscape made a bright tapestry quilted into the emerald green of the grass. Em was reminded of the many shades stitched into her grandmama's quilts. Em made a note to ask Randy to build her a trellis in the spring so she could plant some flowering vines.

Along the river the willows had begun to turn yellow, their long branches reflected in the placid eddies of the dark water. The blue of the sky was so vibrant it seemed as though it couldn't be real. Em was left to her own thoughts in the backseat of their Rambler as Randy and Margret chatted and laughed together. The James River was so different from the Sacramento and the Mokelumne Rivers of the delta. Those rivers were beautiful, but lazier than the James River, as it rushed to the Atlantic. It was as though this river had a purpose, a reason for being, while the delta rivers were somnolent, meandering along in no hurry. The falling leaves reminded Em that soon all the trees would be bare, skeletons standing starkly against the dimmed hues of the world. Eventually, her eyes grew heavy, her body exhausted from her long night of reading and wandering their cabin. She dreamt of Dani and Julia. She saw them in the moonlight together somewhere, perhaps in a large field? Columns of tall trees laced the edges of the field. The moon shone brightly, making shadows appear ghostlike and surreal.

"Sweetheart, we're here. Come on, sleepyhead," said Randy. Em opened her eyes to another lovely sight. "Oh, what a charming restaurant." Margret's eyes sparkled. "I couldn't wait to bring you here, Emeline. When I woke up this morning, I knew this was a perfect day for leaf peeping. This used to be a little cottage, an actual home, right here on the James River. The owners built their new home nearby and turned this into a restaurant, The Woodbine Cottage. Its menu reflects that of the Michee Tavern, which is further away. We'll go there sometime, maybe take a weekend trip?"

"Oh, yes, I'd so love that, Margret. Thank you. It's been ages since Randy and I have gone anywhere except Charles Town." They walked up an oyster shell path to the Woodbine Cottage entrance, the name confirmed by blooming clusters of yellow woodbine, red trumpet flowers, and purple wisteria. Virginia creeper had turned bright red and climbed the walls of the restaurant. Clusters of pink roses bordered the path. Bunches of yellow and pink lantana climbed trellises which led their way to the restaurant welcome sign at the end of the path.

They were escorted into a quiet, elegant interior. Wood-paneled walls were lit with sconces filled with thick, golden candles. The dining room was dominated by a large brick fireplace. A bright fire warmed the room and added ambience and comfort to its interior, the huge logs of wood crackling merrily. Em couldn't remember being in a more beautiful inn.

"We'd like the terrace room, please," Margret said to the hostess.

"Of course," said the hostess. "And I do believe I've met you before? Didn't you used to come with an elderly lady?"

"Yes. That was my Aunt Clarissa. She's gone now and I'm the elderly lady accompanying my son and daughter-in-law." Em was surprised to hear the pride in Margret's voice. Randy, looking spiffy in a camel-hair sports jacket, smiled down at Em, reading her thoughts. He whispered in her ear, "See? I told you. You've made my mom so happy." She kissed him in thanks, then followed Margret and the hostess into a long room. The entire length of the room was illuminated by eight-on-eight windows. No adornment decorated the windows— no shades or curtains—allowing the beauty of the James River to shine through each window. A grassy expanse of lawn led down to the river, where Appalachian chairs, just like Em's, lined the sandy shore at the River's edge.

"Oh, Margret, what a beautiful place. Thank you so much for sharing this spot with us." Em admired everything on the table when they were seated. The heavy linen tablecloths, the thick pink linen napkins, and a ceramic candle holder painted in a colorful design decorated the table. Em realized the candle holder was much like those she and her mama had loved and had discovered at thrift stores in the delta. Those were Mexican ceramics brought from over the Mexican border to San Diego. Most of all, Em adored the miniature bouquets of flowers set in small pitchers, the size of doll's play-sets of dishes. *I can do this at home when I have a dinner party*, Em thought. She picked up the small ceramic pitchers and each tiny cup of varying patterns that adorned the place settings. The pitchers and little china cups were filled with delicate arrangements of Sweet

William, wild pink roses, baby's breath and freesia. All were nestled in the center of tiny ferns. Em thought she had never seen more beautiful flower arrangements. The dishes on the table Em recognized as Blue Willow, one of her mother's favorite designs.

The meal was delicious. Em ordered braised Trout crusted with sliced almonds. Randy had the 1780s Fried Chicken and Margret the Yankee Pot Roast. All were served with fresh vegetables cooked to perfection. After Margret shared a taste of her Yankee pot roast, Em thought to herself that her recipe was better than The Woodbine Cottage's. Both her mother-in-law and Randy voiced Em's thoughts. Randy wolfed down his fried chicken, obviously too deeply immersed in his meal to pay attention to his mother and Em, who conversed warmly.

"Em, I want you and Randy to come for Thanksgiving dinner," Margret said. "It's a month away, I know. However, one must plan for the holidays in advance, especially now that I have something to plan for. I'm so happy you're in our family, dear." Much to her surprise, Margret reached out and held Em's hand in her own. Tears momentarily appeared in her mother-in-law's eyes, which Em pretended not to see.

"Margret, thank you so much. For everything, not just taking us to this wonderful restaurant and showing me the James River and the Plantation, but for everything you've done for us. I hadn't realized how beautiful Virginia is."

"Well, I told you, Em," Randy said through a mouthful of fried chicken. Margret ignored her son. "I thought it would also be a nice Thanksgiving turkey lesson for you. You and Randy should come early, and I'll teach you how to cook the entire Thanksgiving meal, along with all the fixings. I'll teach you all the old family recipes. We'll make Bourbon Sweet Potatoes, Sausage stuffing, fresh green beans with mushrooms, and pumpkin pie for dessert. Oh, it will be such fun. What do you think?"

"I'd love that," Em replied happily. "But only if you come to our home for Christmas dinner, as long as we're planning ahead. I'll invite some of my friends, too, for you to meet. We can open gifts together and Randy can light the library fireplace."

"I'd like that very much, dear Em." Em brightened with another thought. "I know. For Thanksgiving, I'll make yeast rolls for dinner and will bring over an apple pie. How about that?"

Margret laughed. "Oh, yes, I'd love that. I never was much of a baker. Pumpkin Pie is about all I can manage."

Randy watched the two most important women in his life enjoying one another's company. The move to Virginia was turning out to be even better than he had hoped. Thank goodness Em was truly beginning to love his mother. He knew Margret could be difficult. Em not challenging her territory and being more loving had certainly paved the way for their warming relationship.

The three were surprised when they left the warm fires of the Woodbine Cottage and were greeted with the evening chill. The sun was just beginning to lower in the sky, bringing along the coolness of the coming night. The maples, willows, Aspen and the setting sun gilded the bright blue rippling waters of the James River in gleaming shades of gold, red and amber. It had been another perfect day.

* * *

Bright and early Monday morning Em and Randy headed down their dirt road towards Charles Town. "Randy, this car is a mess. You've got papers all over the place! How can you find anything? I'm going to throw everything out."

"Oh, no you don't. This is my office. I need all this stuff. I just don't have a place to put it. I'll clean it up later."

"Later. Sure." Em retorted grumpily. She stared out the window, keeping a hawk's eye out. As always, she was searching for any possible cabin, drive, or path where Felice and Zuma could be hiding. Em knew Felice would be riding out the coming cold days, cozy and warm, in her little home, wherever that was. "I just don't understand it, Randy. Felice must live out here somewhere."

Randy glanced at his perplexed wife. He'd noticed all the changes in her since their move to the holler in the early spring. She had metamorphosed into a strong woman. He realized how much a part of her life Felicity had become, and how much she had added to the changes in his wife. He was joyfully swimming in the wake of each of Em's new adventures. He loved her more than ever. What had happened to his wife, who had once cared far more about the color of toenail polish than the contents of a book or learning to cook? But then, of course it was Felicity who had helped to bring about these changes. Gently he reached out and touched Em's curls as she mumbled to herself, staring out the window. "Love, sometimes people just don't want to be found," he said quietly. "Everyone's entitled to their secrets, their own places to hide away. Don't be sad. I'll always be here for you. You know how much I love you, don't you Em?"

"Ha! You only love me because I've become such a good cook!" she teased. They laughed together companionably. "Well, yeah, that helps. But it's more than that. You don't seem, I don't know, so lost and disconnected from life anymore. You seem to miss your mama less. Oh, don't get me wrong. I know you still think of her and get lonesome for her. Just not in that hopeless way anymore. More like in a happy, remembering kind of way."

With a start, Em realized Randy was right. He had made a shrewd, sensitive assessment of her state of mind. "Randy, you've changed, too. You're not such a braggart, a buffoon anymore, like you were in high school."

"Oh, that was ages ago. Having to learn how to sell cars without pushing people around has helped, I guess."

"Yeah, that's it, exactly. You don't have to pretend anymore to be someone you're not. You've become more, oh, I don't know, quiet? Thoughtful? Introspective?"

"There you go again, using your expanded vocabulary on a dumb rube from the delta." Em playfully punched Randy as he pulled into the car lot. "Well, a dumb broad from the delta oughta know! After all, we grew up together in the same mud!"

They kissed their goodbyes as Randy got out of the driver's seat. "Hey, you forgot your briefcase." Em called after him, holding out a grocery bag she had filled with all the papers from the floor of the car. Ever since Randy's faux leather briefcase had been dropped in the driveway one evening and not discovered until Randy drove over it the following morning Em had teased him. "Highest quality paper bag, sir. Impressive office attire."

"Ha. Very funny. I'd hate to look pretentious with my grocery bag full of paperwork. I think I'll leave it here, but thanks for the thought."

"Oh, my. Look at you, using big words. Guess my smarts are finally rubbing off on you!" With a smirk and a backward wave Randy walked across the parking lot, greeting other salesmen cheerfully.

Adrian was pleased to see Em waiting for him as he opened up the library. "Well, aren't you the early bird? Isn't this about the time you're usually rolling over for another hour of sleep?"

"Don't get smart with me, Mr. Adrian. I'm up by seven every morning." Em followed Adrian around the library as he went about his tasks. She told him all about the Woodbine Cottage and the drive along the James River and the James River Plantation. She shared her story of Felicity's retreat until spring, her friendship with her, and her great desire to unravel the mystery of her friend's life, and her whereabouts. "Jeeze, girl. Slow down," he said. "Felicity said she hides out in her cabin every November till Spring? Like Persephone?"

"Who's Persephone?" Em asked.

Adrian was happy to further Em's education. "Greek mythology. Wonderful stories created to explain the seasons, astrology, cosmology, you name it. Persephone was a willful Greek goddess. Hades was the master of the underworld, whose rules Persephone wouldn't follow. After she disobeyed him by eating four sacred pomegranate seeds, he banished her from the earth. He further punished her by forcing her to reside in his kingdom in the underworld from November till March. She wasn't allowed to return until the first green shoots of new life burst through the soil and the leaves began to bud on the trees."

"That's crazy." Em retorted.

"Maybe. But Greek mythology served its purpose. Could be that's what Felicity's doing." Em's scholarly friend continued.

"I hate to think of her all alone, banished till spring. She didn't look well the last time I saw her. Like she was fading, growing weaker, right before my eyes. I worry about her being alone and sick in some far-off cabin. How can she get groceries?"

"Calls Gillinghams like every other old lady in Charlie's Town does. Has 'em delivered."

"As though Charles Town is some great metropolis? You really think Gillinghams delivers?" Em said, not without a bit of scorn in her voice.

"Hmmpf. Like you know everything about Charlie's Town! Gillinghams and any other exclusive upscale store delivers if you pay enough."

Em dismissed the discussion. "Yeah, right. Anyway, I've got a favor to ask. I need your help. You're a librarian, so you know where to find stuff, like land records, births, deaths, old census records, graveyards. I want to find out exactly where Felice lives. I want to find the graveyard, Heaven's Gate, she talked about. I bet she lives close by. She can't be far from our cabin. Then I could keep an eye on her, without her even knowing it."

"You mean spying on her? Honey, it doesn't sound like your Felicity wants to be found. Have you thought of that? Why don't you just leave her be. Like Persephone, she'll be back in the spring."

"That's what Randy said—that I should just leave her alone, not look for her." Yet a nagging suspicion and unquenchable desire to unearth *something* about Felice wouldn't die in Em's mind.

"Well, what about Heaven's Gate Cemetery? That shouldn't be too hard to find in land records. Felice said the path was overgrown and all the graves went untended. I'd like to at least find the graveyard. You could figure out where it is, right? That would answer a lot of questions. There's a grave I'd like to find." Em looked at Adrian imploringly, hoping for his understanding of the importance of her solving this mystery.

"Whose grave? What questions do you want answered? From what you've said, that graveyard has been abandoned for years. You won't find anything there but sunken ground and maybe a few worn-down headstones."

Em wasn't ready to share anything from *The Book of Memories* or her knowledge of specific graves there. "Maybe. But I'd like to learn to do gravestone rubbings. Best place to do that is in an old graveyard."

"Do what?"

"Gravestone rubbings. You tape rice paper over the gravestone and make an imprint of the stone with gravestone rubbing wax. The words on the stone appear on the paper when you rub the wax over the letters. It's like making an actual copy of the gravestone on paper," Em said, now impressing Adrian with her newfound knowledge.

Adrian was not impressed. "Now you're just being morbid. Where on earth did you come up with this idea?"

"Oh, I read about it," Em said, still determined to keep her secret book discovery to herself. *After all*, she thought, *it was a diary and a very personal one, written for and about the dearest of friends.* Emeline felt it was a secret for her alone. No one else, not even Randy, needed to know the mysteries in the little book. Adrian didn't respond. Em tried another tactic. "Oh, Adrian, come on. You're so smart. You know how to look for things."

"Flattery will get you everywhere. Well, what's Felicity's, or is it Felice? What's her last name?" Em realized she had called her friend by the shortened, more intimate name, *Felice.* She continued, "Her legal first name, I guess you'd say, is Felicity. I don't know her last name."

Adrian's brow furrowed. "Well, did she have any kids, certainly they'd still live around here. Nobody seems to ever leave Charlie's Town, for reasons I have yet to understand."

"She was married, I think, but I don't know her husband's name, either." Em thought for a moment, chewing her lip, and continued. "Addie, let's just call this the Felicity Project. Maybe we'll find her, maybe we won't."

"Girl, you expect miracles, not research. So, I'm supposed to look up birth and death records, or census reports and land records, going on only a first name and a hunch? And, on top of that, you expect me to discover the whereabouts of some old graveyard? You're really losing it, sweets. Not a bad thing, mind you. Some of my closest friends are crazy."

"That's what Julia says," Em muttered, immediately angry with herself for letting slip Julia's name. Adrian looked at Em carefully but said nothing. *Who the hell is Julia?* he wondered to himself, and then changed the subject. "Why don't you just ask Felicity what her full name is?"

"Aren't you listening to me? I told you! I won't see her till spring! Come on, promise me you'll help?"

"Oi Vey. Okay. I'll look up land records for a graveyard so you can do your morbid gravestone robbing."

"*Rubbing*, not robbing, you cretin!"

"Oh, goodness, how hast thy vocabulary grown!"

"Adrian, please?" Em whined.

"Okay, YES! I promise. Now get out of here before Genevieve shows up. Yesterday she made me dust all the shelves, again. If she finds me chatting with you, she'll probably assign me to clean the bathrooms." Emeline couldn't resist pushing her luck. "Dearest Adrian, do you have any discards for me?"

"Don't I always? A real find this time." Surreptitiously he looked around the stacks, even though they were the only two in the library. From under the reference desk, he pulled out a small pile of books. "I found a whole set of the *Little House On The Prairie* books. I thought you'd like them, since you're living in a cabin much like the one described in these pages. You'll just have to read through the coloring. Some darling young artists didn't realize that books are for reading, not art portfolios. Thanks to this blooming young artist you get the books instead of our putting them back on the shelves."

"Oh, Addie! You're wonderful, I will adore these!" She hid the books in her cavernous purse which also served as a bookbag. Impulsively Em threw her arms around Adrian and gave him a kiss on the cheek. "That reminds me. I want you to come for Christmas dinner. I know it is a ways off, but please put it on your 'social calendar' as you call your leather book with all the empty pages."

Adrian smirked at Em, then thought for a moment. "Those pages are filling up nicely, by the way. Can I invite Nils? That is if we're still a number."

"Addie, I do believe you're blushing."

"Don't be silly. But who knows what the future holds? Can he come?"

"Of course. Invite whoever you want." She raised her eyebrows at him. "You and Nils certainly seem to be an 'item'." Adrian replied, "Mind your own beeswax, missy." Em replied with a chuckle, "I'm not your missy, mister," causing them both to laugh, shattering the silence of the library. "Point taken, madam," Adrian replied. "Oh, I almost forgot." Adrian continued. "Here's the latest list of old biddies who want their chairs caned. And I need more of your little announcements for chair caning business with your phone number. They're all gone."

"Wow. Amazing! Thank you so much!"

With a lighter heart and a heavier purse, Em nearly skipped through the library doors. She was certain Adrian would shed light on the Heaven's Gate Cemetery. On top of that, she might have more chairs to cane. Em made her way to the *Inn and Out* to see Sadie. Her friend was thrilled to see her, but the diner was so busy that Sadie had no time to chat. For once, all the seats were taken.

"Meatloaf day," Sadie informed Em. "We always sell out unless folks get here early. Stop by later before closing? I'll save you some pie."

"Of course. And I've got something I need to ask you."

"Oh, keep me in suspense, why don't you," Sadie said, hugging Em warmly just as the order-up bell dinged. "All right already, I'm coming. Keep yer pants on," quipped Sadie rolling her eyes at Em as she hustled to the pick-up window.

Em's next stop was the Sew What to check on her caning supplies. The brightly colored yarn in the shop window had given Em a plan. She'd crochet scarves for Adrian, Margret and Randy for Christmas, even Nils, as it looked like he'd be coming to Christmas dinner also.

Mary, in all her elegance, impressed Em all over again as she entered the shop. On this particular day, Mary was wearing an emerald green dress. The buttons were oversized and bright gold. The dress flowed around Mary's legs gracefully. On her feet, she wore beaded moccasins. In her ears were gold earrings that matched her dress. Her raven-black hair was French-braided and a green ribbon held her braids in place. To Em's surprise, Mary was delighted to see her, grasping Em's hands in her own.

"Lovely to see you, dear. Oh, and I have great news. More of your caning supplies have come in. I'll bring them out." Em thought the sight of the different sizes of caning was just as beautiful as the shades of yarn in the Sew What window. "Mary, I can't thank you enough for finding me a cane supplier." She then stared at Mary, which caused the tall woman to laugh.

"Dear, what on earth are you staring at?"

"It's just that you're so...well, beautiful, yes, but more than that. So exotic. Have you and your family always lived in Virginia?"

"Yes, for generations, for more years than you can imagine. I'm part of the Monacan Tribe, loosely related to the Mannahoac and Powhatan tribes. We originally settled north of the James River. So, you see, my family has lived in Virginia for many generations. We're Native American. That's *really* old family." Her musical laugh trilled throughout the store.

"Wow. I had no idea there were Indians...oh, I'm sorry, Native Americans, living in Virginia."

"Oh, yes indeed. Many of us left, that's true. As for me being exotic, I think that's probably just the way I dress. I design and create all my own clothing. That's why you might think they're exotic. Others just think I dress outlandishly, like a crazy lady."

"You dress beautifully. I can't believe you make all your own clothes. That reminds me. I was thinking of crocheting Christmas gifts for my family. I thought I could make a hat for my husband, and a shawl for my mother-in-law. I have other friends I'd like to make scarves for. But I don't have a whole lot of money right now. What with the caning supplies and all."

"That's not a problem. I'll help you pick out colors and we can put the yarn aside so they'll be in the same dye lots. Just pay for new yarn when you need it. I have plenty of backup yarns in the back."

For the next half hour, Em and Mary picked out shades of yarn to match each of the personalities she would be crocheting for. By the end of her visit, Em felt as though she had made another friend, not just a woman to order cane from. She happily left the shop leaving Mary standing in the doorway waving goodbye.

After grocery shopping, Em made her way back to the Inn and Out. Sadie was sitting at one of the tables, a piece of pie in front of her, her feet propped up on another chair. She bounced up to greet Em with a hug. "So glad you came back. I was about to start the closing routine. Come, sit, I'll get your pie and coffee. Just let me put the CLOSED sign up now that the cook's gone back to his bottle upstairs."

Suddenly, Em felt timid about the question foremost in her mind. *Don't be silly,* Em admonished herself. *After all, Sadie is a good friend.* After finishing her pie and coffee, Em waited for Sadie to end her chattering news about her 'girls' and how well they were doing in school. Em laughed at their antics, especially Mary Ann getting into Sadie's makeup. "You should have seen her, she looked like a clown, perfect for Halloween. Guess I'll have to teach her how to use it properly. God knows I never bother with it here."

"Sadie, I have something personal to ask you. I wouldn't ask, but there's no one else. Do you have an ob/gyn in town? I need to get my birth control pill prescription refilled."

"Of course, love. There's only one in town. My child-birthing days are over. I got fixed after Mary Ann was born. No point taking chances. That is, if I ever met someone I'd like to bed down with, which is doubtful." Sadie laughed, her large breasts jiggling beneath her stained apron. "Dr. Lockehart. I don't know if he works every day, but I'll give you his number. He's a good guy, pretty cute, too. He'll fix you up."

"I'm so grateful. I didn't know who else to ask. I was going to ask some of the wives of the guys that Randy works with at the employee picnic, but somehow I never got around to it."

"What picnic? I've never known Bert to spend money on his employees."

"It was actually a pot-luck last month. Bert didn't pay for anything. All the women brought dishes. The guys brought booze, beer, and fireworks. You know, the usual guy stuff."

"Huh. Last month? Whatcha been doing in the meantime, if you don't mind my asking? I mean, for birth control." Em blushed deeply, which Sadie noticed.

"Oh, sweetie. Don't mind me. None 'a my business. Give Dr. Lockehart a call. Let's clean this place up and get ready for the breakfast rush tomorrow." Sadie quickly rose to her feet. Together, they cleaned the tables. Em filled the salt and pepper shakers and folded paper napkins while Sadie filled the dishwasher. She came out of the kitchen wiping her hands on her stained apron.

"Well, that's all done. Thanks, lovie. I have to admit, this has been a great day. I didn't break a single dish, cup or glass." Sadie laughed her boisterous laugh, her round face becoming close to beautiful with her gleaming, bright eyes.

Sadie was right. It had been a great day. The future was full of new projects and adventures. Hopefully Em would get another chair-caning order. She had Christmas gifts in mind and had thought up the perfect gift for Randy. Even better, she could have Adrian help her pick it out at *Going Places Leather and Luggage Specialists.* It would give her a chance to personally ask Nils to come for Christmas dinner. It would be a very special holiday season, the first in their new home and life. She had so much to look forward to!

Chapter 14
Adrian's Quest

Adrian was on a mission. His excitement was overwhelming, bubbling up like an overflowing champagne flute. He would find this graveyard that was so important to Emeline. He'd doggedly chase his goal in every way possible through research and digging into the past. As for finding Felicity, that didn't seem possible. He'd start with the easier task of finding the Heaven's Gate Cemetery. And what better place to begin his quest than in his own place of employment, the Charles Town Public Library? That meant he'd have to align himself with the greatest keeper of history. Genevieve, his cautious mentor, chief librarian, and an antique herself, might help. However, he was timid about asking Genevieve for assistance on what she might consider a misuse of his library time.

Genevieve noticed Adrian haunting the history stacks one morning. Curious rather than annoyed, she left him to his secretive adventure in the dustiest, oldest part of the library. He was hard to miss. Genevieve chuckled over his pretending to be dusting and cleaning the old stacks. His sneezes alerted the Head Librarian to wherever he was lurking. Intrigued by his surreptitious scurrying about the stacks she finally confronted him.

"Adrian!" He dropped the large book he had been searching through and looked up guiltily, as though he had been discovered doing something elicit, rather than perusing *Charles Town: 200 Years of History.*

"Jeeze! Genevieve! You scared the hell out of me!" He waved his neglected feather duster, causing a dust storm to settle on his hair and shoulders. He sneezed again.

"What on earth are you doing? I never knew you to be so interested in our local history. And if you're supposedly cleaning, why are the stacks still covered in dust?"

"Just acquainting myself with our oldest reference book, so I can be of greater service to our library patrons." Genevieve picked up the book from the floor where Adrian had dropped it. She read the title. "Hmmm. *200 Years of Charles Town History: Early beginnings, settlers, properties, tales true and imagined.*" She examined the books Adrian had neatly assembled on the floor, noting the cushion placed on the step stool for his comfort.

"Really, Adrian? You're suddenly displaying an unquenchable thirst for Charles Town history? I thought you felt our little dell was beneath you and your big city rapport. Come on. What are you really up to?" Pointedly she looked at the cushion, step stool and pile of books. "Looks like you've made yourself quite comfortable. How long have you been working on this project, whatever it is?"

"I was checking these old books to see if they should be discarded, or saved, or archived."

"I'm waiting." Adrian pulled himself to his full height of five-foot ten-and squared his shoulders. Dust and a feather floated from his head. Genevieve remained undaunted by his rooster-like fluffed up appearance.

"Oh, all right. It's for Emeline. She has this crazy idea to find out all about the old cabins where she lives in Heaven's Hollow. And she wants to find this old graveyard that's supposed to be out there somewhere."

"My, what an admirable quest for our little Emeline. She's becoming quite the historian, then? What an improvement over her earlier choices of reading, like *Illicit Pairings.*"

"Genevieve. I'll thank you to give Em more credit than that. She's been reading books from D.H. Lawrence to Simone de Beauvoir for months, as you are aware. She's become a veritable bookworm, I swear. Her thirst for books seems unquenchable." Genevieve looked Adrian over with fresh eyes. She cocked her head, her gaze flitting from his mahogany curls to his Italian loafers.

"I'm sorry, Adrian. You're quite right. I can be judgmental. Emeline has come a long way. But why this sudden interest in our history?"

Adrian brightened immediately and began the long tale of Em's roaming the little village of cabins and the surrounding countryside along with her desire to learn more of the earliest residents and to discover the location of the old cemetery. By the end of Adrian's story, he and Genevieve were sitting together in a dim corner of the library. The sky outside the windows had darkened and rain slashed the building, making music on the roof and rattling branches. They stirred the cups of tea Genevieve had prepared as they listened to the symphony roaring above them. Adrian could see Genevieve was struggling with a question her eyes held. He waited until she finally spoke.

"Adrian, please stop me if I am being impertinent. I don't like to intrude on your privacy. Feel free to stop me in my queries if I have crossed a line of propriety. Shall I continue?"

"Of course. I'm bursting with curiosity." Adrian's warm smile encouraged and warmed Genevieve. He felt as though the older woman was opening a crack in a door toward the future of a closer friendship between them. Genevieve carefully placed her teacup on the table between them. "I've known you for years now, Adrian. What I've noticed is how you've become softer, more congenial to our library guests. If I may say so, lately you seem to have opened yourself up more. I've noticed this especially with your interactions with Emeline. And Nils, when he comes by to take you out to dinner. You seem like a man in love. But with whom, I wonder? Emeline or Nils?"

Adrian nearly spat out a mouthful of tea. "What?" he sputtered. "In love with *Emeline*? She's a friend, a dear one, I will admit. And, she's married. As for Nils, well, if I too can be perfectly honest, that's none of your business."

Genevieve brightened as though a lamp had been turned on behind her eyes and pale features. Adrian had never noticed the deep green shade of her eyes until that instant. "I knew it!" she chortled. "Now, mind you, in my days of courting and romance, I never would have dreamed of imagining such a relationship between two men. But times have certainly changed. If one strives to remain young, one must change with the times."

Adrian felt a spreading flush to his cheeks, traveling upward to his hairline. Genevieve reached out and touched Adrian's hand, much to his surprise. "Adrian, I'm happy to see the changes in you, whatever the reasons. Your efforts in assisting Emeline in her odyssey into the past is commendable. Now, how can I help?" Adrian nearly jumped for joy. He did need help, of that he was certain.

"Oh, Genevieve. Yes, please. I'd especially like to find the whereabouts of the old cemetery in Heavenly Hollow, Heaven's Gate Cemetery? And learning the stories of the neighborhood, and the current and recent residents of the cabin village would be so helpful."

For the next hour, Genevieve outlined a plan of action, carefully delineating a list of resources and goals on a yellow legal pad. Adrian rose to help the occasional library guest who ran out of the storm, splattering raindrops from their umbrellas and clothes. Finally, Genevieve was finished and handed her legal pad to Adrian. "I'll most likely come up with more ideas, but this is a good start. As you can see, my number one priority for you is people. The oldest residents of the cabins have lived in the valley for decades along with their ancestors. You'll need to interview them first. Living history is your greatest resource and they won't be around forever."

"I'll warn you, though, they generally protect their secrets and are reluctant to share their stories. Of course, some aren't exactly in their right or most agile minds. I've compiled a list of the names I'm aware of and remember. You'll have to research the records for more names and addresses. Or just go door to door in Heavenly Hollow and ask people what they know. I have no idea where the cemetery is, or even if it still exists. I haven't visited the hollow in years." She handed her legal pad to Adrian. Smiling brightly she said, "You're on your way, young man."

Adrian scanned the list of names. "Thank you so much, Genevieve. Would you mind if I interviewed some of the people here in the library? It would provide more validity to my quest. And I was wondering. What if I put a notice on the bulletin board? It certainly is working for Emeline's chair caning business. I imagine if people see the notice the word would get out and folks would just come by."

"Of course, please feel free to do so. The pursuit of historical knowledge is a worthy cause. Some of our oldest citizens would most likely be happy to talk about the past. We elderly do get lonely, you know." Adrian studied Genevieve again. Her cheeks appeared rosy now, matching her pink lipstick. She was, as always, tastefully dressed with a carefully arranged silk scarf, her pink cashmere sweater and gray wool skirt. "I can't thank you enough, Genevieve."

"Oh, no. Thank you for letting me in on your great adventure. I am thrilled that you are allowing me to delve into your psyche and plans." Genevieve sensed Adrian wanted to hug her. She quickly rose and picked up their teacups, the china clattering on her tray as she turned toward the library kitchen. She then turned back to Adrian, smiling warmly. "Now, off with you. I'll close up. You have a lot of work to do and I am proud to be your assistant historian."

Adrian made his way through the stacks. After the rain, sunbeams shone through the windows, chasing away the gloom. It had been a wildly unexpected day and he had a lot to think about. Like love. He thought he was, indeed, falling in love with Nils. He also loved Emeline, her sweet ways, her developing mind, the way she teased him. Over the past months she had coaxed him from the cynicism and taciturn refuge of his mind. He had been hiding from the world for years and she had dragged him out of his safe cocoon. Had this not happened would he have been so open to Nils? Could he have become so close to him so quickly? The anonymous partners of his past had quenched his desires momentarily. Caring for another person, and a woman at that, had been his invitation to the open world. He had softened. He was more confident to allow others—Em, Sadie, Nils—and even Genevieve to see him more clearly. He was not as afraid to show who he was or to laugh at himself. He was allowing himself to play. He could be a jokester or one striving for the rudiments of knowledge and deeper sensitivity and intelligence. People were beginning to notice the changes within himself. So was he.

Adrian quickly crossed the wet, gleaming streets as he departed the library. He waved happily to Sadie as she was turning the OPEN sign to CLOSED. She congenially waved back. His smile brightened as he saw that Nil's had not yet put up his Closed sign at Going Places Leather and Luggage Specialists. As he entered the shop Nils was clearly happy to see Adrian and blew him a kiss. He rolled his eyes at his customer who was meticulously inspecting leather lounge shoes. "Of course, Mrs. Carter. I promise you these beautiful slippers were crafted in Italy. If they don't fit, they can be exchanged. They'll be a perfect Christmas gift." Nils made the universal circular finger sign for *crazy* behind Mrs. Carter's back. Adrian happily wandered the shop as Nils completed his sale. As soon as Mrs. Carter had departed, leather lounge slippers secured in her tasteful Going Places bag, Nils put the CLOSED sign on the door. Nils and Adrian hugged briefly, then Nils laughed. "Oh, I'd love to see her husband's duck feet trying to fit into those elegant slippers. He won't have the heart to return them and will be forced to wear them on Christmas day and long after. I can think of someone much more worthy of such a beautiful gift." He winked at Adrian as he cleaned up his desk and put his receipts and cash from the register in his hidden wall safe behind the poker-playing dogs painting. Adrian could contain his exuberance no longer. "Oh, Nils. It's been the most incredible day. I have so much to tell you!" Nils looked at Adrian lovingly. "I can't wait to hear it all, sweetie. Let's go home and I'll make you a fabulous dinner. I've brined the chicken for twelve hours. It will melt in your mouth!" As Adrian helped Nils close up the shop and put merchandise in their proper places, he felt his heart was close to exploding. He had never been happier. He had become part of a life, part of a love.

Arm in arm they walked down the street, Nils humming one of their favorite songs which he paraphrased with his own touch, *"Oh it's a fine day, for chasing the blues, yes, it's a fine day, for buying new dishes...* It's a good day to celebrate. Let's pick up a special bottle of wine at Gillinghams." Adrian couldn't hold in his joy. "Every day with you is a good day to celebrate, Nils." He was rewarded with Nils' misty-eyed grin, filling Adrian with love, yet again.

Over the following weeks Adrian's sign on the bulletin board drew in some of the library patrons who spread the word to their older relatives. Slowly, they began to visit the library and share their stories with either Genevieve or Adrian. The most elderly came with relatives, leaning on them for support. At first, reluctant to tell their stories, they relented when their relatives prodded them to share their past. Adrian's first question was always the same. "Do you know anything about an old cemetery called Heaven's Gate in the Hollow?"

"Nah. We don't go up there. I wouldn't even know where to find it. I'll tell you what, though. My grand-daddy told my pappy to never go there. My grand-daddy came here all the way from Wales. The stories he could tell! We kids was forbidden to go up there. That ole graveyard was for the negroes, so we had no business in those parts. Besides. They's spirits up there. The place is haunted. My grand-daddy tole my pappy he'd seen lights in the middle of the night lighting up the graves. As a boy he snuck up there on Halloween with a few of his friends. They saw it with their own eyes. Flames coming from outta the old graves. Corpse candles, corpse fires, he called 'em."

Adrian wrote down the stories which sometimes Genevieve would enlarge upon. He said, "Can you believe that old coot? Flames coming out of the graves? These old folks are crazy. I don't know if I'll ever get anything out of them that's useful. No one seems to know where the actual graveyard is."

Genevieve clucked at Adrian. "Dear, keep an open mind. There actually is some truth to that tale." Adrian looked at Genevieve as though she too was addled. She laughed in his face.

"They *are* called corpse candles. But there's nothing mysterious or ghostly about them. It's from gasses erupting from the graves when bodies are buried without caskets, just placed in the ground. The gasses from the decomposing corpses sometimes, if conditions are exactly right, turn to flames and light up the graves. The local black people still used that graveyard, albeit surreptitiously."

Adrian was shocked and intrigued. "Jeeze, Genevieve, I should be interviewing you."

"In due time, Adrian, in due time. For now, I think you're making great progress. You might want to go to the county records office to see if you can discover where this graveyard is. Although you still haven't told me why this hidden graveyard is so important to Emeline."

"She's got some crazy idea that she wants to do grave robbing up there."

"I beg your pardon?"

Adrian laughed. "Oh, that's what I call it, just to tease her. She wants to do grave *rubbings*. For some reason, she got it in her head that it would be the best graveyard to make imprints from the oldest headstones."

"How very commendable of her to preserve the past in such an artistic manner. I'll have to look up some print books for our young Emeline. I'm sure there's something in the library that would be useful to her."

More stories began to flow in from the old-timers. "Look for a corpse road if you want to find that old graveyard. The way will be lit with lights from the home of the person about to die all the way up to the graveyard. I spek someday soon my door will be lit with lights leading me up to that old graveyard." Adrian listened intently, writing down every detail from each elderly visitor.

Another woman explained to Adrian that he'd find the graveyard by looking through the old lanes for coffin trees. "They're a lane of trees that were planted near the front door of every cabin. There would be one for each member of the family, starting with the husband and wife, with a tree added for each child. As each family member died, a tree would be cut down for the making of a coffin. By the time the whole family was gone, the trees would be, too. Maybe there are one or two left, if there were no longer living family members to cut down the last tree, to make the last coffin. Look for a row of coffin trees on either side of a road and you'll find the graveyard. It was forbidden to cut down coffin trees that led to a graveyard. The trees showed the way for the funeral marches to travel to the gravesite."

Adrian was surprised by many of the tales, saddened by others. The tale of the coffin trees filled him with sorrow. The world contained numerous tragedies he had yet to experience. He found he was learning the value of mortality, the sacredness of life and the necessity to enjoy every moment of living. He shared his stories with Nils, who was equally touched by the tales.

"Skull Fences. That's what I remember," said the querulous old woman, leaning on a cane and then poking Adrian with it as he sat at the little table he had set up for his interviews and note-taking.

"Pardon?" Adrian said, trying to keep the skepticism out of his voice.

"Skull fences. My grandma told me about them. At the Negro cemetery. Oh, mind you, this was years and years ago." Finally, Adrian felt he had a clue he could follow. "Please tell me. What is a skull fence? Where might this skull fence be found?"

"Oh, I surely don't know. It was an African thing, my grandma told me, and her mama told her, who was a slave until she wound up at Mildred Hanson's plantation. Those old slaves brought all their ancient stories and customs with them." Now Adrian's curiosity was fully engaged. "Please," he implored the woman, "can you tell me more about these skull fences?"

"Well. She told me the negroes needed a graveyard and it had to be protected. So, the oldest slaves, the ones who could remember the tales from Africa, said they had to have a graveyard no whites would enter. Those days, you know, a cemetery full of negroes could be attacked. Whites didn't like the negroes, dead or alive. So to protect the graveyard and frighten away the whites, they put old skulls on fence posts surrounding the cemetery, animal skulls, even humans. She never did say where those skulls came from and no one ever asked. Dint wanta know, if you get my meaning. Musta worked. No one knows where that old graveyard is. I surely ain't never been there. Anyway, no one in my family living down there in the Hollow would have ever wanted to venture forth into an old graveyard." As quickly as she had arrived at Adrian's desk, she skuttled away, her cane knocking along the wooden floor.

One day Adrian was certain he had a solid lead: an old gentleman had stopped by and said he had actually visited the graveyard. "Yup. I been there. Only a young pup, I was. Maybe fourteen, fifteen or so. That was eighty years ago. Me and my friend, Abraham, was his name. Or was it David? Now who was I with that night?" Adrian tapped his foot.

"You say you've actually visited that graveyard, the one in the hollow?" The elderly man grew annoyed. "Well, that's what I said, dint I? Now where was I?"

"You were with Abraham."

"That's right. It were me and Dennis. We had these two gals with us, it was the night before Halloween. All Hollows Eve, my grandma called that night. Now, my great grandma, she was Mexican. You know, came here all the way from California. She was a good old gal. Made the best fry bread this side of Virginia."

Adrian was about to give up getting further information from the old coot and began shuffling the papers on his desk.

"Yup. Went up there with them two gals. All Hollows Eve. Big night for Mexican folk, you know. We thought maybe we'd scare the girls and get a kiss or two. Boy, was we ever wrong." The man's eyes grew misty in memory. He seemed lost again to Adrian. Finally, the old man seemed to awaken and became excited. "We was up there, all right. Skulls on the fence and all, that scared the girls so we figgered we'd get some lovin' for sure. Ha! We was walking through that graveyard when all a sudden a bunch of white things flew right out of a grave. Well, those gals did scream and so did Albert and me. We ran. Left those gals behind. Never did see them again. Now, what was their names? I know one had the pertiest gold hair."

Adrian could hold in his annoyance no longer. "Are you saying you saw something white float out of a grave, like a ghost?"

The old man laughed a phlegmy chortle. "Ha! Nah. What we later found out was they twerent any ghosts, they was geese! They lived in the graveyard and used to settle in to the sunken graves at night. When we was walking through the graveyard, we skeered 'em up and they flew out of the graves! Near about made me piss my pants. Come to think of it, I did." The old man laughed again.

"Well, do you remember where the graveyard was?"

"Hell, no, sonny. That twere eighty years ago. I got a great memory for names, all right. But I disremember places." Adrian rolled his eyes. Genevieve appeared behind the old fellow and gave Adrian a warning glance. She placed her hand on the gentleman's shoulder as she wagged a reprimanding finger at Adrian.

"That's a lovely tale, Mr. Stephens and you tell it so well. I'm sure it will help Adrian in his search for the graveyard."

"Yup. Happy to help Miss Gertrude. Happy to help." With that, the old man nodded to Adrian and cheerfully said his goodbyes.

Adrian muttered under his breath, watching the old fellow depart. "Okay, Gertrude. Point taken. I'll do my best to listen better and be more patient with the old folks." They hid their laughter until the elderly gentleman exited the library.

"Gertrude, indeed," Genevieve said, as she watched Adrian sort through his notes. She was proud of his dedication in helping with Emeline's search for the old cemetery. A lightbulb went off in her head.

"Adrian! I think we've been going about this all wrong. It's fine to get the local elders of Charles Town involved but I think you'll have to go right to the source." Adrian was feeling grumpy over the lack of any real information discovered. "And what might that source be elder librarian?"

Genevieve swatted him. "I am not an elder anything. At least not in *my* mind. What I just realized is that you need to go to Richmond to the Virginia Department of Historic Resources. I have a dear friend who works there and I'm sure he'd be happy to help out. The problem is Heavenly Hollow is an unincorporated part of Charles Town, so virtually no records will exist by street names. None of the roads have proper designations. The only real records would be of Mildred Hansons' plantation, and the immediate surrounding area. None of the land was deeded to existing cabin owners, only their ancestors, whose names probably changed through marriages. All the cabins are only numbered, with no family names, making your discoveries more difficult. But a graveyard would have to be recorded. I'm sure if I give my friend a call he'd help you go through the archeological records, for below-ground archeological sites. He could provide you with all kinds of information, maps, old slave cemeteries, even old photographs and newspaper clippings, if any are available."

Adrian jumped up and to their joint surprise, hugged Genevieve. "Oh, that is a stroke of genius. No wonder you're the Head Librarian. But I'd probably have to take a day off from work to go up to Richmond." In his mind, Adrian was already planning. He could invite Nils and they'd make a day of it. After going through the archives, they could go shopping and have dinner.

"Tell you what," said Genevieve. "I'll give you the day off with pay. This is a valid librarian's duty to provide history and research to our patrons. I'll let you know when I get hold of Don, Donald Fraser, at the Department of Historic Resources, that's who you'll be seeing. We'll make an appointment for you and you can spend the day."

A week later Adrian and Nils set off in Nils' Mercedes. Two more excited men could not be found in Charles Town as they set off on their adventure. It was their first road trip together. Nils had prepared a cooler filled with Brie, Camembert, fresh peaches and chilled Pinot Grigio. Adrian contributed chocolate from Ghirardelli's. In a picnic basket, Nils had carefully placed crystal wine goblets, cloth napkins, a red and white checkered tablecloth along with a special treat for Adrian from Flaky Foreigners Bakery.

The trip had been a chatty one, about their mutual friends, the best choices for cold cuts and olives, and whether Gillinghams or the Piggly Wiggly had the greatest variety of cheeses. Nils planned on touring Richmond shops and checking out restaurants while Adrian met with Donald Fraser to investigate archeological below-ground records and land use records of graveyards. Nils noticed that the closer they came to their Richmond destination the quieter Adrian became. He studied his silent boyfriend until finally curiosity overcame him. He reached out and touched Adrian's hand.

"Sweetie, what is it? Why the Sphinx mode?" Adrian seemed to awaken from his thoughts. "Oh, nothing," he replied, turning his eyes from the car window to Nils, to reassure him. It didn't work. Nils allowed Addy his solitude, having guessed the reason. He had discovered the timidity and vicissitudes of his lover's ways. Finally, as the more intuitive and vocal of the two, he voiced his thoughts. Nils had learned that Adrian often hid his deepest thoughts behind his jocularity. "Addy, stop worrying. We'll get to Richmond in plenty of time, I promise you. Donald Fraser will be thrilled to meet you. How many archeological history investigators do you think wander into his office?"

Adrian roused himself and flashed a smile at Nils. Through the windshield Adrian noticed continuing highway signs and weary-looking trees. They drove by fewer palatial mansions and began seeing more urbane buildings. He sighed deeply. "It's not just that. I don't want to disappoint Genevieve. What if her friend thinks I'm a moron? What if he's disgusted with my lack of knowledge?"

Nils looked over at Adrian and was surprised to see the depth of the worry lines around his eyes and mouth. "Okay, that's it. Time for a break," he said, pulling off the highway onto a dirt lane bordered by old maples, now naked of their bright leaves that had been shed in the recent October storms.

"No, we'll be late!" Adrian protested.

"We'll most likely be an hour early. Grab the picnic basket from the back seat, open it and sniff its contents. There's a surprise in there for you. I'll get the cooler." Adrian did as he was told.

"Oh my goddesses! Chocolate croissants from Flaky Foreigners. Okay, I'm all in for our picnic. Guess I didn't need the Ghirardelli, huh?"

"Love, you've taught me that one can never have enough chocolate." By the time their meal was over, enjoyed in a soft meadow off the road, Adrian was rejuvenated and recharged. The chilled wine and dessert of croissants, accompanied by a thermos of hot coffee made a perfect ending to their meal.

"Now I'll be so wired I'll be bouncing off the walls. But you're right, I do feel much more confident," he told Nils.

They arrived at the Virginia Department of Historic Resources. As Nils dropped Adrian off he reassured him: "You got this, Adrian. Really. I just know you'll end up having a terrific time."

Adrian found his way to Donald Fraser's office and was met by a jovial older gentleman wearing a tweed sports jacket and a red bow tie. Adrian immediately felt at home with Donald's warm friendly welcome in his art-filled office. For the next hour he and Adrian went over various types of records the historian shared with him. Then, Donald led Adrian to the crypt of old records beneath the building. "Now, remember," he said, "the area you're looking into is unincorporated. There most likely will be no street names, only land records. Your best bet will be to search for any land designated as 'sacred, family cemetery or public land designated as burial sites'."

"Why would there be no street names?" Adrian asked, feeling dejected with the enormity of his task.

"RFD, Rural Free Delivery of mail. The only sign of a family would be that they would receive their mail via RFD in a mailbox they registered with the Charles Town Post Office. I've learned that many in these smaller communities prefer not to be found, so they won't have a mailbox. They pick up their mail from their post office boxes. Mailmen only deliver to registered names on the mailbox, if they have one. If they don't have one, it's as though the family and the property don't exist, except under the property records of the current owner, whoever that might be."

Donald saw Adrian's dejected look and sat down next to him, pulling out the first voluminous, dusty book of *Surry County Property Records, Deeds and Titles, 1826-1977.*

The older gentleman continued his instructions for Adrian. "These records haven't been updated by the Clerk of the Court in two years, but I don't think that matters. If what you say is correct, this graveyard has been around since the 1830s, at least. There will have to be a record somewhere. Concentrate on the earliest recorded years."

He patted Adrian on the back and handed him a magnifying glass. "I'll check back in an hour," he said reassuringly. "If you find anything of value I'd be happy to copy the maps or deeds for you. Just focus on Charles Town RFD routes and designated sacred places or family burial plots. You'll be sure to find an area of no cabins. Search the uninhabited locations, anything that sounds like it could be a graveyard. Concentrate around the area of Mildred Hanson's property, which is clearly shown on the land records." With that, Donald departed the depths of the county records department, leaving Adrian in a funk. How on earth was he going to be able to go through all these maps and records? The old handwriting was almost indecipherable.

Three hours later, Adrian, in a state of excitement, walked out the building with a sheaf full of maps, land records and clippings of ancient death notices. Donald had copied everything for him which could provide clues which might lead to the actual graveyard. He walked to he and Nils' designated meeting place, the Sea Hag Restaurant. Nils was already comfortably settled into a booth. The restaurant was one of Nils' favorites, tucked away among larger establishments with a view of the beautiful old downtown Richmond buildings. Adrian was practically floating. He was so excited he pecked Nils on the cheek, even though he knew of Nils' timidity of outward affection in public.

Adrian couldn't conceal his joy. "I found it! I'm certain! And look, Donald made me a map of what he and I both believe is the old slave cemetery. It's never been listed as an historic cemetery but as part of Mildred Hanson's original acreage. In the maps and the Hanson deeds, it's listed as 'a sacred resting place'. I never would have found it without Donald. I didn't even know what an RFD was!"

"RFD?" Nils asked. Adrian was happy to educate him, sharing all he had learned, pulling out maps and land deeds and pointing to the most likely possibility for the old graveyard.

"How are we supposed to find it when there are no road names, just RFD mailboxes, if mailboxes like that even still exist?" asked Nils.

"Oh, I'm not going to worry about that now," Adrian replied. "This will be Em's Christmas gift, absolutely the best present I could ever give her. The three of us will just go traipsing around the hills until we pick up on all the clues in the maps and land deeds. We'll find Heaven's Gate. I just know it." Adrian's excitement was infectious. They spread all the papers across the antique ship-hatch table and only moved everything aside when their lobster arrived. Their lobster bibs did not protect butter from seeping onto Adrian's shirt, but Nils didn't care.

Arm-in-arm they left the restaurant, full of lobster and the discoveries Adrian had unearthed.

"I hate to say it, but should I be jealous? What does Donald look like? How old is he?" Nils questioned his sweetheart.

"Yeah, yeah, I know. Don and I really hit it off." He was thrilled with Nils's words and sang to reassure him, 'You're the only one...' "Nothing like that, honey. Don was so happy to have what he called, 'a fellow historian'. Can you believe it? Me, a historian? I can't wait to show all this to Genevieve. Don and Genevieve went to college together where they both studied Library Sciences. He had nothing but kind words to say about her. I wonder if they dated, or were lovers?" Adrian had never imagined Genevieve in a relationship, but why not?

Nils raised his brows, "Hmm, could be. After all, they went to school together."

Adrian continued to erupt in excitement as they returned to the car. "Next thing I have to do is buy a nice leather scrapbook for Em and I'll put all the documents in it as her Christmas gift. Now, if only I knew where to purchase fine leather?"

Nils punched Adrian affectionately on the shoulder. "You're only going to one shop to buy your leather, and don't you forget it." Adrian's eyes melted. He was certain. He was falling in love with this sweet man. He fervently hoped Nils felt the same. "I wouldn't dream of shopping anywhere else, love." They drove off into the sunset, exhilarated with the day's events and whatever the future held.

Chapter 15

Em studied her wall calendar intently. It was the first of November and her cottage industry of chair-caning had taken off. She'd received a call that morning to cane four chairs by Thanksgiving. The order would bring in $200, a boon right before Christmas. She was thrilled, but nervous. That's a lot of holes to fill in just over three weeks she sagely informed Rhett, who was lovingly washing Scarlet under the kitchen table. Rhett did not reply.

For the first time in five years, Em was excited about Thanksgiving and learning to cook a turkey with 'all the fixins'. Margret had been thrilled and wanted nothing more than to share old family recipes from the Sacramento Delta to Virginia with her new 'daughter'. She promised to teach Em everything from Turkey prep to sausage stuffing mix to turkey roasting, side dishes of cranberry orange nut relish, green bean casserole and Bourbon Sweet Potatoes. In return, Em was excited that Margret had agreed to come to their first Christmas in their new home. Her relationship with her mother-in-law had improved enormously since Em had begun to view Randy's mom with more empathy, seeing her as a companionable and lonely elderly woman, rather than an old lady of cranky competitiveness. Randy was thankful that it was no longer his role to play referee and interference in the older and younger women's blossoming, if cautious, relationship. The day at the Jamestown Plantation and The Woodbine Cottage dinner had cemented the warm feelings between the two.

Several times prior to Thanksgiving Randy had come home to find cane soaking in the kitchen sink and Em fast asleep with a half caned chair in front of her. It was a sweet sight of his wife enveloped in light from the lace curtained window, her head nestled in the seat cushions behind her on the old Lincoln rocker. "Em, Em..." he'd gently shake her. She was always surprised she'd fallen asleep, leaving dinner uncooked and a chair unfinished.

"Sweetheart, I think you're working too hard. Can't you take a break?"

"I can't. The money will be a huge help. Mrs. Conover needs the chairs completed by Thanksgiving. I promised. Caning just tires me out."

Em was also concerned. She was much more tired than usual these days and her effusive bouncy self that arose every morning had escaped her. Often she would fall asleep on the couch by 9pm, the blare of the TV not disturbing her slumber.

"I'll take tomorrow off, I promise. I have to go into town to see Adrian anyway. I want to stop by the *Sew What* for yarn. I've decided I'm going to make your mom a shawl for Christmas. Maybe something real soft and warm, like mohair. Think she'd like that?"

"Oh, Em, she'll love anything you make for her. That's a great idea." Em puffed up with Randy's praise. She was becoming a real artisan, she happily told herself.

"Maybe I'll make her a little basket of my homemade jams, too. And a loaf of my honey wheat bread."

"Perfect. She'll be overjoyed."

Em grew quiet, then decided to plunge ahead with the thought that had been on her mind since her invitation to Adrian, which she had not shared with her husband. "Randy, would you mind if I invited Adrian and Nils for Christmas? Addy doesn't have any family except Nils. I think Sadie and me are his only friends in Charles Town."

"I thought he has friends in Raleigh?"

"Oh, I don't think I'd call those guys friends. More like flings," Em replied with a chuckle. "If you gather my meaning."

"Yuck. Yeah. I get it. Sure, invite him and his boyfriend. Just tell him not to make a pass at me. I'm a taken man, you know."

Em enfolded him in a hug. "And don't you ever forget it."

The next day Adrian was thrilled to see Em enter the library. Em was not thrilled with Adrian's lack of progress on 'the Felicity Project'. Adrian smiled inwardly, thinking how much fun it would be to surprise Em with his discoveries, even if they didn't include Felicity.

"Honey, how am I supposed to figure out who this Felicity is when you don't even know her last name?"

"There can't be too many Felicities around. It's not a common name."

"And you have no idea where she lives! I'm a good researcher, sure. But I'm not psychic. What, do you expect me to channel this old lady? Get my Ouija Board out and ask for a last name or address?"

Em slapped him playfully as he tucked his chin onto his chest, eyes closed. "Ooooommmm, Felicity, wherefore art thou? Show yourself…ooooommmm."

"Well, surely the graveyard must be on an old map or city plat somewhere. Maybe if we find the graveyard, I'll discover some historical stone to preserve in a rubbing."

Again, Adrian glowed in his subterfuge. He countered thoughtfully. "Well, how many people could be buried in that old graveyard? It's been abandoned for years. There can't be that many graves, historical or otherwise." Adrian was beside himself with inward glee, luxuriating in his knowledge of having discovered exactly what Em was looking for, old maps and information on Heavenly Hollow. His discoveries at the Virginia Department of Historic Resources convinced him there were trails leading to Heaven's Gate Cemetery. He kept a straight face, keeping his perfect secret masked. "Besides, everyone in Charlie's Town gets planted at either All Saints or Grand Finale Cemeteries. That's where you might find important, historical founders' graves. I'm sure you could do your grave rubbings there, right?"

"Grand Finale?" Em asked, puzzled.

"Well, the name is actually Grand Father's Friendly Acres. I like the Grand Finale better," he informed Em with a smirk.

"You're incorrigible," she replied, shaking her head at him.

Inwardly, Adrian chuckled, happy in the knowledge of his Christmas surprise. Em had no idea what he had been up to. "Okay. I'll give it a try but only because you invited us for Christmas. You are a dear."

"Margret, Randy's mom, will be there, also. Maybe you and Nils could pick her up on your way over? It would save Randy a trip. That way he could help me out with getting everything ready."

"Of course, no problem."

Em chewed her lip, thinking of the absence of her other friend, Sadie. "I'd love it if Sadie could come, but she's going to her aunties home from Christmas Eve to New Year's Day with the girls. Her Aunt Divinity's got a beautiful home on Cape Henry, right on the water. They go every year."

"Wow. Her auntie must have some bucks. That's a very exclusive area. Oh, speaking of money and your little enterprise, that reminds me. I need more of your chair caning cards. They've flown off the bulletin board."

"Good grief. I have four chairs to finish by Thanksgiving with only two completed. I've got to run."

At Sew What, Em was rewarded with lovely balls of mohair yarn in sunset shades of pinks, lavenders and blues. The colors would be perfect for Margret with her white hair and rosy complexion. Em picked out the wildest Hawaiian colors of yarn she could find to make a scarf for Adrian, and more refined colors of yarn for Randy and Nils. Worries overcame her. *Jeeze, how am I ever going to get all this finished by Christmas? At least I'll have more time after Thanksgiving, though, once the chair orders are all completed.*

"Excuse me?" A woman looking through a bin of yarn examined Em fearfully. Crazy people who talked to themselves tended to knit and crochet. She knew that from experience.

"Oh, nothing. I was just talking to myself. About caning four chairs by Thanksgiving and making shawls and scarfs by Christmas."

The woman lit up. "You're the young woman who lives in the holler and canes chairs." Em brightened. "Yes, I am," she said proudly. The woman continued. "Well, I'll be. I know there used to be an old lady up in the holler who had a shop and caned chairs years ago. I didn't know anyone else had picked up the art. My name's Daphne." She reached out her hand and Em warmly accepted Daphne's handshake. "Really? You mean Felicity? Or Julia, the woman who knew how to cane chairs and had an antique shop?"

"Oh, I can't recall names. This was years ago." Em's spirits were dampened as quickly as they had risen. She then put on her newly adopted professional demeanor. "I live in Heavenly Hollow. I've been getting a lot of orders lately, with Thanksgiving and the holiday season coming up. People are pulling old chairs out of attics to be repaired for their Turkey Day dinner parties."

Daphne looked Em over, examining her. *She seemed like an awfully young woman to be an expert at chair caning.* "Well, I have a Lincoln rocker I wanted repaired for my grand-daughter's Christmas present. She just became engaged, and I thought it would be the perfect family gift. It's an heirloom. Could you do that?"

Em's mind raced. A Lincoln rocker. She'd never attempted one before. That was a lot of work and she'd just told Randy she'd take it easy. But it would certainly give her practice on repairing her mama's Lincoln rocker which she couldn't use unless the broken seat was layered in cushions. With more bravado than Em felt, she replied, "Well, I'd have to see it to give you an estimate. I could do the rocker, but it would be at least $75. Maybe more."

"I could bring it into the Sew What if you'd like so you could give me a more accurate estimate. I live in Charles Town. It would be no trouble at all."

Em chewed her lower lip, then smiled gratefully as she replied, "Yes, that will work. How about next Tuesday?" By Em's calculations she would be finished with the third chair by then, with only one more to cane. She decided to brave her fears and accept the offer.

"That would be perfect," replied Daphne.

"Until Tuesday, then." Em floated out the store with her purchases, bags stuffed with bright colored yarns, heart overflowing with hope, dollar signs in her head. She had Felicity to thank. Her wise friend had paved the way for Em's blooming bank account. She couldn't wait to tell the news to Felice when she reappeared in the spring. Her first Lincoln rocker! She hoped Randy would be as thrilled as Em was.

Em worked herself to a frazzle but managed to get all four chairs completed by Thanksgiving. Her customer was thrilled and promised to tell all her friends of Em's prowess with caning. The Lincoln rocker now waited for her touch. With materials and labor, the job would bring in a $125 windfall. Randy was ecstatic but continued to worry about Em working too hard. The night before he had again found her napping when he arrived home at 5:30 to a darkened house and a cold stove. Em was sound asleep with *Revelations, Diaries of Women* resting on her chest. He watched her breasts push the book up and down as gentle snores fluttered from her lips.

"Em. Wake up sweetheart."

"Huh, what? Oh, damn, dinner time and I haven't started a thing."

"That's okay, love. I'll make grilled cheese sandwiches. How does that sound?"

"Great. I'm starving," Em happily agreed.

The following Thursday was cold and bright, perfect for Thanksgiving. Em and Randy arrived at Margret's home at 10:30 so Em could look over all Margret's recipes and assist her as her prep cook, or 'sous chef' as her mother-in-law called her. Margret bustled around her large sparkling kitchen. Her joy in sharing her family recipes with Emeline was palpable and she was nearly bursting with excitement and cheer as she instructed Em on each step of the meal. Randy ambled off to the TV room, intent on watching the pre-Thanksgiving football chatter.

"Now, dear, first you take out the giblets, the liver, all that stuff. I don't use them for stuffing. Instead, I use sausage meat, celery, onions, mushrooms and stale bread cubes. Just stick your hand in the turkey and pull out all that slimy stuff. Then check inside the neck to see that it's clean."

Suddenly, Em felt overwhelmed by the task. The fat white bird lay in the sink, legs splayed, neck gaping, remnants of feather follicles decorating one wing. Nausea and a strange faintness washed over her. Margret noticed at once. Em's pale skin turned a sickly greenish white. Margret quickly pulled a chair out for her to crash into. The remnants of liver, kidneys, gizzard, and a bony turkey neck spilled onto the floor from Em's hands. Margret cleaned up the mess and then pulled up a chair and sat down opposite Emeline. She placed a cold wet dish towel on the back of Emeline's neck as Margret instructed her to keep her head lowered. Slowly, Emeline revived.

"My dear, you look like a ghost."

"I'm okay. The smell. It just suddenly got to me. And the innards. I'm so sorry about the mess you had to clean up. Oh, I do feel sick. Randy thinks I've been working too hard on chair caning because I'm always so tired."

"My dear, I hope I'm not being intrusive. But is there any chance you could be expecting? You have all the signs. I think. Have you missed...?"

Em, in a panic, calculated backwards. "Well, I had a period in early October. I'm pretty irregular, even with the pill. But it wasn't like a real period. I'd run out of my birth control pills and had an appointment for a refill, but I had to cancel. I was so busy getting those four chairs caned. I don't know, I haven't thought about it. I might have missed this month."

"Oh, my sweet child. I do believe you're pregnant. What a Christmas gift for Randy, and oh, yes, for me, too."

Em roused herself, the thought of being pregnant sent a cold shock through her being, replacing the nausea. "I'll get my prescription refilled this week, I promise. Please don't say a word to Randy about your suspicions."

"Of course not. This will be our little secret," she enthused. "Meanwhile, have a nice glass of milk and some crackers. That always helped me through the nausea. I'll show you how to make cranberry relish. No more raw turkey and gizzards for you!"

Em gratefully accepted the milk and crackers. Her mind was in a tizzy. A baby. Oh my God. Could it be true? Was she ready? Was Randy? Was this what she really wanted? I'll think about that tomorrow she told herself, mimicking Scarlet O'Hara. Then she realized if Margret's suspicions were true, this was something she could not put off. She had to think about it now, not tomorrow. She had to plan. First things first. Doctor's appointment. In the meantime, who knew? Maybe she'd get her period.

"Dear, promise me you'll let me know the minute it's confirmed. I won't say a word to Randy. I'd never steal your thunder. If you are pregnant, that is." Margret judiciously intoned.

Em laughed. "Of course, I will, Margret. I'll be wanting to tell someone."

"Please, dear Emeline, call me Mother, or Mother Margret. After all, I'm the only mother you have now." Em's eyes filled with tears as Margret enfolded her 'new' daughter in a warm hug. She whispered into Margret's ear, "Thank you, Mother. You're right. You are the only mother I have now." They returned to making the Thanksgiving meal, both ignoring what was screaming in their minds. Margret thought the meal was made only more delicious by the secret she and Em shared.

That night Em's mind raced, keeping her from sleep. She calculated the dates when she was 'safe' as her mama had described the 'rhythm method' to Em, which she claimed had never failed her. Em laughed at the memory. Her mother had conceived three babies during those 'safe' times. But Emeline knew. She was certain, even without a blood test or an exam. She was pregnant. She didn't know whether to be happy, sad, frightened, exhilarated or angry.

What an idiot. Expecting a baby? How had she let this happen? Well-known words from *Gone with The Wind* returned to her. "I don't know nuthin 'bout birthin babies, Mz. Scarlet." Em had no experience with children, let alone babies! As a thirteen-year-old, while other girls in the delta were taking babysitting classes and making money, Em had been doing her usual wandering through the delta collecting bird's nests and spying on baby birds. Not baby people. The thought of pregnancy frightened her. She didn't know if she was ready. Yet she had to admit to herself that she felt the truth of her pregnancy, the knowledge and feel of another person living in her body, her heart and soul. She had no doubts. Had she delayed in refilling her birth control pills on purpose? That was a sobering thought.

The following morning she dug into her mind, examining her memories, her future. She was ashamed to admit her complacency about her own body. She should have weighed her and Randy's sexual desires against the possibility of having a child. Had her procrastination made the decision for her? To have a child sooner, rather than later? Yes. Her lack of attention to her health had made that decision for her. Randy never thought about birth control. That was her job and she had always accepted that responsibility. Was she trying to fill some unexplored gap or emptiness in her life? How well did she really know herself? That was the most frightening thought of all.

She was able to get a doctor's appointment quickly. As the receptionist chuckled and said, "September and October are our busiest months. You know, nine months after Christmas and New Year's celebrations. This being early December we can get you in right away." Em giggled. Yes, that made sense.

A week later she entered the chaos of Dr. Lockehart's office, the only ob/gyn within a twenty-mile radius of Charles Town. The waiting room seemed more like a family gathering than a doctor's office. Two toddlers sat at a small child's table, happily clamoring with a plastic teapot, cups and pastry tools. Three hugely pregnant women sat together on the largest couch, feet spread wide, hands resting on their tummies. Em watched as they warmly chatted together. Other women sat comfortably in their varying stages of pregnancy. A middle-aged woman waited with a teenage girl, probably her daughter. As the younger woman snapped her gum her mother sat by with a worried expression. She sighed deeply and began to read Glamour Magazine over her daughter's shoulder.

Where do I fit in? Em wondered. She thought of all the books she had read and the women she had met on their pages. Simone de Beauvoir, George Sand, Lady Chatterley, Ma, from *Little House On The Prairie*. Had all the women in her books, pregnant or hoping to be, with children or childless, led her to this office, to this moment in time? *Was* it the best time to have a baby? Was this truly what she wanted?

Her thoughts were interrupted by the woman perched behind the receptionist window. "May I check you in?" Em approached the woman who was wearing a yellow smock decorated with storks carrying pink and blue bundles of cherubic babies. As Em waited for the receptionist to write down her information she noticed the other women working in the office. They chatted and laughed together familiarly, all wearing the same smocks in pastel colors.

"Mrs. Upswatch, please make yourself comfortable. I'm afraid we're running about a half hour behind. At least, no one's in labor right now so Dr. Lockehart won't be rushing out the door. The doctor does like to chat with his patients, so sometimes his appointments go longer than expected." All three women in the office turned to Em and laughed. "That's an understatement. We call him Chatty Larry," one said. The second woman whose auburn hair was French braided placed her hand on the receptionist's shoulder and said, "And that's why everyone loves him, right Diana?"

Em settled into a loveseat in a corner where she could observe everyone in the crowded waiting room. Her book rested in her lap, unopened. She noticed a large poster on the wall titled, 'Very Important Moms'. The poster was of smiling women all holding babies. Em was surprised to see Sadie's photo among them, then admonished herself. Of course, Dr. Lockehart had been Sadie's obstetrician even before her girls were born. Em discovered MaryAnne and Alison's baby photos with a proudly grinning Sadie. Suddenly feeling nauseous Em pulled out a package of saltines from her purse and began nibbling. The woman next to Em leaned in and patted her hand. "It gets better dearie, you'll see, as soon as the nausea ends, at about three months or so. How far along are you?"

Em stammered. "Oh, I'm not sure. This is my first visit."

The woman smiled hugely at Em. "Oh, what a wonderful adventure you're embarking on." Another woman joined in their conversation. "Is that what you call it? An adventure?" They both laughed together, and suddenly Em felt special, included in this warm family of women.

As soon as Em met Dr. Lockehart, she understood his appeal. His round face and merry blue eyes put her at ease immediately. With his bristly mustache, he reminded her of an otter like the ones who used to swim and play in the Sacramento River. She noticed that under his lab coat he was wearing a vest of the same material as his staff's. His tummy pushed out the fabric of the vest much like the pregnant women in his waiting room. Em couldn't help but compliment the uniforms he and his nurses wore.

The doctor chuckled and pulled at his vest. "Oh, that's thanks to Mary. She's the owner of the Sew What shop in town. It was her idea. She makes all our uniforms. Mary said women should be happy contemplating their new bundles of joy. I think she was right, by the reaction of my patients."

"They remind me of my third-grade visit to the principal's office," Em replied. "I made the mistake of telling my girlfriends that babies didn't come from storks."

Dr. Lockehart laughed heartily. "No, indeed they do not. That's what keeps me in business. How did your visit to the principal turn out? You must have been a precocious child."

"I guess I was, come to think of it. The outcome was my mama enrolled me in another school, a Montessori. So everything worked out just fine."

Dr. Lockehart then became serious as he looked over the information Em had provided three weeks ago when she had made her first appointment. "So, I see you're here for an annual exam and a renewal of your birth control prescription."

"Well, not exactly. I think I'm past the time for birth control. I needed a new prescription when I made the appointment a while ago." Em's voice drifted off. She chewed her lip and felt tears crowding her eyes. It seemed lately she cried over just about anything and everything. The doctor noticed her tears.

"Now, there, there. Let's have a look. When was your last period?"

"Well, I thought it was about a month ago. But it was weird, not really a normal period. I hardly bled at all."

"Uh huh."

"And I've been nauseous, tired, and I cry a lot."

"Well, you certainly have all the signs." Minutes later Dr. Lockehart confirmed Em's suspicions. "Yes, dear, you're right. I'd say about seven weeks. And that bleeding? Probably due to your little one latching onto his or her new home in your uterus. Just settling in, getting cozy for the long haul to delivery."

Em wasn't sure how to feel as Dr. Lockehart watched her reaction closely. He cleared his throat. "There are other options, of course. After all, 1979 isn't the dark ages. What does Mr. Upswatch think?"

"I haven't told him yet. I wanted to be sure." Suddenly Em felt elated. Randy would be thrilled. This baby *was* at the right time. They had a perfect nest for a new life in their home and lives. And, as Felicity had said, Em could always cane chairs when pregnant. She couldn't wait to tell Margret. She'd tell Randy on his birthday just a few weeks away. Could she keep her secret that long? At least she had Margret, her 'new' mother to confide in. That would make the wait easier. Again, tears came to her eyes along with laughter.

"Oh, I am happy, really. My husband will be thrilled. Even though I guess I knew, this is still a shock being told for certain that I'll be having a baby."

The doctor took both of Em's hands in his large soft paws. "Welcome to a new world and a new chapter of your life. I'll be with you every step of the way, steering your ship into a safe harbor." Em completely understood why Dr. Lockehart's patients didn't complain about waiting to see him. He truly had a heart of gold, and she was sure he took great pains to make every woman feel special. That reminded Em of Sadie's photo on his wall. Before the doctor turned to leave for his next patient, Em stopped him with her question.

"I wondered, my friend—Sadie's photo—is on your wall with a lot of other photos of new moms with their babies. Something about being your Very Important Moms? What does that mean?"

Dr. Lockehart turned and looked nonplussed. He cleared his throat before continuing. "Oh, that's my philosophy, which I usually share when a second pregnancy is diagnosed with one of my patients. Now, I don't like to lecture, but since you've asked, I encourage all families to only have two children to replace themselves. Overpopulation is a great concern of mine, especially due to my chosen profession. My VIMs, Very Important Moms, are those committed to only having two children. Sadie is a real star. She had her tubes tied after her second child was born. Don't get me wrong. I realize the number of children one brings into the world is a very personal decision for each family. I try to gently point out the importance of preserving our planet from overpopulation, overuse of resources." He stopped, thought a moment longer as though deciding how to continue.

"You're a friend of Sadie's? She's a great gal. So cheerful, always made me laugh. How is she? And that husband of hers?"

"She's terrific, always makes me laugh, too. She pretty much runs the diner in town, do you know it? The Inn and Out? But Ralph is no longer her husband. They divorced a while back. She's happy as can be without him."

"Hm. I don't doubt that. She's still at the Inn and Out? I'll have to stop by some morning for coffee. It would be nice to catch up on her life."

Em noticed the faraway look in the doctor's eyes and her female intuition kicked in. She wondered if there was a Mrs. Lockehart. "I'm sure she'd love to see you again. You really should stop by."

"Yes. Well. I'll try." The doctor became business-like as he headed toward the door. "Oh, and my heartfelt congratulations. Call me with any problems or concerns. Diana at the front desk will schedule your next appointment in four weeks." He handed a prescription form to Em. "Instead of birth control, here's a prescription for prenatal vitamins. You're on your way, young lady." He patted Em once again on her shoulder, the paper drape crinkling under his touch.

Em dressed slowly, going over the news in her mind. If only she could share this with her mama. At least she had Felice. In the spring, when Felice came out of hiding, she'd be…Em counted on her fingers…how far along? Her dates matched Dr. Lockehart's projected due date of June 15. She'd be five months pregnant in March, early spring. That was right around the time Em had first met Felicity. Wouldn't she be surprised and thrilled to see Em pregnant?

On her way out of the office, Em floated, smiling at all the waiting women. She was now part of them, this tribe of mothers. Dr. Lockehart was right. A new chapter of her life had begun.

* * *

By December 22, Em had everything ready for Christmas. The Lincoln rocker, her greatest caning achievement, had been delivered to her client on time. The warm hat for Randy, the colorful scarves for Adrian and Nils, and the pretty shawl for Margret had all been lovingly crocheted. She was proud of each beautiful accomplishment. The colors of every gift matched the hues of their personalities, in the brightest and warmest shades. Em had crocheted a shell border on Margret's shawl with pink, complementing the blue and violet shades. Adrian's scarf could have matched the turquoise, green, and yellows of his favorite Hawaiian shirt. The scarf for Nils was more refined, with tints of moss green, heather, and golden brown. Randy's hat was in bright greens and blues, a perfect hat to tame his unruly curls while keeping his ears warm.

The baskets for Margret, Adrian and Nils were filled with wild Strawberry, Blackberry and Blueberry jams. The only Christmas gift she had yet to add was the braided honey wheat bread she would bake Christmas morning.

She had taken special pride in the decorations she had made for their homey cabin. She had threaded cranberries and popcorn together for decorating their little Christmas tree, right out of the *Little House On The Prairie*. She had even found time to make calico placemats and napkins in shades of reds, greens and golds for Christmas dinner. Randy's special gift, a leather briefcase with his initials on a brass plate, had been her greatest investment. It was one she could afford now with her chair-caning proceeds. She may have even picked up a new chair-caning customer at Going Places. It would be a perfect Christmas with love overflowing their little cabin. Em hadn't told Adrian or Sadie her news yet. That would be another wonderful thing to share with her friends to make the holiday perfect. Margret had been so overwhelmed and ecstatic she had broken down in tears, which made Em cry, also. Another special bond between the two women: weeping together.

Em had only one thing left to do, give Randy his most important gift to be shared with just the two of them. She had prepared a surprise for his birthday, December 22 and she had planned his gift to perfection, down to the last and most delicious detail.

That evening all she had to do was remain awake until Randy arrived home. Dinner of Lentil Soup was kept warm on the stove next to a fresh loaf of Onion Bread, filling their home with heavenly scents. She relished her surprise under the quilts on their bed wrapping her nakedness in delicious warmth. She would *not* fall asleep. She was excited to share her wonderful news with her best friend, lover and husband. How had she come to this point in time? At the age of fourteen her tenderness for Randy had begun through her attempts to protect him from the scorn of their classmates. She well remembered her mama's words from her childhood days:

"You should always protect the underdog. You'll never love or be loved more than by someone you've helped to grow into themselves. Your friendship will honor you both."

It was true. She and Randy had been through so much over these last six years, two of them married. There were times she hated his buffoonery and wondered why she had ever married him. Their battles were sometimes fierce with both near tears and not speaking for days on end. Yet it was always Randy who crept back into her heart with a gift of flowers, one of his silly poems left on the kitchen table, or merely an apologetic hug. He was always there for her. Slowly, he had learned to trust his own intelligence and insight, leaving his mask of 'Randy the Dandy' in the past. He had opened himself up to learning from others. He listened to Em's rantings, her book discussions and neighborhood discoveries. He had taken note of the changes in his wife and had changed and grown along with her. When memories of her mama left her heartbroken all over again, he didn't ignore or scold her. He held her, told her he understood her pain and let her cry. He put up with her anger and her insults when he was unable to sell a car. He listened, in pain, when Em questioned their marriage or feared for their future. Yet he was happier with Em than he had ever been in his life.

Randy's new approach with customers—with humility and listening—had succeeded. Now he was a top seller who was proud of his accomplishments. He had grown into Em's hopes for him. On her part, Em had learned patience. Knowledge came to her from Felicity and books. The authors and characters had made her explore new places, circumstances and lives. Pride grew from her accomplishments in cooking, making a home, learning to cane, launching her business. Yes, it had been a fruitful year of lessons learned for both of them. She knew she was ready for a baby, toward this next step in their life's journey.

She was just drifting off to sleep when the sound of the Rambler's tires crunching up the gravel driveway brought her fully awake. The house was darkened, lit only with fire and candlelight. Em had lit the fireplace in the kitchen. She had then made a trail of candles from the kitchen, down the hall to their bedroom. She waited for Randy in their quilted bed, the little cabin aglow with soft light. She heard Randy's entrance as she waited, toasty in the beauty of the candlelight and the thrill of her surprise.

"Em? Are you trying to burn down the cabin? Where are you?" She heard him hit his foot on the kitchen chair and giggled into the soft quilt with his complaint, "ouch, damn chair…too dark to see a thing in here. Em?" Slowly he followed the trail of candles, finally standing at the foot of their spool bed.

"Happy birthday, dear husband," Em greeted him.

"Sweetheart, the cabin looks beautiful, really. But isn't this a fire hazard? Why are you in bed? Have you tired yourself out from all your Christmas preparations? I told you I'd help and not to overdo things, you being so exhausted lately."

"Oh shut up and get out of those clothes and into bed. Come snuggle under the covers with me. In a flash, Randy was undressed and in bed, nuzzling Em's neck, moving his hands over her body.

"OW! That hurts!" Randy quickly removed his hands from Em's full and tempting breasts.

"Hurts? I'm sorry. I'd never hurt you, darlin'. Never hurt before when I enjoyed your beautiful boobs."

"That's because I've never been pregnant before. Happy birthday," she sang sweetly. It took a moment of absolute silence, astonishment, a mixture of joy, and something else. Fear? Racing across Randy's features before he spoke.

"You're joking. No, you would never joke about anything this important. Are you sure? When…how did this happen?"

"The usual way." Em giggled. "I was on the pill, but remember I ran out of my prescription? And I was using the rhythm method, like my mama did."

"Yeah. You said we were fine, you were in your safe zone. You couldn't get pregnant for a week after you had your period. Right?"

"Maybe it was more than a week. You know how I lose track of things. It was the night I made you that big thick ole steak, remember? You said the red meat made you strong and lusty." Em giggled at the remembrance. "And you were. Lusty, that is."

"Oh, yeah, I remember." A happy grin replaced his astonishment. "That was a good night. How do you know for sure?"

"I saw the Obstetrician in town, Dr. Lockehart."

"Oh, Em, I was hoping you'd want a baby sooner rather than later. This is the best birthday gift you could ever have given me." He whooped with joy and gathered Em into his arms gently. Together they examined her body for any tell-tale outward signs of pregnancy.

"Well, your tits seem even more of a handful than before."

"And they ache, they're so tender. Just look at the color of my nipples, they're brown, not your 'pink roses' anymore."

"God, I can't believe I'm even saying this. A baby. We're having a baby, is it really true? When are you due?"

"Well, the doctor thinks it's mid-June. But I think maybe later, if my memory is right. I know I made that steak dinner in early October, or late September, when I got one of my first caning checks. Are you really happy?"

"Oh, sweetheart, how could I not be? A baby that you and I created? If it's a boy, we could name him Porterhouse."

Em slapped him playfully. "I think not. It's too early to think of names, anyway. Let's just enjoy the moment."

Randy placed his head gently on her tummy. "Hello in there, little Porterhouse. This is your daddy."

"Well, I know I look a little different on the outside. But I'm sure there are no big changes yet on the inside one could notice, yet."

"We should investigate that possibility, don't you think? And who would know better than me?" Their lovemaking had never been sweeter and more tender. Later, they fell asleep in the glow of candles with their secret cuddled between them. Randy woke first and rose from their warm nest to leave Em gently snoring. He lovingly kissed her forehead and pulled the quilt up to her chin.

"I'll be up soon…feels so good," Em mumbled, then promptly fell back into a snore. Randy retreated quietly to blow out all the candles except for the fat rose scented one on their bedside table. He felt as though he were walking on air as he followed the trail of candlelight into the kitchen. Quietly he set the table, readying it before waking Em. Maybe he'd just bring her dinner on a tray in bed for them both? His thoughts ran wild.

"A baby. Our baby. Can't believe this is true. A baby, a baby, became his quiet refrain, like a song, which sang through his head as he warmed up the Lentil Soup and Em's freshly baked Onion Bread. Yes, he would bring dinner to Em in bed where they'd share their meal. After all, she needed her rest. *A baby, a baby, a baby…*" His song continued its refrain in his mind.

* * *

Christmas morning Em and Randy opened their gifts in front of the library fireplace. Freshly baked cranberry nut bread laced the room with the sweet scent of Christmas morning. Em had baked the braided honey wheat bread for Margret the day before. She had little to do today except simple cooking and enjoying the day with family and friends.

Em opened Randy's gifts slowly. They were beautifully wrapped with Christmas paper and satin ribbons. A pale blue cashmere sweater matched her eyes perfectly. A delicate gold chain with a locket brought tears to her eyes. But the best gift was *Living on the Earth* by Alicia Bay Laurel. "However, did you know I was pining for this book?" Em asked.

"Adrian told me. I visited him at the library and asked him what you'd like. I ordered it at the *Book Nook*. I was really sweating it out, afraid it wouldn't arrive in time."

"Oh, sweetheart, I love it. Now I can learn all sorts of new homespun arts." She pored over the pages, her fingers touching the sweet images of tie dying, blouse making, gardening, canning, and best of all, making looms and weaving. "Look, I can learn to weave if you help me make the loom! I'm so excited! But you sneaky man, you told me you'd never met Adrian."

"We all have our secrets, don't we? I love my gifts. A real leather briefcase, with my initials. The guys will be jealous. This briefcase will take care of all my papers I throw all over the floor of the Rambler. And this hat and matching scarf are great. You really outdid yourself, sweetheart."

Em wore her new sweater over a long wool skirt she had discovered at Thrifty Threads. The cold of Christmas morning had laced their cottage windows with hoarfrost. The ground had frozen but snow had not yet arrived. Em longed to see their first snowfall together. Randy had never seen snow. Em had seen the world changed by snow only once on that fateful trip with her mama and papa to the Sierra Nevada up Donner Pass. She couldn't wait for Randy to see the miracle of the world wrapped in white. She shivered at the window, watching Randy as he collected wood from the woodpile. He brought in the cold along with the split logs and kindling.

"You certainly are becoming a homesteader, aren't you?" Em teased as he walked in the door.

"Yes, ma'am. One has to protect their family." They shared a broad smile.

"Can we tell Mom today? It would be a perfect Christmas gift, don't you think?" Randy said hopefully.

"Yes, of course. It will be. Adrian will be excited, too. I think. And Sadie will be beside herself. I can't wait to tell her. Too bad she'll be at her aunt's place till New Year's Day." Em chuckled to herself, wondering how Margret would pretend she wasn't fully aware of Em's pregnancy.

By two that afternoon, Margret, Adrian and Nils had arrived, with warm hugs and Christmas cheer. Margret felt like a queen, being picked up by two handsome men in a Mercedes. They admired all the decorations Em had worked so carefully to create. "Your sweet cottage looks like a snow globe, without the snow. You've made this cabin into a beautiful home, Emeline. And whatever you're cooking smells divine." Margret's eyes grew misty as she smiled at her daughter-in-law.

Adrian also sniffed appreciatively. "Do I smell ham? And sweet potatoes?"

"Good snout, Addie. You're right. Bourbon sweet potatoes and Miss Magnolia's Honey Glazed Ham. With my piccalilli relish, homemade bread, and Mother's green bean casserole." She and Margret exchanged a warm smile.

"My, you really have become quite the chef, my dear," Margret praised Em, as Em placed two fresh pies on the kitchen fireplace hearth. Adrian scrutinized the pies. "Oh, yummy, apple and pecan? You'll have to teach me how to make pie crust. You must give me your recipes, where did you get them? Old family stuff?" Nils slapped Adrian's hand away from the pecan pie, knowing his love's penchant for sweets.

"You know perfectly well where my recipes came from. Your library. On my very first visit when I met you. *Cooking for the Soul: Recipes for the Down at Heart,* by Miss Magnolia."

Adrian picked up the book from the kitchen counter. "Jeeze, Em, you've beat the hell out of this cookbook. Isn't it time for a new copy?" Adrian thumbed through the stained, worn and food crusted pages. "Wow. This was published in 1956? I doubt I can find you another copy, but I'll try. Antique booksellers in Raleigh might have one or know where I can find one."

"Felicity said it was used in the local high school home ec classes. It was the first book I ever bought at your library, remember? Just for $1. It was pretty worn out then. Apparently, Miss Magnolia was Charlie Town's only celebrity." Nils examined the cookbook with Adrian. I love the title. *Cooking for the Soul: Recipes for the Down at Heart."*

Em replied thoughtfully. "Me too. I think it fit my life when we first moved here, 'recipes for the down at heart'. So much has changed in these last ten months."

"More time than it takes to make a baby," Randy said, joining the conversation. Emeline glared at her husband as Margret raised her eyebrows. Adrian looked perplexed. *Who needs babies?* he thought ruefully.

"Come on. Let's open our gifts in the library under the tree. Randy has already lit the fire."

The next hour was all Em had hoped for. Her dear friends loved their crocheted gifts, which Adrian insisted on calling an ascot, not a scarf. "It will look divine with my new leather vest." He and Nils shared a special smile. Em smiled at Nils with mischief. "I wonder, how much did that new leather vest set Addy back?"

"Never you mind, missy. Open your gifts," Adrian jauntily replied.

Margret's gift was perfect, a gift certificate from Gillinghams. "Now you can pick out something special for your beloved kitchen, dear. They have the most gorgeous salt glazed stoneware. And they just got in the new all-the-rage Le Creuset pots and pans in every color imaginable! And beautiful Quimper Ware dishes."

"Wow, with one-hundred-dollars I can surely buy a lot of goodies. Maybe I can find a big glass jar for fruit liqueur. I found a recipe for it, Rumtopf. It takes months of adding each season's fresh fruit to Brandy. Next year's Christmas gift." Em smiled in pleasure, thinking ahead to another holiday season with all her loved ones, *and* a new baby.

Adrian was so excited over his gifts for Em he could barely contain himself. Em opened Nils' gift first which earned a scowl from Adrian.

"I know what this is, nice and fat and heavy. A book!" She unwrapped a beautiful copy of John Steinbeck's *East of Eden*. "Oh, Nils, thank you so much. What a lovely gift."

"Adrian told me it was perfect for your history. It takes place in your beloved California, in Salinas, the lettuce fields and the sugar factory, Monterey and the countryside all around the coast. It's an epic family story, lots of heartbreak, secrets, scandals, joys. Addy thought you'd like something to remind you of the delta with all their farms."

Adrian's excitement over his gift to Em was so overwhelming that he giggled, causing everyone to laugh. "Now be careful, this one's fragile," he said. Carefully Em unwrapped the elaborately wrapped gift. She gasped when she saw the contents. Inside was a beautiful leather portfolio. She opened it, her eyes widening and her mouth dropping open.

She began looking through the papers in the portfolio. "Oh, my god, is this what I think it is?"

Adrian was bursting. "Yup. It's the plat map of Heavenly Hollow from the Virginia Department of Historical Records, in Richmond. Nils and I went there after Genevieve gave me the name of a friend who could help me research. Don, Don Fraser. He copied the maps for me of Mildred Hanson's plantation acreage."

Adrian proudly pointed out the special aspects of the map along with the clippings of death notices and the roads running throughout Heavenly Hollow. "It's like a treasure map we can explore. All the little roads all up and down Heavenly Hollow. Look, here's your cabin, see? Number 25. Most of the cabins don't have numbers anymore." Em was speechless as she traced her fingers over the map, clippings, and notes.

"Best of all, look at this plat map of Mildred Hanson's acreage, with 'sacred grounds' noted. I'm sure we'll be able to locate Heaven's Gate Cemetery. We'll check all the roads and lanes around. One of these cabins has to be Felicity's. We'll canvas the whole area. I would imagine most of the roads are overgrown and hard to locate. But we should be able to find Heaven's Gate and whatever else you're looking for. It will just take a while."

"Adrian. What an incredible gift. I can't wait to get out there and poke around." Em grasped the beautiful leather portfolio to her breast in happiness.

Nils then handed Randy a large fabric cylinder. "I got this at Gillinghams, for such a special occasion. First time I've had a Christmas with anyone for I don't know how long."

Randy opened the fabric and was thrilled to see a very expensive-looking bottle of Champagne. The bottom of the bottle was ensconced in a silver base, carved with ornate curlicues. The heavy green glass of the bottle was painted with flowers and vines.

"Oh, Nils. It's too beautiful to open." Em gasped. Randy was too dumbstruck to say a word.

"You certainly will open it. Especially as Adrian and I won't be around to ring in 1980 with you guys. We're going to Richmond to explore a bit more. There are some wonderful little inns there and we're dying to tour all the historical buildings in town." Adrian put his arm around Nils affectionately. "Nils surprised me this morning with his gift. He said he thought it was perfect for a budding historian." He grinned mischievously at Nils. "I can't wait for our New Year's eve celebration! You know what they say, whatever you're doing at midnight is what you'll be happy doing the rest of the year." Nils attempted, and failed, to nail Adrian with a scorching look. They all laughed at the futility of making Addy behave.

Randy cleared his throat and looked sternly at Em. "Anything else you want to share this Christmas, sweetie? Don't get over-excited or plan on traipsing all over this valley. And you won't be drinking any champagne on New Year's eve. Remember, your health."

The time had come. Em had never been good at keeping secrets and she had been bursting to tell this one. "I'm pregnant!" Stunned silence, then hugs, tears and laughter. "You never could have given me a more wonderful gift, dearest daughter Emeline," Margret said, kissing Em and then Randy warmly. Her tears reaffirmed her overwhelming joy.

Adrian smiled ruefully and a bit sadly, at Em. "Guess I'll have to start looking for baby book discards. Randy's right. There won't be much exploring for us now."

"Don't be ridiculous, Addy. I'm pregnant, not an invalid. Besides, I feel so well and strong. I'm almost in my second trimester and not due until June. That gives us plenty of time to find out what's in 'them thar hills'."

"I'll come too," Nils said, bursting into the conversation.

"Of course, you will, sweetie." Adrian said, patting his hand affectionately.

A scowl of worry overcame Randy's features. "Em, never go by yourself. Ever. I'll go with you, or Adrian and Nils. Promise me you won't go wandering off whenever the urge hits you."

"Oh Randy, Don't be silly."

"I mean it. Promise," Randy said sternly.

"Yeah, fine, I promise," Em countered. Randy knew Em well enough to understand that she really hadn't promised anything. She'd be off with or without company at her first opportunity.

"*I* promise," Adrian said with a grin.

"Me, too," Nils agreed.

"Great. Two men to worry over me," Em replied.

"Three, sweet pea. Don't forget me." Randy spouted proudly. "After all, I am the daddy."

The rest of Christmas was a dream come true. Her grandmama Muriel's antique table was lit with candles. Her mama's best and rarely used Christmas holly china sat on Em's freshly sewn Christmas placemats. Em had retrieved the old felt-lined wooden box of family silver from under her and Randy's bed. The ornate silverware, safely secreted in the old felt lined box, shone at each table setting enfolded in the new Christmas napkins.

Miss Magnolia's Cookbook, as always, had not let her down. There were hardly any leftovers. When they all hugged their goodbyes at the kitchen door, fat snowflakes had begun to fall. The beauty of the scene—the snow quickly decorating the magnolia tree, the cabin lights illuminating the snow-covered drive and the hush of the falling snow—was a perfect end to the day.

"Now your little home really is a snow globe, my dears. Thank you for the most wonderful Christmas of my life," said Margret, her eyes once again filling with tears. Margret and Em hugged long and warmly. Randy joined their embrace.

"Me, too." Adrian whispered into Em's ear as he said his goodbye. "Can't wait to get into those jams and your bread. You're a sweetheart. I'm so happy for you and Randy, really. Just can't imagine me as 'Uncle Adrian'." Em hugged him tightly. "Thank you for *you,* Addy. You'll make a great uncle. And so will Nils."

Em and Randy stood arm and arm in the doorway of their little home. The snow silenced their world as their cabin lights welcomed them back inside.

"Coming to the end of 1979. It's the first snow Mom said she could remember in years. That's a good omen, sweetheart," said Randy, shutting the door on the cold. Rhett and Scarlet, having hidden under the bed until company left, raced into the kitchen and wrapped themselves around Em's ankles.

Em bent down and rubbed her furry family. "Yes, our first snow together is a good omen. There's nothing that could possibly go wrong. We've come a long way since the delta."

"And a long way to go. But what a fun ride this has been so far," Randy added.

When Em turned to kiss him, she had tears in her eyes. Yes, and what a fun ride it will be with the man I've grown up with, she told herself.

Their world had never been brighter or filled with more love. Their home was embraced with gently falling snow and hope.

Chapter 16

True to his word, Adrian discovered *Journey to Motherhood: Great Writings on Pregnancy Up to Baby's First Day of Life.* Not to be outdone, Randy had found *The Panic-Free Pregnancy* at the *Book Nook*, which he felt was a book more in keeping with who he had become. The expectant, frightened, bewildered father trying not to panic.

Em relished the *Journey to Motherhood* book which shared expectant mothers' thoughts at each stage of their pregnancies. The words of other women uplifted and excited her. She was frightened, too, but mostly enthusiastic about what the future would hold. Sometimes, Em felt as though she were a science experiment, amazed to learn all the changes her body would undergo over the next months. Her due date was five months away, enough time to cane plenty of chairs *and* make a baby she happily told herself.

"Randy, listen to this. My pelvis will loosen up and expand to help with delivery, like a gate opening."

"Well, my mom always said you had great childbearing hips."

"Good grief, look at this photo. My boobs are going to be enormous," Em said, pointing out a photo to Randy.

Randy glanced at the photo and winced. "Well, I guess there's nothing wrong with that, right?" His initial unease with the graphic photo quickly changed to awe as he anticipated the enlargement of his favorite parts of Em. She rewarded him with her most stern look.

January brought other changes. A bleeding episode tore at Em's heart and filled them both with gut-wrenching fear. When the episode ended following Dr. Lockehart's advice of bed rest for a week, they found that the bleeding stopped as quickly as it had begun. Their relief was as overwhelming as their fear had been. It was then they both realized how in love they already were with this tiny developing miracle, their baby.

Em sympathized with Randy. He was not able to have the first-hand information and emotions she felt about the changes within her body. She felt and listened intently to her body's messages. She strained to hear, as though she could interpret their baby's development through sound and thumps. The baby became fully real in late January. At first, Em wasn't sure—was that a muscle spasm? Gas? Or the baby? When the fluttering butterfly movement continued and grew stronger she knew it was their baby, announcing its life and viability, as if saying, "I'm here."

Em felt as though she were a conqueror. She was strong and healthy. She could do anything. Her energy amazed her. She patted her tummy, only slightly protruding, as she spoke to her baby. I love the term, 'with child'. That's what I am, sweet little thing, with you in every sense, every day, every moment. I am *with* child, not just pregnant. She kept her little heart-to-heart conversations with the baby to herself. Her words and thoughts were too sacred to share.

Randy had no such qualms and talked to the baby through the microphone of Em's tummy. "Whatcha doing in there? Did you like that pot roast mom made? Pretty yummy, huh? Just wait till you get here and see all the great meals she'll make for you. When you're older, of course."

Randy's enthusiasm and connection with their baby sweetened Em's soul. She loved to watch the way he looked at her, tenderly, frightened, sometimes awestruck or panic struck. She remembered his reaction when she had retrieved the step stool to reach a high shelf.

"What are you doing! Are you crazy! I'll get whatever you need. Sit down right now and I'll make you a cup of raspberry tea. That's what mom says you should drink. It will strengthen your uterus." *Oh, jeeze*, Em thought ruefully, but accepted the cup of raspberry tea Randy had prepared.

Then, some strange events began occurring. Early one morning when Em opened the kitchen door she discovered a perfect dead mouse on her doorstep, as though left there as a gift. Her cats, who had been indoors all night sniffed the mouse and seemed as perplexed as Em.

Another morning after a light snow she discovered pawprints, like those of her feline family, imprinted across the front porch and driveway. Once or twice when Scarlet and Rhett ran out the door and into the field beyond the house Em thought she saw Zuma. She dismissed the thought quickly. Couldn't be Zuma, can't imagine her coming here in the snow. Besides, Felice's cat probably has a wealth of relatives in the area who looked just like her. Still, she was puzzled about the strange cat-mystery events occurring around their cabin.

Em was impatient about staying inside all the time and Randy didn't trust her driving in the snow. "You're not going anywhere around Charles Town if there's snow or ice on the roads. I've got two to worry about now, remember?" When Randy kissed Em goodbye, she often felt like a prisoner in her own home. Without telling Randy, she convinced Adrian to begin their exploration of Heavenly Hollow. She had studied Adrian's gift of maps and clippings since Christmas and was ready to set forth.

Early one warming February morning she and Adrian began the first of many excursions throughout the Heavenly Hollow neighborhood searching for Heaven's Gate Cemetery and Felicity's cabin. With maps in hand, they began investigating the lanes, roads and overgrown paths closest to Cabin #25. On the least used trails and lanes, they climbed over fallen trees. Addy was fearful and cautious, like a mother hen, holding Em in check. He admonished her frequently.

"No! Stop! Wait for me! Get away from that pasture until I check it out first. That's a deer trail, not a road. We're not going anywhere that's not on the map."

Finally, in early March on their fourth expedition, Em had enough. "Adrian, for God's sake. I'm not made of glass. I'm pregnant."

"You're fragile," Adrian retorted.

"No I'm not!" Em yelled at him.

"What would Randy say if he knew you were out here in the middle of nowhere attempting to climb over stone walls?"

That silenced Em's complaints but not her grousing. "This is our fourth exploration. We couldn't be here at a better time. Frozen ground, no snow, bare trees. We can see for miles. Has anything difficult happened during our last three searches?"

"No. But that doesn't mean something won't happen. STOP! Look out for that cellar hole!" Em glared at him but stopped climbing over the wall. Adrian caught up to her and helped her, complaining all the while. "You're impossible, you know that, right?" Adrian complained.

"That's what Randy always says. Just what I need, two husbands. I don't understand why we can't find the graveyard or a cabin that could be Felicity's. And why hasn't Felice returned?"

"Like me and Randy keep telling you. Maybe she doesn't want to be found and it's still too cold for her to venture forth. Didn't you say how frail and thin she is? Of course, we'll find the cemetery. Stop being so impatient." Adrian pulled his eyes from the distant stone wall and followed Em to where she was peering into the darkened window of a dilapidated cabin. "Looks abandoned. Why would anyone leave furniture? I'd love to get my hands on some of these old chairs."

"You've got enough to do. You shouldn't overtax your strength. You already have the new orders I brought you from the library. You don't need any more work."

"I know. And another woman called from Sew What. Mary has certainly been a great saleslady for my business. I'm saving all the money for when the baby comes. Then I'll stop caning for a while. Randy's going to start building my loom this weekend. Why don't you and Nils come over for dinner Saturday night? I know Randy would be happy to see you. The three of you men can discuss all the ways to keep me safe and sound."

Adrian glowed. His grin was enormous. "Can't. I have a dinner date with Nils. At my apartment. For the first time, I'm cooking. In fact, I wanted your advice on an easy but elegant meal."

They climbed up a small hill to survey the surrounding paths. Adrian seemed immersed in the view. It was beautiful. The stark surroundings should have appeared cold and forbidding. Instead, the sun filtered through bare branches and created a magical view. With every breeze, slim branches performed a ballet. The light created a painting, splashing blue shadows on the frozen ground. They breathed in the freshness of the scented woods, the perfume of dead leaves, moist earth and evergreens. The world was illuminated by the bright blue sky.

Adrian ended their idyllic musings. "I want the meal to be special for Nils. Did you know his last name is Beddekker? A delightful Scandinavian name. He's a Viking, or at least his ancestors were. Do you think I should make something Swedish? Like meatballs, or herring?"

"Sounds like you two are getting pretty serious. Any future plans?" Em asked nonchalantly, not wanting to appear like the snoop she was.

"I don't kiss and tell, but we do have such fun together. The trip to Richmond for New Years was very special. Since then, we've spent most of our free time at Nils' apartment. Compared to mine, his place is like the Taj Mahal, so tidy and eclectic. He has an awesome record collection. When I'm at his place, we dance and talk for hours. He's a fabulous chef. I worry about my place. I'll have to do a deep cleaning, throw a bunch of crap out. The more I get to know him the more I enjoy his company. And he's so smart! I love that! Who knows where this will go. I'll admit it's exciting to have someone special in my life. I just don't want him to think I'm some slob who can't even cook. Well, maybe that's true." Adrian kicked a stone in their path dejectedly.

"Stop being silly. You know how much Nils cares about you. I've seen the way he smiles at you. I can't believe the great Adrian is so melodramatically fearful. Just be yourself. That's who he cares about, not your apartment or your cooking."

"Do you think so, really? I don't know why I feel so insecure sometimes. I've never been in a serious relationship before. I hope we'll be together for a long while."

"Addy, you're the sweetest man I've ever met, besides Randy. Stop worrying. You're irresistible." So much hope, joy and expectations were brewing in both their lives. Deep personal knowledge of one another fueled their thoughts.

Adrian patted Em's enlarged tummy. "You're my dearest friend and confidant. You know that, don't you?"

Suddenly Em felt guilty. Here she was dragging Addy all over the countryside and she hadn't confided the true reason for her search.

"Addy, there's something I have to tell you."

Adrian looked concerned. "Did I overstep a boundary? But you are my dearest lady friend. Was I wrong to say that?" Adrian said, worry in his eyes.

Em rewarded Addy with a warm hug. To outsiders they would have appeared to be lovers enjoying an intimate moment in a fairyland setting. Then she said, "No, love. I'm honored you feel as close to me as I feel to you. That's why I have to tell you about this little book I found in our cabin." For the next half hour, they sat together in the little clearing as Em confided bits and pieces, but not the whole of *The Book of Memories*.

"So, you think this lady, Julia, the one who lived in your cabin is buried there? Along with her friend, Dani?"

Em sheepishly nodded. "I should have told you sooner. They might be there, I don't know for sure. Julia said in the diary she wanted to be buried next to a grave that just says, 'Damn She Was Good'. She wrote that it was in the old Heaven's Gate Cemetery."

Adrian scratched his head and looked completely perplexed. "Wow. That's quite a story. It is kind of a wild-goose chase. Never thought about someone who lived in your cabin buried in the old cemetery."

"Are you mad at me, Addy?" Em asked.

"No. No, honestly. I'm glad to know the story."

Em chewed her lip, knowing she had not told her friend the whole story of the protracted death of Dani and Julia caring for her. "You'll keep helping me find the cemetery?"

He laughed at Em and hugged her again. "Of course, I will. But no more secrets, okay?"

"Well, there is one more thing." Em replied quietly. "I haven't told Randy about looking for Julia's grave based on a hunch from the old diary we found. He just thinks I'm only looking for Felicity's cabin and a cemetery where I can do rubbings, which he doesn't approve of. Please don't mention it to him." She noticed Adrian's scowl and quickly said, "Oh, don't worry. I promise, I *will* tell him, at the right time."

Adrian thought for a long moment. "Promise me you'll tell him."

"Pinky swear. I promise," Em said, holding out her hand.

Adrian brightened as he took her pinky in his own. "Sweetie, even if we haven't found Heaven's Gate, Julia's grave or Felicity's cabin, I so love our walks and our time spent together." Em put her arm through Adrian's as they made their way down the hill toward cabin #25. For the next few moments, Em was deep in thought. Then she brightened. "Roast chicken."

"What?"

Em laughed at Adrian's perplexed look. "Roast chicken. That's what you should make for Nils. It's easy. Just throw it in the oven for a couple of hours and baste every twenty minutes for the first hour. I've got a great stuffing recipe Margret gave me. Chicken and stuffing, gravy, mashed potatoes, frozen peas, unless you can find anything fresh. Don't do the elegant route. Go the homey way. When he walks into your apartment and smells that chicken roasting, his heart will melt."

"You think so? Is it really easy? I wouldn't mind his heart melting. What about dessert?"

"I'll make an apple pie; you can pick it up in the afternoon before he comes over. Just tell him you made it."

Adrian looked at Em sternly. "No, I can't lie. Besides, he loves your pies and would know I couldn't make anything as delicious."

By the time they returned to Em's cabin, they were chilled to the bone. As soon as Em opened her kitchen door, the cats ran down the steps and into the field. What the hell's gotten into them? They hate going out in the cold. Em forgot her feline family as she made tea. She took apple muffins leftover from breakfast from the oven. As Adrian and Em warmed themselves over tea and muffins, they made plans for their next trek.

"Same time next week? We're so slow at the library. No one wants to come out in the cold. Genevieve told me I could take next Tuesday off. She's been very supportive of our efforts, almost as excited as we are. I'll study the plat map some more. Maybe we're missing something."

Buttering another muffin Em said, "Sure, next Tuesday is great. Don't forget to stop by for the pie on Saturday. And be sure to get a nice fat roasting chicken. Don't get a fryer, they're too small and scrawny. Come by about three to pick up the pie. I'll have it baked by then. That will give you plenty of time to get the chicken in the oven in time for dinner around six."

"Yes, ma'am." Adrian hugged Em warmly at her kitchen door, throwing his Christmas scarf around his neck. "I do look dashing in my ascot, do I not?"

"Scarf, you idiot. You look warm, I don't know about dashing in those colors, but they do match your audacious personality well. Off with you!" Adrian stopped on the top step of the porch and pointed to an amazing scene to Em. "Hey, Em, aren't those your two cats with that big orange cat?"

To Em's surprise, there was Zuma, palling around with Rhett and Scarlet. The three were in the middle of the road, cozily soaking up a puddle of sunbeams. "Oh, my goddesses. That's Zuma! Felicity's cat! I can't believe my eyes! They're like old friends." Scarlet and Rhett contentedly looked at Em as Zuma raised up on her paws and stretched.

"Well, I'd say it looks like you have three cats now." Adrian remarked.

Em walked toward her kitty family but Zuma took off. Rhett and Scarlet watched her depart and then followed Em into the cabin. She wondered if she would find Felicity's cabin if she followed Zuma, but put the thought away. No way would she be traipsing across the countryside after a cat, even if it was Zuma. She waved goodbye to Adrian and shut the kitchen door against the coming twilight cold.

The following week was a blur of activity in Em's chair-caning business. She finally made it to Sew What to deliver an order for two chairs. Mary was becoming a friend whose company Em enjoyed more and more. While there she purchased the softest yarn and a number of baby sweater patterns for crocheting.

Mary had promised to help her with the task. "Feel how soft this yarn is, dear? It's perfect for either a boy or girl with these lovely multi-colored pastels." Em placed the yarn against her cheek. "Oh, it is delicious. I still can't believe we'll be having a new life in a few months." She patted her tummy protectively. "It's a girl, Mary. I just know it. Besides, I can't imagine having a boy."

"Well, one never really knows. But I certainly believe in a woman's intuition," Mary said, placing her arm around Em's shoulder affectionately.

Just as on every other town visit Em stopped by to see Sadie. They chatted and laughed as Em helped clean tables and refill salt, pepper and ketchup containers at the end of the lunch rush. Sadie was thrilled over Em's pregnancy.

Em had an intuition of her own about her friend. She suspected that Sadie had a secret as she was even bubblier than usual. The two friends sat together over coffee and pie after Sadie had finished her diner chores. For the next hour, they chatted companionably. At times, Em felt as though Sadie was a mother to her. She was full of great advice and warm, loving hand-holding moments.

"Isn't it wonderful that you're showing? I always loved that time of being pregnant." Sadie reminisced.

"I am loving it. I no longer feel as though I'm carrying a secret. I adore the way other women smile and cluck over me. I feel, I don't know, magical, powerful, as though I could do anything."

"What does Randy think?" Sadie asked, stirring her coffee.

"He's so cute. He worries constantly but is also in awe of what's going on inside my body. But he's a wreck. He drives me crazy watching over me, not letting me do everything I want to do."

"Yup. Men are like that. They always want control, and there's no way to control a pregnant woman's body or a baby's development. Just enjoy every minute, honey. When the baby arrives, your lives will change as though you've been hit by a freight train. Amazing how one tiny baby can change your world. Make the most of this special time. It's the last time life will only be just the two of you."

"I know. I love reading about what's coming, but I'm a bit frightened too. Labor, how bad will it be? The journals of women during their pregnancy is my favorite book, reading other women's hopes and thoughts. I haven't gotten to the labor chapter yet. Randy, on the other hand, can't get his nose out of *The Panic-Free Pregnancy* book. I think he hides his own fears well by being absorbed in that book. I wish he'd stop reading it. He's learning too many scary things. I refuse to look at it."

"You'll be fine," Sadie said absentmindedly, wiping pie crust crumbs from her empty plate. Em examined Sadie closely while trying to appear casual and not curious over Sadie's demeanor. Finally, she said, "What is it, Sadie? You look like the cat that swallowed the canary."

Sadie blushed, then giggled, "Oh, nothing."

"Out with it, woman."

Sadie took her feet off the chair and leaned forward excitedly, grinning hugely at Em. "Larry. He's been coming by almost every morning for coffee before he goes to his office."

"Larry?"

"Yes, Larry, Larry Lockehart, your obstetrician!"

The light dawned on Em. She remembered the way he had asked about Sadie at her first appointment, but never again. Em had imagined he had a wife and that to him Sadie was just a patient.

"He invited me out for dinner Saturday night! I'm so excited! But I need someone to watch the girls. Do you think…"

"Of course! Randy can come with me. It will be a great exercise in fatherhood for him."

"Oh, I don't know about that. The girls will probably run rings around Randy, then will try to get him to do all the things I don't let them do, like eat ice cream right before bed and not brushing their teeth. You're the one who will have to rein them in. Ralph can't come over. I think he's jealous that I actually have a date. Can you believe it? He made up some stupid excuse but that's fine with me. I don't think Larry liked Ralph very much when we were married, and even less when the girls were born. Is seven okay? Larry's picking me up at 7:30."

"Perfect. Better give me your address. I've never been to your house, you know."

"Oh, jeeze. I guess not. Well, we'll have to change that now, won't we?" Em felt another door opening in the home of their friendship, another room to be explored with Sadie. She felt that her friendships and life were blooming along with her body.

Em stood in the doorway of the baby's room. She stroked her tummy. The room was almost ready for its new resident, although the addition to their family wouldn't arrive for another few months.

She admired the room. The baby's crib sat below the windows, catching the light through the tree-laced shadows. The pale-yellow walls held framed prints Em had discovered at the Antique Life shop in Charles Town. One print was of the Water Babies by Arthur Rackham. A tiny baby floated contentedly, sound asleep, in her basket, moving down a stream. Faeries watched the baby protectively, holding the sides of the tiny boat.

Em imagined what it would be like to have their baby nestled into the little crib in this room. She walked across the threshold and settled into her greatest accomplishment, her mama's Lincoln rocker. Repairing and caning this chair had been a labor of love.

Cleo had nursed Em in this rocker. Her mama had shared with Em the stories of her as a baby. Once asleep, her papa would gently lift sleeping Em from Cleo's arms and carry her to her crib. Em remembered her mama's words, "Honestly, sometimes I think your papa was so proud of you that he thought he had carried and birthed you himself!" Em always laughed over her mother's words.

Em suddenly realized how many years and memories were woven into this chair. Visions floated into her mind. This had been the only place her mama could rest once cancer began eating her up, wracking her with pain. In the last months prior to Cleo's death, she had often fallen asleep in this rocker. Just as her mama had rocked her to sleep as a child, Em had rocked her mama to sleep in the last weeks of her life.

The baby within her thumped about, then settled in quietly as Em continued rocking. Sunlight filtered through the antique lace curtains, reminding Em of Felicity.

Suddenly, Em realized the room was filled with three mothers, four, including herself. She felt the presence of both her mama and Felice. She closed her eyes and could sense their presence. She was certain these two dearest mothers of her heart were watching over her, keeping her safe. The third mother was the newest one, Margret. Her mother-in-law was as excited over the baby as Randy and Em were. She called frequently to see how Em was feeling and to ask if she needed anything. Em found she loved the attention as much as Margret loved hearing of the progress of her pregnancy. She felt safe and cherished.

Randy found her there, gently snoring when he came home. He had picked up a casserole for dinner from Margret. His mother had newfound energy and loved cooking for them to keep 'Em off her feet'. He had another surprise for his wife. He had also begun to haunt the thrift stores and antique shop in town and had discovered an old wicker dresser. It was wide enough to cover with a soft towel for changing the baby. "Em, wake up. Come see what I found."

"Damn. Mama's rocker always puts me to sleep." Randy helped Em up and excitedly led her to the yard where their Rambler was parked. Proudly he opened the doors to show her the pretty white wicker chest of drawers he had purchased. Em was thrilled but was immediately struck by a thought. Her mouth fell open as she looked at the old chest.

"Sweetheart, what's wrong? Are you feeling sick? You look like you've seen a ghost. Don't you like it?" Randy said worriedly.

"Nothing's wrong, really. I love it, it's perfect. It will fit so well in the baby's room."

What Em didn't say to Randy, as she had still not shared the *The Book of Memories* with him, was that this wicker chest could be the work of Julia, the Wicker Queen. Em had buried *The Book of Memories* in her great-grandmother's hope chest, not wanting Randy to discover the secrets that lived in these rooms.

"The lady at the shop said this chest is a real antique. And being white, I thought it would be perfect for the baby's room. It can be a changing table, too." Randy looked crestfallen, the sparkle and joy collapsing on his face. "You don't like it, do you?"

Em returned to herself, giving Randy a warm hug and sweet kiss. "Honestly, I love it. It's absolutely perfect. Where did you get it?"

"At Antique Life in town. You know, the place right next to Thrifty Threads? The lady said she'd had it forever but put it in the back room to make way for newer stuff. That's where I unearthed it. She gave me a great price, especially when I told her what it was for." Randy was now in complete excitement. "You go throw the casserole in the oven and I'll set the dresser up in Porterhouse's room." He chuckled, knowing that would raise Em's hackles.

"This baby will NOT be named Porterhouse! Besides, we're having a girl. I know it." Em huffed, taking the casserole from Randy.

"We'll see about that," he replied, smacking Em on her nicely rounded buttocks as she turned toward the kitchen.

When Randy set the little dresser up in the room it completed the nursery. Em was thrilled but couldn't shake the feeling that Julia had worked on this antique wicker chest. She wondered if it had 'come home'. A shiver raced up her spine but she chased the coldness away. She ran her hands over the top of the dresser and opened all the drawers, thinking of the fun she would have filling them up. She had already made three tiny peasant blouses from the pattern in Alicia Bay Laurel's book, *Living On The Earth*. On her next trip to Charles Town, she planned to visit Mary at *Sew What* to purchase embroidery thread to embroider feather vines, leaves and love knots onto the tiny bodice of each blouse. As Em turned to leave, she once again felt as though other presences were gracing the room. "Great," she said to herself. "Now Julia's here too. For a room meant for only one tiny baby, it's getting pretty crowded." Gently she shut the door and returned to the kitchen to warm Margret's beef bourguignon.

Within all the adoration and excitement from Randy, Margret, and Adrian— and others who saw her growing pregnancy—there was only one voice, one presence, Em longed for: Felicity. She remembered all their conversations. Where was she, her dearest friend, mentor and observer of her life? Walking in the woods, washing dishes, reading or sitting on the loo, all of Felice returned to her in random images. Em knew Felicity would not return until the weather warmed up later in the spring. She longed for her company. She couldn't wait to show off her pregnant self. But she knew she had to be patient until her dear friend reappeared, in her own good time. Sharing aspects of Em's life right now was impossible, but what a lot she'd have to share at their next visit. In the meantime, Em had no choice but to respect her friend's escape into her own seclusion and solitude. What would happen if by happenstance Em found her? That could ruin their friendship. She would wait for warmer weather to arrive, hopefully along with Felice. For now, she followed Randy and Adrian's advice, "If someone doesn't want to be found it's best not to look for them."

Adrian called two nights later filled with excitement, she could hear the joy in his voice.

"Addy, I'm guessing your roast chicken dinner was a big hit. Tell me."

"Oh, yes, of course, it was great. I was right though; Nils isn't crazy about my little apartment. And *you* were right. The smell of that roasting chicken when he walked in made him melt."

"Did you make everything like I said? Did he like my pie?"

"Yes! Honestly, we had a fantastic time. I'll never be as good a chef as he is, but he loved everything about the meal. It *was* easy and it certainly did warm his heart." Adrian chuckled at the memory of their evening.

"I'll wager it warmed other parts of him as well." Em quipped.

"Now who's the randy one? Excuse the pun…but there's something else I can't wait to tell you. Em! I figured it out! We're going about this all wrong. We're looking at the roads and lanes and trails on the map below the mansion, in the flatlands. Didn't Felicity tell you the graveyard was up a hill somewhere right *below* the mansion? Made for the residents of the plantation? We need to look around Mildred Hanson's property. I looked on the plat map, and sure enough, in a tiny old English script there's a spot that says, *Sacred Ground,* just like Don Fraser said. What else could sacred ground be but a cemetery? It's there below the old mansion, not in the hollow where we've been looking. We have to find *that* path going *up* the hill."

"What makes you think 'sacred ground' isn't the Hanson family graveyard?"

"Because it's not near the Hanson Mansion, it's *below* it. A family graveyard is always near the house, even right next to it or on a high rise overlooking a home."

"You're a genius. Why didn't I think of that? Felicity was always so vague. She said it was 'up there, over the hill'. I didn't think about the hill being where Mildred Hanson's plantation and mansion were. Let's see if we can discover a lane that goes uphill in the direction of the Hanson property. It shouldn't be that hard to figure out." Little did they know how difficult this seemingly simple task would turn out to be. It took them three more excursions before they finally found the clue they had been searching for.

On a bright April morning, they set off again. Em was feeling dejected, wondering if they would ever find the graveyard. She longed to try her hand at grave rubbings, something else she could show off to Felicity when she reappeared in the spring. She also wanted to continue Julia and Dani's tradition of cleaning the old graves, paying tribute to the dead. How could she do so if the graveyard was completely lost and buried due to years of neglect and over growth? Maybe they'd never find it. She was seven months pregnant and knew she shouldn't be walking around these woods too much longer.

The day was warm, and tiny white and purple violets were scattered throughout the green of the new grass. Curled fiddlehead ferns tickled their ankles as they walked through the deepening woods. While Adrian groused, as he looked down at the ground for clues and kicking stones, Em looked up. She was moving slower due to her advanced pregnancy. Lumbering or not, she was determined. Suddenly, Em stopped dead in her tracks. "Addy, Addy, come look at these trees!"

"We're looking for a path. There are trees all over." Adrian snapped. They had come to a small plateau in the woodsy path, a secret room set in the serenity of green. They were surrounded by a little forest of fiddlehead ferns, some still furled, others opened completely. Their serrated lacy green leaves stretched to the sun, spears reaching for light. Em and Adrian stood stock still in the scattered light and shade which enveloped them. The niche in the deep woods at the end of the path felt sacred.

Em pointed to a welcome sight. In the distance, she had spied the tops of white tombstones glimmering in the sunlight. She turned to Adrian, excitedly dragging him to where she was standing.

"Look UP. What do you see?" she said as she pointed up the hill.

"Two columns of trees going up the hill. They've obviously been here a long time and were planted carefully for a specific purpose, like coffin trees?" Adrian remarked, smacking a mosquito alighting on his arm.

"Coffin trees. That must be what they are. Remember you told me about the old timers at the library talking about how trees were planted to be used as coffins and to mark a lane to a graveyard?"

Adrian agreed. "Yup, you're right. An aisle of trees, coffin trees, on either side of the road. Not a very big road, but wide enough for carriage, foot or horse traffic."

"Look harder up the hill. What else do you see, Addy? TOMBSTONES!! We found the graveyard. Up over the hill, see? Just the very tops of a few bleached stones."

Adrian looked up, his eyes following Em's. The sight of stones they had been searching for months catapulted them onward with renewed energy. "Wow. You're right. You've got the eyes of a hawk."

"That's what my mama used to tell me," Em said proudly.

The lane was overgrown, barely more than a path. The tall maples and oaks clearly delineated a passage from the cabins below. The trees paraded to the right, then disappeared out of view.

"Come on, let's go."

"No way would I let you, in your condition, climb through all this undergrowth. You're seven months pregnant for heaven's sake. Have you no caution? What if you fell? What would I do? Carry you down the hill on my shoulders? I think not."

"I'll go myself," Em replied, setting forth.

Addy raced after her. "You will not. I'll make you a deal. I'll walk up a bit further to see how bad the path is while you wait here. Then we'll go up together, depending on the precariousness of the territory."

Em stopped and glared at Adrian. "No matter what you say, if you don't go with me, I'll go alone."

"I'll tell Randy."

That immediately put an end to their discussion. The last thing Em wanted was to halt their adventure when she was so close to discovery. Just then, Adrian stopped abruptly and stared intently into the distance. Em followed his gaze through the bare trees.

"Oh my God. Em, do you see that?"

Em squinted, looking carefully into the woods. "No. I don't see a thing. What?"

"Sweetie, that's skull fence or a ghost wall," Adrian said.

"What? Where? What the hell is a skull fence?"

"One of the old ladies I interviewed told me about skull fences. Her great-great grandmother was from Africa and had told her the story. Look, there, along the lower end of this hill, maybe ten feet in front of us."

Finally, Em saw it. A number of wooden fence posts, many fallen over but one or two still stood with the horrifying decoration, a skull cracked and hanging sideways on posts. One appeared to be face down at the top of the fallen post, decorated by fallen leaves and vines woven through the eye sockets.

"That has to be the most horrifying sight I've ever seen. Why on earth would someone do such a thing?" Em asked.

"They were for protection," said Adrian. "In the 1800s and earlier, these old traditions came all the way from England, Wales and Africa. Slaves, especially, brought their superstitions and history with them. Skull fences were built to scare off enemies and intruders. They used animal or even their own ancestors' skulls on top of the posts. It was like a warning to trespassers on family land. Some say it was also a way to protect the dead and ward off evil spirits."

Em shivered and placed her hands protectively over her pregnant tummy. "I don't like it. Way too creepy. It's scaring me off, that's for sure."

Adrian placed his arm around Em. "It's history. But yeah, I have to agree. Pretty spooky. We're not going up any path I haven't checked out first. Anyway, this is out of our way. Come on but be careful. We must be getting close. I'll go on ahead."

A few moments later Adrian cried out happily, "Look, there's a cabin hidden down that trail. Right now I'd rather explore that than any skull fence."

"Oh, all right," Em muttered, then brightened, wondering if it could be Felicity's cabin. She watched Addy's back as he wove his way up the meager path, entwined by vines which tripped him. He turned a corner, escaping from Em's view. She leaned against a tree; her eyes focused on the tops of bleached stones. "They have to be gravestones," she told herself. Suddenly she heard a loud whoop from Adrian, echoing down the tree lined passageway.

"EM! You're right!" She anxiously listened to him crashing down the hill through the undergrowth.

"I found it. There's an old rusted sign, fallen over at the top of the hill. It's right in front of that old cabin. looks like it's been abandoned for years. The sign is written in early American script, Heaven's Gate Cemetery: Final Resting Place for Free People. Established 1842."

Em nearly cried with joy and relief. "Oh, Addy, you found it. I knew you would."

"No, you found it, you saw the row of coffin trees. We'll come back with tools to cut away the undergrowth. I promise. I'll ask Nils to come with us to help."

Reluctantly, Em agreed. "I guess it will still be here next week."

"Promise me you won't come out here on your own," Adrian warned her.

Em remained silent. Adrian pressed his case. "Look, you can't do this alone. I'll come sooner, Nils takes Sundays off and that's only a few days away. We'll clean up the trail. I won't have you tripping over these vines. Randy would shoot me."

"My goodness. Two mountain men. How can I resist? Especially since I'm such a woman in distress," Em teased.

Adrian preened, flexing his muscles to illuminate his new status in Em's eyes. "Yup. Mountain Men. That's us! Nils will get a hoot out of that!"

Em laughed at his ridiculous pose. "All right. You've got a deal. But remember, this is still our secret. We'll tell Randy you want to show Nils the neighborhood. How special it will be for the three of us to find the cemetery together."

"What if Randy wants you to stay home on Sunday? Or decides he wants to come along? I don't like keeping things from him," Adrian replied.

"He won't. Sunday he's planning to go over to Margret's and help her with some gardening, household stuff and repairs. He'll be gone for hours." At the bottom of the hill, Em stooped down and placed a small pile of stones at the beginning of the trail they had discovered. Adrian rushed to her side and helped her up as she wobbled.

"Just a little off center, is all. Don't be such a mother hen," Em grumbled.

"Please, love. Let me help you whenever I can. I feel as though this is my baby too. Belongs to all of us. Sadie and Nils are about as excited as you, Margret and Randy. This is a big event. Not many babies are born at Washington Memorial in Charles Town. Mostly just old folks visit the hospital when they fall and break their hips."

"You're right. Mary is excited, too. Even her knitting circle is thrilled. I think they're up to something," Em replied.

Adrian said thoughtfully. "Well, not many childbearing younger women in these parts. A new baby is special. You're so isolated up here you don't know what goes on in Charlie's Town and how few exciting new events there are."

"I think that's why I love it here, because it *is* isolated. You can hear the silence. I relish that." A quick breeze rattled the branches of the trees, reminding them of the late hour and the coming twilight. As quickly as Em's rotund body would allow they made it back to her little nest before Randy got home.

The following Sunday after Randy's departure for Margret's, Nils and Adrian arrived. Em had made sandwiches and filled a thermos with iced tea. Under the checkered cloth and napkins she had placed a small gardening saw from the shed. With excitement and trepidation, the three set off.

With Nils and Adrian trailblazing, it took less time than Em had imagined to reach the top of the road where the protective maple and oak trees abruptly ended. A large field strewn with early wildflowers opened before them.

"Doesn't look like a graveyard to me." Nils observed.

"But I saw the tops of stones. Addy found the sign. It's here. We just can't see anything, yet. We have to get right to the top of the hill and into that field. We're not up high enough and the trees are blocking the view."

Nils looked skeptical. "Well, it does look like an excellent place to have lunch." Adrian set down the basket he had insisted on carrying. When he looked at Em, he was surprised to see her in tears.

"What is it? Are you okay? You're not going into early labor, are you? Sit down this instant." Both men helped Em settle into a soft pallet of grass, tears streaming down her face.

"All this time we've looked. What if this isn't the right cemetery? Or even a graveyard at all?" Em said, wiping her eyes.

"Of course it is. Look at the top of the hill. I saw the sign, remember? Heaven's Gate Cemetery for Free Persons."

It was Nils who first noticed the large stone mansion above them. "Addy, come with me. I think I see something." Nils pulled Adrian to his feet and they walked around a bend in the path and a few feet up the hill. There it was. Mildred Hanson's home. The roofs and four chimneys announced the presence of an opulent mansion just beyond the tops of ancient trees. Walking a few steps higher the men saw the old manse in all its deteriorating majesty. The bright April sun shone off white, crumbling walls. Slate was missing on parts of the roof and a small tree appeared to be growing out of the front steps leading to the large ornate front door. Bricks had tumbled from the chimneys onto the roof and the ground below. They raced back down the hill to where Em was setting their lunch onto one of her brightly-patterned antique tablecloths.

"Em, we found the mansion! The cemetery can't be far since it was part of the mansion grounds."

"What are we waiting for! Let's go!" Em began to rise in her impatience.

"No, sit right back down. It will wait but I can't. I'm starving and the baby probably is, too." Adrian clucked over Em until she settled back down into their meadow nest. He noticed Em's fresh tears. He took one of Em's checkered napkins and wiped them away. "Silly girl," he admonished her. As Em turned, she noticed an orange cat lurking behind a tree.

"Oh, my god. Look, that's Zuma, Felicity's cat."

Nils and Adrian followed her gaze. Adrian said, "I don't see a thing. Anyway, it was probably just a fox. Didn't you say Zuma was orange? Foxes look orange in the light."

Em ate quickly, her eyes scanning the field, hoping to catch sight of Zuma, or the fox, again. She began to notice rose bushes, obviously planted years earlier. Willow, Magnolia and golden aspen were interspersed at intervals in the field. What other reason would flowers and trees be planted so randomly if not over a beloved's grave? Em knew she was right. Before Nils and Adrian could stop her, she wobbled to her feet and set off.

"Wait for us! You know how clumsy you are!" Adrian called after her as he frantically threw everything into their picnic basket.

Em turned to glare. "I am not clumsy. I'm just off balance sometimes."

"I think she's always a little off balance, pregnant or not, if you ask me," Nils said, sharing a chuckle with Adrian as they scrambled up the hill. Nils reached out his hand to help Adrian up. "Don't know why I let you talk me into these crazy expeditions."

Adrian kissed his cheek gently. "Maybe because you care?"

Em called to the men. "I'll go up the center. Nils, you take the right flank; Adrian, you take the left."

"Yes, General!" Nils rolled his eyes. Adrian came to Em's defense. "Be nice. She's been looking for this graveyard forever and we've found it, once and for all."

The three set forth, eyes at the ready. "Look! Here's another old sign like the one I told you about at the beginning of the trail. It's identical to that one." The three stood over the rusted piece of metal. Em gently lifted it from its grave of weeds and dead leaves. "We should put the sign back up, don't you think?"

"Next visit." Adrian promised.

Nils found the first grave, only part of it showing through the tall grass, a stone beacon worn and bleached of words. He was so excited he could do nothing but jump up and down and scream.

"A grave! I found one! No writing on the stone. Looks like the words are all worn off. The stone fell over. I almost tripped over it. It's definitely a grave."

Em and Adrian raced over to inspect the site. As they examined the grave they noticed more stones, some standing, many toppled by age and weather. There were depressions in the field here and there, clearly old collapsed graves. Then they discovered the first grave which still had discernible words engraved into the old stone:

"Eliza A. BORN: Feb. 15, 1812 DIED Jan. 30, 1903.
The waves of trouble how they rise
How loud the tempest roar.
But death shall land our weary souls
safe on the heavenly shore."

The three stood, silenced by the words etched into the stone. "Wow. That's pretty creepy. It's like we're on a scavenger hunt. Em, are you sure this is the right thing to do? Aren't we desecrating this sacred place?" Nils said, as he looked doubtfully around the field.

"Hogwash," Adrian scoffed.

"I agree," Em said. "Whoever lies in these graves would be happy to know we're here to honor their resting places. Oh, why isn't Felice here now? I was sure she'd return by March. She'll be so thrilled. We can come up here together and clean the graves and plant them with fresh flowering plants, like begonias."

They soon found other graves with their verses intact:

"Elizabeth R.
Wife of Rev. T. Bishop of the Virginia Conf. A.M.E. Church.
Fell asleep in Jesus' Arms, January 24, 1894. Aged 41 yrs.
Faithful unto death. She had nothing left to do but die."

A chill ran up Emeline's spine. "Wasn't this the grave Julia had written of?" She was certain they would find what she was looking for, the gravestone in *The Book of Memories,* 'Damn She Was Good'. They were getting close. Em could feel it. Adrian and Nils were not so certain they should continue. Nils looked nervous and Adrian had placed his arm around his sweetheart's shoulders.

"It's getting late, Em. One more hour and that's all. We've got to get you home before Randy. You know he'd have a fit if he knew you were traipsing up these hills." Em had to agree with Adrian. They worked diligently and separately for the next half hour. Em was thrilled to find gravestone after gravestone. Some with names and verses intact:

"Stop, my friend and you shall see. As I am now so you shall be."

They found more graves with eerie messages and admonishments to the living. Em couldn't wait to come back and do gravestone rubbings. She had already ordered the materials from The Book Nook's art shop. The next stone saddened her deeply.

"In memory of OUR MOTHER

Mrs. Eliza Adkison, Born January 1, 1820; Died June 20, 1882.
Good bye dear Mother you have left me. No more on earth your face
I'll see. Your tender voice is always with me. Through your illness I
was absent yet you asked for me. My tenderest thoughts was ever with
you though I was far across the sea."

Em sat in front of the grave, tears streaming down her face. Nils sat beside her and held her hand. "Oh, Nils. Isn't that the saddest thing you've ever seen?" He gently rubbed Em's back until she was more composed. She took a deep breath just as they heard Adrian's scream. He ran breathlessly to where Em and Nils sat.

"Em, quick, I found it. Didn't you tell me Julia was 'planted' next to a gravestone that read, 'Damn She Was Good'? I found it!"

Em and Nils rushed to the far corner of the cemetery. The three stood looking over the grave, reading the inscription just as Adrian had said, *Damn She Was Good.* No name, no dates, only that inscription, just as Julia had written. Em noticed that there were three graves next to one another under a large magnolia, with the *Damn She Was Good* grave in the center. Magnolia blossoms were just beginning to fill the tree above with their waxy globes.

Em read the inscriptions on the three graves. To the right of *Damn She Was Good*, the gravestone was marked with only an inscribed name, date, and a few words.

"Julia Anne McNamish 1902-1970. Wicker Queen, Rest In Peace."

Em felt chilled to the bone. "Oh, my God. It's Julia. Just like she wrote in the little book. She wanted to be placed right next to this grave." Slowly, with a sense of dread and excitement, Em knelt before the grave to the left. Adrian stood behind her and read the ornate lettering out loud.

"Danielle Felicity Watts,
November 14, 1902-November 21, 1969
Antique Queen, master chef, friend to all, artisan
lover of all things beautiful. Sorely missed".

The three stood before the grave, speechless. Finally, Adrian spoke, "Em, isn't this your friend Felicity's name? Maybe she had relatives? An aunt she was named after? It can't be your Felicity. After all, years ago, Felicity was probably a pretty common name."

Em had collapsed on the soft grass before the grave. Disbelief and shock flooded her senses. She felt slightly nauseous and lightheaded. This could not be true. There must be another explanation. But in her heart of hearts, Em knew it was true.

"It's her. It's Felicity. She had no relatives. It can't be anyone else. Her grave is so close to Julia's and on the other side of 'Damn She Was Good'. She and Julia were best friends in life. Julia wrote that Danielle hated her name. She called herself Dani. I never imagined Felicity could be her middle name. That's her name, the one she told me. Felicity. How can this be? I just can't wrap my head around it. But it all fits together. It's everything Julia wrote in *The Book of Memories*."

Em was mesmerized, enveloped in shock. Words, names, dates inscribed on a gravestone don't lie. She was stunned to her deepest depths. Her dearest friend, her mentor, was dead. Or not.

To Em, Felicity had appeared to be a living breathing woman flesh and blood. Could she be a ghost? Adrian sat down next to her and gently placed his arm around Em's shoulders. He noticed Em's fresh tears and wondered if she knew she was crying.

"Am I crazy?" asked Em plaintively.

"Pregnancy brain. I've heard of it. Lots of pregnant women imagine all sorts of things. It's like you crying so often. It's a pregnancy thing." Nils offered hopefully.

"No. I'm not crazy and this is *not* pregnancy brain. I met Felicity in late March, after we first moved here last year. I wasn't pregnant then. She taught me how to cane chairs. She told me what books to read. Addy! I gave you her booklist she dictated to me! You know she's real! She was like a second mother to me and the best teacher and friend I've ever had. I love her and miss her. How can this be real?"

Silence enveloped the three. Nils was the only one moving, pacing back and forth behind the three graves.

"We know you're not crazy, Em. This is just hard to take in," Adrian said as he watched Nils pacing.

"You're telling me?" Em whispered. "My best friend is a…*ghost? A spirit?* And the Friendship Book, *The Book of Memories,* that's real. All the stories in the book fit with these graves." No one answered. The only sound was the rustling of the magnolia leaves overhead.

"Come on, sweetie. We better head back. Randy will be home soon." Adrian reached out a hand to help Em to her feet.

Quietly they gathered up their picnic remnants and gardening tools. Em gave one last look at the three graves. She saw that the magnolia tree over the graves would soon be fully engulfed in blossoms. A stray breeze kissed the back of her neck. The three were silent, a contrast from their earlier joyous walk up the trail.

"Em. I believe you," said Adrian. "Tell you what, now that we have Felicity's full name, dates of birth and, uh, death, I can look her up."

"No Addy. That's sweet of you, but no. I just want to remember the Felicity I know, or knew. My mom told stories to everyone who would listen about the fancy ladies long gone who worked at the old Ryde Hotel. Everyone said the old Ryde was haunted. Mama used to say that some people have the gift of moving between worlds and dimensions. She said the spirits found receptors, living people they knew who could see and hear them. And Felicity told me herself that she believed there were parties among the dead right here in Heaven's Gate Cemetery."

Nils joined in. "My grandmother told me the same thing. I used to think it was all just some crazy old Scandinavian tale. Now I'm not so sure. Nana said it was a privilege to see and hear the dead. A gift they bestowed on special spiritual people. And my grand pop-pop, he was from Wales—told stories about 'thin places'—spots between where the line between the living and dead is permeable, always near. I never believed them, till now. Just keep an open mind and remember who your mama and Felicity were to you. Some relationships are too strong to die."

"That's exactly what Felicity told me. I guess I believe it now," Em said.

Slowly they gathered up their picnic basket and gardening tools and made their way toward the bottom of the hill. Em was silent the entire walk. Adrian's heart went out to her as he and Nils exchanged worried looks. Nils whispered to Adrian, "So this is why you met up with Don Fraser to find Em's dead friend? Researching old land plats and graveyards? You certainly hit the jackpot."

"Shhh," Adrian whispered back.

Finally, they reached the bottom of the hill and the dusty road to Cabin #25. Adrian stopped abruptly and examined Em carefully. She seemed a million miles, or worlds, away.

"Oh, come here, my little plump pregnant love." Adrian enfolded Em in a tight embrace. Nils joined in. The three of them were dappled with sunlight through the clearing in the welcoming aisle of tall trees.

"You're not crazy. But you will be in trouble if we don't get you home," Adrian said, as he kissed her forehead.

Back home again, Em waved goodbye to Adrian and Nils as they drove off. She felt more alone than she had since her mama's death. She felt as though she herself were dead, covered by a shroud of sorrow.

Just then the first of the blooming magnolias fell at her feet, its perfume scenting the air on descent. She remembered it had been Felicity who had shown her the beauty of the magnolia tree over her head. She had never noticed the enormous tree prior to Felicity walking up her drive to pick the blossoms. That was a year ago. So much has happened since then. Em stared at the blossom and picked it up. The scent was intoxicating. Tears once again filled her eyes as she picked a few blossoms from the lowest branches of the great magnolia. "Thank you, Felice," she whispered.

Em walked into her kitchen and pulled a blue glass vase from her shelf, an heirloom passed down to her from her grandmama and mama. She placed the blossoms in the vase. It was the first magnolia of the season to adorn her kitchen.

Felicity would be pleased.

Chapter 17

Em still hadn't confided Felicity's true identity to Randy, but knew she couldn't keep this secret from him much longer. It was eating away at her soul. Randy noticed her sorrow, and was perplexed and concerned.

"Sweetheart, are you worried about the baby? You know you're doing great, having a perfect pregnancy now that the little episode of bleeding is over. Dr. Lockehart was so pleased at our last visit. You know you can tell me anything. What is it? You're so quiet lately. That's just not like you."

"I'm fine, really. Just have a lot on my mind." Em knew the truth. She was grieving. She would never see her friend again, never have a conversation or laugh together in her kitchen.

They would never pick magnolia blossoms together. She was gone. Em knew it was time to share her secret with Randy. Em retrieved *The Book of Memories* from her grandmama's hope chest.

"Randy," she said. "I've got something to show you. Remember that little book we found on the top shelf of the kitchen pantry?"

"Huh? No, not really." He turned the book over in his hands. "What's it about?"

"I can't begin to tell you. You'll have to read it yourself. Then we'll talk about it."

Just as Em had sat down to read the book from start to finish, so did Randy. As he turned the last page of the book, he looked more perplexed than ever. "Does this mean these two old ladies lived in this cabin, Julia and Dani? And one of them died here? That's sure creepy. But then, it is an historical cabin. Probably lots of people died here back in the old days. Huh. Old days. It was 1970 when Julia died, 1969 when her friend Dani died. That's only what, twelve years ago?"

"Looks that way," said Em, concentration furrowing her brow. She wasn't ready to share more with Randy at the moment. But she knew the perfect way to share the rest of her tale.

Bright and early the next morning Em was up and bustling around the kitchen getting breakfast ready, determined to put Felicity behind them, for the time being. "Honey, can I drop you off at work? I need to get out of the house for a while. Stop at the library, maybe visit with Sadie."

"Of course. That's just what you need, get out and have some fun. Tell Sadie I said hi, and Adrian, too."

There was only one thing left to do, for herself and for Felice. The next day Em picked up her order of rice paper and gravestone rubbing wax at the *Book Nook Art Corner*. She would complete this task alone and secretly. This was a final tribute to Felice she couldn't bear to share with anyone else, not even Adrian. She sat in the car and read the instructions carefully on the box of Gravestone Rubbing Wax.

"Clean gravestone carefully with a small brush, removing lichen, debris and leaves without damaging stone. Adhere the rice paper gently to the stone, securing all edges with masking tape, making certain the rice paper is completely flat on the surface of the stone. Leave overlap of paper at top and bottom of stone. Slowly and with utmost care rub wax gently over rice paper. Do not tear paper. Examine your work frequently making certain all impressions from gravestone are pressed onto paper. When completed and all inscriptions and embellishments are clearly visible on rice paper, carefully remove the masking tape from stone without tearing the rice paper in the process. Roll up rice paper with gravestone print, wax image facing the inside of the roll." Em carefully placed the roll of rice paper and the box of gravestone rubbing wax, back in her *Book Nook* bag. "I can do this," Em confidently told her image in the rear view mirror.

This was a personal and private endeavor Em wanted to share with no one. She also knew that at almost eight months of pregnancy she would be taking a risk. If Randy knew of her plan he would forbid her from walking up the long hill to Heaven's Gate Cemetery alone, but Em was determined to do so, anyway.

The following day before walking up the hill Em reread *The Book of Memories* and cried over the reality of Dani's identity as her dearest friend, Felice. Into her bag she placed her small clippers and trowel, as well as a sealed canning jar filled with water for collecting wildflowers.

She added her rolled rice paper, her small brush, gravestone rubbing wax and masking tape and set off up the hill with a mixture of worry and anticipation. The April day was bright and sunny and perfumed with a flower-scented breeze caressing her as she walked out of the yard. Em looked at the small garden plot Randy had dug for her next to the cabin. She had planted a few spring vegetables, with their seed packets gaily adorning sticks Randy had placed in the rows. The lettuce and spinach were beginning to poke their young shoots up through the soil. Her tomato plants were beginning to bloom with tiny star-shaped blossoms. Everything was thriving, including the weeds, which Em knew she should tackle. She had lost all gardening enthusiasm once she had discovered Felicity's grave. She was saddened to realize since her discovery she had lost a zest for just about everything.

Em took her time walking toward Heaven's Gate Cemetery. *Snap out of it!* She angrily told herself as she walked up the path. She would enjoy this day. She would celebrate Felice, not mourn her. She perked up and began noticing the colorful carpet of wildflowers and flower gardens along her journey. Lilies, violets, daisies, and dandelions grew wildly and in pretty cabin flower beds along the Heavenly Hollow road. She picked a bouquet of wildflowers from the side of the road and placed the blossoms in her jar of water. The colors and the scents of the flowers cheered her. They would look beautiful on Felicity's grave.

She meandered through the aisle of maple and aspen trees, glowing and showing off their fresh green spring wardrobes. Occasionally she would surprise a chipmunk or a bird, who would race off at her approach. A mockingbird warily watched her, sang his song to Em and departed, leaving her with a strange stillness after his cheerful song had long floated away. She felt as though she were walking into a special, spiritual place, almost like an outdoor church, open and nature-filled, a meeting place of nature, beauty and light.

At last, she reached the graveyard and made her way to Felicity's grave. She sat before the gravestone, not caring that she was probably sitting on top of Felicity, six feet under. She cried, the tears running slowly down her cheeks. It was hard to believe her best friend, her *other mother*, was gone. The loss of one mother was enough, how could she cope with this loss of two? The baby gave her a solid kick, reminding her that she would be a mother herself before she knew it. You're right. Better get with the program, Em reminded herself, not for the first time. Her quickly approaching motherhood frightened her. She shivered at the thought. Am I ready? Is any woman ever ready?

She rose, and gently cleansed the stone of debris. She taped the rice paper tightly to the gravestone. She was tired but elated. She would have something of Felice, after all. A physical sign that she could touch, hold and prove to herself that Felicity had once been alive. The baby kicked methodically, then stopped.

"Good girl. Time for your nap while mama works."

Em began to rub the wax over the rice paper, picking up the words from the stone. As if by magic, the vines, interspersed with flowers and hearts, rose from the stone onto Em's rice paper. Slowly, the beloved name, Danielle Felicity Watts, letter by letter appeared. Painfully, the dates also rose. From time to time, Em would struggle to her feet and step back to examine her efforts. She would then return to her task, kneeling and becoming more excited as the words and decorative flowered vine fully materialized onto the rice paper. Birds sang and chattered vibrantly overhead. She recognized the song of the cardinal, its full-throated serenade erupting loudly from the Magnolia tree. She followed the voice and discovered a male, dressed brightly in red, the female close by. The hushed silence of the graves seemed to be listening to his song as closely as Em. The leaves rustled and waltzed to and fro. The Aspen trees at the edge of the graveyard were a fresh spring green, unlike their golden jeweled foliage of the fall. Their symphony was a gentle whoosh, like waves, coming over her, enveloping her completely as she worked. A foolish squirrel raced up the magnolia tree and scolded her loudly, rebuking Em for his interrupted peace.

She traced her fingers over Felicity's name once again. She felt as though she were raising Felicity from the dead. Suddenly she felt another presence and fear leapt into her throat, chilling her. *Oh, please, let me be here by myself,* she begged silently. The last thing she wanted was another visitor to the cemetery. Of course, this graveyard wasn't hers alone. Others must know the location of their family's graves and would visit, now that the spring weather had arrived. When the feeling persisted, Em turned and looked directly into Felicity's eyes.

"Lo, Darlin'," Felicity said with a smile, as she always had.

Em gasped, placed her hand over her pregnant belly to quiet the awakened acrobatics of her child within. The world became completely silent. Gone were the birds, the squirrels, the breezes. Everything came to a standstill yet seemed to swirl around Em. She felt as though she were in a kaleidoscope in a soundless vacuum. Her mouth was agape as she stared into Felicity's granite eyes, saw her familiar pale face, her lips in a wide smile. Her hair was even the same, those gray curls, with their white wings at her temples. The barely-blue striped shirt, the faded cotton pants, the old Keds. She was exactly the same as Em remembered Felice through all the months of missing her.

But Em was sitting on Felicity's grave, not on her front porch or under her magnolia tree. Felicity sat down beside Em. *Why should I be shocked?* Em wondered silently. I always knew she was alive in my life. Then she burst into fresh tears.

"Oh, Felice. This can't be true. I've missed you so much. How can this be possible? You look like you always have. A real, living, breathing..." Em stopped. *How do you name a spirit, a ghost?*

Felice's voice was as musical as Em remembered. "Ghost? Remnant? Spirit? Someone who doesn't know how to rest peacefully? That's what I am, darlin'. Now you know. And call me Felice, love, as you always have."

"But, how—why did you choose to visit me? To become my friend, my dearest friend?" asked Em.

"You needed me, pure and simple. Oh, I've been hanging around Julia's cabin and our little neighborhood since I left. I never showed myself to anyone except you. I just contentedly haunted about by myself."

"You've been around our cabin all along?" Em asked incredulously.

"Yes, love. Love and energy don't always disappear. They just take another form. Sometimes a spirit, a love, or friendship is so strong that it doesn't end. The essence of some is breathed into a home, a sacred place, becomes part of the fabric, enters it, revels in it. The presence of a well-loved person never leaves when there has been too much love in that place to let one depart. You just have to look for old friends and loved ones in forgotten, hidden places. You might catch a glimpse, or a shadow, a scent or vibration, like smoke, disappearing as soon as you enter a room. That's a powerful soul. That's *my* soul."

"Initially, I had to keep an eye on Julia. I knew every nook and cranny of cabin #25. When she died, there was no reason to haunt about. Yet I couldn't leave. I had to keep watch over the place where I had lived and died. I was never more thrilled than when Randy carried you over the threshold of Julia's #25. Wonderful! A new couple worthy of Julia's home, I told myself. I exulted in your young presence. The first time I presented myself to you was because I knew you needed a mother in your life. You also reminded me of the daughter I had always hoped to have, but never did."

Felice stopped for a moment to study Em. She gently reached out and touched Em's cheek, wet with tears. "As time went by, I noticed every one of your sweet and lovely decorative touches. I realized you had talents you had not yet discovered. When Randy first carried you over your threshold, your aura was bright and sunny. Then, suddenly your aura turned dark. You were cloaked, drenched in sorrow. Poor child. How you missed your mama. That's when I knew I had to act. I needed you. I needed someone to guide, to teach, and you were that naive little girl who cried out for me. You just didn't know it."

"I did miss Mama," Em said through her tears. "Still do. But you helped me so much, to read, and to understand life more fully. You gave me new ideas, a fresh journey to travel. You taught me to cane chairs!"

Felicity chuckled her deep and throaty laugh Em remembered and loved so well. "Yes, love, you were an excellent student. And look at you now, with your own chair caning business." Felicity gently touched Em's tummy. The baby quieted her acrobatics. "And here you are, about to have a child of your own. You're ready now. You weren't ready when I first met you, darlin'."

"I knew you desperately needed guidance the day I saw your most important task was in choosing which color to paint your toenails. I was positive there was more in life for you. You only needed someone to lead the way, to gently push you in the right direction. Cabin #25 was my haunt, Julia's home and my responsibility. There just hadn't been anyone who lived there before you to interest me. I continued to exist within the dimensions of that space. At first, I kept my presence a secret."

"You chose me? Because I needed my mother?"

"Because you needed a mentor, a friend, another mother. Yes, sweet child. Your heart and soul called out to me. I answered your call. You were so needy and unobservant. You didn't even realize your magnolia tree was in full bloom right over your head. You became more to me than a student, but a friend through life. I came to love you, dearly, like a daughter. Still do."

Impulsively Em grabbed Felice's hand. "You're ice cold."

"Of course I am, deah. I'm dead," Felice said with a chuckle.

"I just can't wrap my head around—you being—*gone.*" Em couldn't bring herself to say 'dead'. "Yet I know you. I know who you are. There's no mistaking the books you told me to read, the caning lessons, the supplies you found in the shed. And then you directed me to *The Book of Memories* and I read about Dani. That was you, wasn't it?" It wasn't even a question because Em knew the answer. She thought a moment longer as she looked around searching the graveyard.

"Where's Julia? Shouldn't she be here with you?" Em half expected Julia would appear, joining Felicity at their graves.

"Julia never came back. She was ready to go. She wanted to depart. Not me. I was too angry to leave. I wasn't ready to die. My life had been perfect; my business was thriving. I had Julia to laugh and talk with. One damn fall, hitting my head brought all that to an end. Anger kept me wandering after death. I wasn't ready to go, then."

"Anger? You mean over dying?" Em asked.

"Yes, of course. But not just over dying. About the way I went. ALS was a horrible death sentence. I wished that my mind could have departed long before my body. The cruelest aspect of the disease is your thriving, alert brain. You are forced to witness every deterioration of your body. It is torture. You are watching yourself become diminished, bit by bit. You lose more functions every day. Finally, you can't talk, swallow, eat, or breathe. And you watch it all. I didn't deserve that death. Nor did Julia deserve to watch me die, that way, to hope, to care for me endlessly. There was no hope. We both knew it."

"Oh, Felice, the little book…"

"I've always loved that you called me Felice. No one else knew me by that name. Only you. Yes, *The Book of Memories*. Julia wrote that book for me. She wanted to memorialize our friendship, and she did. Until you came along, there was just no one to share it with. I showed you where it was. By then, you had grown so much, learned so much. You missed your mama still, but not in the heart-wrenching way you had before. You had become an intelligent, inquisitive woman. Your aura became a bright shining star. You were ready to learn the history of the rooms in which you lived. I was almost finished with your education. I think it all worked. Look at you now!"

Felice's well-remembered broad smile lit up her face. Again, she reached out and touched Em's tummy. The baby immediately awakened and rewarded Em with a strong kick. They laughed together as they had so often in the past.

"If it's a girl, and my heart tells me the baby is, we're naming her Felicity. Lissa for short."

"That's the greatest gift I've ever received in my life. Or in my death. Thank you, sweet Emmy, for such a tribute. That's another reason I'm ready. Because of you, I am grateful. Now that I have helped you in your world, I can rest. I am ready to depart. As Julia grumbles at me from time to time, 'Shoulda done that a long time ago, Dani'."

"What do you mean? Why should you be grateful to me?"

"You let me in. You gave me purpose. I'm your Juno, your guardian spirit. You don't need me anymore. I've completed my guardianship. In my gratitude to you I can rest easy. Oh, cranky Julia, she'll be so pleased! She's tired of me roaming around. She never understood the light. I was never afraid of death. You know, from the worst fears arise the greatest hopes. I had nothing to hope for until you came along. Some folks say dying is a radiant light at the end of a tunnel. For me, it was the light I refused to enter. Like candlelight in the corner of the room of a dying person. When the candle blows out, another soul goes to heaven, so the story goes. Well, I'd be damned if I was going to heaven or anywhere else. I wisped about, ghosted between dimensions, in the breezes, in the shadows or in the blink of an eye. Until you came into my dimension, and I saw clearly that you were a receptive soul. I remained angry, and aloof. Then, you showed me the way to peace and restfulness." There erupted that deep throaty laugh Em so missed, although Felice sounded a bit more hoarse than she remembered.

Suddenly another thought flew into Em's mind. "Felicity, what about Zuma? Is she a real, living cat? I think I've been seeing her around our house, even on the hill to Heaven's Gate. I wondered if it was just my imagination playing tricks on me."

Felice chuckled again. "Oh, yes. She's alive and real all right. She was my cat and adored me. All the stories I told you about Zuma are true. Animals have greater receptibility to spirits than humans. Zuma never left my side while I lived and was not ready to do so when I died. She was always happy to accompany me in my wanderings. After my final November departure last year, she hid around your cabin, hoping I'd return. When I didn't, she adopted you and your cats. She's still young, by cat years. Zuma's mama lived to be twenty, almost as old as your mama's cats. I imagine she'll be gracing your home for the rest of her life. By the way, thank you for leaving food out for her."

Em shook her head in amazement. No wonder Rhett and Scarlet had befriended Zuma. They realized Zuma could be a new feline friend and one who needed to be fed. It was her furry family that Em had left the food out for when they foraged overnight. She had never imagined she was also feeding Zuma.

Em looked at the rice paper still taped to Felicity's gravestone. "I brought flowers to place on your grave. And I promise I'll come by as often as I can, to clean the graves, just as you and Julia did."

Felice's smile was a beacon of light, yet tears glistened in those familiar granite-gray eyes. "My deah, deah lovely child. You've done a fine job of everything. I would be thrilled if you would keep up our tradition of honoring the dead." Felice lightly touched Em's shoulder as together they admired her gravestone rubbing.

"Oh, Felice. I still can't believe this is happening."

"Yes, you can. And you will. You'll remember it all when I flit away. You don't need me anymore, darlin'. You've grown into a mature, intelligent, talented and loving woman. You're going to be a wonderful mother. You'll never forget me, or your mama."

"I wonder who I would have been without you in my life?"

"Probably a girl still deciding over toenail polish, never having read a book, not learning to cane chairs nor enlarging your horizons so completely."

"Or bake biscuits! You even taught me how to cook! Through *Miss Magnolia's Recipes for the Down at Heart.*"

"Yes. I was in the library with you that day. Didn't you think it was strange when that cookbook flew off the shelf and landed at your feet?"

"How could I have known? I thought the book falling was the fault of the way the librarian stacked the shelves. Then I met Adrian."

"Yes. He is a dear man, and an important friend in your life. As are all the friends you've made and welcomed into your heart. Never underestimate friendship or the strange places friendship blossoms and grows. Adrian would go to the ends of the earth for you as would your dear sweet Randy. After all, it was Adrian who brought you to me here in Heaven's Gate. You even found my cabin, though you didn't know that at the time. You looked through those old cobwebbed windows and noticed the chairs and antiques I was unable to refinish. After all, the dead don't own nuthin'. No one ever moved in. Julia and I chuckled over that. 'Guess you never left so anyone else is afraid to move in. Felice continued, "You've helped Randy to mature too. To learn to trust and love and be comfortable in his own skin. You've all grown up beautifully. And you finally opened your heart to our old librarian, Genevieve, who you used to make fun of. And Sadie, who you thought was only a waitress. You learned she was so much more."

"And let's not forget Mary at the Sew What. As with most Native Americans, Mary is a very spiritual and receptive person. She sees far more than you can imagine. Mary filled your orders for caning and pushed you forward into your

310

career path. She recognized your talent and your sweetness, your bright aura. Of course, Randy was the one who gained the most with your renaissance. He may have had grandiose ideas which annoyed you. Loving you unequivocally was probably his greatest challenge. He persisted in courting you long after you were married. Deah, you finally learned how lucky you are to have a man who was happy to grow and change to make life better for you both. He's a keeper, although there were times when you didn't always think so."

"With your help," said Em. "It's true. Randy and I *have* changed, grown up and become closer. We should with this baby six or so weeks from being born. I worry about what's coming. I haven't been around kids much. How can I possibly be a good mother?"

"Oh, you will, love. All first-time moms feel that way. You've got the heart and the desire to be the best mother any child could hope for. Just follow your instincts. You'll be fine."

Em looked at Felicity closely, examining every line in her well-loved face, her deep gray, almost black eyes, her full mouth, her sculpted cheeks, her Roman nose. She wanted to memorize every aspect of her dearest friend. A beautiful face, Em suddenly realized. How had she not noticed before?

"Darlin, I won't be seeing you again. Oh, I'll be around, rest assured. I'm tired. It takes a great deal of energy to appear in your world, to flit between dimensions. Most importantly, my purpose as your Juno is fulfilled and your gratitude has allowed me to rest. I've loved every minute of our friendship. You're the daughter I never had. I may have raised you, Emeline. But you raised me from the dead. For that I am forever grateful."

Suddenly they were interrupted by a chattering squirrel overhead, squawking at a Blue Jay. Em and Felicity's eyes gathered in the magnolias, the clouds overhead and the breezes in the surrounding trees. "It's a beautiful world, isn't it, sweet Emmy?" Silence enveloped the two until Felicity spoke again.

"It's time for me to follow Julia to rest in peace. My anger is dissipating. There's nothing I can do about being dead or how I died. It is what it is. Most importantly, I've fulfilled the most important purpose in my spiritual, ghostly, and very real life."

"Will you be near me? Can I talk to you?" Em asked querulously.

"I'll always be around you. Just look for me in the things most beloved to you. When you love someone deeply, they never depart. Remember how you always laughed about talking to yourself? You were really talking to your mama and I'm certain she always heard you. I will always hear you in the same way. Oh, you might catch a vision of me from time to time, but only when you need me. Or when I must celebrate with you." Felice looked completely at peace. She grew silent and became lost in thought.

Felice's silence, her contented seat upon her own grave and her Mona Lisa-like her smile reminded Em of a Maxfield Parrish painting, a moment in time, tinted with colors of the past. Em could only stare at this soul-filled vision before her.

"You are my dearest friend—my other mother," Em said.

"Thank you for your gratitude and love, my dear sweet Emmy."

"I'll miss you. I *have* missed you terribly," Em said, her eyes filling with tears again.

Felice smiled. "But you've survived. You've learned some of life's most important lessons. You've made a business, a home, a marriage and a new life. You've made friends to fill in the empty spaces. You can always talk to me. You'll hear my replies in your heart. And in noticing different things, just like the first magnolia blossoms. You finally saw them without me having to show them to you this year, didn't you?"

They laughed together again. Em reached out and touched Felicity's cold hand. She began to cry when their laughter ended.

"Don't grieve, darlin'. Look in your heart, I'll always be there. Keep growing and learning. Continue your good work of keeping our graveyard tidy. Julia will be so pleased."

"There's so much more to say," Em said, not wanting to relinquish Felice's presence.

"No, there isn't. We've said it all in one way or another. You'll bring me with you wherever you are, wherever you go. I'll always be around, I promise. Didn't I promise I would return to you in the spring? I kept my promise and I will continue to do so. You just won't always see me. It's time for me to rest. I'm tired." Felice seemed to fade along with her quiet words.

She examined Em's rubbing of her gravestone. "You've done an excellent job, deah. Thank you for etching me into immortality and into your heart, soul and life. My work is completed. You don't need me anymore, which is a wonderful thing. And if I do say so, my task of raising Emeline has been a successful one." They shared the sort of smile reserved for only the dearest of friends.

"Now be very careful when you take the tape off the stone and paper. Remove it slowly so the rice paper doesn't tear," Felice said, returning to her role of instructor and mentor.

Em struggled to her feet and began the slow task of removing the paper from the stone. A light breeze lifted the curls from the back of her neck and blessed her forehead like a kiss. The scent of the blooming magnolias overhead mingled with the breeze.

Em turned and saw nothing but an empty cemetery. Felicity had left, departed, returned to wherever she had come from. Em smiled. *At least, I know she can rest in peace now. So can I, knowing she'll always be with me.*

Em picked up her belongings in a dream-like state. She carefully rolled the rice paper and placed it in her bag along with her other gravestone-rubbing tools. As she placed her bouquet on Felicity's grave she noticed the cacophony of natural sounds erupt again. The cardinals, the squirrels, the wrens, a mockingbird, the breezes brushing the Aspen—all created their own ruffled music. The scent of early Magnolia blossoms drifted. Everything returned to this small spot in time, this vacuum Em had been immersed in.

She made her way slowly down the hill, her pregnant tummy leading the way. Spring breezes followed her all the way home, lifting her hair and racing about her feet. By the time she reached Cabin #25, Em had made her decision. At first, Randy might think she was crazy, but it wouldn't be fair not to tell him the truth. She'd show Randy the rice paper rubbing of Felice's grave tonight, the testament to her life. She was ready to share the truth of Felicity's existence with Randy, her husband, dearest friend and love. He had the right to know as much as Emeline did. After all, he was her partner in life and the father of their child. They didn't need secrets between them when there was so much in life to share now, and in all the years ahead.

What if he thought she was crazy? Well, she might be about other things, but not about Felice. Em trusted her other mother, and herself, enough to know Randy would also trust and believe in her. Em carefully carried her rubbing of Felicity's gravestone into the cabin where she would share the final secret of Felicity with her husband that evening.

Em was unusually quiet when Randy arrived home from work, worrying him. "Sweetheart, are you feeling okay? You're not getting any pains, are you?" His voice awakened Em from her reverie. "Oh, I just have my mind on something

I want to show you." Randy looked at Em quizzically but kept his questions and unease to himself.

Em was not certain how to approach Randy. She decided it was best to show, rather than tell her husband, what was troubling her. When he went to the fridge to get a beer, Em unfurled Felicity's gravestone rubbing on the kitchen table. Turning from the fridge, beer in hand, Randy asked quizzically, "Hey, what's this?"

Em took a deep breath. "Randy, sweetheart, there's something I've been keeping from you. This is Felicity's gravestone."

Hesitantly at first, and then in a great rush of words Em confided how she, Nils and Adrian had discovered not only Heaven's Gate Cemetery but thegraves of Felicity and Julia. It was a long painful discussion between the two of them. Randy read the words on the rice paper over and over again, shaking his head. "Are you sure this is the right gravestone? It could be anyone's."

"Yes, I'm sure," Em said, tenderly touching the epitaph on the rice paper.

Randy shook his head and then realized what Em had done. He became angry with the risks she had taken. "You mean to tell me you've been running up hills and valleys in your condition, looking for this *cemetery?* With two men I trusted, Adrian and Nils?"

"Don't be mad at Addy and Nils. They knew I'd take off by myself and really risk my health if they didn't go with me. I'm very grateful for their presence during this whole adventure. I'm in great health. Remember? Dr. Lockehart said I'm having a perfect pregnancy. Just think of it as exercising when I was walking up the old lanes."

Em laced her story with hand-holding, tears, and all the tales her mother had told of the Ryde Hotel, along with snippets of stories and research Addy and Nils had provided. She described everything Felicity had told her of spirits and love that was too strong to end with death. When she was growing up, Em hadn't believed her mama's ghost tales, either. But she had *wanted* to believe Felicity, in hopes that her mother, and now Felicity, would always be near her, even after death. The gravestone rubbing resting on the kitchen table finally convinced Randy, along with everything Felicity had told Em at her grave. He still wasn't entirely sure his wife was not crazy and hallucinating.

Gradually, Randy calmed down and turned to the greater issue of Em's dearest friend residing in a cemetery, under the stone rubbing which was now spread across their kitchen table. As Em prepared dinner they argued for the better part of an hour. Em finally convinced Randy that she had actually visited with Felice. After dinner, with the rubbing carefully rolled up and placed under their bed for safekeeping, Randy finally calmed down. For now, he believed his wife and knew eventually they'd visit Felicity's grave together.

"I guess it was a good thing Adrian and Nils were with you. I shudder at the thought of you traipsing around all on your own." Randy scratched his head. "I don't know, Sweet Pea. It's just a lot to take in. I never really believed in all that stuff your mama used to tell everyone, but I know other people sure believe in spirits. Jason always jokes that he sells more cars because his dead father hangs around the car lot, giving him good luck. Mom swears she sees Clarissa in her old house sometimes, but I've never seen her. Who knows what goes on between lives, dead or alive, right?"

A tinge of anger returned to Randy's voice. "You *must* promise me that your walking all over the holler and up in the hills is over until after the baby comes. Promise me, Em. I mean it. And don't make me have my mother stay here to keep an eye on you."

That sobered Em. "Of course, I promise. You don't have to worry about me. I'll behave."

"No more visiting Heaven's Gate until after the baby's born." Em hugged Randy tightly. "Oh, sweetheart. Thank you for believing in me. For the time being, let's just put it in the back of our minds. We've got lots more important things to think about."

"Ain't that the truth," Randy said ruefully. He was relieved that his wife would settle down in their home, and not traverse the countryside for the rest of her pregnancy.

"As if I don't have enough to worry about," he said to himself, as he settled in front of the couch and turned on reruns of *The Andy Griffith Show*.

Chapter 18

"Why on earth can't your mother come here? I'm so fat and disgusting, I don't want to leave the house."

Randy provided Em with one of his sternest looks. "Because she has asked you to visit for one last time before the baby arrives. She wants to show you my baby album and make you a special meal. And you don't look fat. You look adorably, plumply, pregnant. You'd really hurt Mother's feelings if you refuse to go. You know she invited us two weeks ago and you said it was fine then. We can't bow out at the last minute."

"What do you expect me to wear? A tent?" Em said testily.

"Just wear your maternity jeans and that pretty blouse you made."

Em wanted to smack Randy. "Do you actually think that blouse I sewed two months ago will fit over these enormous boobs?" When Em saw how crestfallen and miserable Randy looked, she relented at once, saying, "I'm sorry, sweetie. It's fine. I know it's hard for your mother to come here to cook. She really made a mess the last time, not knowing her way around my kitchen. It ended up being more work for me to clean up after her. It will be fine. I'm sure we'll have a great visit."

"There's my sweetheart. Just wear that Hawaiian dress Adrian bought for you," Randy said hopefully.

"It's a moo-moo, made for cows, is what I told him. Perfect for me now. Moooo!"

Randy laughed in spite of himself, then sobered. "Stop that this instant. I told you, you look adorable."

"Yeah, right. Blindly in love, as usual," Em said, kissing Randy sweetly.

The next afternoon, Em and Randy arrived bearing their gifts of lettuce and early tomatoes from their garden. Soon after their arrival, Em understood the real reason for their visit to Margret's.

Mother Margret opened her front door and was nearly jumping with excitement. "Oh, Emeline, how wonderful, thank you so much for coming and for the fruit of your garden. You look wonderful, absolutely blooming."

Em felt grouchy and enormous. "Jeeze, it's only lettuce and tomatoes. Not such a big deal. And I'm not blooming. I'm a whale."

"Oh, Emeline, you're pregnant and healthy. And as for your garden contributions, it *is* a big deal because you planted and grew them yourself," Margret said, embracing Em in an awkward hug.

Em continued, "Randy did most of everything in the garden. I'm too damn big to weed anymore. Gravity will pitch me face first into the manure. I'll just put the veggies in the kitchen." As Em walked by the dining room door, she heard a giggle, then loud screams, "SURPRISE!" Em stood in the formal dining room with her mouth agape. She promptly dropped the lettuce and tomatoes and started to cry. They were all here, Sadie and the girls, Adrian, Nils, Mary, even Genevieve. They rushed out to embrace their dear friend. Sadie carefully wiped her tears away, and whispered in her ear, "We're all here because we love you. I know those are tears of joy." Em immediately brightened as she reached out and held Sadie's hand.

"Oh, you look wonderful! I haven't seen you in a month!" Mary laughed as she patted Em's tummy.

"I'm an elephant."

Sadie, as always, shared her motherly wisdom. "Sweetie, every pregnant woman feels the same. Just remember that after the baby's born and you're nursing this baby body will only be a memory."

"I think you look adorable and so does Nils." Nils looked at his beloved in shock. Adrian poked Nils, who then agreed. "Yes, honestly, Em, you look beautiful."

"You never could lie well, Nils." Em's mood quickly changed when she realized all the trouble her friends had gone into planning her baby shower. They led her to the sun porch where balloons were hung along with pink and blue crepe paper. In the center of the room was a pile of gifts in a baby bathtub. All her friends chatted happily together as they settled Em in Margret's favorite loveseat. Randy sat down next to Em and gloried in the party. Alison and Mary Ann happily skipped around the gift-filled baby bathtub in the center of the room. "Open ours first! Open ours first!" they yelled.

"I'm amazed you managed to keep this from me," Em said to Randy reproachfully.

"You're not the only one who can keep secrets, you know." Randy raised his eyebrows, reminding Em of the secrets she herself had kept. She touched his cheek and gave him a gentle kiss. "You really are the sweetest man. I'm so lucky to have you. No more secrets between us, I promise."

They sat together happily on the love seat as Em opened her gifts. Mary had made her a beautiful quilt for the baby's crib and had brought along an afghan made by the knitting circle. "The knitting ladies declined to come to the shower. They took months to make their gift for you. Each one had a specific number of afghan squares to knit, all in different shades of pastels. They were so proud of their work and loved keeping it a secret each time you came into the shop."

Genevieve gave Em and Randy a beautiful set of Beatrix Potter Books. "Perfect for reading to infants and young children. It's never too early to begin teaching literature to babies," Genevieve said judiciously. "Definitely, I have a whole bookcase waiting to be filled with children's books," Em said happily.

Sadie gave Em onesies, tiny booties and socks, bibs and 'belching towels' as she called them. "And look what Larry gave you," Sadie said, handing Em an envelope. Before Em could open it, Sadie excitedly said, "It's a gift certificate for meals from the Inn and Out for six months."

Em laughed at Sadie. "Did you have to pull his leg for this gift on one of his many visits to, uh, have coffee with you every morning?" Sadie blushed as Adrian and Nils picked up the thread. "Oh, really?" said Adrian in mock surprise. "A romance in the wings? Sadie, I thought you were waiting for me to switch teams." Nils smacked Adrian soundly and pretended to glare at him, which made everyone else guffaw. "No one's switching teams in this room," Adrian said, placing his arm protectively around Nils' shoulders.

Alison and Mary Anne continued to jump around the room excitedly. Finally, Sadie acknowledged their gift. "The girls picked out the bathtub and the baby toys themselves. They had so much fun shopping. Then Alison decided to stuff a pillow under her blouse which I didn't realize until the storekeeper asked me if Alison was pregnant. I could have killed the kid." Alison and Mary Anne giggled. Alison, hands on her hips, scolded her mother. "Everybody else thought it was funny, Mom."

Margret glowed with joy. "We have another surprise for you, sweet Emeline. Everyone brought frozen casseroles. We'll replace them for a couple of months, until you're on your feet."

"Oh, what a wonderful gift. That's perfect. Between your casseroles and Larry's gift certificate I won't be cooking for ages." Em couldn't imagine not engaging in her favorite hobby of trying out new recipes. She realized once again just how much her life was about to change.

Shyly, Nils came forward with a large, beautifully wrapped package. Em opened it carefully and gasped when she saw its contents. It was a handsome leather photo album, the surface etched in gold with figures of cherubs floating on clouds. Adrian couldn't hide his excitement. "It's a photo album for all your baby pictures. It goes with my gift." Em opened the small box Adrian handed her, which held a camera. "It's one of those instant Polaroid cameras. You can take tons of photos and they'll be developed in a minute. We expect to see all the baby photos in the album," Nils joined in happily.

Margret's gift was a year's subscription to a diaper service, which Em knew would end up being her most appreciated gift. "Nothing worse than washing diapers, day after day," Margret said, as she gave the certificate to Em. "Just put the pail of rinsed diapers out once a week and they bring a clean, fresh supply. Sure wish they'd had that in my day."

The rest of the afternoon passed in a blur. Sadie had made delicate and delicious tea sandwiches. There were fruit and vegetable salads, ice tea, and wine for the adults. Sadie became tipsy and joined her daughter's chorus, the three singing together loudly and off key.

In the corner, Nils, Randy and Adrian quietly discussed Felicity. Randy was still having a hard time accepting the reality of Em's departed friend showing up at her own grave.

Nils shuffled his feet and looked at the floor until Adrian poked his love. "Nils, tell him." Nils cleared his throat before straightening and facing Randy. "My Scandinavian grandmother believed in spirits. She said they made their appearance only to very special people. Addy and I think that's true, too. My grandma called it Viking love. It never ends, but has the strength, like a warrior, to live through the ages."

Randy looked skeptical but saw how strongly Nils felt. Randy smiled as he said, "You're right. Em's mama believed in ghosts and swore she had spirit friends at the Ryde Hotel. I guess my Sweet Pea is pretty special, too."

This was a secret only the four of them shared, as Em had made Randy, Nils and Adrian promise that they would never reveal the details of Felicity's life and after-death visits to anyone else. Em imagined that everyone in the room, except Mary, would think Em was crazy.

Sometimes even she wondered if she had imagined Felice. During those moments of doubt and loneliness she would pull out Felicity's gravestone rubbing and read The *Book of Memories*. Her friend's love would return in full force. And at those times, Em was certain Felicity was in the room with her, just as Em now realized her mama probably had been, too, for years.

* * *

Em had never felt so full; enormous, fat, and lazy. At nine months, five days of pregnancy, she felt she had the right to relax as much as possible. Her hospital bag was packed, the baby's room readied, diaper bag stuffed. The crib Margret had given them was under the windows, complete with sheets. Mary's baby quilt decorated the little mattress. The afghan made by the knitting circle was draped over the end of the crib, the mobile floating overhead. The white wicker dresser was filled with baby clothes, diapers, baby powder and creams. The Lincoln rocker sat in a corner of the room next to the crib. All Em had to do now was wait. She was tired of waiting. For the third time that day, she stood in the doorway of the pretty little nursery. The cat mobile over the crib gently swam in a breeze from the open window. The prints on the walls would tempt any baby's eyes. It was the perfect place for welcoming their new life. All they needed now was the baby.

She waddled into the library where Rhett, Scarlet and Zuma were napping. Em opened the library Dutch door to allow the June breezes to race from the open kitchen screen door to the sunlit library. Settling into the window seat with her most comfy pillow, her mind scuttled about, like a quick mouse on the hunt for cheese. She curled into the warmth caressing her, feeling the first meanderings of sleep overtaking her. Her mind did not agree and continued to race, fighting the peace she so desired. One contemplation after another crowded her mind.

To and fro, her thoughts, like a song or a lullaby, mingled in her mind. Was she ready? A little late for that now, she chuckled, as she caressed her pregnant tummy. As always, she admired this most special room, her library. One entire bookcase was filled with library castoffs and books she had managed to purchase as well as the gifts of others. Another bookcase was mostly empty.

"That's the one we'll fill up, baby, with all kinds of books and stories I can read to you. I've read fairy tales and poems to you already. I've told you stories from your grandma Cleo and Felicity. We'll fill this bookcase together. It will be yours to help fill over the years. Oh, just like I'm so filled up now." Em shifted the pillow under her head, hoping sleep would empty her mind of anything but dreams. Instead, she continued her conversation with her unborn child.

"Remember how afraid I was of you? Not any longer. Now I can't wait for you to arrive." The sun glazed the walls with ruby and golden light. "Wasn't it sweet of your grandma Margret to give you so many wonderful gifts? The *Pat The Bunny* book, your little night light with the lamb jumping over the moon, the mobile over your crib and that Cadillac of a carriage. Your grandma Margret has certainly outdone herself. I can't wait to dress you in those adorable little outfits from Auntie Sadie and show you off in that carriage on walks through the neighborhood. Everyone thought of everything. You're going to adore your grandma and all our friends just as everyone already adores you." She remembered Randy's excitement over all the frozen casseroles. No more KFC for dinner for at least a few months. She had placed one of the casseroles in the sink to defrost. Don't have to worry about dinner tonight, Em said sleepily. She yawned, enticing sleep to take over. "I think you're a girl. Can't wait to find out if I'm right."

The warmth of the room and the fragrant scents from the fields finally overtook her and Em fell to sleep, her mouth gaping open as her gentle snores filled the room. A dream enveloped her. Her mama and Felicity were sitting at her kitchen table drinking tea. They were wrapped in a golden glow. Their conversation came to Em clearly.

"You've done a great job raising your daughter, Cleo," said Felicity.

"Glad I had you to help," said Cleo. Felicity stirred the tea in her ramblin' rose teacup. Flashes of light swirled in rainbows across the kitchen walls.

"I only finished the job you'd begun," Felicity said, reaching out to touch her mama's hand.

Cleo chuckled in that old familiar musical way Em remembered. "We couldn't have done it without one another." Felicity shrugged, a smile gracing her pale face, her granite eyes lit from deep within.

"Thank you, Cleo."

"Thank *you*, Felice." The two women touched their teacups together, toasting their accomplishment of raising Emeline.

At that moment, Em awoke with a start, feeling the rush of warmth between her legs.

"Did I pee myself?" She stood up on wobbly legs and crossed the room toward the bathroom. Immediately, she realized what was happening. "Oh, my god. My water broke. You're coming. What a mess we've made of my window seat." Then the first stab of pain flew through her entire being.

"Oh. OW!" was all Em could say. When the pain subsided, she walked as quickly as she could to the bathroom, threw her maternity shorts in the sink to soak and noticed her panties were blood stained. "Yup. You're definitely on your way." She quickly changed into a more relaxed tent-like dress. She was overcome with fear, but also excitement. Her three cats followed and watched her nervously.

She made her way to the phone in the kitchen. She noted the time on the wall clock. "Got to time the pains. 11:17," Em said to her feline family. She stood by the kitchen sink, wondering when the next pain would arrive. When nothing happened, she thought perhaps she had imagined the pain. Maybe this was just another Braxton Hicks contraction. But there was no imagining her soaking wet shorts.

Em took deep breaths as she moved about. First to the bedroom to retrieve her little suitcase. Then to the baby's room. She stood in the entrance of the room and noticed the way the cavorting kitten's mobile was swaying over the crib. She picked up the diaper bag, which was fuller than her own suitcase. All three cats swarmed around her ankles meowing their concern.

She walked into the kitchen to check the clock. The next stabbing pain arrived at eleven-twenty-nine. Twelve minutes apart. As soon as the pain subsided, she noticed a different pain, an agonizing ache in her lower back. Definitely time to call Randy.

Randy could barely talk. "Are you sure?"

"Yes, goddammit. Of course, I'm sure. Come home. Now. It's time. I soaked the window seat in the library. I put my shorts and panties in the sink to soak. Pains are coming twelve minutes apart, so I don't have time to chat until the next one. Just get here."

"I love you. I'm on my way."

As she hung up the phone another contraction wracked her. She moved to the old Lincoln rocker in the baby's room and checked the nursery clock. Her pains were now about ten minutes apart. Between pains she rocked. The Felix the Cat clock's tail in the baby's room kept time with her rocking. When the pain had subsided, it was almost as though she had imagined it. When the next pain arrived, she knew this was no hallucination. Randy wouldn't be home for another twenty minutes. She was as ready as she could hope to be. All the books she had read, her classes in Dr. Lockehart's office, her classmates' stories of their deliveries had prepared her. She was once again overwhelmed with pain. She was frightened by this agony, even though she was well prepared. How long would their baby take to arrive?

Even to the experienced admitting room nurse the scene in the Washington Memorial waiting room was one of the strangest mix of family and friends the nurse had ever seen. The husband, a sweet nervous fellow, as all first-time fathers are, had just been thrown out of the labor room in a wifely fit of rage. Everyone in the waiting room heard the exchange. Only Margret continued to crochet calmly, as though she hadn't heard a thing.

"You did this to me! Don't try to be nice to me now! Out! Get out!" He was led from the room by Em's sympathetic labor room nurse.

"Now, dear," the nurse comforted Randy. "Don't take it too hard. Many women feel this way when they're approaching transition and close to pushing. You'll both forget this little fit as soon as you hear your baby's first cries. Just be thankful your Emeline didn't throw her bucket of ice chips at you as the last mom did." The nurse smiled at the memory. "Now that was a mess to clean up. Poor Dad was still damp when their baby arrived." She shook her head, chuckled and returned to Emeline who was begging for drugs. "Forget this natural childbirth crap!" Em screamed as her contractions became unending, with no respite between pains. The labor nurse's pace also picked up. "I'll call Dr. Lockehart and tell him she's getting close."

Sadie heard the exchange between two nurses in the hallway. She called out to them. "I already did. He's on his way," she said with authority.

"That's my job," the nurse replied testily. "Who the hell does she think she is?" she asked her co-worker, who shrugged noncommittally.

"He's my boyfriend," Sadie said with a grin. That shocked both nurses. They turned and scurried back to Emeline's room, anxious to share this news with the other staff.

Randy sat dejectedly with his mother and Adrian. His mother sat serenely and contentedly, crocheting yet another baby cap, this one pink. Margret had finally followed Em's instincts and allowed that the baby was a girl if Em said so. Adrian tapped his feet incessantly and wandered to and from the snack machine. The admitting room nurse had thus far counted three Snickers bars, one Mounds and one Almond Joy consumed by the gentleman in the Hawaiian shirt.

The door burst open and an extremely handsome tall, blond man rushed in. He stopped dead in his tracks, and glared at Adrian. "Just couldn't help yourself, could you? Even on this most momentous occasion."

Adrian stared back at Nils, open mouthed. Chocolate speckled his chin. "What?" he asked his love.

"LIME green pants? And what thrift rack did you grab that horrendous Hawaiian shirt from? Could any more color have been vomited onto that excuse for apparel? Fuchsia? Canary yellow? Turquoise? Really?"

"I dressed for the occasion," Adrian said, looking down at his ensemble.

"Now, Nils. I think Adrian looks quite lovely. His attire perfectly suits his *joie de vie*, his exuberant and celebratory personality."

"Thank you, Mother." Adrian sniffed.

Mother? Randy thought. When did that begin?

"And Nils, wherever did you find that exquisite pinstriped oxford? The stripes are so fine as to almost be a mirage. And they so perfectly match your tailored slacks."

"Thank you, Mother. Lord and Taylors, the last time Addy and I were in Richmond." Nils smiled apologetically at Adrian as Randy glared at *his* mother who had happily returned to her crocheting.

Adrian licked his lips, tasting chocolate. Nils apologetically said, "I'm sorry, sweetie. I'm just nervous." He sighed, taking a handkerchief from his pocket. "You're a mess, you know that?" Gently Nils dabbed at the chocolate smears decorating Adrian's lips and chin.

"You think you're the only one who's nervous here, Nils?" Randy spat. All eyes were suddenly riveted on Randy. Margret patted his hand consolingly. "Now, Son. Em and the baby will be fine. I always told you she was made for childbearing."

Mary was the next to arrive, assaulting the waiting friends with questions. "How is she? Is the baby here yet? Not by the look of the four of you, I gather." She noticed Margret's crochet work. "Oh, Margret, I'm so pleased the pink sherbet yarn worked beautifully for your latest cap. It will be perfect with the matching sweater you made."

"Yes, Mary, you were right to entice me with pink. Come sit next to me." Margret dumped all her crochet supplies, purse and yarn from the chair next to her onto Randy's lap. Randy looked at his lap dejectedly. Together the women admired Margret's meticulous crochet stitches. "The men are just cranky." Margret whispered to Mary. "Let's leave them be."

Mary announced to everyone, "Sadie will be here as soon as she drops the girls off at her ex's. She's bringing us all dinner from the Inn and Out."

"Oh, that dear sweet girl. Maybe she'll bring some of those delicate tea sandwiches she made for Emeline's baby shower," Margret said hopefully.

The admitting room nurse viewed the group one last time, shook her head and closed her glass admitting window. She happily returned to her throne of authority and paperwork, shutting out the unusual family in the lobby.

Margret continued Mary's conversation. "Did you close up Sew What early, dear? What time is it?"

Nils glanced at his elegant gold Timex watch Adrian had given him for his thirtieth birthday. "Five-thirty-three, exactly," he said.

"Jeeze, isn't six hours long enough to birth a baby?" Randy groused.

"Now, Randy, darling. Babies take their own sweet time," said Margret. "But since Em threw you so forcefully from the labor room, I'd say it won't be much longer."

Just then Sadie burst in, carrying a basket filled with sandwiches, a thermos of coffee and thick slices of chocolate cake. On her heels, Genevieve breathlessly followed.

"I brought the champagne!" Genevieve cheerfully announced, as she raced into the lobby, lifting a large bottle of Piper Heindecker over her head. "I came as soon as I could close up the library."

The admitting room nurse again rose to survey the scene. Alcohol was strictly forbidden from the Washington Memorial Hospital. She hesitated in her duties, finally deciding not to pitch herself into this situation. She retreated again behind her fortress. "Going off duty in a half hour anyway. Let the night crew deal with these nuts," she muttered to herself.

Sadie settled on the couch across from Margret. "How is she doing? I remember my first. Twenty hours of horrible, screaming, excruciating pain.

Hours and hours of yelling, 'Can't anyone get this baby out of me?' And then all that pushing." Sadie's eyes teared up at the memory. "It was wonderful."

Randy blanched and slouched deeper into his uncomfortable plastic chair to which he had been evicted. He might as well have been absent and invisible, for all the attention he was receiving. What use was he? He had clearly lost all control over the women in his life. Wasn't he the father of this coming baby? Didn't he deserve any credit? Some comfort?

"Tell us about it, Sadie." Nils enthusiastically begged. Adrian elbowed his beloved and nodded to Randy's blanched face. Nils ignored him as Sadie continued her tale.

"I was torn from end to end." Sadie graphically directed everyone's eyes to her lower extremities. "Couldn't go to the bathroom without terrible pain for days. And the stitches! I could barely walk!"

"My Randy here, now he was a trial. Came fast and hard, just like his dad always did," Margret joined in.

"Mother!" Both Adrian and Nils exclaimed in shock. Nils smirked at Margret. "I do declare you're being overly risqué at such a serious moment," he soberly intoned. Everyone laughed, except Randy, who rose, and said, "I'm going to check on Em."

Almost immediately Randy excitedly ran back to the waiting room. "It's time! They're taking her to delivery! She's ready to push!"

"Oh, my. We'd better begin this delightful repast our faithful friend has provided," Margret said, hungrily eyeing Sadie's basket.

"I'll just have some chocolate cake," Adrian said, pulling the checkered cloth from the basket and eyeing the contents.

"No, you won't. No dessert until you eat something healthy." Nils reproached Adrian, as he tenderly patted Adrian's tummy. "Don't you think you've had enough chocolate, already, dear?"

"There's never enough chocolate," Adrian answered. They dug into their meal and were almost finished with the cake when a cloud of nervousness settled over them. Silence reigned, as palpable worrisome thoughts descended on the waiting room. *It seemed to be taking an awfully long time for Em to push this baby out,* they were all thinking, but no one said aloud.

They were not yet aware of the events unfolding in the delivery room. The baby rested on Em's breasts as Randy held the new mom in his arms. Both Em and Randy were in tears, examining their beautiful daughter, checking fingers and toes.

"Welcome to the world, Felicity," Dr. Lockehart looked up from his sewing to comment. "What a beautiful old-fashioned name. Don't think we've ever had a Felicity before."

Randy and Em shared a smile through their tears. They were too full of joy, emotion and love to speak.

The nurse took the now screaming Felicity to the warming table. "She's really beautiful, Mr. and Mrs. Upswatch. Her eyes are the deepest shade of blue, almost black."

"Got good lungs, too," Dr. Lockehart observed with a smile.

Em and Randy had to agree. She was beautiful and perfect in every way. Her eyes were deep blue, almost violet. She had Em's heart shaped face and Randy's nose. Her mouth was a tiny pink rosebud. She was pink and white all over with light brown fuzz topping her little head. Em's eyes began to close in exhaustion as Randy held onto Felicity's tiny fingers.

The surgical nurse suddenly grew tense. "Magnolias. I smell magnolias, doesn't anyone else?"

"You're just imagining things, Darcy. All I smell is antiseptic. You know we can't wear cologne." Nurse Darcy shook her head as she placed instruments on the Autoclave table. "I know Magnolias and I smell magnolias," she muttered.

Dr. Lockehart commented as he sewed Em up, "Well, they are in season. Just not in here." That drew a chuckle from everyone.

Just then all the lights flickered overhead, plunging the room into momentary darkness. A small breeze arose from nowhere as the lights flickered back on.

Em's eyes flew open as she intently studied the ceiling. She began smiling broadly.

"That's Felicity and Mama, my two mothers," she said, happily seeing her mama and Felicity floating overhead watching Em. Both Cleo and Felicity were smiling through their tears.

"It appears your daughter already has an electric personality," Dr. Lockehart laughed at his own joke over the dimming lights as the nurse returned their new-born to Em and Randy.

"Yes, I'm sure she will have an electric personality. She has two grandmothers watching over her right now. Her full name is Felicity Cleopatra, after the two most important women in my life. My mother and my other mother, my dearest friend. We'll call her Felicity, or Lissa, for short," Em said groggily, smiling at the view overhead while proudly showing off baby Felicity. The new family cuddled happily sharing their amazement at what they had created. Em closed her eyes without letting go of little Felicity's hand until the nurse took her away to place her on the baby scale. She returned Felicity to her father, who was anxiously waiting.

"I assume both the grandmothers are with your extended family in the waiting room?" the nurse asked, readying Em for her transfer onto a gurney as Randy held his daughter for the first time.

"Yes. They're here right now. They're both dead. But Randy's mom, Margret, is in the waiting room and very much alive. Along with the rest of my friends, my second family," Em said sleepily.

"Too much anesthetic," the doctor grumbled quietly. "Nurse, remind me to talk to Dr. Dilettante."

Em knew she was right. Her mama and Felicity had been there, awaiting their grand-daughter's arrival. Em glowed in their presence, knowing her two mothers would always grace their lives. She had never felt happier, more secure or at peace with herself and her world. "You do smell magnolias. Make no mistake about it, lady," Em told Nurse Darcy as she was being wheeled from delivery.

Nurse Darcy looked puzzled, but gratified. "I knew it. She must have used some sort of birthing magnolia scent, snuck it in here at the last minute," she said under her breath.

Em and Randy exchanged a special look with a wink from Randy. Em still felt the protective presence of her mama and Felice as she drifted deeply into sleep, the scent of magnolias surrounding her. In her dreams, she tiptoed through dimensions, talking with her mama one moment, Felice the next. Then she clearly remembered her dream of them at her grandmother's old oak table, sipping tea and chatting happily together. In this dream Felice and her mama were proudly discussing baby Felicity's beauty. Em was nursing the baby, smiling at their assessment of her daughter. The circle of her family of women was complete. The dream had come true. Em had grown up and into this tribe of women. What joy it would be to teach baby Lissa all she had learned in her life.

Randy watched Em sleep and glowed. His life was unimaginably full. He too noticed the scent of magnolias. He looked up happily and said, "Glad you all could make it."

Their new life, full of the past, was ready for the future, whatever it would bring. The ghosts, spirits and protectors of their world would always be there, Randy was certain. He held his new daughter, who had fallen asleep in his arms. He began to talk quietly so as not to wake Em.

"Wait till you meet everyone, your grandmas Margret, Cleo and Felicity, and all our friends. You're going to have a great life, Lissa." Em heard his voice, opened her eyes and reached out to hold his hand. "Yes, a great life. We'll always be together, sweetheart." She fell back to sleep and into her dreams. They were all together, and that would never change or disappear. She said to Randy, half asleep, "Never forget that, loves. We're all in this together in this great adventure of life."

* * *

Cabin #25 waited patiently for the arrival of the new family. The walls were alive with the past. Whispered voices echoed throughout the rooms. The swish of light footsteps sounded their tread in the well-loved cabin. The sunlight lit up the embroidered kitchen curtains and the antique lace adorning the window in the baby's room. The walls shared their secrets with the residents of the past and waited anxiously for the newest resident to arrive, Felicity, Lissa for short. Rhett, Scarlet and Zuma cuddled together happily on the Appalachian rocker on the front porch. Randy had come home early that morning to let their furry family out of the house and promised them he'd be back later that day with their new sister. By five, their ears picked up the sound of the Rambler on their road. Together the cats jumped up to wait on the top step of the porch.

The magnolia tree also waited, its limbs heavy with blooms. Just as the old Rambler arrived, a great and unexpected gust of wind rattled the branches of the old tree on this otherwise still day. Like snow, blossoms floated from the tree, slowly drifting on the breeze. They decorated the walk to the porch and the steps. Zuma batted one away as the three cats ran into the yard. The scent of the magnolias filled the air. The entire path to the old cabin was strewn with white magnolia blossoms, welcoming the newest resident, baby Felicity, to begin the new cycle of life at Cabin #25. Randy and Emeline stood in the continuing cascade of blossoms, astounded by this fantastic sight.

Randy and Em smiled at one another as a blossom fell onto Lissa's tiny head. The baby opened her eyes and looked upwards, seeing the mass of whiteness falling to earth.

"Thank you, Mama and Felice," Em said. "I'm glad you're both here to welcome your namesake." They were home, nestled in the cradle of safety and love, among past lives discovered and a new one to be learned. It was the end of one story and the beginning of another.